Dedicated to Book Tok…thank you for making me a #1 Best Seller this year. And if this book is dirtier than all my other books, I blame you entirely.

LAST ON THE LIST

AMY DAWS

Published by: Amy Daws, LLC
ISBN: 978-1-944565-56-5
Proofing: Julia Griffis
Editing: Jenny Sims with Editing4Indies
Formatting: Champagne Book Design
Cover Design: Amy Daws
Cover Photography: Wander Aguiar Photography
Cover Model: Tanner

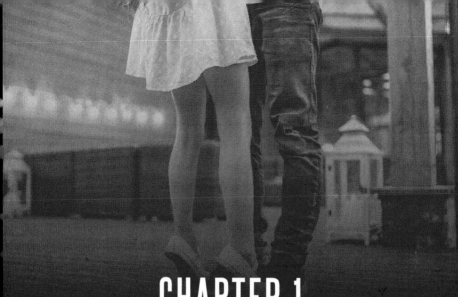

CHAPTER 1

Max

"This is going to be the worst summer of my life," Everly grumbles from the office chair beside me. "I wish Mom wasn't leaving. She ruined my whole summer."

I swivel to face my daughter's slumped frame. Her feet are dangling off the edge of her chair, scraping over the bald office carpet in my boardroom with tiny, frustrated kicks. I reach over and tug on her blond ponytail. "Don't be sad, kid. I have so many plans for you this summer. You're going to be too busy to miss your mom."

My eleven going on twenty-year-old looks up at me with her lethal robin-blue eyes that make me doubt my manhood every single day. "Can't wait," she mumbles flatly.

I sigh heavily and chuck her chin. "We just need to find the right nanny to help us out, and then we're set. It would help if you weren't so picky."

"Dad, the last one said her favorite TV show was *Maury*," Everly snipes, shoving the last one's résumé in front of me. "That's the show that Mom grounded me from watching because one time when I saw it on TV, a woman took out her fake tooth, spanked her own butt, and said she loved doing drugs."

My chest contracts with that horrific image, reminding me yet again of all the things I missed out on after separating from Everly's mom. "I never heard about you watching that."

Everly turns forward with a shrug. "Mom told me not to tell you. She said you were too busy to be bothered by it."

My jaw cracks as I turn my frustration toward the boardroom table instead of my kid. I tap the clicker of my pen insistently. My ex, Jessica, and I have been divorced since Everly was two, and most of the time, we have a great co-parenting relationship. Some would say admirable. But Jess has a habit of placing me in the "need to know" category when our daughter is at her house. She claims it's because I'm busy with my company, and she doesn't want to bother me with things she can handle. But I have told her time and time again, Everly is my exception to that rule every fucking time. I want to know what goes on in her life…even if it's watching a horrible television show.

I'll admit, things are a bit hectic for me. My franchise development company is in the process of partnering with another company in Denver, which would double the size of Fletcher Industries here in Boulder, Colorado. Honestly, the merger is huge for more than just my corporation. It will bring in more jobs and business to the growing city of Boulder and make my corporation that I started in my twenties the largest developer in the Rocky Mountains.

This is huge for me.

Which is why the fact that Jessica took a film job in Bulgaria for three months this summer of all summers is a bit of an inconvenience.

Normally, I only have Everly three out of four weekends a month. Friday night through Monday morning. That was something we set up in our custody agreement once Everly started school. It was important to Jess and me to ensure Everly's school life did not get disrupted too much during the week. And having Everly on the weekends meant I could give her quality time away from my office. I kill myself Monday through Friday so that when I pick Everly up at six o'clock on Friday, I can give her my full attention. I don't take a single work call until she is fast asleep…never mind have a social life. The few friends I have rarely hear a word from me on my Everly weekends. They respect the boundary.

However, it's been ten years since I've had Everly at my house full time. Which means, like it or not, I need to step it up and find someone to help me with her. I want this summer to go well. Everly is getting older, and eventually, it will be her choice whose house she spends more time at. Mine or her mom's. I would love it if, after this summer, she would *want* to spend more time with me. It won't be long before she's graduating from high school and going off to college to God knows where.

My chest aches at that thought, so I clear my throat to refocus on the task at hand before I let thoughts of the future overwhelm me. "Well, we still have one more person to interview. Hopefully, the agency saved the most qualified for last." I clench my jaw to hide my doubt. The agency owner and I haven't exactly been seeing eye to eye these past few weeks. I'd feel mildly guilty about being so high maintenance if she wouldn't have just sent me a candidate who listed the *Maury Show* as her favorite bingeable series.

Jesus Christ.

I glance down at my watch and frown. "Our last interviewee is officially late."

"Might as well scratch her off the list now," Everly drones. "You flip your lid whenever we're running late."

"I do not flip my lid." Those words feel strange coming out of my mouth.

The small smile on the corner of Everly's lips shows me she thinks I'm full of shit. God, she really makes me wonder who the parent is sometimes.

A loud bang thunders from behind us, turning both Everly's and my focus to the bank of glass windows that separates us from the rest of my office. My eyes widen when a blur of orange comes streaking by, running straight for the boardroom entrance. The person flings it open so fast that it thuds against the wall with a thunderous crack and has both Everly and me flinching.

Wide eyes swerve our direction. "Hey girl heyyy!" the woman

says as she waves animatedly in our direction like she didn't just cause a scene.

A sputtered giggle erupts from my kid.

The woman bustles over to us, breathing loudly as she struggles to say, "My sister told me you were a stickler for punctuality." She pauses to take a deep breath, tugging on the chest of her top to cool herself down. "I literally ran down that long hallway for you. For the record, I do not run." She gestures toward where she just came from.

My brows pinch together as I glance down at what I can now discern as an orange tie-dyed sweatsuit the woman is wearing. "Who is your sister?" I ask, glancing at the strip of pale skin revealed below the cropped sweatshirt.

"Rebecca Barlow! She owns the nanny agency." The woman pulls out the seat right next to me and flops noisily down into it. She quickly runs her fingers through her cropped black hair, getting hung up on several tangles.

I glance over at the seats across the table where every other candidate we've interviewed for the past two weeks has sat. But not this one. I adjust my tie and grind out, "Ah…Rebecca."

The woman covers her grimace. "Yeah, I think the feeling is mutual."

"Excuse me?" I ask, angling my head toward her. "What is that supposed to mean?"

"Nothing!" She holds her hands up defensively. "I've just heard you two have butted heads a few times."

I twist my jaw and shove the list of nanny rejects away from her prying eyes. "So I take it she sent you here to let me go as a client? We still have one more nanny to interview. A Cassandra…" My voice trails off when I see the last name.

She holds her hand out to me. "Cassandra Barlow. So nice to meet you, Max."

I reach out and take her offered hand, noticing the slight clamminess from her run while cursing myself for not putting two and two together earlier. "I prefer to be called Mr. Fletcher."

Her plump lips twitch with poorly concealed amusement. "My apologies, Mr. Fletcher," she says in a mock British accent. "That's a great name to say with a British accent." I open my mouth to reply as she adds, "And for the record, I was early, but your receptionist out there wanted to see my ID before I came back here, and I left it in my car, so I had to run back down to get it, and well…that was the two-minute delay. I'm a very slow runner. And I was really bummed I didn't get to hang in your waiting area. It's aces! Did I see kombucha in that mini fridge?" She leans close to me, and the smell of coconut wafts over me as she winks. "Very nice touch caring about your staff's gut health."

"It's not for the staff. It's for clients," I announce. My eyes blink as I try to figure out why the fuck we're talking about gut health. "And most people bring their identification to interviews. And most dress—"

"Dress for the job they want!" Cassandra interrupts, puffing her rather large chest out proudly. "Nothing says number-one nanny like homemade tie-dye."

She looks past me and smiles warmly. "You must be Everly. Love that top, by the way."

Everly tugs on her bright pink tee. "I love yours more. You made that yourself?" Everly presses up against my arm as she struggles to look around me. "That's so cool. I love tie-dye."

"Who doesn't!" Cassandra barks back. "This was actually a reject. You should see some of my masterpieces."

"Didn't think a masterpiece would be good for a job interview?" I grumble under my breath, fully intending for Cassandra to hear me.

Everly pinches my arm through my suit and turns a bright, genuine smile to the orange blob beside me. "So…Cassandra, what do you like to do for fun?"

"Call me Cozy." Cassandra winks at Everly. "I was a really chubby baby, so everyone called me Cozy Cassie…pause for shock and awe." She gestures to her body, which is apparently supposed to confirm her coziness? "Anyway, I decided to rock the Cozy instead of Cassie as I got older. It's more fun, don't you think?"

"Definitely," Everly says with a giggle.

I huff out a forced laugh that Cassandra does not give notice to. She leans past me toward Everly, pressing me back in my seat before she brushes my chest. "You know what I like to do for fun?" She pauses and waggles her dark eyebrows playfully. "Nothing."

Everly jerks back with a puzzled look on her face. "Nothing?"

Cassandra nods and smiles, flashing her round emerald eyes at my daughter. "A whole lot of nothing. My life philosophy is why do more when you can do less."

I roll my eyes and sigh. I'm not surprised. Her résumé had next to nothing on it. This must be some cruel joke Rebecca is playing on me for being a pain in her ass client.

"Isn't doing nothing kind of boring?" Everly asks, her brows pinched together with rapt fascination.

"Only if you have a boring mind," Cassandra quips as she props her chin on her hand and narrows her gaze at my daughter. "Do you have a boring mind, Everly?"

Everly scrunches up her nose as if she's trying to think seriously about this ridiculous question. "I don't think so."

"I don't think you do either...I can usually spot a boring mind." Cassandra's eyes slide to mine, and her intent is as subtle as her entrance into my boardroom.

I clear my throat, knowing I need to take over this interview that's venturing on completely ridiculous with a candidate who listed Subway as her last place of gainful employment four years ago. "I'm afraid our life philosophies don't quite match up, Cassandra. My ex and I like Everly to stay busy and feed her mind. She's on the swim team and does gymnastics. She has piano lessons and her chess club. We have her booked up for several camps this summer. Oh, and her book club—"

"I'm in a book club...What are you guys reading right now?" Cassandra interrupts.

"It's called *Mostly The Honest Truth*...it's kind of sad." Everly looks disappointed.

I frown and open my mouth to respond to that but am cut off once again. "I love a good tearjerker!" Cassandra gushes, adding excitedly, "Especially the kind that makes your nose run. It's like your body's way of cleansing your soul."

"Cleansing your soul?" I mock.

"I never thought about it like that!" Everly peals with a thoughtful smile, erasing the sadness in her voice she had a moment ago.

Cassandra returns Everly's smile and shoots a small wink at me before refocusing on Everly. "It's fun to think about things, isn't it? That's what doing nothing gives you the opportunity to do. Let your imagination run wild and daydream."

"So that's really your proposal with my daughter this summer? To do nothing?" I ask dryly, hoping she has a backup response that she's going to pull out of her back pocket at any moment.

Cassandra nods proudly. "We'll also do a lot of sitting. I'm an expert at sitting," she deadpans.

"Okay…I think we've heard enough, Cassandra." I move to stand, but she reaches out and touches my arm, halting me in my tracks.

"Cozy," she corrects with a wink.

The teasing look in her eyes causes my skin to tighten. I do my best to shake it off as she refocuses on Everly to share with her the last book that made her cry. Her hand slides off my arm, and my eyes lock on the way her index finger trails off the fabric of my suit.

I'm left struggling to shake this silvery feeling her delicate touch has left on my arm, so I take a moment to inspect Cassandra a bit closer now that her focus is off me. Her facial features are round, a faint dimple appearing in her cheek as she talks animatedly to my daughter. Her alabaster skin is a stunning contrast to her nearly black hair cropped bluntly just above her shoulders. She has shockingly plump lips slathered in a pale pink gloss that thankfully doesn't match the orange jumpsuit that looks like something a teenager would wear. Her ample curves indicate she's very much not a child.

"How old are you?" I blurt out and then blanch at how unprofessional of a question that is. I close my eyes and curse under my breath. "I'm sorry, you don't have to answer that."

"I'm twenty-six, Big Daddy," Cassandra replies with another wink and then immediately dives back into conversation with my daughter.

Big Daddy? I frown at that very unpleasant label. Jesus Christ, so unprofessional. No fucking way…over my dead body. This will not work. I click my tongue and bring out my CEO voice. "Cassandra…I thank you for coming in, but I'm afraid—"

"You're hired!" Everly bursts out, standing up so she's eye level with me. She thrusts her hand across my face and reaches for Cassandra's, mimicking me to a T how I've handled many successful boardroom transactions.

My mouth hangs open as I sit frozen, watching Cassandra stand in what feels like slow motion to take Everly's hand and accept the offer.

"This is so awesome!" Cassandra shakes Everly's hand so hard, she starts to giggle. "This summer is going to be GOAT!"

"Goats?" I exclaim, finally breaking free of my stunned-stupid response to my daughter taking over this meeting. How is Everly so charmed by this…this…I don't even know what to call a person like Cassandra. "No one said anything about farm animals."

Cassandra and Everly burst out laughing like they've been buddies their entire life. Everly places her slender fingers on my shoulder in a way that makes me feel like the eleven-year-old in the room. "Dad, GOAT means greatest of all time."

My shoulders slump. "Oh."

Everly leans over to Cassandra and whispers loudly, "I'm so glad this worked out. If we didn't hire someone today, my dad was totally going to get a case of his stress poops again."

"Everly!" My eyes fly wide when Cassandra turns her green gaze to me. I push a nervous hand through my hair and quickly rush out, "I don't get stress poops. I don't know what that kid's talking about."

Cassandra reaches out and pats me on the other shoulder. "Hey Mr. Fletcher, no judgment here. Maybe you should try some of that kombucha out there you won't let your staff have? It's really good for the digestive system."

I groan and pinch the bridge of my nose. This summer is going to be a disaster.

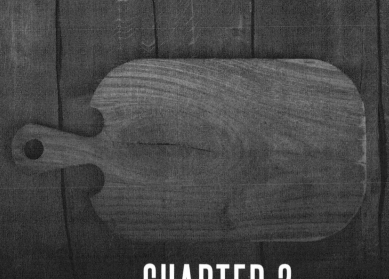

CHAPTER 2

Cozy

"**R**ebecca just told me you're moving into this guy's guesthouse?" Dakota hollers to me from somewhere in my sister's spare bedroom that I've been living in for the past few months. I'm tucked away in the small walk-in closet, so it's hard to hear her.

"Be right out!" I call loudly before grabbing an arm full of clothes on hangers. When I emerge, I peer over the top of my sweatshirts to find my childhood bestie sacked out on my bed, popping one of my sour gummy worms into her mouth. "The guesthouse was a perk of the nanny job I accepted. And really, the only reason I agreed to interview in the first place."

"And because you're ready for a freaking job," my older sister's voice chirps as she pokes her head into my room.

Rolling my eyes, I hook the clothes on a metal bar inside a garment box I picked up earlier today. "I get it, Bec…you're sick of me."

"I'm not sick of you." She pins me with a look. "However, I didn't fully expect my sister to be such an active part of my first year of marriage."

My shoulders sag. "Jacob loves me. We play gin rummy togethe-

"Exactly," Rebecca scoffs. "Maybe I'd like to play gin rummy with my husband?"

"Would you?" I ask, surprised by that remark. Rebecca is more of a Netflix and do her nails type of girl.

"God no, I hate cards." She confirms my suspicion. "But that doesn't take away from the fact that this is the perfect job to get you moving again. There's taking a break, and then there's taking a *break*."

"That's what I've been saying!" Dakota agrees, licking the sour sugar off her fingers.

"Well…I'm still in the middle of my Great Defrost," I huff out defensively and move toward the bed to snatch my gummy worms out of my former best friend's hands. "And moving back in with Mom and Dad would have been hell."

Rebecca sighs knowingly. Our parents are good people, but they live on acreage outside of Boulder with a few farm animals they raise as a hobby along with their day jobs. And as much as I loved doing chores for our small flock of ewes who were all labeled with old lady names before and after school when I was a kid, it just wasn't what I was up for when I moved back home.

Which means that ever since I quit my job in Denver and moved back to Boulder, my mom has been watching me like a ticking time bomb, just waiting to see what I'm going to do with my life next.

"Please just don't screw this up," Rebecca adds, tapping the doorframe. "Max Fletcher, uptight as he may be, is a very well-connected customer. Rich clients have rich friends, and those are the kind of referrals I need for my agency, okay?"

"You know what, Bec?" I scratch my head, my face growing serious. "Until you told me not to screw it up, I had totally planned on screwing it up. So I'm glad you made that distinction before I move in there tomorrow. We really dodged a bullet."

She shoots me a lethal glare. "Just be professional, Cozy. I know how you can be sometimes."

My jaw drops as she leaves me with that bolstering remark. I point at the empty doorway. "Can you believe her?"

Dakota shifts uncomfortably. "Maybe this job opportunity is good timing. I'm sensing a bit of tension between the Barlow sisters."

I prop my hands on my hips, glowering at my sister's guest room littered with my stuff. "I swear she doesn't know me as an adult at all. Why would she act like I don't know how to be professional?"

"Well…" Dakota's traitorous voice rises in pitch.

I shoot her accusing eyes. "What?"

She winces slightly. "Don't get me wrong, I love your 'Great Defrost Cozy.' It's reminiscent of the original Cozy Cassie who I thought was gone forever from our childhood. But a lot has happened in the past six months. You changed from a woman we barely saw for years and was too busy to let her childhood bestie visit her in Denver to…whatever this version of yourself is. It's a lot to take in."

"I know, I know," I mumble, shaking away the memory that always causes a pit to form in my stomach. "But don't worry because Denver Cozy is long gone. And I have my Cozy Cassie hips back to prove it." I bite the head off a gummy worm to accentuate my point before tossing the bag back onto the bed. I glance at myself in the mirror and tug at my oversized sweatshirt. I've gained a solid ten pounds since moving in with my sister, but it doesn't bother me. It's a sign that I'm happy. The slimmer version of myself that I was in Denver was stress-induced. I'd much rather be plus-sized and happy than mid-sized and miserable.

I retreat into my closet for a second armful.

"I do agree with your sister that it was time you finally got a job," Dakota calls to me. "Selling your homemade charcuterie boards every other week was not going to get you out of Rebecca's house anytime soon."

"You know I don't make my boards for the money," I huff, nearly tripping on a dress that gets tangled under my feet as I come walking back out. "In fact, I wouldn't sell any of my boards if you'd stop telling people about my hobby."

"I know it's your 'therapy.'" Dakota finger quotes. "But you're too good at it not to do something with it. I'm telling you, if you worked on those boards more than a few hours a week, you could turn your hobby into a legitimate business. I could help you set up an Etsy shop. Hell, you could sell the boards in my store!"

I eye my best friend with a look that tells her this conversation needs to stop. "This is my year of doing less. It's like a gap year, remember?"

"At twenty-six years old."

My lips thin, and Dakota finally gets the message and holds her hands up in surrender. "Fine, fine, I'll shut up." She pops another worm into her mouth.

I love my childhood bestie, and it's been great to reconnect with her these past six months, but she's just as lovingly pushy as she was when we were kids. She was always like the mini mom of our group, organizing activities for all of us and checking in on the weekends. Harping on us to get our college applications in. Honestly, it's kind of shocking she has such a hip little business now. I swore she was going to go the young motherhood route with her high school sweetheart and have two or three kids by now. But she's single and a boss ass bitch of her own graphic tee shop downtown. She sells the cutest little slogan shirts and does a lot of mail-order business internationally because she teamed up with one of her college friends, who turned out to be this huge plus-sized designer in Aspen.

Tatianna Ashley kind of blew up when she was featured on an episode of *Project Runway*. She specializes in formal wear but has designed a line of size-inclusive tees for Dakota's store that really helped elevate her business from an Etsy shop to a legitimate storefront that has so much inventory she can't run it out of her home anymore. It's amazing.

I'm currently wearing a powder-blue sweatshirt from Tatianna's line that says Aspen Bae. All Dakota's stuff is cozy and chic with lots of retro styles and designs. I want my entire wardrobe to be from her shop. It's like…unpretentious loungewear with a sense of humor. She even has these fun tie-dye classes every week, which is where I made the orange set that I wore to my job interview a few days ago.

The job interview that I surprisingly nailed…with Everly, at least, who seems like a cool kid. Her dad, on the other hand…

"So what do you get paid for this nanny gig?" Dakota asks, chewing on another worm. "Is it a huge pay cut from your previous job?"

A small tremor runs through me at her mention of my past job. "I never asked what it pays."

"Are you serious?" Dakota gapes at me like I have two heads. "Does your sister know?"

I shrug and move over to my dresser to begin emptying its contents. "Probably."

"Your 'do less' vibe is going to be the death of me, Cozy." She sits up and pulls her phone out of her back pocket. "It has to be good. Max Fletcher is like…the only Boulder billionaire in existence."

"He's a billionaire?" I ask, turning to look at her. "No billionaire I ever met interviewed their own staff."

"Met a lot of billionaires, have you?" Dakota quirks a brow at me.

"Just a couple…at the old job." I swallow a knot in my throat. "But it was obvious. They walked around with staff and security. Didn't drive themselves. I'm sure they don't even know their kids. Plus, they're all old. Max doesn't look old enough to be a billionaire. How old is he?"

"I'm internet stalking as we speak." Dakota focuses on her phone intently. "He's thirty-four. Born and raised in Boulder. Net worth is one hundred million. So you're right, he's not a billionaire. What a slacker."

"Yeah…total loser." I force out a laugh.

"Jesus, he's even hotter than I thought!" Dakota's jaw drops as she stares accusingly at me.

"You think?" My voice is weak as my palms start to sweat. Unfortunately, I know firsthand how good-looking Max is, which is why I'm trying *not* to think about it. He's about to be my boss.

She turns her phone to reveal a photo of him in a suit crossing his arms in front of the building where I had the interview at. It's the cover photo of some business magazine. "That dirty-blond scruffy jaw? Come to mama."

Yeah, okay, there's no way I can't not think about him now.

"He had really nice lips too," I muse, my voice getting weirdly breathy as I think back to the way he kept angrily pursing them every time I said something he didn't like. They were like perfectly full. Not too big, not too thin. Just…annoyingly kissable. "His daughter is eleven, though. He must have had her young if he's only thirty-four. Does it say anything about his ex-wife?" I'm dying to see a picture of her, but I can't tell Dakota that.

Dakota shakes her head. "Not that I can find. He has three brothers though."

"Shit, there's more like him?" I feel hot all of a sudden.

"Um…yeah…check it out." She holds her phone up to me again and there's a photo of three burly, Brawny man-type dudes and then Max in a perfectly tailored suit.

"What a gene pool," I deadpan.

"Right!" Dakota confirms and then narrows her eyes at me. "Why were you acting like he's not hot as fuck before?"

"'Cuz it's weird." I look down as my cheeks begin to heat. "And like…perfect, blond model looking dudes with lush, full lips aren't really my type. He looks like an uptight Ken doll. His arms and legs probably don't even bend. He told me to call him Mr. Fletcher. Can you believe that?"

Dakota's brows lift. "That's kinda hot."

"I guess it's better than calling him *Zaddy*, which is what I thought when I first saw him." I cover my eyes and try not to groan with frustration. It's almost not fair that the first job I land has to be with a man I couldn't have even conjured in my dreams.

"What's a Zaddy?" Dakota asks with a wicked smile on her face. "And why did you say it with your nose wrinkled like that?" She giggles, her shoulders hunching up under her ears.

"'Cuz you gotta say it like that for the full effect." I inhale and close my eyes before adding, "A *Zaddy* is a hot, intelligent older man who knows how to handle business inside and outside the bedroom. A little dominant. A little naughty. Makes you wet just thinking about him, and you low-key want to have his baby."

"That's really specific," Dakota sputters, and my eyes pop open to see her face contorting with hysterics.

I swallow thickly. "Sorry, I've been reading straight smut the past six months, and he checks a lot of Zaddy boxes. Did you know we have a famous erotic romance author who lives in Boulder? Her name is Mercedes Lee Loveletter. You need to read her books."

"Cozy…focus! You're calling your new boss Zaddy!" Dakota exclaims and throws a pillow at me, laughing. "You are so screwed!"

"I know!" I say, shoving my face into the pillow to scream. "I basically felt like a pervert during the entire interview. I don't even know what I said. I think I said…why do more when you can do less?"

"You used your new life philosophy in an interview?" Dakota looks horrified.

My cheeks flame with mortification. "It just stumbled out, okay? I could feel his hot, blue eyes staring at me the whole time I was talking to his daughter."

"My God…what are you going to do around him all summer?"

"Nothing, obviously," I snap defensively. "He's rich, so I'm sure he'll be busy and gone most of the time. Also, he looks like a guy who only bags size zero hot models who look like you. I bet he took one look at me and was like, she looks more like a cart horse than a race-horse…she's hired!"

"Shut your fucking face. You're gorgeous."

"Trust me, I'm not fishing for compliments!" I argue. "But I'm a nutritional overachiever, and that type isn't typically a number-one draft pick for rich assholes like him. Do you see anything about a girlfriend online? Maybe he's taken, which will shut my libido down real quick."

Dakota does a quick scan. "No obvious girlfriend in any of his Instagram photos. But look at this picture." She turns her phone to me and shows me a photo of him and Everly at some beach. He's wearing those tiny floral men's trunks that hug his muscular thighs.

I snatch the phone out of her hands as my eyes zero in on his abs. "What kind of dad bod bullshit is that?"

"Right? He really does look like a Ken doll. Hopefully a bit more anatomically correct but a total Zaddy body, nonetheless."

My head snaps up to my best friend. "You just learned that word."

She shrugs. "I'm a quick study."

I glance back down at the photo and lick my lips. His dirty-blond hair is that effortlessly sexy cut that's trim on the sides with natural waves on top. I didn't realize how long it was during my interview because he had it smoothed off to the side. But blowing in the beach wind like it is in this photo, looking artfully mussed with his smiling eyes all crinkly is positively mouthwatering. My hands itch to run my fingers through it.

"Is taking this job a big mistake?" I ask, my voice feeling thick in my throat.

"Why would it be?" Dakota inquires, clearly having no idea of the dirty thoughts going through my mind.

I hand her phone back to her. "Because I'm going to work for a hot, single dad billionaire who represents corporate greed and everything I hate in life?" Not to mention I'm not sure I'll be able to stop my vivid fantasies from living rent free in my imagination.

"He's not a billionaire," Dakota corrects. "He's only a millionaire. You're going to be fine!"

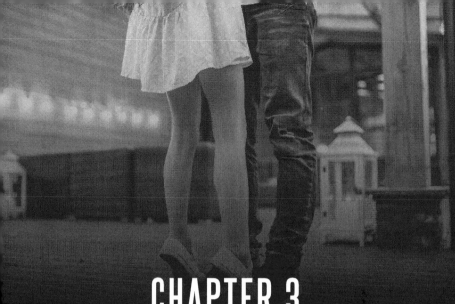

CHAPTER 3

Max

"This looks great, Bettina, thank you," I proclaim, standing in the small kitchenette of the guest cottage located on the backside of my property.

Bettina is my house manager and tends to all things domestic for me. She picks up her cleaning supplies and makes her way out as I walk a couple of steps over to the large sliding glass doors on the backside of the house. It overlooks Boulder Creek that lines about two hundred feet of my property. There's a small, sandy beach area that Everly used to love to play in when she was little. I haven't been back here in years.

This cottage used to be a boat house until a few years ago when I had my brothers turn it into one of those tiny houses that were all the rage on TV. This structure is only five hundred square feet, but with vaulted ceilings, lots of windows, and shiplap on the interior walls, it's bright and airy and feels more like a luxury cabin. I installed high-end appliances, custom cabinetry, and even a small soaker tub with a waterfall showerhead in the bathroom. It might be tiny, but it has everything you'd ever need. The sleeping area even has a king mattress. Hell, I'd live out here. Seems a lot simpler than the eight thousand square feet house I currently live in...*by myself most of the time.*

My brothers did that remodel for me as well. The three of them work under my father's construction company. They specialize in house flipping and remodels all over the Boulder area.

My dad had expectations for me to take the wheel when he retired, but I never pictured myself working on job sites for the rest of my life. As soon as I started business school, I knew I wanted to carve my own path in life. Something that required a suit and tie every day in an office setting. And when my franchise consulting business took off in my twenties, that all but secured the fact that I wasn't going to have an active role in the family business.

Unfortunately for my dad, my three younger brothers seem less than motivated to take on more responsibility. The three of them march to the beat of their own drums. A few years ago, they built these self-sustaining log cabins on a stretch of land up in the mountains outside of Boulder near Jamestown. Now they have their own little commune that they get up to God knows what up there.

Everly loves to stay over. It's like visiting an adventure park to her. I just have to be careful in the winter when we visit because if it snows, we could be stuck up there for days.

Yeah, my brothers and I...very different.

I'll stick to my climate-controlled office and focus on the task of integrating a hundred new employees into my workflow.

"She's here, Dad!" Everly's voice rips me out of my musings, and I turn on my heel to see my kid standing in the doorway next to the new nanny.

Cozy.

It was a whole ordeal deciding to hire her. We had to have a Zoom family meeting with Jessica and the nanny agency owner to make sure Cassandra was actually qualified. I had to double-check because that was one of the weirdest interviews of my life, and I've interviewed plenty of staff. But Rebecca assured us that Cassandra had all the proper qualifications, and her candidates were extensively vetted. Seeing as the owner of the nanny agency is her sister, I guess I took that as a small comfort.

The next ordeal we had to handle was Everly's summer schedule. The kid broke down in tears to Jess and me on the video call, begging us to cancel all her summer activities so she could "do nothing with Cozy." It was hell. Everly crying is like an instant surrender button for me. I will do anything to make it stop. I often use Jess as the heavy in our family, but with her being out of the country already, she couldn't exactly find a better solution. So despite my better judgment, Cozy was hired, and Everly's busy summer plans went out the window.

"Cassandra, welcome," I state, striding to meet her at the doorway. I reach out my hand, and she releases her large suitcase handle to shake it. That silvery feeling is back, so I quickly pull my hand back and slide it into my suit pant pocket. "I hope you'll be comfortable out here."

"Please call me Cozy," Cassandra says, offering a soft smile. Her dark hair is up in a short ponytail today, and she looks exceedingly younger than her twenty-six years.

"Your house is cozy, isn't it?" Everly giggles and grabs Cassandra's hand, pulling her into the small living area. There's a long white sofa that lines the opposite side of the sliders with a great view of the creek, plus a small television mounted over the dining room table that pulls down from the wall in the event you need more floor space. "My uncles built it. It's called a tiny house."

"Your uncles must be very handy," Cassandra responds, walking into the kitchen and running her hand along the white granite countertop beside the stainless-steel fridge. She points at the large wooden ladder that leads to the lofted area. "Is up there where I sleep?"

"Yes, let me show you!" Everly peals and begins her climb.

I walk over to the ladder just as Cassandra does, both of our hands reaching out to hold it steady. Cassandra's green eyes connect with mine, and I swallow thickly before turning back up to the loft, ignoring the scent of coconut that wafts over me at her proximity. "Everly, you don't have to show her that part. I'm sure Cassandra can manage."

Everly's head pops over the edge, her blond hair haloing her face as she peers down at us. "Dad and I had a sleepover up here once."

Cassandra's brows lift in surprise as she looks at me for confirmation. "Wouldn't have taken you for the sleepover type."

I frown at that response. Is she teasing me? "She was eight, and it looked like a playhouse to her when it was all done. She can be relentless when she wants to be. I hope you're tougher than I am."

"I'm sure we'll be just fine." She smiles, almost to let me know she was trying to joke with me, and I relax a bit. Cassandra points at the ladder. "Do you mind if I—"

"Of course, sorry…let me get out of your way," I babble and step back, giving her room to climb. I shove a hand through my hair and force myself to look out the windows and not gape at her legging-clad ass that's currently eye level with me. At least she's ditched the matching tie-dyed sweatsuit. But now I'm face-to-face with her curves that leave little to the imagination. *Fuck.*

"Big bed!" Cassandra calls down.

"With a little reading chair!" Everly exclaims, her voice more excited than it's sounded since her mother left the country last week. "That's my bedroom on the far-right top window. My dad's is down there on the left." I glance up and see Everly pointing at our house that's up the grassy hill and past the pool.

"Do you have more bags in your car?" I ask, feeling a bit stir-crazy down here doing nothing.

"Yes, but don't worry. I can get them."

"I got it." Without another word, I haul ass outside, grateful for the fresh air. I unbutton the sleeves of my dress shirt and roll them up. Why did it feel so hot in that cabin all of a sudden? I should check the A/C unit when I get back.

The sun is just beginning to set as I make my way over the large, manicured lawn that looks damn near electric green in this light. The blue pool sparkles, and I have a moment of brief appreciation for the fact that Everly will finally be here for a decent length of time to use all this stuff I've invested good money in. I barely remember what it was like to be a full-time dad. Shared custody can really fucking suck sometimes.

I find Cassandra's SUV and spot a large box and a duffel bag in the tailgate. That coconut smell hits me again as I toss the bag across my chest and carry the box out back. God, that scent is appealing. It reminds me of vacation and sunshine. I haven't had a real vacation in years.

I hear Cassandra and Everly's giggles wafting out the front door as I return to find them in the living room. Everly is showing her how to use the television.

"Thank you for that, Mr. Fletcher," Cassandra says, shooting me a warm smile as I set the box down next to the closet cabinets that line the hallway leading to the bathroom.

"Don't mention it." I shove a hand through my hair. "Do you want a tour of the main house? I expect that's where you and Everly will spend most of your days."

"Aw, why can't we hang out here?" Everly whines, looking over at me with her lethal puppy dog eyes.

"This is Cassandra's space, Everly. You need to respect it," I state a bit too firmly. Why am I feeling so flustered? I clear my throat. "Also, there's nothing to do out here."

"Exactly!" Everly replies with a smile. "Why do more when you can do less?"

Cassandra bites her lip and has the gall to look sheepish. I hit her with a look, so she knows exactly how I feel about this. Leaning on the dining room table, I cross my arms and inhale deeply. "Look, you're entitled to your own life philosophies, but there will need to be some structure this summer."

Cassandra nods and swallows slowly. "You're the boss."

That label sends a heady jolt of electricity through my body, settling annoyingly in my cock. I clench my jaw and continue, "After your interview, Everly made it very clear she didn't want to do all the camps and activities we had planned for her this summer. So Jess and I came up with some compromises to ensure it's not a completely pointless summer."

Cassandra's head jerks back. "I don't think giving your mind a chance to recharge and daydream a bit is ever pointless."

"I agree!" Everly huffs, crossing her arms and giving me attitude as she damn near snuggles up to Cassandra on the sofa.

"Nevertheless," I continue through clenched teeth, leveling the nanny with a look. "She can take the summer off gymnastics and swim team, but she needs to still be in the pool at least three times a week for exercise." I point at the swim deck up by the main house.

"Swimming is great for the imagination." Cassandra winks at Everly. Everly smiles with glee.

"She must continue with her book club. And do book reports every week. That's non-negotiable."

"Reading is so much fun!" Cassandra replies, but Everly looks less than thrilled.

"And screen time will be very limited. Doing nothing doesn't mean bingeing Netflix."

"I don't even have Netflix," Cassandra says with a shrug. "This sounds great. We're going to have the best summer ever." She holds her hand out to Everly, who slaps it with a high five. "You want to help me unpack, and then we can do the Fletchpad tour?"

"Fletchpad?" Everly giggles. "I just called it a house!"

Cozy touches her finger to her temple. "It's more fun to use your imagination and come up with your own words, isn't it?"

"Totally!" Everly agrees and turns to begin helping Cozy unpack.

I pause at the door, realizing I've never seen my kid get so excited to do a chore. "I'll just...leave you two to it. Oh, and just so you're aware, I'll be working from home this week."

"From the Fletchpad?" Everly asks excitedly, adopting that bizarre label for our home in the blink of an eye.

"Yes, my office is being renovated." Total fucking lie. I just don't trust this chick with my kid. Not yet. I need to see them in action for a bit. Make sure this nanny isn't going to be a total disaster. Do I want to manage the extra work I have with this giant merger approaching from home? No. But Everly is my entire life, and I'm not taking any risks with her this summer. "I'll be around to help you both get settled."

"Sounds good...Mr. Fletcher." Cassandra appears to be fighting back a smile, and my eyes narrow suspiciously.

I'm watching you...*Cozy*.

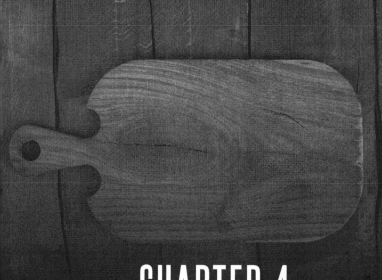

CHAPTER 4

Cozy

"**W**ant to see me do a dive?" Everly calls out from the diving board of the giant Olympic-sized pool that no normal human would have chilling in their backyard. But of course, millionaire Max Fletcher does.

"Heck yeah!" I exclaim from my spot on the edge of the pool, where I'm kicking my feet in the water. "Let's see it."

Everly swan dives gracefully, making the tiniest of splashes. She pops up out of the water and grins gleefully at me before tucking her head down and swimming toward the other side of the pool.

Dang, this kid lives a privileged life. I can't believe she's not more of an asshole. I always imagined kids who lived like this would be bossy and entitled. I'm pleasantly surprised to admit I was wrong about my assumption. I know I'm still getting to know Everly, but I'm usually pretty good at reading people, and she seems sweet and cool and a great listener. Especially for an eleven-year-old who lives in a rustic mansion.

Mr. Fletcher gave me a tour of the Fletchpad last night, and my eyes were in a constant state of orgasm. First of all, this giant house is located just minutes from downtown, but it's tucked away on this private cul-de-sac decked out with mature trees and a creek out back right by the tiny house I'll be living in for the foreseeable future. The location couldn't be more amazing.

While my cottage is white with a splash of adorable Southern charm, the main house has a rustic cedar wood siding. It's quite striking as far as curb appeal goes. The inside maintains that rustic mountain feel with knotty wide-plank flooring and cool modern contrasts like bright white walls, exposed wooden beams in the vaulted ceiling, and unique bronze light fixtures. There's even this ridiculous brick triple fireplace in the main living area next to a bank of sliders that overlooks the pool. Off the living room is a freaking library with a ladder.

A Library. With. A. Ladder.

Upon first glance, most of the books appeared to be boring business books, but I spotted some cozy mysteries in there that makes me think maybe Max Fletcher does know how to relax on occasion. The cutest part is that one giant section of shelves is dedicated to all of Everly's books. It looks like Max has kept them from when she was little because the top shelves are these tiny cardboard baby books and as you progress downward, they mature in age to Judy Blume books, Babysitter's Club books, and even Harry Potter books. It's adorable that in this sexy, masculine library with a pool table in the middle and a wet bar on the side, he has an entire section dedicated to his kid with room to grow.

I may have swooned a bit.

The kitchen is on the opposite side of the living room, and it should come as no surprise that it's a chef's kitchen with glossy white backsplash tiles and a giant bronze hood over the oven. Cute barstools nestle against the white marble island and a matching bronze farm sink. Honestly, this whole house is so extra, and I'm obsessed with absolutely every bit of it.

A wrought-iron spiral staircase leads upstairs to Everly's bedroom and another spare room—both with an en suite, of course. The basement has a workout room with mirrors and all the equipment one could want, plus a couple of more bedrooms and a theater room.

The only part I didn't get to see was the master bedroom through the kitchen, which is apparently where Mr. Fletcher's office is as well.

That's probably for the best. I had a hard time not staring at his sculpted forearms beneath those rolled-up sleeves during the tour. When my nose almost brushed with his ass as we climbed the spiral staircase to Everly's room, I knew I needed to get out of this house as soon as possible. Visions of his abs have been haunting me since I started internet stalking him after Dakota left my room the other day. Those pictures coupled with his seriously expensive-smelling cologne are sending me into a bit of a state. I need to be focused on his daughter, not him. *Damn Mercedes Lee Loveletter for stoking my smutty thoughts.*

However, his bedroom has a slider that opens to the large back deck that overlooks the pool. When Everly and I came out here this afternoon, I caught a glimpse of him through the window at his free-standing desk talking on his phone. He has a perfect view of everything we're doing back here, and it's unnerving. I swear I can feel him watching.

I've felt so awkward that I haven't been brave enough to take off my swim dress and get some sun on my pasty skin. Which is weird because I've never been one to feel self-conscious about my body.

I've always been on the bigger side, but I'm somewhat proportional, save for my DD breasts, so I still wear the clothes I want and rock a two-piece when the mood strikes me. I've never really been self-conscious with the guys I've been intimate with, so it's unsettling that stripping down to my swimwear in front of *Zaddy* is freaking me out so much.

Luckily, Everly doesn't seem to mind me not being in the water, so I'll keep my jiggly bits to myself for now.

Everly swims over to where I'm perched on the edge in the deep end. She treads water in front of me and says, "Do you have a boyfriend, Cozy?"

"Ha!" I bark out a laugh. "That's a big fat no."

"Girlfriend?" she asks, completely straight-faced.

"Nope."

"Which do you like? Boys or girls?"

I smile at her adorable inclusivity. "It's always been men for me."

She nods thoughtfully, her blue eyes matching the color of the water perfectly. "Why don't you have a boyfriend?"

I frown and hold my foot out to her. "Will you come hold on to the edge of the pool? Watching you tread water like that makes me nervous."

"I'm fine," she says with a laugh but listens to me like the sweet little kid she is.

I exhale heavily and try to come up with an answer to her question. "I haven't been back in Boulder very long, so I haven't really made time to find a boyfriend."

"Have you *ever* had a boyfriend?" she asks, her voice rising in pitch.

"I've had a few, yes."

"Did you *loooove* any of them?" she inquires in a sing-songy voice that makes me want to squeeze her.

"Probably not," I reply honestly. "I was too busy working to fall in love." Too busy to fall in love. Too busy to dream. Too busy to even have thoughts of my own.

"You sound like my dad," Everly harumphs and rests her chin on the concrete.

I poke her shoulder. "What about you? Are you old enough to have a crush yet?"

Everly's eyes go wide, and she glances over toward her dad's bedroom. I can see the outline of him standing at the window, looking in our direction while he holds his phone to his ear. "Don't tell my dad, but I have a boyfriend."

"You do?" I ask dramatically before whispering, "What's his name?"

"Hilow. He lives down the street from here. Dad cannot know. He will flip out."

My chin lowers conspiratorially. "Are you not supposed to have a boyfriend?"

Everly shrugs. "I've never asked, so I wouldn't know."

I laugh at that very creative logic. I've used it myself from time to time. "Well, I hope Hilow is nice to you."

"Oh, we don't talk," she says like it should be obvious. "We are just boyfriend and girlfriend."

God, I want to pinch her cute cheeks so bad right now. "Non-talking boyfriends sound like a great idea. I should try to find me one of those."

"I could help you. I found my best friend Brooklyn a boyfriend."

"Well, aren't you a little matchmaker."

She nods and frowns down at my dress. "Do you have a swimsuit on under that?"

"Yes, why?" I ask, clutching my chest self-consciously, worried my tits are hanging out or something, and I'm scandalizing my new charge.

"Because…it's time to swim!" Everly squeals and grabs my legs. She presses her feet to the sides of the pool, and before I can brace myself for what I realize she's about to do, she yanks me straight into the water.

My fingers grasp at air as I try to reach out and catch myself. The blue sky fills my vision as a sharp pain strikes the back of my head. I cry out the moment I'm enveloped by the water and stupidly inhale a large gulp of water to a place that water is not supposed to be in my body. I try to cough it out, which is obviously a bad idea when you're…*under water.*

My head throbs as my body flips upside down. I struggle to get myself turned right side up and blink rapidly to spot Everly's little legs kicking over to the side of the pool. It feels like I'm going in circles, and panic begins to overtake all my emotions, blocking out the pain I feel on the back of my head.

Finally, my feet find purchase on the bottom of the pool, so I push myself up, reaching toward the top of the water with all my might. Just as my face is finally about to break through to freedom, a dark cloud descends over top of me.

A rush of water sends me flying as bubbles impede my vision. When they clear, two arms wrap around me, yanking me back against a hard body. I look down and notice the hands are planted firmly on both of my breasts as strong legs kick aggressively behind me.

In seconds, I feel sunlight on my face as I break through the water, gasping for air and coughing violently. My stomach roils as the water I swallowed earlier threatens to come back up. One of my breasts sags as it's released, so I turn around to discover with great horror that it's Everly's dad swimming me toward the shallow end of the pool.

"Everly, go inside and get the first-aid kit out of my bathroom!" his deep voice bellows, but it sounds muted because I have water in both of my ears.

He finally reaches the shallow end and stands up, turning to lift me up in both of his arms as he makes his way toward the steps of the pool.

Oh, my God, what is happening? I glance down when my body is lifted out of the water completely. How the hell is this man carrying me out of a pool right now? I'm…not light!

Seconds later, I'm lowered onto a lounge chair, and I look up to see the silhouette of Max Fletcher standing before me in a soaking wet dress shirt, tie, slacks, and shoes. His pink nipples are at full salute in his now see-through shirt, and I am mortified. Which can only explain why I can't take my eyes off his wet chiseled chest.

I glance down and see my caftan clinging to my curves and discover with great horror that one of my tits has come completely out of my bikini top and is nearly fully exposed through the V-neck of my dress.

"Shit," I murmur as I unstealthily place my too big for its own good breast back into its cage.

"Can't you swim?" Mr. Fletcher's voice growls angrily at me.

"Um…I can do a halfway decent doggy paddle," I croak, coughing out the last bit of liquid circling my lungs. I swing my legs off the side of the lounger to lean forward, feeling dangerously like I'm about to vomit as I push my hair out of my face.

"Your résumé said you know CPR," he thunders at me.

"I do know CPR," I snap at him because he's yelling at me, and I do not take kindly to being yelled at by a grown man moments after almost dying. "You are aware you can get CPR certified without knowing how to swim, right?"

"What would you have done if my kid started drowning?" His sculpted chest is heaving with rage.

"I don't know!" I screech, tearing my eyes off his pecs to look into his darkened eyes. "Do you have a big pole?"

His face contorts. "A big pole?"

"I mean a life preserver thingy!" I correct, my brain clearing more now. I stand to gain some leverage, but he still towers over me in his well over six-foot, broad-chested glory. I have never felt small at five foot eight, but Max Fletcher must be pushing six two to make me feel like a child getting scolded at this moment. I puff my chest out to match his, noticing his eyes straying to my breasts for a moment too long before he looks up. "Most lifeguards have life preservers strapped to them so when they jump in to save someone, they don't have to grope their victim's tits."

Mr. Fletcher blanches, his hands turning to fists as his eyes cast downward. He clears his throat, looking mildly less angry now. "I'm sorry about that. I didn't mean to…" He pauses and looks away, giving me a profile view of his chiseled jaw. He has a lot of nerve being so attractive while being a class A dickhole. "I looked up from my desk just as Everly pulled you in, and I didn't think. I just reacted."

His face looks tortured, and now I feel bad for being mad at the man trying to save my life. This whole ordeal is probably a fireable offense for this guy.

I cross my arms over my chest and swallow nervously. "I'm sorry I didn't inform you I'm not a strong swimmer. I assumed that Everly being on a swim team meant the odds of me needing to save her were slim to none. But I must inform you that the job application never said I needed lifeguard training."

Mr. Fletcher pinches the bridge of his nose. "An unforgivable oversight on my part."

He looks like he's already made his decision, and I feel horrible. I already unpacked all my shit. And I love that tiny house. It's the nicest place I've ever lived in. My sister is going to lose her shit on me if I come crawling back to her house after one day on the job.

I wiggle my earlobe to drain some water out of it and wince when I feel an ache on the back of my head.

"Shit," he murmurs under his breath and moves to stand behind me. "Did you hit your head going in? You might be concussed." He reaches up to inspect my injury, causing me to shiver as the warmth of his body presses against my back. I'm suddenly feeling light-headed for a whole different reason.

"I'm fine," I croak, catching myself from leaning into his body for comfort. I try to step away, but he annoyingly follows. "I'm not bleeding, am I?"

I reach back to touch the injured area, and his fingers brush over mine as his other hand rests on my waist for purchase. His fingers press into my curves, holding me in place, and I have to swallow my gasp as a current of heat damn near explodes between my legs.

His voice is soft and velvety when he replies, "No open wound that I can see, but you have a decent goose egg."

I lick my lips and nod. "Your kid is stronger than she looks."

Mr. Fletcher exhales through his nose. "That was horribly reckless of her. Everly knows better." His tone is scathing, and I suddenly wish it was directed at me again, not Everly. "I'm sorry for yelling at you. I didn't know you were hurt. We should get this looked at. My friend Josh is a doctor in town. I can run you to his private practice clinic."

"Heavens no, I am fine." I wipe the water off my face and turn, instantly feeling the loss of his touch while noting the genuine traces of concern in his eyes. I offer up a smile as proof of life. "I grew up on a farm. We're built of sturdier stuff than most."

He holds my eyes for a moment, and I swear they shift from that bright ocean blue that Everly's are, into a cloudy mix of bluish green. Almost indigo. They're narrow and framed by long, dark lashes that have no business being on a man with lighter hair. I quickly drink in the rest of his face, noting the worry lines that stack on the center of his forehead. His nose has a faint smattering of freckles over it that I never noticed before. Probably because I was too busy staring at the scruff on his square jaw peppered with light, dark, and gray hairs. And those lips. Those full lips look so soft, I have a strange urge to reach out and pinch them to see how they feel.

I swallow the knot in my throat, and my voice is barely a whisper when I croak, "If you need to fire me, I understand."

A wrinkle forms between Mr. Fletcher's brows as his gaze drops to my mouth. He moistens his lips to reply when a strange noise from somewhere in the distance has both of our heads snapping toward the house, making me flinch as pain shoots down my neck.

I spot Everly seated on the deck steps with the first-aid kit beside her. She's curled up in a ball, her head buried in her arms as she sobs violently.

"Fuck," Mr. Fletcher mutters, making a move to go to her.

"Let me." I grab his forearm and feel slightly woozy from either my brush with drowning or the skin-on-skin contact after I basically just imprinted his handsome face in my mind. I pull my hand back and rush out, "I'm sure she feels awful, and I'm the only one who can forgive her."

The muscle in Mr. Fletcher's jaw jumps. "I'm not sure she should be forgiven just yet."

"Yes, she should," I huff indignantly, my defenses instantly going up. "She's not one of your many employees who need to be written up. She's a little kid who made a mistake." I practically push this grumpy anti-Dadbod, corporate mogul-ass out of my way to walk over to my charge.

"Yo, Sea Monster," I call out, and a red-faced Everly looks up at me, her shoulders shaking with every hysteric sob that wracks her tiny body. "Seriously, you gotta tell me your workout routine. I'm no skinny minny, and you manhandled me into that pool like a boss." I try to laugh as I stand in front of her, but Everly does not take the bait.

"I'm so sorry, Cozy," she sobs and leaps up to barrel into me. She wraps her slender arms around my hips and buries her face in my chest. "I didn't mean to hurt you. I thought it would be funny. I'm so stupid. So, so stupid!"

"Hey," I assert, grabbing her arms and pulling her away from me. I squat down in front of her so I can look her in the eyes. "You are many things, but stupid isn't even close to one of them."

She sniffs loudly, and her little chin trembles. "I'm dumb then."

"You're not dumb," I argue and then reconsider. "Well, maybe you are dumb because stupid and dumb mean the same thing, but we can work on that later."

She begins crying again, and I realize my joke failed miserably. I cup her face and force her to look at me. "I've known you for less than a day, and I can already tell that you have great taste in books, you're sweeter than any kid I've ever met your age, and you swim like a mermaid. Stupid and dumb are not adjectives that belong to you. You got me?"

Her chin continues to tremble. "But I could have seriously hurt you."

"Your Aquaman of a dad could have seriously hurt me," I correct with a laugh. "Did you see how he almost cannonballed on my head?" And then manhandled me in a way no man ever has before. Life-or-death situation or not, I had an out-of-body experience as he carried me across the patio.

She sputters out a snotty laugh, bringing me back to the moment, and looks up behind me. I glance back to see Mr. Fletcher standing there, staring down at us with shocking, red-rimmed eyes that make my heart leap into my throat. I definitely didn't see that reaction from him coming.

Shaking that image away, I turn back and wipe at the tears under Everly's eyes with the back of my finger. "If he had a nice swan dive like you, this all would have been much less dramatic."

Everly wipes her nose on the back of her hand. "I really am sorry, Cozy."

"You are forgiven. And just because we make bad choices doesn't make us bad people." I pull her into a hug, and she falls into me like she can't stand to hold herself upright anymore. It's soul-crushing. "I'm sorry for scaring you like that. I'm not the best swimmer."

"I noticed," she murmurs into my neck.

My body shakes with laughter, and I think I even hear a chortle from grumpy Zaddy behind me. Everly pulls back, and I tuck a wet strand of hair behind her ear. "Why don't we go get dried off and have some hot cocoa. All life-threatening moments seem a lot less scary after chocolate."

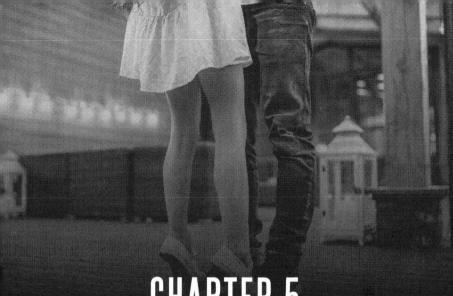

CHAPTER 5

Max

No matter how hard I try to focus back on my mountain of work the rest of the afternoon, it's no use. My eyes are constantly being drawn to what Cassandra and Everly are doing. They're dressed back in their clothes and lying out in the grass, far away from the pool.

Thank goodness.

Jesus Christ, what the hell was all that?

I saw the moment Cassandra was pulled into the water and even waited a few seconds, expecting her to surface. When she didn't, I dead sprinted out of my patio door and straight into the pool, nearly kicking Everly in the head as I jumped over her.

I've had this pool for a decade and never had to perform a water rescue. Day one with the new nanny, and I'm testing the water resistance on my Cartier watch as I save her fucking life.

Can't swim? How the fuck did I fail to include that on my job application? Jessica will kill me when she finds out about all this. This was a horrible oversight. What kind of father am I for not thinking about that?

Cassandra's words play on repeat in my mind, *'Just because we make bad choices doesn't make us bad people.'* Wise words for someone whose life philosophy is "why do more when you can do less." Thankfully, they helped to soothe Everly. I wasn't going to be able to stand by and watch her cry for a moment longer. I know what she did was wrong, but it doesn't change the fact that my kid's tears gut me.

Memories of her being three years old and crying every time I picked her up for her weekends with me still fucking haunt me. She didn't want to leave her mom's and spend the weekend with her dad. It wasn't anything I did or didn't do particularly. She was just a kid who loved her mother. Often, I would cave and let her stay with Jess and miss out on a whole weekend with my kid just so she wouldn't feel that pain. It killed me to lose that time with her, but if Everly was happy, that was all that mattered.

Thankfully, she grew out of that stage as she got older. And we found activities to keep us busy when she was with me so she wouldn't have time to miss her mom. I filled our weekends with trips to the zoo, plays, amusement parks, and weekend trips to Aspen to ski. Anything I could find that kids like to do, we did it. I wanted Everly to leave weekends with me feeling like she had the time of her life.

Now she wants to do nothing with the nanny all summer, and I can't help but draw a parallel.

A light knock on my door has me straightening in my desk chair. Everly doesn't knock, so I can only assume it's the nanny. I smooth down my new tie for the day and attempt to look busy as I call out, "Come in."

Cassandra walks into my bedroom, dressed in a long tie-dyed T-shirt and a pair of black leggings. She glances briefly at my bed and then forces her eyes on me.

"Can I have a word with you, Mr. Fletcher?" she asks, her hands playing with the hem of her shirt as she approaches my desk.

"Yes, of course. Where's Everly?"

"She's reading upstairs," she replies quickly, tucking her damp hair behind her ears.

The smell of coconut invades the room, and I wonder if she's just gotten out of the shower. Not that I should be thinking of my nanny in the fucking shower.

"I was wondering if maybe we could tell Everly I quit?" Cassandra quips, her tone sharp and contained.

My heart rate increases as I repeat her words in my head before I can mutter them out loud. "Quit?"

"Yeah…" she responds, her eyes staring down at the floor. "I'd rather she think I quit than blame herself for getting me fired. She keeps apologizing about the accident today, and I know it's breaking her little heart that she hurt me. If she thinks you let me go because of the pool incident, she'll never forgive herself."

I sit back in my chair, processing everything Cassandra has just said to me. She's known my kid for one freaking day, and she's willing to take the fall for her? I'm rarely speechless, but this situation makes forming a coherent sentence difficult.

I clear my throat. "Do you want to quit?"

"Not at all." Cassandra's round eyes lift to meet mine. The sunlight pouring in the windows behind me makes her eyes look greener than ever. "But I know that what happened today was terrifying for you and Everly. We were lucky you were here. I mean, I don't think I was going to drown. I was getting up to the top of the water before you jumped in. But I fully admit that it wasn't safe. Yes, it's true I'm not a great swimmer. I mean, I think I can save my own life, but if something like this happened to Everly, I'd be terrified of what that could look like. And with how much time you want us to spend in the pool this summer, I realize this makes me unqualified for the job I accepted. Therefore, I take full responsibility and will tender my resignation, Mr. Fletcher."

My head jerks back. *Tender her resignation?* That's pretty official language for someone whose past employer involved making footlong subs. I inhale a deep breath and stand, propping myself on the edge of the desk. "Let's take a breath here, Cassandra," I say, crossing my arms over my chest.

She nods and tucks her hands behind her back, her chest jutting out toward me. I flinch as I recall the feel of her extremely full breasts in my hands. How is it possible to be completely fucking terrified and half hard at the same time? That's really something I should talk to a therapist about someday. But not Josh's wife, Lynsey. Patient confidentiality or not, I don't need her to think I'm lusting after my kid's nanny.

"The truth is, Everly is an excellent swimmer," I continue, refocusing on the task at hand. "An incident like this never should have happened. Everly feels awful because she knows what she did was wrong. She usually has better impulse control than that, but I think she's really excited about hanging out with you this summer, and she got carried away."

"Hey, I've been there," Cassandra huffs with a laugh, her hand pushing into her dark hair as she gazes out the sliders behind me. "I remember pushing my sister off the dock at the lake once. She whacked her ankle on the boat hoist and screamed bloody murder for hours. Even had to get stitches."

I fight back a smile at that very random overshare. "Ouch."

"Yeah…the whole lake heard her battle cry. It was Awkward City. I immediately regretted my life choice that day."

I cringe knowingly, thankful for the turn in the conversation as the tension relaxes. "Kind of like your new boss regretting accidentally grabbing your chest as he attempted to save your life?" My shoulders lift with embarrassment.

"I mean, I was a kid, and you are a full-grown man, but I guess you can still relate." She lets out a soft giggle, and the tension eases between us as I watch her with downcast eyes.

"Awkward what?" I frown and watch her curiously, wanting to know more about her.

"City. Awkward City." The teasing smirk on her face makes it hard to keep scowling.

I click my tongue and sigh, trying to figure out the best way to resolve this. Giving up, I gesture awkwardly toward her chest, trying hard not to look at it. "Well…I am sorry about that."

"It's fine. My tits get in the way a lot." She closes her eyes and shakes her head. "I shouldn't have said that. Can we stop talking about my breasts now?"

"Please," I agree because now I can't stop looking at them and

recalling how the weight of them felt in my hands. Fucking hell…
Awkward City indeed.

"Okay then." She pulls her shirt away from her chest as if she's
trying to conceal her completely un-concealable breasts. "So are you
saying I'm not fired?"

I force myself to lift my eyes to hers, holding her gaze as I push
away my indecent thoughts. "Correct."

"Yes!" She thrusts a fist up into the air. "That is good news."

I laugh. I can't help it. Cassandra Barlow is unlike anyone I've
ever met before.

"I should probably go check on Everly." She gestures toward the
door.

"Yes, you do that," I confirm, my brows furrowing as I try to refocus my thoughts away from the nanny. I lower myself back into
my chair.

She pauses at my door. "Thank you, Mr. Fletcher. I promise I
will be extremely careful from now on whenever we're at the pool."

I nod and smile. "Call me Max."

"Max?" She looks unsure. "You sure about that?"

"Anything but Big Daddy," I reply with a grimace.

She snorts out a laugh. "That kind of slipped out."

"It would have had to."

She bites her lip and waggles her eyebrows. "Does this mean
you'll start calling me Cozy?"

I wrinkle my nose. "I think I prefer Cassandra."

"Fair enough." She taps the wall beside her. "I'll let you get back
to work. Thank you again…Max."

I nod and turn back to my desk, hating how much I like the way
my name sounds on her lips.

CHAPTER 6

Cozy

"Hello, Zaddy," I murmur to myself the next morning as I stare slack-jawed at Max from the grass as he hoists himself out of the swimming pool. Sluices of water ripple down his washboard abs and disappear into his low-slung swimming trunks.

"Morning," he says crisply as he notices me walking over to him. He grabs a towel off the nearby lounge chair and wipes it over his head, mussing his dirty-blond locks.

"Heyo." I swallow the knot in my throat and rip my eyes off his very erect nipples as I stand before him. "You're up early."

"I like to swim laps in the mornings." He wipes his pecs next. My eyes follow his movements for far longer than is appropriate. If there's any length of time that would ever be appropriate for a nanny to look at her boss's big, fat pecs.

Can pecs be fat? Probably man boobs are fat. Max definitely doesn't have man boobs. They are mounds of firm muscle that I would really like to poke my finger into one to see what they feel like. I bet they feel like pound cake.

What is with me wanting to touch various body parts of this man?

"Swimming is nice," I reply, hesitating awkwardly in front of him because it's hard to walk away from such a fine specimen.

"For those of us who can swim." The corner of his mouth pulls up into a teasing smirk like it did yesterday. It might be my favorite expression he makes, and I don't even care that it was at my expense.

I bite my lip and smirk right back. "Maybe I'll learn more than a weak doggy paddle one of these days." *Especially if it would give me a body like his.*

Mirth dances in Max's eyes as he tilts his head and reads the text on my loose-fitting graphic tank. It reads: '*Whatever. I'll just date myself*'

"Nice shirt," he says with a small laugh.

"Thanks! I got it from my friend's T-shirt shop downtown. She has a lot of cool stuff. I was hoping to take Everly there for one of her tie-dye classes."

Max nods. "I'm sure Everly would love that."

"Cool." I pause awkwardly, clutching my Kindle, and am unsure what else to say. "Guess I'll just head inside then to read while I wait for Everly to wake up."

I make my way toward the deck steps and pause when Max calls out. "What's on the agenda for today?"

"Agenda?" I respond, turning on the bottom step to face him. I'm dressed in a pair of tie-dyed shorts, and I swear I catch him staring at my legs. I shrug. "No agenda, I'm afraid. My nanny business model prefers more of a willy-nilly approach."

Water drips off Max's hair as he walks toward me with a dubious look. "What is willy-nilly exactly?"

I waggle my eyebrows playfully. "I suppose you could say it's like an elevated version of YOLO. It allows Everly and me to be spontaneous. I mean...look at this beautiful morning? Why would we want to spoil all its possibility with a stifling agenda? Unless it's for tie-dye classes, obviously."

"Interesting," Max huffs and takes a few steps past me so he's towering over me. His six-pack abs are annoyingly eye level now as he turns back and adds, "If my business philosophy was willy-nilly, I wouldn't have any of the success I have today."

He turns to leave as I can't stop my reply from tumbling out of my mouth. "And that would be a bad thing?"

Turning on his heel, he furrows his dark brow at me. "You have a problem with success?"

"No," I answer and glance back at his giant pool. "But at what cost?"

"What does that mean?" His tone takes a swift turn from pleasant to punchy, and I scold myself internally for not being able to bite my damn tongue.

I try not to squirm under his penetrative glower. "I'm just saying all things in life come with a cost. It's important to determine what expenses are necessary and what expenses aren't. I'm sure I don't have to tell you that material items aren't the only things of value in life."

Max tilts his head, his eyes roving over my face for a long, pregnant pause. He takes a step down, looming over me with his all-business face that I recall him having during my initial interview. "You have a lot of uniquely strong outlooks on life, Cassandra. I can't help but wonder what's inspired them?"

My chest tightens at his pointed question, and I falter for a moment, trying to figure out how to answer him.

"You were born and raised here in Boulder, right? You mentioned growing up on a farm. Is a willy-nilly business philosophy really how your family gets things done?"

"No," I state, my lips thinning with challenge as I watch his pouty lips like a freak. "But country life is very different from corporate life."

Max stares at me incredulously. "And you think you know my business?"

I open my mouth to reply when a high-pitched voice breaks through the moment, "Morning!"

Max and I both spread apart like we were caught kissing. I didn't realize how close we'd gotten until Everly snapped us out of whatever mental standoff we were just in the middle of.

"The Sea Monster is awake," I exclaim with a dramatic flourish to my tone as I march past Max with my chin held high. "Ready for breakfast?"

"Yes, I'm starving." Everly pats her tiny tummy. "Can we do pancakes?"

I turn on my heel and wince. "Is now a bad time to tell you I'm a terrible cook?"

Everly sighs. "Oh Cozy, what are you good at?"

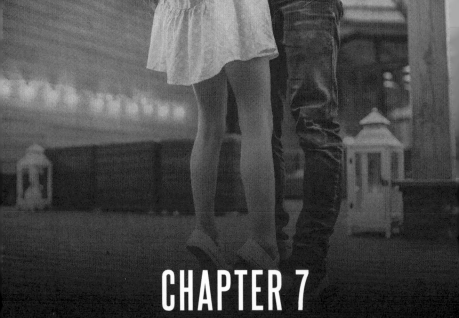

CHAPTER 7

Max

The next few days go a bit more smoothly as we all find our rhythm. Cassandra continues to wake early and is in the house reading a book in the living room before Everly ever wakes up. I often pass her as I finish my workouts but do my best *not* to ask what's on the agenda since that's essentially a four-letter word to the new nanny. It's honestly really frustrating to have such a contradictory employee. However, I allowed Everly to choose Cassandra based on her interview, so it would be a dick move for me to try changing her mindset on week one.

I just need to watch how this all plays out. I have a feeling Cassandra and Everly are going to tire of this willy-nilly summer sooner rather than later. And at that moment, I shall take my victory lap.

Although I will say, yesterday at lunchtime, I found the two of them out on the deck with their eyes closed. When I asked what they were doing, they said they were playing tennis against each other in their minds. Everly's eyes were closed so tightly, her voice deadly serious as she yelled out, "Love all," that I couldn't help but think it was pretty damn adorable. Not that I'll ever admit that out loud. Nor will I admit that I pay for a membership to a country club with professional tennis courts, and it kills me to think my daughter looked happier on that deck with Cassandra than she ever did during all those tennis matches we played together. Being a dad is really fucking weird sometimes.

Everly's book report for the week is already done, and she even made a mood board with photos inspired by the story. She looked adorable as she presented it to me at lunchtime yesterday. When I asked Cassandra where her book report was, because she's clearly an avid reader, she said her books weren't for a child's eyes. And after a slight pause, she smiled, mumbling to herself about how her mood board wouldn't be appropriate for even my eyes.

She didn't think I heard her, but I did. It made me wonder what kinds of naughty stories she might like to read. Not that I'm going to ask. Asking would be inappropriate. As my head swam with those thoughts, I had to scold myself and remind my cock that it's imperative for me to keep a professional approach with Cassandra after practically groping her in the swimming pool on her first day.

Evenings with Everly have been great. Cassandra usually goes back to the guesthouse when my chef shows up to make dinner. Everly does a lot of talking about Cassandra and their "daydreaming sessions." It gets a little old, but I guess it's good to see her happy.

She talks to her mother around lunchtime every day, and I would have thought she'd be homesick for her since Jess has been gone for two weeks now, but Everly seems to be managing okay. That kid is growing up so fast. I'm really cherishing this extra time I'm getting with her.

I even have to admit that working from home has gone better than I expected. It's amazing how much I can get done in a day when I'm not interrupted by my assistant or staff members. As long as I don't have to jump into swimming pools to save grown women, I can get a lot accomplished.

Thursday morning, my phone rings, and I see my buddy Josh's face pop up on the screen. "Well, hello, Dr. Richardson...how the hell are you?" I ask, noticing how bright my tone is this early in the morning.

"Where are you?" Josh inquires, sounding like he's outside.

"I'm home…why?"

"'Cuz I'm at your office."

"Oh, I'm working from home this week."

"I'm sorry, what?" Josh huffs, and I swear I can hear the fucker laughing.

"I am working from home," I repeat.

"Are you sick? Did you catch the bubonic plague? Need me to come examine you?"

"Maybe you should examine your chronic case of assholitis. It sounds like it's flaring up again."

He laughs into the phone. "I'm sorry, but you're never not in the office. You live in the office when you don't have Everly. Plus, don't you have a big merger coming up?"

"Yes, and I am handling it, but I'm doing it from home. I hired a nanny for Everly, and she's kind of different, so I wanted to take the week to make sure she's…sane."

"Jesus. Is she that bad?"

"She's not bad. In fact, I think she might be good. She's just… unique."

"Is she a teenager?"

"No, she's twenty-six years old."

"Kind of old for a nanny, isn't she?"

I shrug even though he can't see me. "She seems mostly professional."

"Mostly," Josh huffs out a laugh. "Glowing review."

"That's why I'm working from home, asshole. I'm assessing."

"Hey, I get it. I'm lucky we have daycare at the practice. Both Lynsey and I can pop in to see Julianna between patients. It's the best. I can't imagine not seeing my kid all day long. That would kill me."

I can't help but smile at Josh's words. He has changed so much from who he was just a few years ago. He used to be a cold, secretive, moody asshole with baggage he refused to unpack from his days as a pediatric oncologist on the East Coast. He moved back to Boulder, and I'd have to beg him to go out with me when he wasn't working at the ER, and even then, he was barely present. Meeting Lynsey and becoming a father has really transformed him. It brought back the guy I grew up with. I'm really happy for him.

"This is the first time in years I've had this much quality time with Everly. I must admit, it's pretty amazing," I reply, standing up to look out the window. Everly and Cassandra are currently having a picnic breakfast on a blanket outside. They've rolled over one of the pool umbrellas for shade and have all of Everly's old stuffed animals I thought she was done playing with surrounding them. The entire scene looks fucking heavenly.

When my eyes wander from my kid to Cassandra, I quickly clear my throat and look away. "Did you call for a reason or just to bust my balls about working from home?"

"I did call for a reason," Josh says with a laugh. "We're watching Lynsey's nieces tomorrow night, and Lynsey was wondering if we could do a barbecue at your house and let the girls swim with Everly."

My eyes widen in surprise. Lynsey has mentioned to me before that her nieces are near Everly's age, and we should get them together to play sometime. I just brushed her off because I usually like to keep it just me and her on my weekends with Everly. But I guess now that I don't have to share her with Jess all summer, I could probably branch out. Let her play with some friends.

"That sounds awesome. I'm sure Everly will love it."

"Really?" Josh sounds shocked. "Shit, that was easier than I thought."

"Well, I haven't seen Julianna in a while, so it'll be nice to catch up. I'll have my chef do all the food, so we can all relax and enjoy ourselves."

"Sweet…umm…okay if we bring some extra people with us?"

I huff knowingly. "The regular crew?"

Josh tsks through the line. "Yeah, Lynsey and Kate are joined at the hip. And you know Kate…she likes to invite everybody."

I nod. Kate Smith, aka Mercedes Lee Loveletter, is a force of fucking nature in Boulder. She's the self-proclaimed resident smut writer at Tire Depot. She's as loud as she is successful in the world of romance novels, and whatever Kate wants, Kate gets.

I met her through my stockbroker, Dean Moser, who I'm sure will be coming tomorrow as well. His fiancée, Norah, is one of my biggest clients at Fletcher Industries. She specializes in a donut, croissant combo, and since franchising her bakery last year, her business has blown up. We're up to twenty-eight Rise and Shine Bakeries now, with one in Canada on the horizon. It will be good to see them again. I have some business to discuss with Norah anyway, so I can kill two birds with one stone there.

I also assume Miles's best friend, Sam, will be coming with his wife, Maggie, who happens to be Miles's sister. Honestly, Boulder is what I call a big, small town. Everyone is connected to everyone. It's a step away from being an incestuous freak show.

Luckily, I've spent a fair amount of time with this whole crew, so I get along with everyone. I even hosted Kate and Miles's joint bachelor and bachelorette party at my house in Aspen. How Kate got me to give up my home for her and all her friends is still a mystery to me. But they're a fun bunch, so even though I act put out, I look forward to seeing them all. Kate and Miles have a baby now, and I must see that in action. Smut writer and mechanic turned parents...I'm sure it's an amazing sight.

"I look forward to seeing everyone," I state honestly.

"Amazing. Text me if you need us to bring anything. Should we say six o'clock tomorrow? After work?"

"Sounds perfect."

We hang up, and I nearly jump out of my skin when I see Everly standing in my bedroom staring at me. "Daddy?"

"Yes?" I notice Cassandra standing at the door with a sheepish look in her eyes.

"We have an idea," Everly chirps.

The hair on the back of my neck prickles. "What is it?"

"Well...Cozy and I were daydreaming, and she told me to daydream what I wanted to do today, and she would do everything in her power to make it happen."

"Did she now?" I level narrow eyes on Cassandra, who looks a bit too guilty for my liking.

"So…I used my imagination and decided we should all go white water rafting."

My head jolts forward. "Your imagination told you that white water rafting was a good idea?"

Everly nods enthusiastically. "You, me, and Cozy."

"She doesn't know how to swim." I point accusingly at Cassandra, whose face falls.

"Hey!" she barks back inelegantly and walks into my room. "I can swim a little. And I'm sure they have life jackets. You just have to bounce off the rocks like a pinball until you can make it to shore. Plus, I don't think it's drowning they worry about…more so the head traumas from hitting rocks."

I gape at Cassandra. "Are you sure you're not concussed from Monday?"

Her jaw drops, but I turn back to my daughter. "We are not white water rafting. Besides, I have to work. This is me working." I gesture to my desk to punctuate my point.

"Fine…I have one more idea," Everly says, her jaw taut with determination.

I flick my pen on my desk. "I can't wait to hear this one."

CHAPTER 8

Cozy

Everly must have magical Sea Monster powers because how she got her father to agree to take us zip lining up in the mountains is beyond all logic to me. Like seriously, I expected Max to laugh in our faces and point at the door. But the website said Everly needed a parent present, and she was determined to get her dad to take the afternoon off.

A girl boss through and through. I'd be proud if I had anything to do with raising her.

So here we are, all tucked into Max's swanky SUV and driving an hour up into the mountains to this adventure course that one of Everly's friends told her all about. Max is on the phone the whole time, and I look like a big kid in the front seat of his car feeling slightly guilty for taking him away from his work when I'm supposed to be the one in charge of his kid.

Plus, this isn't exactly doing "less" like my nanny philosophy promotes, but it's at least recreational. Nothing says broadening our imaginations like an adventure course.

We check in, and Max signs all the waivers and looks decidedly irritated when we get fitted with harnesses and carabiners, plus some weird-looking zip line trolley that you use to attach to the cables that stretch nearly a hundred feet between these giant trees.

We go through a small practice course that Everly breezes through, squealing with laughter as she descends the short distance.

When it's my turn to do the short line, I wasn't expecting the bite of the harness to dig into my thighs so much. I'm more of a mall walker when it comes to exercise choices, so this tree flying stuff is a bit out of my comfort zone.

As I spin around, going backward down the short line, the smile on my face falters as I notice Max's damn near feral facial expression as he watches me go. He looks like he's about to shapeshift into a wolf!

As soon as I stop, I quickly pat my ass, half expecting my bike shorts to be split up the middle with how intense he was staring at me. When all was as it should be, I return to the starting point, wondering if I was seeing things because Max is back to ignoring me.

His entire focus is on our guide, Chad, asking him to make sure Everly's harness was snug enough. Before I can ask Mr. Grumpy if he's having any fun, he scoots by me to climb into the gator with Chad, who's taking us to our first zip line course. Maybe his facial expression had nothing to do with me and more to do with a work issue. That would be far more likely.

"Okay, guys, let me just check your harnesses one last time," Chad says, stopping in front of Everly first. "You're all set, little dudette. Have a killer time."

"Thank you!" Everly squeals and begins climbing the ladder up the first tree.

Max looks up nervously and bites out, "Is that safe?"

"Totally!" Chad bellows with a hearty thumbs-up. "She's all hooked up, Padre. Just chill."

The muscle in Max's jaw tics violently as he watches his daughter climb every step.

"Let me get your other daughter checked out, and then I'm on to you," Chad adds.

"Other daughter?" Max's eyes zero in on the guide in confusion. Chad points at me. "Is this your oldest?"

"What the hell?" Max snaps, his voice gruff. "She's twenty-six years old."

"She looks young…and beautiful." Chad smiles at me, and I hear a growl vibrate from Max beside us. I glance over and begin to fear for the guide's safety at the positively lethal look in his eyes.

"How old do you think I am?" Max is seething.

Chad shrugs. "I don't know, man. I'm not good with ages."

"Fucking hell," Max mumbles under his breath, and a chortle sputters out of my mouth. He looks at me like I've just betrayed his entire family. "Something funny, Cassandra?"

"Nothing funny at all, Big Daddy." I can't help it. I had to poke the bear.

His lips part as he tucks his tongue to the side of his mouth and bites it like he's trying not to say what's on his mind. "You think you're cute?"

I giggle and tug on the short braids sticking out from my helmet. "Chad said beautiful actually…and very youthful looking. Right, Chad?"

"Climb the fucking ladder, Cozy," Max barks, and my heart jolts at his use of my nickname.

Our eyes connect, and for some strange reason, the glint in Max's gaze makes me feel like he's not as irritated by me as I thought. In fact, he looks like he wants to swallow me whole. Like he's a second away from grabbing my harness, strapping me up to the nearest tree, and holding my braids as he runs his tongue over every inch of my body.

That illicit image causes a painful throb to erupt between my thighs as I wobbly attempt to climb the ladder up to the platform. When Max joins me and Everly at the top, he shoots me a knowing look that makes me wonder if he could read my mind a moment ago.

I need to get control of my thoughts.

"Who wants to go first?" Chad asks after he's hooked all our zip lines up to the safety ropes above us.

"Me!" Everly calls out, raising her hand.

I shake my head and look at Max. "No fear."

"I don't know where she gets that," Max says, and I notice a flicker of distress cast over his eyes as he looks down. "We're really high up, aren't we?"

"You're not scared of heights, are you?" I ask, narrowing my eyes as I watch him white knuckle his safety harness.

"I didn't think so…but I'm doubting that fact now." His gaze flicks from me to Everly as she gets into position for takeoff. "Be careful, Everly."

Everly offers up an enthusiastic wave before launching herself down the long cable, squealing excitedly with her hands splayed out wide. Max looks like he's about to crawl out of his skin as he watches her go, his feet moving close to the edge the farther she gets away from us. He's focused so intently on Everly that he doesn't notice where he's standing.

He's about to take another step forward, so I reach out and grab his arm to pull him back. He stumbles into my body, pressing me back into the tree and causing our safety straps to tangle on the line above. Our bodies are flush against each other, so my hands grip his shoulders for balance as his land on the tree behind me, caging me in with his musky, manly scent. He looks down at me in confusion.

"You were about to step right off the platform," I clarify, looking up at him. My eyes zero in on his pursed lips as I struggle to ignore the reaction my body is having to the weight of him pressed snugly against me.

"I was?" His breath is warm on my face as his eyes flick back and forth between mine.

"I basically just saved your life," I answer with a laugh.

Max's mouth pulls back into a surprising wolfish smile as his eyes lower to my lips. "Don't think we're even now."

We stare at each other for a moment in a sort of stunned shock before Chad's voice interrupts. "He was hooked up to the safety line, so he was perfectly safe."

I blink myself out of this trance and mumble, "Thanks, Chad," annoyed that the guide popped our little bubble of…flirting? Was Max Fletcher flirting with me just now?

He gives me a terse look before pushing back enough to give a breath of space between us. But it can't go unnoticed that his hand remains firmly on my hip.

"That was awesome!" Everly squeals, and Max turns to look over his shoulder to see that Everly has reached the next platform and is standing with the guide.

His body sags with relief, and his hand reflexively tightens on my hip before he lets go completely. "Good job, kid!"

"Dad, you go next!" Everly calls back.

Max's Adam's apple slides down his throat as Chad disconnects us to untangle our lines. He attaches Max's zip trolley to the cable next. "Ready, Big Daddy?" Chad says with a dopey smile.

"It's Mr. Fletcher," Max growls at the dude.

"Hey, chica." Chad looks at me. "Smile at this dude again…I think it helps with his mood."

"What?" Max barks, and without warning, Chad shoves him down the cable for his ride.

I laugh at the girlie scream that slips out of Max's mouth when he first takes off. He does not appear to be enjoying himself as he grips his line like he's hugging a security blanket. By the time he makes it to Everly, she's cheering him on and laughing loud enough for the entire adventure course to hear. When he's caught on the platform, her little arms wrap tightly around her dad, so I quickly pull out my phone and zoom in to snap a picture of them. They really are so adorable. I think Chad made a mistake earlier. It's not my smile that brightens Max's surly demeanor. It's Everly's. Without a doubt.

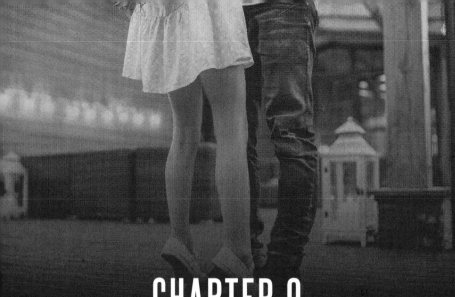

CHAPTER 9

Max

"This looks amazing, Michael," I state, standing by the grill outside where the chef who's been cooking for me for years is grilling up shrimp, chicken, and steak kabobs.

"Wait until you see what we've got cooking inside," Michael says, elbowing me gently and pointing back to a staff member he brought with him tonight.

"Oh, I already sampled the mac 'n' cheese." I pat my stomach. "You do such great work. Thanks for making extra on short notice."

"Anytime!" Michael replies just as my front doorbell rings.

"They're here," Everly peals, running toward the deck from the pool area where she's been inflating floaties for the better part of an hour. "I'll get the door!" She tears past me barefoot in nothing but her swimsuit.

I smile. Damn, I wish she looked that excited every time I picked her up on the weekends from her mom's. Maybe sheltering her away from my friends wasn't the best idea. I join her at the front door and see Josh holding his little brown-eyed toddler on his hip.

"Holy shit, Julianna has gotten big," I blurt out honestly.

"Language, Max," Josh chastises, and I cringe when I see two kids old enough to understand my curse words flanking Josh. They are also brown-haired girls that look a lot like their aunt Lynsey. "This is Lennon and Claire. Lennon is a brand-new teenager, and Claire is a whopping ten years old."

"You don't have to say brand new." Lennon rolls her eyes and crosses her arms over her chest.

Josh shoots me a desperate look as Everly's fingers wrap around my hand. She tucks behind me, suddenly acting very shy. I give her a reassuring squeeze. "Well, Everly here is eleven, so you girls should have tons of things to talk about."

"Dad," Everly groans and rolls her eyes just like Lennon did.

"Do you want to take the girls up and show them your room?" I ask, desperate to get past the eye-rolling phase of the evening.

"I want to see your room," Claire chirps, saving all of us from awkward doom. Or "Awkward City," as Cassandra would say.

Lennon glances up at Josh with a too cool for school look but follows the girls into the house and up the winding staircase.

"Dude…if I end up with three girls in my life…send whiskey. Lots and lots of whiskey," Josh says, shifting Julianna over to his other hip.

I laugh and hear Lynsey's voice squeak from behind Josh. "You're in my way, babe."

Josh moves inside to reveal his wife, Lynsey, weighed down with a beach bag, three life jackets, a pool noodle, and a round charcuterie board overflowing with meats and cheeses.

"I told you I had the food all covered." I cut a look to my buddy as I take the board from Lynsey's struggling hands.

"She wouldn't listen," Josh huffs, eyeing his wife with a knowing look.

"Charcuterie isn't food. It is life!" Lynsey proclaims, looking mildly less stressed now that I've taken it off her hands. "Let's see this big ass pool Josh wouldn't shut up about!"

I place the charcuterie board in the kitchen where Michael's assistant is setting up a buffet and lead Josh, Lynsey, and Julianna out back. Lynsey instantly puts a life jacket on Jules, who's looking pretty comfortable in her dad's arms and nowhere near ready to get in the water. Everly, Lennon, and Claire dart past us, wasting no time jumping off the diving board. I watch cautiously for a moment and feel relieved when I see they're decent swimmers. I don't need to perform two water rescues this week.

Miles and Kate show up next, an adorable redheaded little boy named Tucker in tow. He's four months old but looks like he's going to be a bruiser like his dad. Dean and Norah arrive next, and I take a moment to congratulate them on their engagement that happened a couple of months ago at a concert. I've known Dean for years, and I was certain he would be a terminal bachelor with me until we were old and gray. I guess he fell in love with more than just Norah's croinuts.

I pull Norah into my bedroom/office to have her sign some documents that popped up for her this week.

"This is weird signing papers in your bedroom," Norah says with a laugh. "I couldn't believe you weren't in the office this week."

"Trust me, more work gets done in here than sleep. Why do people keep freaking out about me not being at my office?" I ask, handing her a pen and opening the document to the pages she needs to sign. "I'm not that much of a workaholic, am I?"

Norah's brows lift. "Let's be honest, Max. You're the CEO of Fletcher Industries. You probably should have handed me off to one of your client managers months ago."

I shrug. "I keep all my favorite clients. Plus, I'm an investor in your franchise so helping you helps me."

"I appreciate that, but you're a full-time dad this summer. You need to let some things go and enjoy your time with Everly." She gets a soft look in her eye, and I swear I see her hand touch her stomach.

I'm just about to ask her a question when we're interrupted by Kate banging on the deck slider. She opens it up and her eyes sweep the room. "So *this* is where the millionaire Max's magic happens." She waggles her eyebrows lasciviously and runs her hand along the duvet that covers my king-sized bed. "I like the color. It's very Christian *Grey* of you."

"Would you stop with the Christian Grey jokes?"

"You're the richest guy I know nonfictionally. Christian Grey is the richest guy I know fictionally. I love to draw parallels in my life. Now show me to your red room of pain."

"There is no red room of pain in this house. And no magic happens in this house. This house is for my kid," I groan with irritation, running a hand through my hair. I never bring women back here. Not even when Everly is at her mother's. I prefer to keep my life as a single man in Boulder very separate from my life with Everly. Most of the women I sleep with don't even know I have a kid.

Kate doesn't look like she believes me. "What about that chick in Aspen I met? She's never come to Boulder for a visit?"

"No…what I do in Aspen stays in Aspen."

"So that's where the red room is." Kate laughs, and Norah looks decidedly uncomfortable.

"Let's save the dirty stuff for your books, Kate." I wrap my arm around her and gesture for the door. "This conversation requires alcohol."

"I'm just trying to figure you out, Max," Kate states, eyeing me speculatively. "Every millionaire has a kink."

I exhale through my nose. "Boy, I really love seeing you, Kate."

We head outside just as Sam and Maggie arrive. Sam owns Tire Depot in town and has done all the work on my dad's construction vehicles for years, so I know him pretty well. His wife, Maggie, I don't know as well because she's not originally from Boulder. She's Miles's little sister, and apparently, it was a whole ordeal when the two of them hooked up. But obviously, everyone got over that little hiccup because they were married over the winter and seem to be doing well.

"So Max…Dean was saying that your ex-wife is out of the country for the summer," Kate says, holding a bottle of beer in her hand while her baby is strapped to her chest in a little swaddle wrap. It's a look only Kate could pull off. "What's Everly up to while you're at work all day?"

"I hired a nanny actually," I reply and take a sip of my whiskey, doing my best not to let my thoughts fixate on Cassandra again.

After our little ropes course day yesterday, I gave her and Everly a wide berth today. The thoughts I had watching her lush figure strapped up in all those harnesses were highly inappropriate.

I need to get fucking laid.

Which will be next to impossible now that I have Everly around all summer. So I need to get my dirty thoughts about the nanny in check.

Beyond the indecent thoughts I had about Cassandra, I had some surprisingly wholesome thoughts too. I forgot how fun it is to share the joy of Everly's experiences with another person. I haven't had that happy family feeling since Everly was one and Jessica and I were still married. Every time Everly cracked a joke or giggled with glee, Cassandra and I would share a knowing look that said... *this kid is the best.*

It felt...nice.

Which is why I need to go back to the office next week and stop having happy family moments with Cassandra and Everly. Cassandra is an employee. Nothing more.

"Where did you find this nanny?" Kate inquires, adjusting her red ponytail. "I might need one once Tucker here is a bit older."

"A nanny agency in town actually."

"Oh cool, I didn't know we even had one of those."

I shrug. "The candidates were less than impressive. But the owner's sister interviewed and Everly fell in love with her."

"Huh," Kate huffs. "Are they teenagers or like college students home for the summer?"

I shake my head. "The gal I hired is older actually."

"Like a grandma old?" Kate asks curiously.

"Not a grandma, no."

"She's twenty-six," Josh says, coughing into his fist.

I swerve accusing eyes at him.

He shrugs. "She'll get it out of you eventually."

"Twenty-six? That's not much younger than us," Kate snaps pointedly. "Well, except for Maggie...at least she's older than the wittle baby of the group," Kate says with a baby voice.

Maggie rolls her eyes and leans into Sam as I get a flashback of that fucking Chad guide who accused me of being Cassandra's dad. I'm only eight years older than her. What the fuck was with that guy? The age gap between Maggie and Sam has got to be bigger than that.

"What did she do before she was a nanny?" Kate continues, incessant as always.

I press my finger to my lips. "Would you keep it down?"

"Why?" Kate blinks back at me.

"Because she lives in the guesthouse, and I don't want her to think we're talking about her."

Kate swerves her gaze over to the tiny white house nestled along the flowing creek downhill. "She's in there right now?"

"I believe so."

"Why isn't she out here with us?"

I balk. "She's a daytime nanny. Not a nighttime one. I didn't want her to think she had to work."

"But she's a grown-up. Surely she likes alcohol and adult conversation?" Kate deadpans, looking at me like I've committed some unforgivable sin.

"It didn't seem professional," I argue.

"Good God, men are the worst," Kate snaps and thrusts her beer into Miles's chest and takes off toward the guesthouse, baby still cinched tightly to her chest.

I turn to Miles. "What is your wife doing?"

Miles shoots me a half smile. "If I had to guess, I would say she's going to make a new friend."

"She's totally making a new friend," Dean confirms, resting his hand on my shoulder.

"Can we stop her?" I ask, watching Kate burn rubber all the way to Cassandra's place. I really don't want Cassandra up here right now. I'm trying to get farther away from her, not closer.

Dean sighs heavily. "Kate's been one of my closest friends for years and the answer is always no."

I pinch the bridge of my nose. "I'm so happy you guys came over."

"Me too!" Lynsey says with a bright smile, clearly not picking up on my sarcasm.

Cozy

Music wafts down from the deck of the Fletchpad into the open windows of my tiny house. Max said he was going to have company tonight, and of course I didn't take it personally when he told me I didn't need to join them. I'm just the nanny. I'm not a friend. And honestly, this is my time off. I should be able to relax and kick back and "do less."

Yet still, I find myself peering out the window from my loft bed and enjoying the view of the Edison bulbs casting a glow over Max's big dick…I mean deck! Jesus.

He's amassed a nice little group of friends over there it seems. Most of my friends have moved on from Boulder. I was lucky Dakota was still around because I've lost touch with pretty much everyone else. And I cut off contact with all the people I met in Denver. The more space I get from that life, the better.

The sun is just beginning to set as a couple of girls who look to be Everly's age splash around with her in the water. The scent of grilled meat seeps into my cottage, making my stomach growl.

Ugh, this is stupid.

Why do I want to be out there? Because I think Max is fucking gorgeous and I couldn't stop noticing how he kept looking at my legs in his car on our way back from the ropes course yesterday? Because I loved the way he smiled at Everly instead of the camera every time I took their photo? Because seeing him in a suit is sinfully hot but seeing him in jeans and a gray T-shirt with sweat marks from his harness is the stuff wet dreams are made of?

Ugh. No. I'm disgusting.

I pull out my phone.

Me: You have to take me out next weekend.

Dakota: Twist my arm, why don't you. What's going on?

Me: I can't have a workaholic millionaire having more of a life than me.

Dakota: What's Zaddy doing exactly?

Me: He's having a pool party.

Dakota: And you weren't invited?

Me: Not really…I mean, kind of? But I could tell he didn't want me to come.

Dakota: Why do you say that?

Me: 'Cuz I'm the nanny and it was like a courtesy invite. I hate that I'm here right now. I look pathetic. Let's dress up and go out next weekend. Make it look like I actually have a life.

Dakota: Your wish is my command.

Me: I need to find a guy to distract me from the Zaddy.

Dakota: I knew him working from home this week was going to be a recipe for disaster.

Me: You have no idea. I'll tell you everything over drinks.

Dakota: I can't wait. I'll see what's going on in town. Stay tuned.

A knock on my door has me sitting up in my bed with wide eyes. I glance down from the loft and see a mane of red hair standing outside my door.

"Oh, God," I mumble nervously, lumbering my big ass down the giant ladder to see who's knocking on my door. If I had to guess, the grown-ups want to get drunk, and they are hoping to pay someone sober to watch the children. I hate being a grown-up nanny. It suddenly feels very pathetic.

Begrudgingly, I open the door, and my lips part in shock at the person standing there. "Mercedes Lee Loveletter?" I glance down at the baby strapped to her chest, my brain not quite computing the combination of my favorite erotic romance novelist standing before me…with a baby.

Her lips part into a stunning smile. "Oh, my God, do you read my books?"

"I…I…" My voice gets caught in my throat. "I do. And I follow you on Instagram. So…yeah…I swear I'm not a stalker."

"I love stalkers!" She laughs and takes a step inside. "Mind if I come in?"

"Sure." I stand back and watch Mercedes walk around my tiny house, feeling like I must be in the middle of a fever dream because there's no way the woman whose books I've been reading for the past six months is standing in my place of residence right now.

"Typical Max…can't even make a tiny house look basic." She walks down to the bathroom. "Oh, my God, even the bathroom is sexy!" She re-emerges and pats her baby's back. "This is a sweet pad."

"Yeah, it's really nice," I offer, my mouth feeling dry. "The bedroom is up that ladder."

"Cool." She nods thoughtfully. "What was your name?"

"Cozy," I reply quickly.

"Like warm and cozy?" Mercedes asks.

I nod and smile like an idiot.

"Totally putting that adorable name in a book," she deadpans.

"Will you really?" I respond breathily. My fangirl hysteria is raging at full force.

"Oh, yeah." She nods thoughtfully again. "My real name is boring old Kate. Mercedes is my pen name just so I could feel fancy."

"That's neat." *Oh my God, Mercedes Lee Loveletter just told me her real name. I feel so fucking cool right now.*

"Come up and have a drink with us."

She makes her way out of my cottage, and I pause, shocked that Max is friends with an author. He seems too uptight to have a friend as cool as Mercedes Lee Loveletter.

"I don't want to interrupt," I offer weakly from the doorway as

I glance up to see everyone staring down at us like we're a couple of zoo animals.

"You're not interrupting. You're invited. Formally…by a *New York Times* Bestselling author. Are you really going to say no to having a drink with a bestselling author?"

I lick my lips thoughtfully. "No…but can I be real lame and ask you to sign my books first?"

"You have my freaking paperbacks in there? Oh, my God, yes. I'll sign the shit out of them. Whip 'em out!"

Mercedes, I mean…Kate, signs my books, and we snap a quick selfie in my tiny house before she leads me up to the deck where the party is going on. Everly waves at me from the pool, making me feel welcome, but the look on Max's face has me struggling to walk.

He looks…uncomfortable.

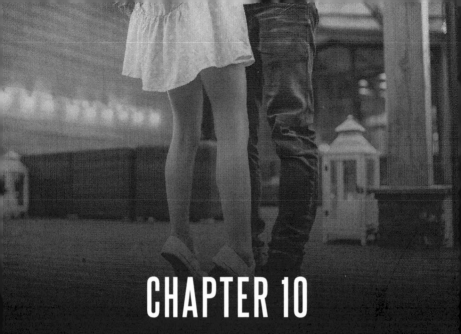

CHAPTER 10

Max

My eyes are locked on Cassandra as she sits with all the ladies and talks animatedly. They erupt into laughter, and from the way she's gesticulating, I can guess she's telling stories about the ropes course. Or maybe her near-drowning experience? Hell, a lot has happened in a week, so she's probably not short on content.

She appears to be charming the fuck out of all of them the same way she's managed to captivate me this week. It's crazy to think that I went from loathing her whole life philosophy and debating firing her to feeling oddly protective over her with all those women. I hope they're laughing with her and not at her.

Not that I think she's laughable. I mean…showing up to that job interview in tie-dye was pretty comical, but as I've gotten to know Cassandra this past week, I can tell this "do less" life philosophy is a front for something. What, I do not know. But I have a strange feeling she's done more with her life than work at Subway. Why she's hiding it remains to be seen.

"Did you hear me, Max?" Dean asks, pulling my attention away

"What? No…sorry. What did you say?"

Dean laughs and hits me with a disbelieving look. "I said we're pregnant."

"Who's pregnant?" I bark.

"Norah and I."

"Are you serious?" My jaw drops, and I look around at the group of guys who all seem to be in the know already.

Dean chuckles and adjusts his dark-framed glasses. "It's not really a thing you joke about, so yeah. I'm serious."

"Holy shit, man, congratulations!" I pull Dean into a hug and slap him on the back. "That's amazing. I didn't see this coming so fast. You just got engaged!"

"I know." Dean laughs again and takes a sip of his IPA. "It wasn't exactly planned, but we're both really happy about it."

"As you should be." I clink my glass with his and have flashbacks of Jessica having Everly. We were so happy back then. And in love. Or so I thought. I never saw what was coming.

I quickly shake that thought away. "Becoming a dad is the most incredible experience."

"Yeah, I can't wait…although I can because Norah really wants to get married before the baby comes."

"I can understand that," I reply knowingly. Jessica and I had a similar situation fresh out of college.

"Which is why I wanted to talk to you." Dean looks at me with an odd expression. "Norah wants to get married before the baby is born, which means by this fall at the latest, and well…all the good venues are booked up already."

"Okay…" I respond, still wondering how this involves me.

"We want something small with room for an outdoor tent… maybe a little scenic view…like a little creek or something."

My eyes lift to the sky. "I see where this is going."

"Something like…" He gestures out to my property with a shit-eating grin on his face.

I sigh heavily. "Dean?"

"Max?"

"Would you like to use my home for your wedding?"

Dean feigns surprise as he places a hand on his chest. "You want to host our wedding? Wow, Max. I mean…boy…I'm not sure…we'll have to really give it some thought…hell yes!"

I laugh and shove him away from me. "You are about as subtle as a boulder falling in my pool, Dean Moser."

"I know." He smiles gleefully and cups his hand to his mouth to yell down to the girls by the pool. "Sugar butt, Max said yes!"

"Yes!" I hear a high-pitched squeal from Norah, and all the girls lean in to figure out what she's excited about.

"Seriously, Max, you're the best." He throws his arm around me and looks toward my sprawling backyard. "This is going to be perfect."

"Do you have a date in mind already?"

"Thinking mid-October, maybe?"

I grin and shake my head. "I'll have my assistant clear my schedule."

Miles holds his beer out. "Congrats, Dean. I'm happy for you. It'll be nice to add another kid to the group."

"Hopefully a boy," Dean says, clinking his glass with Miles's. "Not that I wouldn't love a girl. But I wouldn't trust your son and my daughter growing up together."

"Fair enough." Miles laughs and turns his attention to Sam. "Now it's your turn."

Sam shakes his head. "Just because you nut jobs are all popping out kids doesn't mean we are. Maggie and I are enjoying our time with just the two of us." Sam winks at the group.

Miles groans. "That's my fucking sister you're talking about, bro."

"You just told me you wanted us to have a baby," Sam argues with a laugh. "You do know how babies are made, right?"

Miles looks ill. "I need more beer."

After we eat, it starts getting dark out, so we have the kids change into pajamas and all curl up in the theater room for a movie. Everly looks so happy having friends over. It's not something I've ever really let her do, and I realize I need to change that.

The ladies work on getting the girls settled so I head down to the creek to start a fire on the beach. Cassandra is the first to join me with a fresh drink in hand.

"I'm sorry for crashing your party, eating your food, and drinking your alcohol. Mercedes…I mean…Kate is not an easy person to say no to."

"Oh, trust me, I'm aware," I reply, stirring the fire around with a long stick and sending sparks up into the air. "And don't worry about it. You're not crashing at all. You were invited."

She pulls a face and lowers herself into one of the Adirondack chairs. "I about fainted when I answered the door. I've been binge-reading Kate's books for the past few months."

My brows lift knowingly. "So that's why you couldn't turn in your own book report."

She nods regretfully with a small embarrassed laugh. "I'm afraid so. God, I love her stuff."

"She's very talented…not that I've ever read her work."

"Why not?" Cassandra gazes up at me, her round eyes sparkling in the firelight.

I huff out a laugh. "I don't think I'm exactly her target demographic."

She shrugs and takes a sip of her beer. "Maybe you should. Might help loosen you up a bit."

I pause my work on the fire. "Need I remind you I went zip-lining yesterday?"

"And you screamed like a girl at least half a dozen times." Her shoulders shake with silent laughter as she covers her smile.

I point an accusing finger at her. "You promised me in the car we would never speak of that again."

She bends over, full-on belly laughing now. The sound travels straight to my groin. She composes herself and exclaims, "I promised I wouldn't speak of it in front of other people. I never said I wouldn't tease you privately."

The word private makes me think of my cock. God, I'm a mess. I do my best to scowl at the nanny but the sight of her giggling to herself is too adorable not to smirk at. Her pale skin glows in the firelight and I'm having that issue of seeing her as a woman again and not just a nanny I hired for my kid.

That is not good.

Thankfully, the rest of the group join us, taking seats around the fire and distracting me from my impure thoughts. Miles settles in on his own chair, a fast asleep Tucker nuzzled comfortably in his arms. Kate lays a blanket over them, leaning down and pressing a soft kiss to her son's head before finding Miles's lips next.

I look away, struggling to watch the sight of them enjoying life as new parents. It was never fully like that with Jess and me.

"Julianna fell asleep on the couch," Lynsey says, sitting down on Josh's lap in the chair beside me.

"Is she okay up there alone?" I ask, turning around to see if I can see the kids from down here.

"I can go up and sit with the kids if you like," Cassandra offers, her eyes shifting from Lynsey to me.

"God no!" Lynsey waves Cassandra off. "Lennon is watching her. One big perk about having a teenage niece. Built-in babysitter."

"Did Everly let them pick the movie at least?" I inquire, wanting to make sure she's being hospitable to her new friends.

"She did," Lynsey answers with a smile. "She and Claire seem to be hitting it off. They're making friendship bracelets as we speak."

My eyes find Cassandra's as she glances up at the house, trying to catch a glimpse of the kids as well. I like that she's interested in my kid...even when she's not on the clock.

"Can you believe how much our lives have changed?" Kate says, stretching her flip-flops out toward the fire. "We used to party down on Pearl Street, and now we're talking about kids' movies and built-in babysitters."

"Sam and I can still party," Maggie states with a smile, showing her young age.

"You can party, Sparky," Sam grumbles. "I prefer to stay home with you."

"Poor Grandpa," Maggie teases, reaching out to run her fingers through Sam's red beard. "Are you ready for bed now? Should I bring the wheelchair around?"

"I'm ready for bed with you," he replies, shooting her a wicked look.

"Bro...sister." Miles shakes his head, eyeing Sam with a "fuck around and find out" look that makes the group laugh.

"What's the age difference between you two anyway?" Cassandra asks, watching everyone in rapt fascination.

"Nine years," Maggie answers. "I'm twenty-four, and Sam is thirty-three. He's more than ready for kids, but I want a couple of years with my husband first."

"I'm not complaining one bit." Sam pulls Maggie's hand to his mouth and kisses it sweetly. It's a hard display of affection to watch because I can't imagine ever having that.

"Let's play two truths and a lie," Kate suggests, her eyes dancing in the firelight in an almost scary way. She turns to Cassandra. "Cozy, since you're the fresh meat here tonight, you go first."

"Oh...um...okay." Cassandra shifts in her chair and takes a big swig of her drink as she ponders what she's about to say. I can't help but watch her curiously, selfishly interested in learning more about the mysterious woman I've hired to watch my kid all summer.

"Okay...here we go. I am a skilled woodworker, I got my bachelor's degree at nineteen years old, and I hate popcorn."

The group pauses as they stare at Cassandra like her face will reveal her truth. I narrow my eyes, watching her smirk and chew her lip in that delicious way that always makes me notice how big her lips are.

"The college one is a lie," Kate says, sitting back in her chair. "Your face twitched when you said that one."

"I agree," Lynsey interjects next.

"Let me see your hands," Sam requests, and Cassandra turns her hands upward. "No way you're a woodworker. Your hands look too soft."

I agree with Sam, and when everyone finishes guessing, Cassandra reveals her lie. "I love popcorn."

"What?" the group exclaims.

"You graduated college at nineteen?" Josh takes the words out of my mouth.

She nods and shrugs. "I had earned my associate's degree before I was even out of high school."

"So we're sitting next to a freaky genius?" Kate laughs. "Cool! Say something smart."

Cassandra shakes her head and points at Josh. "I'm seated beside a doctor, not to mention the rest of you who are all highly successful in your fields. I'm just the nanny. The smart thing to do is remain silent."

Everyone scoffs but eventually resumes the game and moves around the circle for more truths and a lie. I try to participate, but my gaze continually turns back to Cassandra. Why would she exclude her college education on her résumé? That makes no sense.

When my turn comes up, I'm so in my own head that I don't even think before I blurt out, "You lied on your résumé."

My eyes laser in on Cassandra, who squirms in her seat. "What?"

"You never listed any college degree," I accuse, ignoring everyone's gaping at me.

She licks her lips and shrugs. "College wasn't a requirement for the nanny position."

"No, but why downplay your education?" I tilt my head and watch her body language.

"Because it wasn't relevant to the job," she says, looking mildly annoyed as she sets her beer down on the arm of the chair.

"It seems like you're being secretive," I volley back.

Cassandra laughs awkwardly and looks around at the group, avoiding eye contact. "I'm sorry, but my life story really is none of your business."

"You're watching my kid for the summer," I snap, my jaw taut with irritation. "You're absolutely my business."

Her eyes widen and jump to mine at my possessive words.

"Max," Josh murmurs from beside me, but I brush him off.

"Why hide that part of yourself?" I continue, unwilling to let this go.

"I'm not healing the sick or climbing the corporate ladder. Why does what I list on my résumé even matter?"

My teeth crack as I struggle not to lose my temper. I don't like that she's keeping shit from me. No, I don't need to know it to trust her with my kid. She's proven herself to me this week, and I feel good about hiring her. I just…want to fucking know something real about her. Anything that will make this person with a willy-nilly business philosophy in front of me make sense.

"What kind of woodworking do you do?" I ask, changing tactics to see if she's going to be secretive about that too.

Cassandra laughs dryly and slaps her hands on the arms of the chair. "I make charcuterie boards, okay?"

"Charcuta-what?" Lynsey interjects, her voice practically squealing with delight. "Are you serious?"

Cassandra's gaze tears away from mine and softens when they land on Lynsey. "Yeah, they're simple to make, and I find the act of sanding wood really satisfying. I used to have a huge collection of boards that I made, but my friend Dakota sold them all from her T-shirt shop downtown."

"Why don't you make more?" Kate asks curiously.

"Because I moved away from my workshop and don't really have a good setup here. Trust me, I'm not complaining." She shoots challenging eyes at me. "I love the guesthouse. But I just haven't figured out another place to work on them yet. I'll find something, eventually. I'm still settling in here."

"That's really cool, Cozy," Maggie offers with a smile.

"And I do have some calluses, I'll have you know." Cassandra turns her focus to Sam. "See?"

Sam eyes her hands closer this time. "Child's play. Come to Tire Depot and sling tires with Miles and me sometime. That'll really toughen up your hands."

"Sounds like a blast," she replies with a smirk that I wish was directed at me, not fucking Sam.

"It's better appreciated as a spectator sport," Kate adds with a wink. "Trust me."

The game resumes, and I sit back and sip my whiskey, brooding over the fact that Cassandra is keeping things from me. I thought after this week I was finally feeling more secure in my decision to hire her, but the more I learn about the woman I practically invited to live with me, the more I wonder who the hell she is and why she'd even want to be a nanny in the first place.

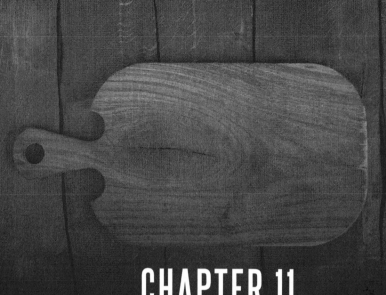

CHAPTER 11

Cozy

A knock on my door Saturday afternoon has me setting my book down to see who it is. My heart rate increases when I see Max's broad shoulders through the window. I snuck off to bed early last night before his friends left because I didn't want to talk to him at the end of the night after how heated things got by the fire.

I don't know what the hell that was. And I hate that fighting with Max in front of all his friends felt like some sort of torturous foreplay that they were all spectators to. Damn, that man can be pushy at times. No wonder my sister called him a high-maintenance client. I sincerely hope he's not knocking on my door to fire me. I've had enough close brushes with that to last a lifetime.

Steeling myself, I open the door and hold the frame for balance because his body in jeans and a T-shirt is stupid. "Hey, I was just going to text you, actually."

"Oh?" Max asks, eyeing me curiously.

My jaw feels taut when I force myself to say what I'm about to say because I need this job. "I'm sorry if I had a little attitude with you last night. I...maybe had too much to drink." Total lie.

Max shakes his head stiffly. "I shouldn't have pried."

"You were just curious. I was rude."

"I was rude." He licks his lips and pauses for a moment. He sighs heavily and adds, "I'm a man who is used to getting what he wants."

My heart lurches up into my throat at the wicked connotation that remark possesses. I steel myself to reply, "I'm a woman who can be pretty stubborn sometimes."

"I noticed." A smile ghosts his lips, and I once again get lost in thoughts of how kissable they look. "Anyway, I didn't come here for an apology. Would you come with me? I want to show you something."

Max steps back, and I frown curiously as I slide my feet into my flip-flops and follow him through the yard and around the house toward the five-stall garage sitting open. He opens a door that leads into a closed-off area of the garage that looks like a little man cave. He steps back and gestures to a large workbench that's ridiculously organized with a pegboard above and a million different tools mounted.

"Before I started my own company, I used to do construction with my dad. A lot of carpentry work and such. Anyway, I don't do much of that anymore, but I still have all this stuff."

"Okay…" I respond in confusion, looking around at the power tools tucked under the bench.

"You can use it," Max adds crisply. "For your…charcuterie boards."

"Seriously?" I turn and eye the space with renewed interest.

"It's just sitting here collecting dust, so somebody might as well make good use of it. You can use this as your personal workshop or whatever. It's temperature controlled over here." He taps on a device on the wall, and a digital screen pops up. He then hands me a garage door opener. "You can keep this to get in and out without having to come through the house."

I hold the clicker in my hand, my eyes blinking back the shock that's taking over my entire body. "Wow…this is…really thoughtful, Max."

"It's nothing," he replies and moves to stand awkwardly in the doorway. He slides his hands into his jean pockets. "If you need wood, there are some scrap pieces on the lower shelf, but several hunks of trees that can be chopped into lumber are also down by the beach.

I just haven't gotten around to chopping them yet. Just let me know how you like it, and I can help you out with that."

"You…chop your own wood?" I ask, my mouth suddenly very parched as I imagine him shirtless and glistening with sweat as he grunts through each swing of an axe.

Fuck, that's a hot image.

Max crosses his muscular forearms and leans against the door. "I do a lot of things on my own, Cozy."

My body hums to life with his use of my nickname. There's something about when he uses it that makes me forget all about the fact that he's a corporate, suit-wearing, power-hungry workaholic who represents the opposite of all I want out of life.

Before he turns to leave, I inhale sharply and say, "Hey…you never had your turn."

"What turn?" he asks, staring curiously back at me.

"The two truths and a lie." My smile feels wobbly as he tilts his head and eyes me with such fierce determination that I think I need to sit down. I lean on the workbench and feign curiosity while wondering if I'm imagining his eyes roving down my body. "Let's hear it."

"Okay…let me think." His brows quirk as he reaches above his head and braces his hands on the top of the doorframe, showing off a sliver of skin on his waist that reveals the deep lines of his hip bones disappearing into his denim. "I graduated summa cum laude. My ex-wife left me for another woman. And I hate anchovies."

I laugh at his horrible lie. Honestly, he's terrible at this game. The man is a millionaire, so clearly very smart, and everyone hates anchovies. My eyes drink in his impossibly perfect body, and I reply, "Your ex is straight, so that's the lie." *Though how she left him, I'll never understand.*

He smirks knowingly and clicks his tongue. "I never graduated summa cum laude. In fact, I barely graduated college at all." He winks and taps the frame of the door before disappearing into the garage, leaving me alone in my workshop with a whole lot of wood.

CHAPTER 12

Cozy

By the end of week two, Everly and I are full-on simpatico. We have perfected the art of sitting, the art of laying, and the art of dancing to Kidz Bop Radio on the deck after lunch. We've even successfully navigated the swimming pool three times. Although it should be noted that a life preserver magically appeared beside the pool on Monday morning that I have no doubt was left behind by an overprotective father. I keep it close by just to be safe.

I even got to meet a few other nannies who are watching some of Everly's private school friends when we all met up for the monthly book club. The kids honored me with the label of "top tier nanny" because I made up a themed charcuterie board to share with everyone. I just took notes from Everly's book report on *11 Before 12* and filled the board with things pre-teens would love. Ring pops to represent boy crazy thoughts, gummy bears to represent helping the environment, and friendship bracelets to remind them all that despite going into middle school next year, their gal pals are their most important allies. Everly helped me shop for all the supplies, and we had a fabulous time assembling it all. I chuckle to myself when I consider what might use for a Mercedes Lee Loveletter-inspired board

Mostly, I was just excited to use the new board I had just made. The workshop Max gave me has twice the supplies that I had in my sister's garage. And when I found a random scrap of maple that was probably meant for some luxury cabinets, I knew I could get it done relatively quick. Everly even helped apply the food-safe wood wax at the end. Our summer of willy-nilly was off to a great start for sure.

I worried that Max would work from home again after our tense barbecue moment on Friday night. But I think gifting me the workshop was his idea of a peace offering and to show me that despite leaving things off my résumé, he did trust me.

In fact, I've barely seen him this entire week. He sent me a text and asked if I could be in the house by six o'clock every morning this week so he could get to the office early. I'd barely catch a glimpse of his perfectly tailored suit before he hightailed it out the door. When he'd come home, he barely made eye contact with me, directing all his attention on Everly.

Rightfully so.

I don't know why I'd want him to look at me anyway. It seems the more I'm around him, the more questions he asks, and that's not really a box I care to open with my new boss.

So instead, I text him updates and photos of Everly throughout the day—what we get up to and how Everly's mood seems. It's usually nothing exciting or groundbreaking. That would go against our "do less" summer motto. But I think that if I had to leave my daughter every day for work, I'd love to see glimpses of her throughout the day. Even if it's just a picture of her reading a book by the creek. It's got to be a healthy dose of serotonin that a full day of the corporate grind requires. Who needs kombucha when you have an adorable blond daughter who looks like literal sunshine?

Also, a side benefit of texting Max all day is that I don't have to have a face-to-face recap with him when he gets home at night. My lusting over him hasn't improved, even after his grumpy, prying questions at the firepit. In fact, I think I like the pushy side of Max Fletcher. More than I should.

Finally, it's Friday, and Everly and I are seated by the creek with our feet in the sand and our nose in our books. It's heavenly. I can't believe I'm getting paid to hang out with a cool kid all summer. This couldn't be more perfect. I glance at the time on my phone.

"Hey…it's almost time for your daily call with your mom. Do you want to head inside?" I ask, waving my Kindle over my face to fight off the heat as the sun peeks through the trees and shines directly on me.

Everly holds a finger up as she finishes her page. Finally, she smiles and closes her book, looking like such a grown-up. "What did you say?"

"It's almost time to call your mom."

"Okay," she says with a yawn and a stretch.

"Are you missing her a lot?" I inquire, feeling a bit nosy because I have yet to actually *see* Everly's mom. Everly always FaceTimes her on her iPad in her room, and it seems intrusive for me to be around while they visit.

"Yeah, but it's been nice spending time with my dad." Everly rests her head on the back of the chair and sighs. "He seems less lonely with me here."

I smile at that thoughtful remark. "What about your mom? I'm sure she's lonely in Bulgaria, isn't she?"

Everly shakes her head. "Her wife, Kailey, is out there with her. They do photography together."

My brows lift curiously. I didn't think Max was lying to me this past weekend about his two truths and a lie, but hearing Everly confirm the fact that her mom is with a woman is still not something I expected. "Have your mom and Kailey been married a long time?"

Everly rubs her eye and nods. "Since I was little. I was their flower girl, but I don't remember it. I've only seen pictures."

"That's fun." I chew my lip thoughtfully. "And your dad? Did he ever get married again?"

Everly's lips smush together. "I wish. Then I wouldn't worry about how lonely he is."

"What makes you think he's lonely?" I ask, watching her intently.

"Because when he picks me up on his weekends, he talks non-stop in the car all the way to his house." She slaps her hands on the Adirondack chair with a little squeak. "Guess what happened at work?

Who did you talk to at school? I had Michael make us fish sticks. Guess what Grandpa did? It's too much."

My shoulders shake with silent laughter at Everly's exasperated body language. "I can't picture this."

"It's like his brain has had no one to talk to all week, so as soon as I get in the car, he blurts out everything he's thought of since the last time I saw him."

"That sounds sweet." My lips turn down as I picture Max sitting in this giant house all by himself just waiting for his time with his kid. It's heartbreaking.

"It's not bad, but I'd still like to find him a girlfriend this summer. I've never seen him with one."

"Really?" I find this hard to believe.

"Yep." Everly nods. "It makes me sad. And after spending so much time with him this summer, it will be really hard on him when Mom comes home, and I go back to her house. That's why he needs a girlfriend."

The thought of Max with another woman makes the hairs on the back of my neck tingle. It's not something I would care to see, so hopefully, if Everly finds someone for him (I wouldn't put it past her), it's after I'm done working here. I shudder to think about him texting me to watch Everly in the evenings so he can go out on dates with a supermodel-looking female who gapes at me like I'm a zoo animal.

I clear my throat and coyly ask, "What kind of girl do you think your dad would like?" Hopefully, Everly isn't as perceptive with me as she is with her father. I'm about as subtle as a freight train right now.

Everly smiles, a conspiratorial glint in her eye that I'm not sure I like the look of. "Someone smart, funny, kind, and sassy. And who can cook for him, so Michael doesn't have to be here every night."

Welp...I'm out of the running.

I've been surviving on lunch meat wraps and ramen in my tiny house for the past two weeks. Max offered food from his chef, but I stupidly told him no, thank you. I'm pretty sure I was staring at his ass when he said it, so I didn't exactly have all my faculties in working order.

I smile warmly and waggle my brows. "Where will we find this magical woman?"

"I'm going to ask my uncle Luke tonight," Everly answers like she's been working on this plan for a while. "He's taking me out tonight, and he's had *lots* of girlfriends. Dad can maybe have one of his old ones?"

Oh, this sounds like a Mercedes Lee Loveletter original in the making.

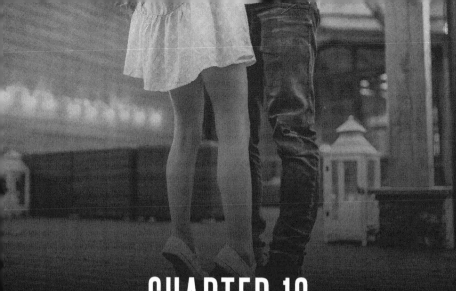

CHAPTER 13

MAX

Me: Can you possibly come up to the house for a moment? If you're not busy?

Cassandra: Sure! Be right there.

Me: Come into my bedroom.

I wince as soon as I send that last text and my hands shake violently as I quickly try to fix my error.

Me: Everly is in here with me.

"Dad, just watch the video one more time," Everly whines from her seat on my bathroom countertop. Her sundress is bunched up around her lap, and her bare feet are curled inside the sink as she holds the iPad up above her head for me to see.

The tiny red rubber band snaps on my fingers. "Dammit," I mutter under my breath. "This little thing hurts!"

"You're stretching them too much."

"My fingers are too big for this, Everly," I growl, my temper at a breaking point as I make eye contact with my kid in the mirror. "Why can't we just leave your hair down?"

"Because Uncle Luke is taking me to dinner and a movie, and I want to have cool hair."

I curse a million different words under my breath because what was supposed to be a night off every week has now turned into more work for me.

My brothers decided to start a weekly rotation of taking Everly out for an evening. The group text said something about teaching her how she should expect to be treated by men.

Like an eleven-year-old needs to know that already.

In truth, I think my brothers are just trying to get in some extra time with her while she's with me all summer. She's the only child in our family and spoiled rotten by all three of them and my parents. The best part, though, is that any one of them would drop everything they're doing for Everly. Spoiled or not, it's pretty great.

Except for the fact that now I'm being forced to teach myself how to do bubble braids. Who came up with this fucking hairstyle? It looks like it belongs in a sci-fi film.

A faint knock on the door has Everly and me calling out in unison, "Come in."

Cassandra appears in the doorway of my master bath. She's dressed in a pair of thin cotton shorts, a tank top, and a jean jacket that couldn't even begin to button over her definitely more than a handful of breasts.

Breasts I really shouldn't be looking at right now.

"Daddy can't do bubble braids, Cozy. Can you help?" Everly wastes no time throwing me under the bus. "He's really bad at this."

I let go of Everly's hair and toss the tiny rubber band onto the counter that's littered with ones I've already broken. "These damn rubber bands suck."

The corner of Cassandra's mouth curls up as she holds my gaze. "I'm impressed you were even trying."

"Believe me, I tried to talk her out of it." I roll my eyes and shake my head. "I'm not bad with a curling iron as long as I wear that little glove it came with. But she could not be convinced."

"I want bubble braids," Everly repeats for the fourth time in the thirty minutes I've been attempting this hellish activity.

"I got this," Cassandra says, rushing over and assaulting me with that heavenly tropical scent of hers.

I step away from the bathroom counter to give her room to work. Leaning against the glass shower door, I note Cassandra's hands making quick work of the mess I left behind. She begins to talk to Everly about how to do this hairstyle on her own, and I can't help but be impressed. As Everly is an only child, I just do a lot of things for her. It gets done properly that way, and since I only have one kid, it doesn't really take that much time. Hell, she still wasn't even tying her own shoes in third grade. I remember her teachers telling us at her conferences that she should have been doing that in kindergarten. I guess both Jess and I spoil Everly a bit too much. It's bizarre that Cassandra is the one who makes me realize there are so many things I don't even consider showing Everly how to do for herself. I should give her more credit. And Cassandra.

I reach back to rub a stress knot in my neck, and my gaze inadvertently travels down Cassandra's backside, lingering on her ass. It's impossible not to look at. She has…a great ass. It's big and round, making her waist look small by comparison. Her ass is certainly something I'd have to work hard at to possess with any measure of authority. That realization has my cock thickening in my jeans.

I always did love a challenge.

Jesus, she's been here for two minutes, and I'm already overwhelmed with indecent thoughts about her. Have I ever been this turned on by a woman? The answer has to be hell fucking no.

In truth, most of the women I've dated in the past haven't had the curves Cassandra possesses. They're usually super-toned gym rats or they barely eat and walk around like they could blow over at any second.

Cassandra is not them.

She's full in all the right places. Her breasts alone are something I could get lost in and feel deliriously happy about. They're far more than a handful, and I fucking love the thought of struggling to possess them. For the better part of two weeks, I've lost count of the number of times I've pictured burying my face in them and tasting their softness.

Fuck, I'm fully erect now.

I pull my T-shirt down over my groin to conceal the reaction I have whenever I'm near this woman. I didn't think I ever really had a type, but Cassandra is making me doubt that fact now. It's not just her luscious body that turns me on, though. It's the way she seems so comfortable in her own skin. Effortless. She doesn't doubt herself at every turn. Hell, I've made more money than I ever dreamed possible, and I still fight imposter syndrome nearly every fucking day of my life. Then there's Cassandra, who exists like she knows exactly what she was put on this planet to do.

And the natural comfort she's found with my kid in only two short weeks causes a warmth to bloom in my chest. She's not just a nanny. She's become Everly's friend. The two of them interact like they've known each other their whole lives.

How did she fucking do that?

Granted, I've never introduced Everly to any women I've dated in the past, so I don't really have anyone to compare her to. And I use the word "dated" loosely because I don't really do relationships. Women I've slept with have always been a matter of convenience. And if they didn't have any expectations of me, then I went for it. I scratched that un-scratchable itch I had to fuck someone. Hard.

Unfortunately, that spark I feel for them fades quickly after sex. It's like as soon as we have sex, a light switch gets flicked on and casts ominous shadows over everything that doesn't work about this person in my life. Namely, that she's not good enough for my kid. And I'm only getting divorced once.

Which is why I've resigned myself to a life of bachelorhood. I don't need another person to take my attention away from what matters most. My daughter and my company. In that order.

Consequently, these dirty thoughts I'm having about the nanny need to go the fuck away. And soon.

"What do you think?" A voice cuts into my inner reverie, and I'm forced to tear my eyes from Cassandra's ass to look up into the mirror. Her green eyes captivate me as the blood rushes out of my cock and back into my lust-filled brain.

"Beautiful," I blurt, my gaze never leaving Cassandra's.

"You really like it, Daddy?" Everly's innocent tone interjects.

My blood rushes to my ears as I look at my daughter's hair for the first time and realize what I just did. Licking my lips, I do my best to sound aloof. "You look like you're ready for a space adventure."

"Dad," Everly drones, clearly not amused by my dad joke. She twists around and hops off the bathroom counter to wrap her hands around Cassandra's hips. "Thank you, Cozy."

Lucky hands.

Fuck, I'm a pervert.

The doorbell rings, thankfully snapping me out of the mental stroke I must be in the middle of to let my thoughts wander again. Everly takes off running, so I shove my hand into my pocket to hide my hard-on and follow my kid.

"Uncle Luke!" Everly peals, opening the front door and hugging my youngest brother.

"Evie girl, holy shit, you're huge!" Luke says, grabbing Everly's hand and giving her a spin.

She giggles proudly.

I turn back to Cassandra. "Don't mind the language. My brothers work construction, and I'm afraid it's just something I gave up on correcting long ago." I turn my eyes to Everly. "Luckily, Everly knows what words are for grown-ups and what words are for kids, right?"

"Uncle Luke lets me swear sometimes," she replies with an evil snicker.

I swerve accusing eyes at my brother. "What the hell, Luke?"

"It's therapeutic." He shrugs, reaching up to scratch his chin that's covered in a thick dark beard. "Kids get angry too, and sometimes fart whistle just doesn't cut it."

"Fart whistle?" I jerk my head back in disgust. "I think I prefer the swear words." I hear Cassandra laughing behind me and quickly step back to introduce her. "Luke, this is Everly's nanny, Cassandra."

"You can call her Cozy," Everly corrects.

"Cassandra, this is my youngest brother, Luke."

Cassandra walks over and shakes his hand. I bristle slightly as I watch him rake his eyes down her body. Luke is Cassandra's age, so something about seeing the two of them next to each other irks me. I wonder if he would be Cassandra's type?

He's about an inch shorter than me but has me beat in the muscle department. When he's not flipping houses with my brothers, he's at the gym, religiously. I'd probably work out more too if I had the time. Even my morning swims seem to be few and far between these days.

"There are two more brothers, right?" Cassandra asks curiously.

"Yes, Wyatt is number two, and Calder is number three," I answer.

"And you're number one?" Cassandra looks at me with her round eyes that look so fucking innocent, I can't help the reply that tumbles from my lips.

"I'm always number one." I wink and feel a rush of attraction surge through me when crimson climbs up Cassandra's neck all the way to her cheeks. *Fuck, that's hot.*

And...*fuck* do I immediately regret saying that out loud. Especially when I turn to find my brother staring at me like I've grown a second head. His eyes dart from me to the nanny.

"Let's go, Uncle Luke," Everly groans and grabs my brother's hand to pull him out the open door.

"Okay, Evie! Keep your shirt on." Luke laughs and shoots me an odd look.

"I'm wearing a dress." Everly spins to show it off.

"So you are. You look beautiful." Luke tugs on her bubble braided ponytail before turning to leave. I walk to the door to close it behind them and hear the rolling of distant thunder.

"Careful out there, it looks like it's going to storm," I say, just as a flash of lightning illuminates the twilight sky.

Luke waves me off. "I checked the radar, and it'll be done before we're out of the movie. Plus, I've got the truck, so we'll be fine. See you in a few hours."

I close the door and turn back to find Cassandra standing in the foyer. She wrings her hands awkwardly in front of her.

"Thank you for your help with her hair." I slide my hands into my pockets and walk toward her. "I know it's your night off, so I hope it was okay I texted you."

"Text me anytime." Cassandra smiles, and I see her neck contract as she swallows. She chews her lip nervously. "It's Friday night. No big plans for you?"

I inhale a deep breath and shake my head. "I'm having the guys over here for poker next weekend, so I'm planning to lay low and hydrate before I assault my liver with too much whiskey."

"That sounds smart." Cassandra licks her lips and shoots me a shy smile that I feel right in my groin.

"You?" I ask even though I don't know if I want to hear the answer.

She hooks her thumb over her shoulder. "I'm going out tomorrow night with my friend Dakota, so I'm probably going to hydrate tonight too."

"That's good," I state stupidly.

"Yeah," she confirms.

A moment of silence falls between us, and I have to press my lips together to stop myself from asking if she wants to watch a movie with me. It's a bad, bad idea to hang out with the nanny when Everly isn't around. Plus, if I sit on that couch with her, there's no telling what might happen underneath a blanket.

I blow out a slow breath. "I'm gonna go hit the shower." Cold shower. Arctic, blazing, ice-cold shower.

"Right, sorry. I'll get out of your way," Cassandra stammers and turns on her heel, nearly tripping over her flip-flop as she hightails it out of my house.

And I watch her leave...*boy, do I watch her leave.*

CHAPTER 14

Cozy

The raging thunderstorm outside is the perfect soundtrack to the ridiculously erotic Mercedes Lee Loveletter book I'm currently reading in bed. After the awkward tension I felt at Max's house tonight, I had to do something about the overwhelming emotions coursing through my body.

So as soon as it was dark outside, I slipped into my sexy chocolate satin night dress, the one that barely covers my breasts that Dakota forced me to buy a couple of months ago because *"all single girls needed a sexy nightie to stay in touch with their 'womblands.'"* Something she heard on Tik Tok, I'm sure.

But she might be onto something because wearing this and climbing up my loft ladder to reread my favorite erotic romance novel in bed feels exactly like the kind of "self-care" I need tonight.

It's a little odd reading this book after meeting the author last weekend, but I love this story too much to let that ruin my favorite dirty book.

The two characters are currently at a sex club, and the alpha hero is forcing his new submissive to watch two couples having sex.

"Does my little slut like that?" His voice growls into her ear as his

hand reaches across her chest and dances up to her throat. "Does my little precious whore like to watch a woman get fucked in the mouth by a big cock until she chokes?" His grip tightens around her neck, and he growls into her ear. "Answer me, bitch."

"Yes!" she garbles out, his hand tightening more around her delicate neck, causing black spots to form in her vision. She sags in his arms, and he loosens his grip, allowing her to gasp for breath.

In a flash, he turns her around, his hand back on her neck as he backs her up to a wall and tears off her top with his free hand.

I flick the button on my battery-operated device, the low hum causing my thighs to rub together in anticipation as I slip it under the covers. I press the vibration to my center and feel overwhelmed at how close I am to climaxing already.

Jesus, I'm keyed up tonight.

My tight bundle of nerves throbs so much that I can barely read the words in my book. My eyes shift to the white shiplap ceiling flashing bright in the lightning. Rain pounds hard onto my tiny house as my pelvis thrusts greedily upward.

A loud crack of thunder shakes my entire house, and I distractedly notice that my lamp downstairs kicked off and the air conditioner hum is no longer present. The power must have gone out. My vibrator is still alive and well, though.

God bless batteries.

I close my eyes and attempt to put myself back in my story. I know the entire thing by heart. I don't need to read the pages to recall the delicious dirty things the hero says to the heroine.

But my traitorous mind has other ideas.

Namely…Max…*in his shower.*

That clear glass shower with glossy charcoal tile that I tried not to stare at when I walked into his bathroom tonight. Never mind the moment I had walking into his bedroom when I paused by his bed and inhaled his masculine scent. I have no idea what cologne he wears, but his room is completely drenched in it. Before I entered the bathroom, I debated lying on his bed and rolling my body all over just so I could take home a hint of that intoxicating aroma he carries with him everywhere he goes. It's a heady mix of smoky woods with an exotic scent that I can't even begin to place. It gives total mafia boss vibes, and my body reacts damn near carnally to it.

Or maybe it was that smoldering look in Max's eyes when I finished doing Everly's hair. It reminded me of the look I saw when we were zip-lining, but I was close enough to confirm this one. Max was staring at my ass. Without a doubt and without any ounce of shame. And when his eyes caught mine in the mirror, and he said "beautiful," he wasn't talking about Everly's hair.

I nearly came on the spot.

Okay, that's not true. There was a child in the room, and I'm not a complete pervert!

But my stomach was doing cartwheels for sure. I can still feel my pulse racing in my veins, thinking about how I noticed him letting that CEO guard down for a moment. With one expression, he confirmed that the chemistry I've been feeling between us for the past fourteen days hasn't all been in my head.

If only he'd have asked me to stay with him tonight. A shock runs through me as my thighs clench around my vibrator at the thought.

I imagine him grabbing me by that hand and walking me into his shower, stripping off my clothes as he explores my curves. The image of that causes me to gasp, feeling myself grow wetter as my nipples tighten beneath the taut fabric.

With my opposite hand, I caress my stomach, imagining they're his masculine fingers working their way up my chest. I shudder against the vibrations between my legs as my breath quickens, feeling my orgasm just on the crest.

My own fingers wrap lightly around my throat as I imagine Max whispering every dirty word to me the character in my book whispered.

Lifting my hips, I chase the orgasm that's right there...that's almost...

A loud bang on my door just as I was about to reach the precipice has me screaming. Full-on blood-curdling scream.

"Cassandra, what is it?" Max's voice booms as he bursts through my unlocked door with a flashlight in hand. He shoots the stray light beam all over my tiny house, seeking out the cause of my apparent stress.

"Max?" I barely hear my voice over the pounding of my heart. From my almost orgasm or from being scared half to death, I'm not sure.

I shoot up out of my bed and drag my blanket with me to cover my scantily clad body. Peering over the railing, I see my boss. The grip on my blanket tightens as I take in his completely soaked white T-shirt and a pair of gray sweatpants.

I sway heavily against the railing feeling my center throb at the real-life fantasy standing in my living room.

He shines his light toward me, and I lift my hand against the brightness. "What are you doing here?"

"The power went out," he answers, pushing back his wet hair as he lowers the light. A security light down by the creek casts a bluish glow through the windows enough for me to make out the features of his face. He looks stressed when he adds, "I was coming to bring you a flashlight. I heard you scream, and I thought something bad was happening."

I swallow nervously, thinking about what was about to happen, and shift the blanket to cover my hardening nipples nearly falling out of my nightie. "Sorry, I was just—"

A loud thunk down by my feet has my eyes moving from Max to the floor where my pale pink vibrator has come loose out of my blanket. Eyes wide, I pray his light didn't catch it before it hit the floor. Hastily, I bend over to grab it so I can stash it safely back in the folds of the blanket.

As I bend, the blanket falls over it, making it hard to see with only the light from below as my guide. I kick my foot out to move the blanket aside when it connects with the vibrator.

To my great horror, I watch in slow motion as it falls through the railing right toward where Max is standing below me.

With a loud thud that echoes through my tiny home, it hits the floor.

"I got it," Max says, moving toward the device that now resides on the main floor.

"Just leave it," I nearly scream as I drop the blanket and scamper my ass down this stupid fucking ladder that I thought was charming until this very moment. Now I hate it with the fire of a thousand suns. "Please...don't touch it!" I gasp loudly out of breath as I fumble for the next rung on the ladder.

"It's no problem," Max offers, walking over to the kitchen area that's under the ladder.

"Please, for the love of God!" My feet thump on the hardwood floor as I jump off the ladder with three rungs to go.

A tingle shoots up my feet as I make a dive for the vibrator just as Max bends over. Our heads instantly collide, causing him to drop the flashlight onto my bare foot.

"Ouch!" I squeal, bending over to grab my tingling foot as I hop awkwardly and grip the ladder for balance.

"Shit, Cassandra, are you okay?" Max's eyes find mine in the darkness, his gaze shifting to my chest.

I glance down, and my heart rate skyrockets because my right breast is completely exposed. Nipples and all. "Holy fuck," I cry, dropping my foot to yank my nightgown over my chest. "Oh, my God, this is so embarrassing," I groan, feeling more horrified than I have ever felt in my entire life.

Scratch that.

There's more.

A faint noise permeates the air, breaking through the mortified ringing in my ears.

The distinct, unmistakable tremor of...

...*vibrating*.

Max's brow furrows at the noise, and without pause, he bends over and picks the device up off the floor. His lips part with an audible pop as he holds it in front of his face, staring at it like it's an alien life-form.

With a frustrated growl, I snatch it out of his hand, quickly pressing the off button to stop the soundtrack of my complete and utter demise. I slam it down on the counter and push my tousled hair out of my face before releasing a groan of agony.

"Cassandra, are you okay?" Max's deep voice asks, his scent invading my senses that are already at a hair-trigger level.

"Obviously not." I turn to face him and struggle to fight back the knot forming in my throat. The emotion causes my skin to tighten as my nipples pebble beneath the satin. I close my eyes because his handsome, confused face is just too much for me to bear. Why do I keep finding myself in awkward situations with this man? What have I done to deserve this level of torture from the gods?

Max's voice is hoarse when he inquires, "Were you—?"

"Max." I inhale deeply before opening my eyes to look at his devastatingly sexy face. The lines on his forehead are creased in such concern, I feel mortified all over again. "Please don't speak."

"Why not?" His gaze darkens as drips of rain fall down his face.

My eyes begin to sting as I fight back the tears. Tears that will sprout likely from searing pain on my foot, the dull ache on my forehead, the damn near crippling mortification…

…and sexual frustration beyond my wildest dreams.

The past two weeks have been the best and the worst kind of torture. I don't know what end is up anymore.

My eyes lift to his, searching back and forth and wishing I could say what I need to say without uttering a sound. "Don't ask me what I was doing or if I'm okay because you're not going to like the answer."

Max's chest heaves as he holds my gaze, taking a step toward me, clenching his jaw with each excruciating second that passes. "Tell me anyway." His voice is soft compared to the hard lines of his furrowed brow.

A crack of thunder shakes the roof over our heads, and I expel a deep breath, feeling the last shred of my dignity leave the tiny house to be swept away by the storm. On an exhale, I give in and groan, "I was pleasuring myself, okay?" He stares at me without a word, making me angry that I had to confess at all when the evidence of what I was doing is sitting on the counter. My voice grows louder with my irritation. "Are you happy? Have you succeeded finally at discovering one of my secrets? Do you feel superior now knowing that you drive not only my mind wild but also my libido?" I'm practically shrieking at him as his eyes storm with something I can only assume is repulsion. "Does it make you feel like—"

"Enough," Max growls, cutting me off as he reaches out to grip the back of my neck and haul me against him.

My startled gasp is engulfed as he crushes his lips to mine and thrusts his tongue deep into my more than accepting mouth. It's a "zero fucks given" kind of kiss. No gentle coaxing, no tantalizing sample. It's the kind where you don't know where your mouth starts and his begins.

His fingers dig into my flesh as if I'd try to get away. I wrap my arms around his shoulders, practically crawling up his damp body as he folds himself over me, making me cry into the kiss as the sensations overwhelm me in the best way.

The texture of his damp shirt against my breasts chafes against my hardened nipples as he squeezes me to him. He makes a guttural noise as he sucks on my lower lip before plunging his tongue back into my mouth.

I faintly consider pushing him away. I'm kissing my boss. He's a corporate-greed asshole whose child I care for five days a week. This is not a good idea!

But my traitorous pelvis has other ideas as it grinds into him like his dick is a magnet and I'm made of fucking metal.

Oh, my God, he's hard.

He's hard because of me?

A rush of heat spreads through my center as his hard cock presses so close to where I need him.

My hands slide up around his neck, scoring over the planes of his muscles while his tongue continues to claim me, his head turning from side to side like he can't decide which angle he likes better. An image of his cock fucking my throat hits me, and my hands slide from his neck to his arms, my fingers digging into the muscly firmness of him and wanting so much more than a kiss.

His grip skates down to my back to palm my ass as he twirls me until my back hits the ladder that's secured to the floor above. He hooks one of my legs on his hip and presses his cock into my center.

The hard ridge of him thrusting forward as I brace myself on the wood, gasping for air before he finally breaks our kiss.

"Christ, do you have any idea what you do to me?" he pants as if in pain while staring down at my breasts. His hands scale up my ribs to cup the sides of them. He presses inward and forms a long line of cleavage very nearly causing my nipples to pop out of my nightie. He dips his head to press hot, open-mouthed kisses on my chest, running his tongue down the fall of them all the way to the very edge of my nipple but never actually getting to the good part. He murmurs reverently, "I could get lost in these."

Whimpering, I release the ladder and score my fingers through his damp hair, tugging softly at the longer strands on top. The musky smell of his cologne, the rain, and the arousal pooling between my legs is enough to have me fall apart with just a little tongue play.

He returns to my lips, sealing our mouths together once again as his hand that was holding my leg moves to graze my inner thigh.

"Max," I moan as my head falls back in total ecstasy.

"Were you thinking of me with that vibrator?" he asks, his voice a growly, sexy rumble that I want to feel on my center as he dances his fingers along my flesh. My skin feels like it's going to burst into flames.

I squirm with need and rest my head against a ladder step, my chest heaving under the clinging satin. The sinful look in Max's eyes is something I need to imprint in my brain right now.

"Maybe," I offer, my voice breathy.

The corner of his mouth twitches, causing another onslaught of butterflies to take flight in my belly. He likes when I think of him?

"I was thinking of you earlier...in my shower." He leans down and sucks harshly on my breast, causing me to yelp in pain. He pulls back and stares down at the red welt already forming. His eyes look electrified as he gazes back at me. "I stroked my cock and pictured your tits covered in my cum."

This has to be a dream. I am going to wake up any second and curse Mercedes Lee Loveletter for writing such descriptive books that have turned my imaginations into hallucinations. Seriously, do they make medication for this?

His fingers finally slide upward to brush my bare center, and I cry out, bracing myself on his sculpted pecs that most definitely do not feel like pound cake. They feel like rocks. Hard as stone boulders rivaling his impressive cock that's going to rip through those cotton pants any second.

He sinks a long, delicious finger inside me and groans, "Soaked." He drops his forehead to my chest and rolls his face against my cleavage. "Are you soaked for me, Cassandra?"

"Yes," I cry out as he thrusts into me once again, his thumb scraping over my sensitive bundle of nerves. "All for you."

He pulls back and bites his lip, looking down at my face as he pumps his fingers in and out of me, watching me fall apart with every thrust.

"Max," I whimper, unable to look away from the desire in his eyes. I can't believe I'm about to say this but, "I'm going to—"

"Come for me, Cassandra," he commands, his voice powerful and everything I want at that moment. "Come on my fucking hand right now."

"So bossy," I moan and rock into his touch, feeling light-headed as my orgasm threatens to come barreling through at any second.

His hand then stills inside me, and my eyes pop open to find that his expression has completely shifted. That wickedness, that slight curve of his mouth, that darkened look in his eyes…it's all gone. And it's been replaced with the most horrific thing I can imagine at this moment…

Regret.

"I shouldn't be doing this," he croaks, pulling his hand literally out of my body like a bucket of ice water has been dumped on him. I fall forward when he moves away from me quicker than lightning. His arms are bowed out at his sides as he looks around the tiny house like he's just snapped out of a fever dream. "Fuck, this was stupid."

"What? Why?" I ask, struggling to stand upright on my wobbly legs, still feeling the aftermath of what his fingers almost accomplished as my sensitive clit throbs from being denied once more.

"You're my employee," he snaps, his tone morphing from sexy Max into grumpy CEO. "Fuck, you're my kid's nanny. This is ten kinds of fucked up."

He turns on his heel, and his hands form into tight fists at his sides. Lightning flashes through the windows, illuminating his tortured pose. My God, he looks as though he's just found out his house is on fire. This has to be about more than just the fact that I work for him.

My voice is weak when I offer, "I was a willing participant."

"It doesn't matter," he thunders back, his eyes haunted. "This was inappropriate. I should have known better."

The chastising tone of his words pierce through any shred of dignity I had left. I feel dirty and ashamed as he looks at me like I'm the worst mistake of his life. Is hooking up with me really such an appalling concept to him? I realize he can get girls ten times hotter than me, but to act like I'm some kind of disgusting mistake is a degradation I can't stomach.

"You need to go," I state through clenched teeth, willing my voice not to shake from the rejection blanketing over top of me.

Max turns around, looking guilty, which only makes this situation ten times worse. "Cassandra, I'm so sorry."

"Max," I grind out, holding my hand up to stop him from trying to talk his way out of this. "Just…go."

He closes his mouth and nods woodenly, giving my body one last glance before tucking tail and damn near running away from me.

I exhale a trembly breath as I huddle against myself, alone in my tiny house. I am a confident female. I look in the mirror every day and I like what I see. I know my worth.

But being so swiftly rejected by Max Fletcher has somehow managed to poke tiny holes in all those confidences I've worked my entire life to build.

CHAPTER 15

Cozy

"**Y**ou are the dumbest smart person I know," Dakota jabs, taking a sip of her second cocktail that was delivered smoking inside a glass dome on a platter for dramatic effect.

It's Saturday night, and we're currently at a place called *License No. 1*. It's a dark, sultry, Speakeasy-type bar located in the stone basement of a historic hotel in downtown Boulder. There's a live jazz band playing on the small stage, and the place is brimming with couples.

Clearly, Dakota and I are not joining the couple crowd anytime soon. In fact, I'm debating joining the friendship crowd because with every judgmental word Dakota shoots my way, I realize I might be in the market for a new best friend.

"Thanks, bestie," I snap, grumpily sipping my lavender gin cocktail in a fancy coupe glass.

She rolls her eyes. "Like honestly, all those romance novels you've been reading lately should be making you more confident, not less."

I eye her warily. There is just something righteously irritating about childhood best friends. They think they can voice any opinion about you because they happened to wear a heart-shaped pewter pin with your picture in it on their sweater to school every day in fifth grade. Apparently, that level of bestie devotion means they can make scathing remarks on your personality or lack of emotional intelligence while smugly insinuating they know you better.

Even tonight, when we were looking at the extensive cocktail menu, I struggled with what to order, so Dakota just picked one for me while in the bathroom without even asking me.

It was fucking delicious.

Damn her.

"I thought you were supposed to be making me feel better about my situation, not worse." I slide my finger along the fancy charcuterie board that we demolished within moments of the server setting it down in front of us. I really love how they added handles to the sides. I should shop for hardware tomorrow to add that to mine.

Dakota reaches out and touches my hand. "Focus, Cozy. You just told me you had a hot make-out sesh with Million-Dollar Max that involved loads of heavy petting and a hickey souvenir." She giggles on the last word, and I debate punching my best friend in the nose. "And then he just freaked out and bolted?"

My hand touches the space on my chest where the red welt is, and images of last night explode in my mind. His body, his tongue, his teeth, our breaths. I close my eyes and swallow the knot in my throat. "That about covers it."

"And you think it's because he's out of your league?" She stares at me in disbelief.

I shrug and nod, forcing my chin not to wobble with the overwhelming sense of raw vulnerability I'm feeling right now.

"Hi, Crazy, I'm Dakota. It's nice to meet you." Dakota holds her hand out for me to shake, and I smack it away. She sighs heavily. "Honestly, Cozy, I don't even understand this side of you. Our whole lives, you've never been insecure. It's the thing I admire most about you. Not your freakishly smart brain that seems to be both analytical and creative, not even your insane ability to make a stunning charcuterie board, or the fact that you know how to show sheep because of the years you spent in 4-H. It's your strikingly effortless confidence that gets my panties wet."

I pause before putting an olive into my mouth. "That was a bit too specific."

"Well, it's the truth," she huffs indignantly. "You're hot, but your confidence makes you a total catch. Which is why I'm struggling to get past the comment you made about being 'too fat' for Max Fletcher!"

"Would you keep your voice down," I hiss, leaning across the table to shoot daggers at her. It took a lot for me to admit that insecure thought but hearing her say it back to me fills me with regret.

My stomach sinks as I prepare to reveal the dark truth that I haven't shared with my questionable best friend tonight. The truth that's been living rent free in my mind all day long.

"It's not just the physical aspect." I blow a slow breath out of my mouth and continue, "It's the fact that Max is a multimillionaire with a successful company. He has a gorgeous home, a sweet daughter, an ex-wife who, by all accounts, he gets along well with. He has his life together, and here I am, a twenty-six-year-old nanny who just moved out of my sister's spare bedroom into a tiny house on his property that is nicer than anything I've ever lived in before. I have absolutely nothing to offer him. It's no wonder he took a second look at me and ran for the hills."

Dakota's features soften. "Need I remind you that your circumstances are by choice right now?"

"I know that." I groan and push my hands into my hair. "But he doesn't."

"So then tell him," she presses.

"Absolutely not. If he's going to be a shallow asshole who won't sleep with a girl because he thinks she's beneath his station like we're in the middle of some Regency romance novel, then fuck him."

Dakota laughs. "Regency romance couldn't handle the likes of Cozy Barlow."

"And those corsets can go to hell." I pop another olive into my mouth, and we both giggle like schoolgirls. It feels good. It's the first time I've cracked a smile in twenty-four hours. And I love to smile.

A thoughtful look crosses Dakota's face. "If you ask me, this has nothing to do with your body, your looks, or your current career choice. I think this has to do with his position over top of you and him not wanting to take advantage of you."

"I want him to take advantage of me!" I exclaim as her words elicit a graphic image of Max over top of me, causing heat to pool in my belly. "I want him to finish what he started. I want to scratch this itch, so he can stop consuming my thoughts day and night. If we hooked up just once, then maybe I could go five freaking minutes without thinking about how he looks in his swim trunks or now…a wet fucking T-shirt."

"Yeah, I'd pay to see that." Dakota's eyes flare with heat before she shakes that image away. She eyes me over her cocktail as she takes a sip. "So are you saying you'd be up for a one-night stand with a millionaire?"

"Yeah, who wouldn't be?" I reply with a laugh. "Trust me, I'm not looking to become Everly's new mommy. And I certainly don't want to be a second wife to the corporate grind. Not to mention, I need to get my life together long before I could ever seriously date anyone, let alone a single dad. But CEO Max is clearly not up for sex with a nanny."

"I wouldn't be so sure about that." She presses her fingers to her lips, clearly deep in thought.

I roll my eyes. "What is running through that hamster wheel of a brain you have?"

She quirks a challenging brow and props her elbows on the table. "Just that men are essentially cavemen who learned how to dress. And what do cavemen do?" She sits back and smirks. "They hunt."

I chew my lower lip nervously, knowing that I shouldn't encourage Dakota because when she puts her mind to something, she often succeeds. But I can't help the question that tumbles out of my mouth. "So what does that mean for me?"

"It means you need to make them chase you a bit before you write him off for good." She winks coyly. "Because I have a feeling he's the kind of guy who goes after what he wants."

I shake my head and press my fingers to my temples. This is a bad, bad idea. I am not as skilled at playing men like Dakota is.

"Should I even want something to happen between us? I mean…he is my boss and I love Everly."

"So what! You're both mature-ish consenting adults." She waves her cocktail to the server who's passing by, indicating we need another round. She turns back to me, not missing a beat. "Since you've already crossed the line, you might as well make it to the finish line. A fling with a millionaire sounds like the perfect Great Defrost life experience for Cozy Cassie."

Butterflies erupt in my belly at just the idea of this happening. It's been so long since I've had some good, mind-blowing sex.

In the past, I never made much time for men. My studies were my main priority in high school, and then after that, a job took over my whole life. Sure, I had the odd boyfriends, but they never lasted more than a few months. I was usually too mentally exhausted to give the relationship any sort of attention. When I was home, I was in sloth mode, so the idea of a booty call or a late-night hookup was the last thing on my mind.

With Max, it's a completely different story, and I am a completely different person. I'm someone who wants to make time for carnal pleasures. And something tells me that Max would be very good at delivering on that.

"How do I make him chase me exactly?" I ask, cringing inwardly because I can't believe I'm entertaining this idea.

"Look, it's not rocket science," Dakota laughs, noticing my anxiety-ridden face. "But a hot Zaddy like Max probably has women throwing themselves at him every single day."

A pang of jealousy over that thought hits me out of nowhere so I quicky chug down the last of my cocktail.

"So if you want him to come to you, you need to be aloof. Hard to get. Unapproachable. You need him practically panting for your attention, wondering what's going on in that pretty, dark-haired, green-eyed, pouty lipped little head of yours."

A pleased smile lifts my cheeks. "I have pouty lips?"

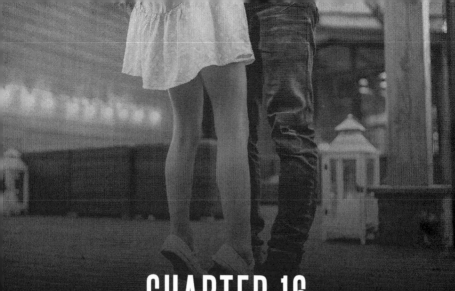

CHAPTER 16

Max

Monday at noon, I shoot off yet another email to Jenson Hunsberger, the CEO of All-Out Properties, the Denver company that we're due to merge with in less than ninety days. They are a commercial real estate firm with properties in over one hundred countries. Having this level of commercial real estate options at our fingertips with no competitors will be tremendous leverage for Fletcher Industries.

When I first launched my business, I started in real estate development. I wanted to be a brand with widespread recognition so when people were looking to buy up properties for personal use, they came to me. That earned me my first million faster than I thought possible. And a hell of a lot faster than flipping houses like my father and brothers.

Then when I was twenty-six, I was approached by a colleague about becoming a regional hub for a franchise developer that has been helping businesses grow globally for years. When I signed with them and became a franchise consultant, I went from a millionaire to a multimillionaire. Not only did I help businesses expand, but I was also able to invest in the ones I found the most promising. The monthly distributions I receive through those various investments are enough to set Everly up for life.

Adding All-Out Properties to my portfolio will make my multimillionaire status a thing of the past. This will be a game changer for my company.

I press the assistant number on my phone. "Marcia, can you please follow up with Jenson Hunsberger's assistant and let him know that I emailed him again about the quarterly tax reports for last year? We have asked for it three times already, and our lawyer is growing impatient."

"Yes, sir."

"Thank you." I sigh and sit back in my chair, pinching the bridge of my nose.

"And sir, did you decide on bringing a plus-one for the Rainbow Project Gala in Denver? The event is in four weeks, and they need your headcount."

I exhale heavily. I've been avoiding this RSVP because I don't particularly want to bring a date, but Jenson Hunsberger will be at my table with his wife. I've learned from attending enough of these events that it's much easier to talk business when the partners have someone else to visit with. And Jenson and I will surely have a lot of business to discuss with the impending merger.

Maybe I can bring Henley over from Aspen for the night. I met her years ago when I was selling one of my properties there. She was a broker for a couple who was interested in buying my place. That deal never panned out, but the deal for Henley and me to be fuck buddies when I'm in town ended up okay. She'd be good at an event like this.

"You can put me down for a plus-one," I reply to Marcia crisply. "And will you call Bettina about having my tux dry-cleaned?"

"Yes, sir."

I pull out my phone and shoot a quick text to Henley. She responds almost immediately, confirming she is available and would love to come. Good. That's sorted. Now if only I can get Jenson to follow through with the fucking documents I still need. If I don't have them before this gala, I will certainly be cornering him at that party to make it happen.

The ache of an oncoming headache hits me, so I reach into my drawer for some Excedrin. I never felt this stressed when I was working from home a couple of weeks ago. Probably because I had a lot to distract my thoughts every day.

Namely, the hot nanny.

I glance back at my phone to see if I have any texts from Cassandra. Last week she would periodically send me photos of her and Everly's day. She'd keep me posted on what they were up to and cute things Everly would say. On Wednesday she asked me to text Bettina to pick up more fruit because she thought Everly was constipated. Then she texted me two hours later...

Cassandra: Abort fruit gathering mission. Everly has made a deposit at the porcelain bank! Turns out she's rich! Poop emoji. Poop emoji. Poop emoji.

I was equal parts horrified, amused, and appreciative. I've never had this much communication about Everly's day-to-day life with Jessica. She and Kailey do their thing when they have Everly, and I guess I do mine. But having Cassandra's regular text messages pinging me throughout the day made me feel connected to them, even from my office. And it sure as hell took away from the stress of my workday.

Now I've gone all morning without a peep from her and I have no one to blame but my fucking self.

I check my phone to read the last messages I exchanged with Cassandra.

Me: I'm sorry about last night.

Cassandra: I know, Max.

Me: Are you okay?

Cassandra: Why wouldn't I be?

Me: Because of what happened between us. Because of what I did.

Cassandra: Relax, Max. I'm not a sexual harassment case you need to worry about. I was a consenting party.

Me: I understand that, but I would also understand if you wanted to quit.

Cassandra: Do you want me to quit?

Me: No…Everly loves you.

Cassandra: The feeling is mutual, so you're going to have to fire me if you want me to leave.

Me: That won't be happening. I don't want to lose you.

Cassandra never replied to that last message, and I spent every minute of today wishing I could unsend that last fucking text. It was too much. "Don't want to lose her?" My God, I sound like a creep.

She probably thinks I still want her.

And regrettably, I do.

I freaked out Friday night when I realized I attacked her like a starving psychopath…*as her boss.* Nanny or not, that's not the way to get into a woman's bed. She would be well within her right to file a sexual harassment charge against me. I deserve it.

But whether I want her or not is irrelevant. She is Everly's nanny. We need to stay professional.

My phone beeps before Marcia's voice echoes through the speaker, "Mr. Fletcher?"

"Yes?"

"You have a surprise visitor out here. Can I send them back?"

"Who is it?" I ask, my brow furrowed.

Everly's voice whispers so loudly, I can hear it clear as day. "Don't tell him, Marcia. It has to be a surprise."

I hear Marcia laugh and then say, "It's a surprise, sir."

"Send them in." I sit back, my heart full because I'm excited to see my kid. Unfortunately, my stomach is in knots because I'm also about to see Cassandra for the first time since Friday night.

"'Tis I!" Everly peals as she bursts through my office door. She dead sprints through my expansive space and around my large mahogany desk to throw herself into my arms.

"What a surprise!" I exclaim, my hand cupping the back of her head and noticing she has two bubble braids in today. I pull her away from me to get a look at her as she sits on my lap. Her long legs dangle to the side in a way that makes me sad because she's growing up way too fast. She beams at me. "We brought you a picnic lunch!"

"Did you now?" I reply and see movement in the doorway.

I glance over to see Cassandra standing there looking somewhat awkward but just as cute as Everly. Both of them are dressed in floral sundresses, and Cassandra's dark hair is pulled back into two short bubble braids to match Everly's.

They look fucking adorable.

"Hi, Cassandra." I try to sound casual instead of sexually frustrated by the sight of her.

"Dad, will you ever call her Cozy?" Everly whines.

I smile nervously. "She looks like a Cassandra to me."

Cassandra clears her throat and glances down at her feet. "The lunch surprise was Everly's idea, so why don't I let the two of you have a daddy-daughter lunch date alone. There's a coffee shop across the street I can go to. Just text me when you're done."

"Are you sure?" I ask, hating that she's trying so hard to get away from me. "I don't mind you joining."

"Yeah, Cozy. Eat with us! You made most of it."

Cassandra gets a nervous look in her eyes and murmurs, "That's what I'm afraid of."

The corners of my mouth lift. "Well, if you made it then you have to join us."

She sighs heavily but nods. Everly cheers like this is the best day of her life, and all we're doing is eating lunch. Do less, indeed.

The three of us walk out of my office building to a little park beside a dog park. I have a perfect view of this area from my office window, and every time I look out there, I have to fight the urge to buy Everly a puppy. She's always wanted one but knowing the time I have with her is limited, a dog would be sorely neglected when Everly's not with me.

Everly grabs a plaid blanket out of the large tote Cassandra holds open and spreads it out on the grass even though there are perfectly good picnic tables not far away. I slip out of my suit jacket and lay awkwardly on the blanket, propped on my elbow with my legs stretched out. Cassandra kicks her flip-flops off and sits as far away from me on the blanket as she can get, her pink-painted toes hanging off the blanket and into the grass.

"I did this part," Everly says, pulling out a small vase with daisies that grow on the bank by the creek. She sets it down on the blanket and then retrieves some paper placemats with pictures drawn on each one. She points at the first one. "This is Cozy and me on the deck playing tennis." *They're just sitting.* "This is me and you having supper with Michael." *Dad can't cook, nice touch.* "And this is you saving Cozy's life!" She laughs and rests her hand on my shoulder, sighing like it's the funniest story in the world.

I shoot a wooden smile to Cassandra, who is distracted with the sandwiches she's placing on the placemats. She pops open a Tupperware of fruit and something else I can't quite discern.

"Great drawings, Everly," I declare with a smile. "You'll have to draw a picture of this picnic. Everything looks great."

Everly settles in the space between us, sitting criss-cross and biting into her sandwich enthusiastically.

"Is it okay?" Cassandra asks nervously.

Everly's brows shoot up. "It's delicious!"

Cassandra looks relieved.

Around a mouthful, I inquire, "What have you guys been up to this morning?"

"Cozy showed me the charcuterie board she's working on, and it's so cool, Dad!"

"Oh? Did you find some wood that worked? I told you I can chop something if you need it."

"I'm good," Cassandra says, avoiding eye contact with me.

"She let me sand it, but I got a splinter." Everly thrusts her finger into my face, and I can't tell where the splinter was, but I grab it and kiss it away anyway.

My brows furrow as I look over at Cassandra. Last week, this would have been something she texted me about. Now this week, she can barely make eye contact with me. Goddammit, I fucked shit up.

"But don't worry," Everly continues. "Cozy got the splinter out, and I didn't even cry."

I set my half-eaten sandwich down and nod. "Well, that sounds like a busy day already. What's the plan for the afternoon?"

"Probably swimming," Everly peals excitedly and then looks over her shoulder. "Cozy, can I go play at the park?"

Cassandra's eyes lift. "You should ask your dad, Sea Monster. It's his lunch date."

"Yeah, go play, kid," I answer, my heart sinking a little over how Everly defaulted to Cassandra for permission instead of me. It's to be expected when she's in charge all day, but it still stings. I want that dynamic to change between Everly and me before the summer is over.

Cassandra and I sit in awkward silence as we watch Everly run on the playground from one obstacle to the next. I consider broaching the subject of Friday night, but that seems inappropriate. Plus, what else is there to say really?

I'm sorry I'm a horn ball fuck up who attacked you like I've never had sex in my entire life? I sigh heavily. Somehow, I was able to stop it before we had sex which is a painful reminder I'm going to have to live with every second I'm with her. Especially after getting a taste of her pouty lips and how she felt in my arms.

Frustrated with my stupid fucking thoughts, I open the second Tupperware. It looks like some sort of potato soup that's...cold? I shrug and stick my fork in it to give it a try.

When the mushy particles hit my mouth, I instantly freeze and can feel Cassandra's gaze on me. Fighting the urge to gag, I point at the container and mumble, "What is this?"

"It's supposed to be potato salad," Cassandra offers, her eyes watching me intently. "Is it not good?"

I press my lips together and nod, my face contorting in agony as I turn to look at her.

"Oh, come on. It can't be that bad. I followed my mom's recipe."
She grabs a fork and takes a drippy bite, instantly hunching over in
shock. Her cheeks puff out as she garbles, "Oh, my God."

I nod sadly.

"Oh, my God!" She quickly grabs a napkin to spit into. "I must
have put in too much apple cider vinegar. That tastes like poison!" She
hands me a napkin, but I've already swallowed. It was a sad swallow.

Her eyes are severe when she realizes what I've done. "That was
a mistake."

I quickly grab a bottle of water to chase the awful concoction
down my throat. "I hope I don't regret that later."

"You will," she huffs, replacing the lid on the Tupperware and
tossing it into the grass like it's going to infect us if we sit too close
to it.

Silence descends for a moment before I catch her gaze out of the
corner of my eye, and then, in unison, we burst out laughing. Her
face lights up as she covers her flaming red cheeks, and the knots in
my stomach begin to unravel at the sound of her happy voice again.
It gives me hope that we can move past the whole Friday night disaster and get back to normal.

"A for effort, Cozy." I sigh, lifting my bottle of water up to her
in a mock toast.

Her smiling eyes fall, and she blinks quickly before moving into
a standing position.

"Where are you going?" I ask, looking up at her and trying not
to stare at her legs.

She tugs on one of her braids and stammers, "To check on Everly."

"I can do that." I set my water down and stand.

"It's my job, Mr. Fletcher," she says crisply and then takes off,
leaving me standing alone with the poisoned potato salad.

CHAPTER 17

Cozy

The scent of charred wood makes me horny.

Which is problematic because a large part of my charcuterie board design technique is to torch my boards with a weed burner. Burning helps the natural grain of the wood pop out, achieving a unique zebra stripe appearance to the boards once they're finished. I used to use a smaller flame torch, but it would take me hours and I'd be dripping in sweat with cramps from hunching over by the time I was done. This torch has a three-foot pole and much larger flame, so it's cut my burning time in half.

Plus, I feel like a badass when I'm operating it.

Who knew all that time I spent taking college courses as a young teenager would result in me finding my passion for making charcuterie boards of all things? Skills I achieved from doing 4-H projects with my father on the farm, not taught by a professor in a college lecture hall.

When I was a kid, my dad and I did all sorts of woodworking projects in the machine shed. Various shelves, cutting boards, benches, and stools. Some cheesy decorative items like snowmen and would enter them as 4-H projects in the county fair, and I'd always earn a blue ribbon and oftentimes, best of show.

My sister was the girlie daughter. She enjoyed baking and cooking with Mom, so her 4-H projects would be of the consumable variety.

In hindsight, I should have had a better balance between wood-working and kitchen projects because the putrid look on Max's face when he sampled my potato salad earlier this week is burned into my memory. And the moment I realized that we were bonding over my failed attempt at a classic salad is when I knew I'd failed misera-bly at Dakota's plan for me.

"Be aloof. Be unavailable. Don't say much to him."

Ugh, I should have gone to the coffee shop like I planned. But when Everly turned those baby blue eyes on me, I couldn't say no. Plus, Max's entire office was drenched in his intoxicating scent, and I could barely form a coherent thought, let alone come up with an excuse for why I shouldn't go with them on their picnic.

Heavy sigh.

I've done a better job the rest of the week at avoiding him and acting indifferent. I even declined a dinner invite from him last night when Michael made too much homemade pasta. Saying no to fresh pasta about killed me. But I was in survival mode after what I had witnessed the other night.

When I stumbled upon Max...*chopping wood.*

Yep. That's right. The millionaire really did chop his own wood. It wasn't total bullshit. I nearly dropped my bag full of dill pickles that I had just picked up from the grocery store when I caught sight of him down by the creek. He was dressed in jeans and a flannel, even though it was a warm summer night. He had clear safety goggles on and was working in front of a large tree stump situated beside a log rack with rows and rows of freshly chopped wood.

I watched in awe as he bent over to pick up a giant log that looked much too heavy to manhandle. He grunted as he set it on his chop-ping station. Then he picked up the axe propped on a nearby tree, spread his legs, and inhaled a huge breath before winding the axe back and crashing it down on top of the wood.

I nearly came on the spot.

He would mumble curse words for every log that didn't split open on the first swing. I know because I stood there watching for far longer than was appropriate. It was like a lumberjack fantasy and a Zaddy fantasy were having dirty sex in my brain, and I couldn't walk away until they both had their happy ending.

He stacked the freshly chopped wood up in a wheelbarrow, and when he propped the axe up on the tree and bent over to push the wheelbarrow up to the house, he caught me standing there, staring at him.

I nearly tripped on my feet as I hurried off to my tiny house with my pickle jars clanking in my bag like a disgusting pervert who got off watching her boss swing an axe.

It was ridiculous. I'm a grown woman. Why is this man unnerving me so much? Surely, I've seen grown men chop their own wood before. I mean…not in person but on the internet and stuff.

And obviously, most fathers' eyes light up when their children come running into their office to surprise them with a picnic lunch. That doesn't make Max special. That doesn't make him sexier than all the other single dads who look stupid hot in suits.

It makes him average. Max Fletcher is an average human.

Which is why it's good I'm out here in the garage working on more charcuterie boards. It's not the most exciting Friday night activity, but I need the distraction, and my vibrator is still in a time-out for misbehaving last week.

If only this smoky wood aroma didn't remind me of Max.

Ugh. Now I'm sweating. Yes, I'm working with a flame so that could be the cause of it, but there is air-conditioning in here and a strong evening breeze coming in through the window I opened for ventilation. I'm afraid this sweat dripping down my chest has a lot more to do with the fire I feel for Max than the flamethrower in my hands. I wonder what his tongue would think of the under-boob sweat I'm currently rocking?

"What's on fire?" a voice yells, causing me to jump out of my skin as I nearly drop my flamethrower on the concrete.

"Holy shit!" I exclaim, quickly recovering my grip on the dangerous tool. I bend over to shut the gas off and wait for the flame to go down. I place the long, hot tool on the sawhorse that's holding my charcuterie board and push my safety goggles up on my head.

I turn around and have to remind myself to breathe because seconds ago, I was falling deep into yet another Zaddy fantasy. And now that fantasy is standing right in front of me.

I drink in the sight of a barefoot Max in faded jeans and a white T-shirt. His broad frame stretches the white fabric as his pecs rise with each intake of breath. My fingers itch to run through his sandy hair that looks soft and rumpled on top of his head. It's my favorite look on him. Even better than the hot, tailored suit and side-swept hair. He looks like he was enjoying a quiet Friday night until I ruined it. I glance at the clock and see it's almost ten, so I suspect Everly is in bed already.

"Nothing is on fire, I promise," I reply, pressing a hand to my heart that's still racing from the shock of his presence.

Max's indigo eyes seem to darken under the fluorescent lights as his gaze drops down my body. Honestly, I didn't expect anyone to see me like this. I'm sure I look like a hot mess. My hair is in a low messy ponytail stuffed under a backward John Deere hat that has seen better days. I'm wearing a black sports tank and yoga shorts with my old Doc Martens boots, and I have this tan leather apron that my dad gave me years back to help protect my clothes when I work.

At least the apron is hiding the under-boob sweat.

Max seems at a loss for words as he opens his mouth and struggles to speak. Finally, he stammers, "Um…good. I just smelled something, so I wanted to check."

I gesture to my charred board. "Yeah, sorry. I was just doing some burning on this piece I'm working on. I opened a window and thought that would help. I can take this outside, though."

"No, no," Max rushes out, holding his hand up. "It's fine. I was just…worried."

I rub my lips together, ignoring the intensity of his eyes. "Sorry."

"I said it's fine, Cassandra." He breaks eye contact and stares down at the floor by my feet. "I've seen a lot of tools in my life, but this one is new."

I laugh and move to pick it up. He walks over to inspect it, and the scent of his cologne mixing with the smell of charred wood has my legs feeling like they could give out at any second.

I swallow the thickness in my throat. "It's a weed burner. I use it to torch the wood and give the grain pattern more pop. I saw you had a regular torch in here, but it takes forever with those tiny things. This big guy gets the job done much quicker."

His brows flicker slightly at my last comment as the corners of his mouth turn down. He runs a hand over the charred wood.

"Careful, it might still be hot."

He pulls his hand back, rubbing black ash between his fingers before sliding them into his pocket. "You really love doing this, don't you?"

"It's my therapy," I answer honestly, and he turns curious eyes to me, his gaze roving over my face, probably covered in sweat and soot.

"What do you need therapy for?" His question is gentle and different from the way he's pried into my personal life before.

I shrug. "Various reasons…but I think everyone needs a release of some sort, don't you?" *Why does everything I say sound so sexual?*

His eyes fall to my lips, and my stomach swirls with desire. When his gaze travels even lower, I think he's noticing the beads of sweat falling down my cleavage, but I inhale sharply when I realize his eyes are zeroing in on the faded hickey over the swell of my breast.

Fuck.

His jaw muscle pops, and he quickly snaps his focus back to my board. With a raspy voice, he breaks the heavy silence. "At some point, are we going to get back to normal?"

My head jerks back as I stare at his chiseled profile. "Why do you think we aren't normal?"

He moistens his lips before turning to look at me. "You haven't been texting me this week."

"What?" I ask, taking a step back to get some space from his intoxicating smell so I can understand what he's saying.

"The Everly update texts." His face looks vulnerable and younger than I've ever seen it before. "You haven't sent me a single one this week. Last week those texts were the best part of my days."

"Oh…" I blink back my shock, my pulse quickening in my veins at his shocking admission. "You never say much back."

"I'm usually in meetings," he replies, his jaw taut. "But I see them. I see them all. And I reread them before I fall asleep every night. It makes me feel like I'm a part of her whole day."

My heart lurches at the image of Max lying in bed rereading my messages. He's probably shirtless, wearing a snug pair of Calvin Klein boxer briefs. Maybe he even sleeps naked. I shake that thought away, and my voice is wobbly when I respond, "I didn't realize you enjoyed them so much."

"I love them." He inhales deeply and turns to face me head-on, maintaining eye contact that I find impossible to look away from.

"I'll start sending them again next week," I rush out and chew my lip nervously. "I'm sorry for stopping them."

The corner of his mouth morphs into a thoughtful smile. "Thank you."

Shame blankets me that I went an entire week without updating him about his kid. It's unforgivable. "And I promise you that's the last time I ever let anything that happens between you and me change what I share with you about Everly." Max frowns curiously as I take a step toward him. "I'm upset with myself for doing that. I let my own emotions get in the way of my job, and I assure you that's out of character for me."

"I deserved it," Max replies through clenched teeth.

"No, you didn't." I steel myself to say the next bit. "What happened between us was nothing I need to be coddled over. It was two consenting adults who had a moment. Nothing more. I promise you, I'm not some love-sick female looking for a relationship." I take a deep breath before revealing the next bit. "The truth is, I'm in a bit of a transition in my life."

"Okay…" Max looks perplexed, and it's kind of adorable.

"I mean, honestly, I don't even know why I was so upset." I laugh and adjust the hat on my head. "Sexual frustration, I suppose." *Good Lord, did I just say that last part out loud?*

"Sexual frustration?" He quirks a brow.

Yep. Said it out loud. Best own it now.

"Yeah…sexual frustration." I remove my goggles and slide them over the edge of my apron, feigning indifference like I talk about sex all the time. "Women experience blue balls too, Max."

"They do?" He looks shocked again, and for some reason, I'm enjoying the way his feet are shuffling uncomfortably. If I have to live with that hot kiss in my mind all day, so can he.

"Sorry, I'm oversharing." I offer a rueful smile as my cheeks heat and that under-boob sweat returns with a vengeance. I need to re-direct this conversation before I say anything else. "I just mean, you don't have to worry about me anymore. I'm not looking for anything from you—you made it clear that I'm not what you want, which is all good! In fact, I've decided that I'm on the hunt for a casual summer fling with a stranger. So rest assured, you are off the hook."

I laugh awkwardly and realize I'm still oversharing. My God, Cozy. *Shut up.* This is like bad interview 2.0. Just abort this conver-sation. He doesn't need to know about the epiphany you just had. Simply reassure him that you're going to be a good nanny and you can both move on with your lives.

"And I promise you that when I find a guy, it won't get in the way of my time with Everly," I blurt out, feeling like I need to bring the focus back to Everly, not Max. Everly is who's important here.

"*When* you find a guy," Max repeats as he scratches his fingers through the whiskers on his jaw. His forehead lines stack on top of one another, and I hope he's not thinking about firing me again. "Okay then."

"Okay?" I reply with relief and smile warmly. "Great! I'm glad we had this talk. I feel so much better."

"Yeah." His face looks pensive, but he's probably just still in shock about my comment about women having blue balls. He can Google it later.

For now, I think I need to stop playing games and actually do something for myself.

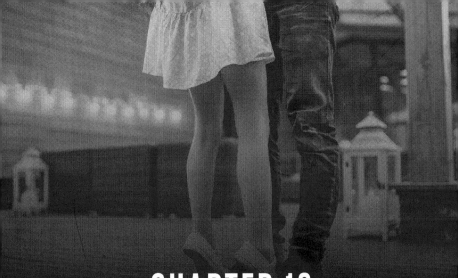

CHAPTER 18

Max

Whiskey burns on my tongue as I hold the amber liquid in my mouth and watch my brother Calder deal out another round of cards for our monthly Texas Hold'em meetup. His inked arms are swift as he deals me in, my other two brothers, plus Josh and Dean, who join us every time it's my turn to host.

The other person who joined us tonight is the tiny human working hard to take all our money this evening.

Everly sits at the head of the table, her feet swinging off the edge of her chair, as she dons Luke's baseball cap backward over her blond hair. She looks like Cassandra did last night in her workshop, and I can't help but notice how much the two of them seem to be morphing into each other this summer.

Everly grabs a handful of popcorn as Luke explains the rules to her for the twentieth time.

"But Uncle Luke, why can't I see the cards in the middle before I bet?" Everly asks, her tongue sticking out of her mouth as she holds her two cards out for the whole table to see.

"Because then it wouldn't be gambling," Luke says, pushing her cards to her chest and trying not to look at them. "Don't be showing these cheats your cards, or they'll take your money."

Luke looks at me with an exasperated expression, and I shrug. "You guys were the ones who asked her to play." I glance at my phone to see it's venturing on nine. I typically let Everly stay up until ten or eleven on weekends, so this will be a long night of card playing with her. She looks adorable, though, and I'm more than thankful to have brothers and friends who have zero issues with her hanging around. She is the princess of the group, after all.

"She needs to learn the art of a good poker face," my brother Wyatt suggests, his face unreadable. Wyatt is the king of a poker face. I think that the secluded house where he lives in the mountains has sucked away his limited social skills. It's either the cabin or the fucking goat named Millie he bought that's turned him into a full-fledged grumpy mountain man who's hardly fit for polite company anymore.

Everly adores him.

"Uncle Wyatt?"

He grunts.

"Will you tell me what your cards are?"

He slides unamused eyes to Everly and shakes his head stiffly.

She sticks out her lower lip.

He sighs heavily and turns his cards to her.

"This is why she keeps winning!" Calder barks, slapping his hand on the table, his competitive nature in full throttle tonight. "This is total bullshit."

Josh tosses his chips out onto the table, shaking his head at the spectacle of my family. "All right, everyone…place your bets."

I match him and glance out the window toward the guesthouse for probably the twentieth time tonight. It's dark out now, and I can see the lights on inside. Every once in a while, I spot the silhouette of Cassandra's body through the windows, and I can't help but wonder what she's doing in there. Is she thinking of going out tonight in search of that "summer fling"?

I inwardly groan. That was quite the conversation we had in the workshop last night. First, I walk in on some fucked-up version of a porn scene. Didn't think a female doing woodworking was my kink but seeing the round ass of Cassandra hunched over a slab of wood that she was lighting on fire in that backward hat and those clear goggles made me see otherwise.

Fuck...I was done for.

Then she tells me women get blue balls right before she mentions she's looking for a summer fling. I didn't know what end was fucking up by the end of that conversation! I'm certain this isn't the type of relationship most single dads have with their kid's nanny, but I'm also certain most single dads don't leave fucking hickeys on the person they've employed to watch their kid for the summer either.

Fuck.

After we cleared the air, I thought I would feel better, but then she had to overshare about her goals to hunt for summer dick, and now my mind is consumed with thoughts about her with another guy.

"Why do you keep looking outside?" Dean asks, adjusting his glasses as he glances at his cards. Josh looks over his shoulder to see what I might be looking at.

"Just watching the weather," I mumble and turn my focus back to my cards. I spy Luke staring at me, so I sharply decide to ignore that nosy fucker.

The rest of the table finishes placing their bets just as the doorbell rings. I frown, wondering who that could be because everyone I know is already here.

I open the door to find a lanky blonde standing on my front step. Her eyes widen obnoxiously as she leans against the door and purrs, "Hello, Maxamillion."

"Do I know you?" I inquire curiously.

She huffs out a laugh and then clears her throat. "Sorry, I'm Dakota, Cozy's friend. I'm here to pick her up."

She reaches out to shake my hand, and I can't help but notice this girl looks like she's dressed for a night out on the town. Is Cassandra going to be dressed like her? I shake my head and reply, "Cassandra is out back in the guesthouse."

"No worries! I just texted her and told her I was up here. She said she'll be right up."

A loud argument breaks out behind me that has Dakota frowning curiously. "Sounds like you're having a party," she says, trying to peer over my shoulder.

"No party, just poker night. Please, come in," I respond woodenly as I step back and guide her over to the dining room table that's covered in snacks, poker chips, and cards.

"What do we have here?" Dakota sweet-talks, propping her hand on the back of Wyatt's chair. Wyatt hides his cards from her.

Calder fiddles with the sleeves of his flannel and flashes her a wicked grin. "You got any money?"

"I do, but I usually make the man pay for me," Dakota answers with a flirtatious wink. "It's possibly anti-feminist of me, but I figure taking a man's money is also a way to fuck the patriarchy."

"What's a patriarchy?" Everly's voice interjects as she returns to the table from the bathroom off the library.

Dakota's eyes widen in horror. "Oh, my God, I'm so sorry! I didn't see you there." She covers her mouth and shoots me a guilty look.

"It's okay," I reply, sitting down in my chair and shooting my cute kid a wink as she resumes her spot at the table too. "Everly knows what words aren't for her."

"Is patriarchy a bad word, Daddy?"

I frown at that. "Kind of? But it's not really a curse word, so you can feel free to use it."

Calder taps the cards on the table. "You want me to deal you in, Blondie? I like to fuck the patriarchy too."

She laughs. "Not tonight. Cozy and I are meeting some people in a little bit, and I wouldn't want to be late."

Her eyes turn to Everly, who has turned Luke's baseball cap forward now, pulling it low over her eyes. She has a piece of licorice hanging out of her mouth, and she's staring at her cards like she's about to bet her mortgage payment on them.

"So you're the infamous Everly," Dakota says, her voice rising excitedly at the end. "I've heard a lot about you."

Everly looks up at Dakota, giving her body a once-over. "Still don't know what patriarchy means."

It's Wyatt's deep voice that pipes up next. "It's a social system where men have power over everything in a society that wrongly oppresses women." His jaw tightens, and he adds, "Though the fact that I gave you the definition instead of the other female in the room means that the patriarchy is sadly ingrained in all of us."

Silence descends the table for a moment before Everly looks back to Dakota and notes, "Cool shoes."

Dakota smiles and glances down at her strappy sandals. "Thanks...I like your hat."

"It's Uncle Luke's," Everly replies distractedly. "Now...can someone tell me what two A's mean again? That's not a number, so I don't know what to do with them."

The table groans as several of the guys toss their cards down in frustration.

I smile proudly. "Everly has a case of beginner's luck."

"Or maybe lady luck," Dakota offers.

"Dakota." Cassandra's voice cuts in behind me as the slider door to the house opens. "I told you to text me when you were outside, and I would meet you at your car."

Dakota shrugs. "I wanted to meet the kid you won't stop bragging about."

Warmth blooms in my chest at the fact that Cassandra brags about my kid. Unfortunately, that sensation is quickly stamped out when I turn and see Cassandra's outfit.

Double fuck.

She's wearing a long brown skirt that instantly reminds me of that nightgown she had on the evening of the storm. It was a flimsy little thing that would have tumbled off her body had I just blown on it sideways. I'm sure I would have gotten to that, but I was too busy assaulting her with my tongue first.

The skirt has a sexy rouching on the side that splits apart into a wide slit up her leg. The fabric hugs her hips and ass perfectly, and she's paired it with a snug black, long-sleeve top that her ample breasts do a good job testing the stretch of the fabric. It has a high neckline and reveals a sliver of her abdomen above the skirt's high waist. I wonder if she wore that shirt to cover up the mark I left on her? Why does my mark on her make my cock stir every time I think about it?

Jesus, I'm such a fucking creep.

"You're the nanny?" Calder balks, his eyes nearly bulging out of his head. I glance around the table and notice most of the men are gaping at her as well, and my fists clench.

Cassandra's strappy heels clunk on the hard wood as she walks over to join her friend. "Yes, I'm Cozy. And you are?"

"I'm Calder," he answers, standing and leaning across the table to shake her hand. Her breasts nearly brush Wyatt's ear as she reaches past him to take his hand. Calder sits down and points. "That grump is Wyatt...there's baby Luke. Do you know these two boneheads already?"

Josh and Dean roll their eyes and ignore my obnoxious brother.

"Yes, we've met," Cassandra says with a smile. "And I met Luke last week. Nice to see you all."

"Nice to see you too. Both of you." Calder shoots Cassandra and Dakota a boyish smirk that I'd really like to punch off his face. He's always the fucking flirt. Seriously, anywhere we go where there's a single woman in sight, he will abandon whoever he arrived with and go into fuckboy mode.

His eyes move to mine as he shoots me a weird look. Seriously, what the fuck is with my brothers looking at me like that tonight?

"What's your plan this evening, ladies?" Luke asks, lifting his brows curiously. "Hitting up Pearl Street?"

"Yes, we are," Dakota answers, grabbing Cassandra's arm. "But first we're meeting a couple of guys for drinks. A little double-date action. Haven't been on one of those in ages."

"They don't need to hear about our night." Cassandra laughs, shaking her head. She looks uncomfortable but not irritated.

I'm irritated.

In fact, I'm downright bothered.

She wasted no time starting the hunt for that summer fling she mentioned. And I can't help but wonder if that's a good idea? My hickey is still on her body, for Christ's sake.

"That's good you're going on a date, Cozy," my daughter's voice chimes in, ripping my eyes away from Cassandra's body in that outfit. "You said you haven't had time to find a boyfriend since you moved back to Boulder."

Moved back to Boulder? When did she leave? And when was she looking for a boyfriend? She said she just wanted a summer fling. What the actual fuck? How does my kid know more about the nanny's life than I do? I'm the one who pays her every week.

Cassandra's cheeks flame red, and her eyes notably flash to mine. "It's just for drinks."

"But it could turn into a boyfriend, and I think that's great," Everly sings merrily like she's a step away from being the flower girl at Cassandra's wedding. "Now I don't have to find you a boyfriend like I did for my friend Brooklyn."

Triple fuck.

"What do you know about boyfriends?" Calder takes the words right out of my mouth as all eyes swerve to my child.

Everly's lips part. "Um…" She looks up at Cassandra like she's going to save her.

"You might as well just tell them," Cassandra whispers.

The hairs on the back of my neck stand up. "Tell us what?"

Everly looks decidedly guilty. "I have a boyfriend."

"Who?" my brothers and I all bark in unison.

"Hilow from down the block."

"The Fredrich's kid?" I ask, and she nods. "Absolutely not."

"They don't talk," Cassandra interjects with her hands raised defensively. She moves to stand by Everly as she shrinks further and further into her seat. "They are literally the non-talking kind of boyfriend, girlfriend. He's not even a contact on her kid's messenger app. I checked."

I exhale a slow breath to calm down the anxiety that bubbled up to the surface at the idea of my eleven-year-old having a boyfriend. She's too young for boys. If she starts now, who knows what she'll be getting up to in high school.

"Are you certain?" I nearly growl, shooting angry eyes at Cassandra for not telling me this fun fact. She texts me about Everly's bowel movements, but this doesn't warrant a message?

"We don't talk." Everly's nose wrinkles like the idea of it disgusts her. "Because…fudge the patriarchy!" She thrusts a tiny fist up high, and I think I have a mini stroke.

Cassandra's eyes widen as she looks at me. "I didn't teach her that."

"That was me!" Dakota cheers, thrusting her fist into the air in solidarity.

I cradle my head in my hands, my head whirring with all that's coming at me within the span of five minutes. My God, I run a company with nearly a hundred employees, but a hot nanny and one night of poker with my kid has me seeing spots.

"Anyway…we best get while the getting's good," Dakota sings, grabbing Cassandra's arm and dragging her away from the table as she waves. "Don't want to be late for our date."

Without thinking, I stand and blurt out, "What about your shirt?" My eyes are locked on Cassandra's as blood roars in my ears.

"My what?" She looks curiously at me and then at her friend.

I can feel everyone's eyes on me, but I figure I'm all fucking in at this point. "That tank top you wore the other day by the pool."

A wrinkle creases between Cassandra's eyebrows. "I literally have no idea what you're talking about."

"It said something about you only dating yourself," I sputter, sounding like a complete moron, so I add weakly, "Or something like that."

Her smile fades, and I swear the pupils in her eyes dilate as she gazes back at me. Her tone is soft when she replies, "It was just a shirt, Mr. Fletcher."

Fuck. Fuck. Fuck. Fuck.

CHAPTER 19

Cozy

Jeff Holsburg from high school. Jesus, I never thought I'd see him again in my entire life. We went to junior prom together, and I remember deciding to give him my virginity that night and then panicking at the last minute because I wasn't ready. He didn't even have a chance to get the condom on.

Thankfully, he was really decent about it. But I swear I saw a tear in his eye when he crawled off me in the tailgate of his pickup truck out in the middle of a cornfield.

In hindsight, I wish I had just had sex with him because my first time was with a boyfriend who told me I was fat after I broke up with him. That's one of those insults that will always stick with you no matter how much self-love you have.

But as far as double dates go, Dakota didn't do too bad. Jeff is apparently home for the summer, taking a break from getting his law degree in Utah. He's sweet and a little timid, just like he was in high school. I remember having to ask him to prom because he didn't have the guts. Evidently, he'd hoped to make me his girlfriend after prom, but when we didn't have sex, he thought that meant I didn't

The guy designated for Dakota was a few years older than us in school and is the bartender at the place we are currently sitting at—good old Pearl Street Pub.

Not gonna lie, I'm overdressed for the location.

But I love Pearl Street Pub. It's a typical dive bar with sticky carpet, well-worn booths, a giant buffalo hanging from the walls, and multicolored Christmas lights that stay up year-round.

Apparently, Mr. Manbun Randal gets off at ten and will join us on the other side of the bar when he's relieved. For now, I've been catching up with Jeff and watching Dakota out of the corner of my eye snap selfies with Randal, who she's clearly hung out with before.

"So Dakota said you were nannying this summer?" Jeff asks, his brown eyes blinking back at me curiously.

"Yeah. It's been fun. The kid is great."

"What happened to that big corporate job you landed in Denver?"

I smile around the straw of my drink. "I just wanted a change. It feels good to be home, doesn't it?" I divert the conversation back to him. "Are you staying with your parents?"

He winces slightly. "I'm afraid so. It just makes the most sense not to spend the money on rent when I have to go back to school in the fall. Are you with your parents too?"

"No, I'm in a guesthouse of the guy whose kid I'm nannying."

"Guesthouse?" Jeff huffs. "Guy must be rich."

Oh, if only you knew, Jeff.

"So one more year of law school, and then you're fighting crime?"

"I guess so. I have to pass the bar exam first."

"You were always so smart in school. I'm sure you'll do well."

"Not as smart as you," Jeff replies knowingly.

I laugh that comment off and recross my legs, noticing Jeff's eyes linger on my leg. Disappointment casts over me when I realize that I don't get that warm feeling in my body that erupts whenever Max looks at me.

Honestly, I'm not sure anyone has ever looked at me the way Max does. He looks at me like I'm some sort of foreign creature he has to study to understand. What's worse? *I like it.*

Which is stupid because I'm moving on from Max. He made his

intention very clear last week. Plus, Dakota said it herself, women probably throw themselves at him every day. He could easily find someone who's a lot less complicated than his kid's nanny to hook up with. And a hell of a lot hotter.

I pull the front of my shirt off my body, feeling flush all of a sudden. "Should we get another drink?"

"Definitely," Jeff answers, bouncing his knee nervously.

Unfortunately, this feels a bit like it's going to be a repeat of junior prom night, and that wasn't a happy ending for either of us.

CHAPTER 20

Max

My mood is markedly different for the rest of poker night. For starters, my daughter left with Wyatt. She got bored of playing cards shortly after Cassandra and her friend left. Then out of nowhere, Wyatt asked if Everly wanted to help him bottle-feed his baby goat Millie in the morning. We all call Millie a dog goat because she acts more like a pet than a farm animal. Which means my kid packed her overnight bag in less than ten seconds.

They took off over an hour ago, and since then, I have nothing to distract my poisonous thoughts, so I'm just brooding over Cassandra out on a fucking date. I'm also losing a shitload of money because I'm too distracted to pay attention to my cards.

"Max, what is your problem?" Josh barks, snapping my eyes up from the spot on the table I'm burning a hole through.

"Nothing, I'm fine," I snap, frowning at him.

Josh looks at Dean. Those two used to hate each other back when Dean offered to be Lynsey's baby daddy over Josh, the actual baby daddy, but now they seem in cahoots with each other. I don't like it.

"Are you bothered about Everly at Wyatt's cabin?" Dean asks, watching me pensively. "Your brothers' cabins are kind of in the middle of nowhere, right?"

"Yeah, but I'm not worried about that. Everly loves it up there."

"Then what has your panties in a twist?" Calder inquires, his brows wagging like he already knows the answer.

"Let's play another hand. Whose deal is it?"

"Yours," they all answer in unison.

Rolling my eyes, I grab the deck of cards and begin aggressively shuffling. Cassandra has been out for over an hour now. If it was a bad date, she'd likely be home by now, right? My house isn't far from downtown. A five-minute Uber ride at best. Maybe she needs a ride? I haven't had any whiskey in a while, so I could pick her up. Maybe I should text her to make sure she's safe. She does live on my property, so that makes her my responsibility.

Me: Do you need a ride home?

I hold my breath when I see the typing bubbles pop up and then instantly deflate when they go away. I'm staring at my phone as I try to shuffle again and curse when cards slip out of my hands and clatter to the floor.

"Fuck," I growl, pushing my chair back to pick them up.

"Jesus Christ, I can't watch this anymore," Luke bellows from the far end of the table. "You were barely fine before the nanny left, and since then, you are low-key losing your fucking mind. Just admit it already."

"Admit what?" I grab the cards and shoot a murderous look at my baby brother.

"That you want to nut the nanny!" Calder cajoles.

"That's enough," I bark, dropping the cards on the floor again. "Show some fucking respect, asshole."

My hands are shaky as I pick up the cards and picture her laughing at some guy's joke. The young guys in Boulder are douchebags of top variety. They're Instagram success stories who like to jog, pretend they like IPAs, and they likely have a dog they're obsessed with. Basically, Dean fucking Moser.

He's my friend, don't get me wrong, but he owns the Boulder

scene like no one's business. And men outnumber women here by like five percent so if Cassandra's "date" doesn't work out, I'm sure all she'll have to do is turn her barstool around to find another douche who claims to love brunching.

A bead of sweat forms on my brow as I sit up and find everyone staring at me.

Josh is the first to break the silence. "I saw this coming on the first weekend. You were way too interested in her backstory. Obsessed almost."

"I wasn't obsessed. I was annoyed because she's secretive as fuck. She makes me crazy." I toss the cards down on the table with a huff.

"Something's already happened, hasn't it?" Dean leans forward and eyes me closely.

I clench my jaw and debate the fallout of answering this question. Telling them I attacked Cassandra in the guesthouse isn't a good look for me. But these crazy thoughts aren't going away, and if I can trust anyone with this heavy burden on my mind, it's the men at this table.

Shoving a hand through my hair, I mumble, "I stopped it before it got too far." And I've been living in a constant state of regret that usually ends with a hard-on after I replay every second of that night in my mind.

They all make knowing sounds.

"And you let her go out on a double date with Blondie?" Calder hooks his thumb over his shoulder. "Rookie mistake, man."

"What was I supposed to do? Club her over the head and drag her back to my bedroom? She's my kid's nanny."

"Who cares?" Dean asks seriously. "I was an investor in Norah's bakery and look how we turned out."

"What you and Norah have is not what I want with Cassandra." It's not what I want with any woman. I grip the back of my neck and sigh. "I just…can't get her out of my head. And last night, she told me she was looking for a summer fling, and ever since then, I can't fucking see straight."

"If she said she was looking for a summer fling, she was giving you the green light, man," Calder declares knowingly.

"I hate to agree with him, but I do," Josh confirms. "Plus, she's not some young chick fresh out of college who you're taking advantage of. She's a grown woman with life experience. Hell, she graduated from college at nineteen."

I lock eyes with my best friend, whose words are never given lightly. Josh is a zero-bullshit kind of person and does not shy away from conflict. If he thinks someone is phony, he'll say it.

So the fact that he doesn't think it's fucked up of me to pursue the woman taking care of my kid for the summer gives me the glimmer of hope that I've been denying myself for the past twenty-four hours. Hell, maybe even the past three weeks.

Cassandra Barlow has consumed all my thoughts with her lush curves, her tropical scent, and her insane ability to make even the most mundane tasks interesting. Maybe if I fuck her, I can get past this ache in my body and feel like myself again.

Dean laughs as he stares at his phone. "Got it."

"Got what?" I ask, my brows furrowing.

He turns his screen to show me an Instagram story of Cassandra and Dakota taking a shot at the bar. There are two dudes with them, and they all laugh as Cassandra begins to gag and whack the tall guy with long brown hair tied up in a bun for forcing her to take the shot. I narrow my eyes to look a little closer and recognize the place they're at.

"That's some stealthy fucking internet trolling, my dude," Calder says, bowing his head to Dean like he's bestowing him with some great honor.

"All in a day's work." Dean adjusts his glasses and turns to me. "Now the only question is, what will you do with this information?"

I look around the table at everyone staring expectantly back at me. I have never been inspired to stalk a woman before. In fact, I rarely even have to try to get the women I'm interested in. Going to the bar she's at would be seriously fucking insane. But perhaps Cassandra's weird brings out my weird.

I shove my chips into the middle of the table. "Fuck it. I'm all in."

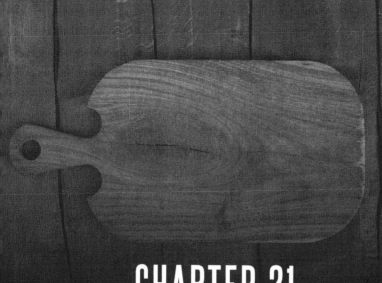

CHAPTER 21

Cozy

Booze makes Jeff funnier, which is highly important because Dakota's lips have been permanently locked with Randal's for most of the night. Honestly, it's like we're back in high school again. If they're not making out, they're whispering into each other's ears and giggling like a couple of school children. It's highly annoying.

But I'm not going to begrudge her making a connection with the guy. I'm happy for her. And I'm happy to be out with a group and enjoying life outside of Max Fletcher's bubble.

Sure, Jeff doesn't give me that warm, gooey sensation whenever he looks at me. But I'm having a nice time with him, and that should count for something.

This is exactly what I needed to get my mind off Max. I just had to put myself out there and remind myself I am capable of flirting and finding a summer fling without crazy mind games. This is the kind of shit you do on a gap year!

"Jeff, I have to ask you a strange question," I blurt out, taking a sip of my drink.

"I love your strange questions," he muses and sips his IPA beer.

I lean forward and run my finger along his brow line, my eyes marveling at how perfectly shaped they are. With a giggle, I ask, "Are your eyebrows natural, or do you use a serum because I've never seen such full eyebrows in my entire life."

His shoulders shake, and he nearly falls off the stool with a bizarre silent laugh. He presses a hand to his chest, and his voice is high-pitched when he cries, "What the fuck is a serum?"

"Like something that makes eyebrows grow thicker!" I reply, laughing hysterically at his comedic reaction.

His smiling eyes widen. "People actually want big eyebrows?"

My nose wrinkles as I chuckle. "Yes. Seriously, if you're using a product, fess up because you have the most stunning brows I've ever seen on a man or a woman!"

He props his elbow on the bar and covers his face, still in stitches over the topic of our conversation. He's obviously drunk, but it's cute, and I live to amuse.

He wipes some errant tears out of his eyes and sighs loudly. "You are one of a kind, Cozy Barlow."

"I've been getting that a lot these days," I murmur as Max's annoyingly handsome face invades my thoughts.

A clammy hand lands on my bare leg, and I look over to see Jeff no longer smiling. In fact, his face has grown super serious. His eyes are hooded and locked on my lips. "I'm so glad this is finally happening, Cozy."

"What do you mean?" I try to laugh to lighten the mood.

He hiccups and glances down at my chest. "You and me. A redo."

"A re-what?" My back straightens with his forced proximity.

"I was so awkward in high school. So inexperienced." He closes his eyes and shakes off the obvious embarrassment before resuming really intense eye contact. "You would have been my first, you know."

My head jerks at his sharp vibe change. I look over my shoulder to see Dakota walking toward the bathroom while Randal is scrolling on his phone. Guess I'm stuck here alone with a drunk Jeff who wants to have a walk down memory lane. Jesus. I need to get control of this conversation.

I heartily pat Jeff on the shoulder, hoping I'm giving out platonic friendship vibes because that is most certainly all I want from him. "I was awkward too, Jeff. But you were cool and a total gentleman."

His head bobs up and down. "I'm not so much of a gentleman anymore."

"Oh?" My nose wrinkles.

He licks his lips and leans in close, the skunky scent of his beer wafting over my face as he murmurs, "I've learned a thing or two since junior prom."

Suddenly, his damp palm inches up my thigh, and I slap my hand over his to stop its pursuit. I'm just about to tell him this isn't happening when a large body presses up against him.

"Your cab is here, pal," a deep voice utters, and my eyes nearly pop out of my head when I see Max's broad frame standing beside Jeff. He grabs Jeff's hand firmly and yanks it off my leg before helping him up out of his stool.

"My cab?" Jeff's immaculate brow furrows in confusion as he looks at me. "Are we leaving, Cozy?"

A weird chirping sound emits from my lips because I can't find any words to make sense of this situation.

"Not her. Just you. I'm afraid the bartender insisted. She's sorry for overserving you."

Jeff shakes his head, voicing his denial, "You think I'm too drunk?"

"Yes, we do," Max answers, placing a hand around Jeff's back to lead him toward the door. "We thank you for stopping in, but we'd appreciate your cooperation. We wouldn't want to get the police involved for disorderly conduct."

"The fuzz?" Jeff bellows, gripping the sides of his head. "No, no, no, no. Don't call the cops. I'm in law school, bro. I can't have a criminal record." His voice cracks on the end as he adds, "Plus, my mom will kill me if I'm dropped off at home by a cop."

Max nods crisply. "I understand. Then just please make your way out to the cab outside. It's already paid for."

Jeff's head is bobbing in terrified understanding as Max releases him, but he turns back toward me before he leaves. "Cozy, can I get your number?"

"No time for that," Max barks, stepping between Jeff and me. His shoulders rise with determination as he points at the door. "You need to leave, sir. Now."

Jeff holds his hands up and nearly falls backward as he scrambles out of the bar without looking back.

When Max turns on his heel and lowers himself into the seat Jeff just vacated, like nothing happened, I wonder if I've somehow drunk myself into an alternate universe.

He casually holds a finger up to the bartender, and I faintly hear him ask for a whiskey on the rocks. Though my ears are doing this annoying ringing thing, so I can't be sure. I watch in astonishment as he takes a sip of the amber liquid before rolling up the sleeves on his black button-down.

Finally, he turns his indigo eyes to me and offers an easy smile. "Hello, Cassandra."

My lips open and close multiple times, and I fear I might be doing a good impression of that cheesy singing bass wall mount that my dad has hanging in his machine shed. "W-W-What are you doing here?"

His lips turn down curiously as he shakes the ice in his rocks glass. "Having a drink."

"Why?"

"Because we're at a bar." He looks around at all the patrons with a smug look of contentment. Just then, Dakota comes strolling back from the bathrooms, and her jaw drops when she spots Max. She points at him obnoxiously and begins making lewd gestures and thrusting her hips forward.

Thanks, bestie.

"I know we're at a bar. I've been here all night," I snap, my hands balled up into fists on my lap. "Why are *you* at this bar? How long have you even been here?"

He shrugs dismissively. "Maybe an hour."

"Who are you here with?"

"You." His gaze lowers to my legs, and my body heats involuntarily.

"Who's with Everly?" I ask, my chest rising and falling with rapid breaths I can't seem to get control of.

Max sets his glass down and runs a finger around the rim. "Everly is having a sleepover at Uncle Wyatt's."

"Oh," I reply dumbly.

"How was your date?" Max's eyes narrow as the T on date seems to be difficult for him to say.

"It was okay until a few minutes ago."

The muscle in his jaw jumps as he inhales deeply through his nose. "Were you flirting with him?"

His question catches me off guard. "When?"

"When you touched his face," Max responds instantly, his eyes holding mine captive as the entire bar seems to fade to darkness all around us.

My voice is weak when I stammer, "I...touched his eyebrows."

"You touched his eyebrows?" Max repeats the words like they're curses. He shoots me an exasperated look and pinches the bridge of his nose. "Why would you touch his eyebrows?"

"Because they rival Eugene Levy's from *Schitt's Creek,* and I wanted to see how they felt," I blurt out honestly because I have no idea how else to explain my behavior. It is undeniably weird.

His head turns forward as his jaw shifts from side to side, his body vibrating with irritation. "You can't just go around touching men's eyebrows, Cassandra."

"Why not?"

"Because it makes them think you want to fuck them." His voice is acidic as he stares broodingly back at me.

I inhale sharply at his vulgar response. It's definitely not the way I'm used to him speaking to me. I'm also not used to seeing him at a bar. At *my* bar specifically. Which is why his opinion on this situation doesn't mean anything to me.

I jut my chin out defiantly. "Other men's thoughts are not my problem."

"No, but they're mine," he growls and then swivels in his stool. His denim-clad legs straddle me as he hovers closer, blanketing me in his mouthwatering cologne and the spicy scent of the whiskey on his breath. His brow furrows as he scrutinizes my entire face. "You would really hook up with another man with my mark still on you?"

Jaw? Meet floor.

Blood rushes in my ears as my hand moves to my chest to cover the mark he's referring to. I've been concealing it all freaking week and doing my best to forget about its existence. But him throwing it in my face right now thrusts me right back to that stormy night in my cottage.

That sinful, wild, unforgettable night.

My heart thunders beneath my palm as I attempt to find the breath that has vacated my lungs. "It's not like this is a brand, Max."

His eyes flinch as his gaze drops to my hand. "You sure about that?"

Liquid heat pools between my legs, and I have to fight the urge to rub my thighs together. His eyes are smoldering. On me.

Any other man who would have the nerve to say this to me would probably get a drink thrown in his face.

Max is another story.

I struggle to swallow the knot in my throat. "A week ago, you couldn't get away from me fast enough."

His eyes darken as he quirks a brow. "Things change."

Anxiety stirs in my belly at the words coming out of his mouth. They are words I've wanted to hear ever since our first kiss. Yet still, they're hard to believe, hard to process, hard to compute. Is this really what I even want anymore?

I turn in my chair, my head whirling with the unmistakable intention in Max's eye. I can't think with him staring at me like that. I need space. I need time. I need… "To pee."

I'm not sure which of those words I said out loud as I stand, my ankles wobbling in my heels as I use stray barstools for balance to make my way to the dingy dive bar bathroom located in the basement. I can feel Max's eyes on me as I walk away, and I have to stop myself from looking back at him.

Clicking the lock on the bathroom door, I flatten myself against the wall, trying to catch my breath and figure out what the hell just went on up there?

Why is Max here? Why did he send Jeff home? Why is he looking at me like that after blowing me off once? I hate that I have insecurities bubbling up, but rejection does funny things to people. And I refuse to put myself in the position to be humiliated again.

I pull my phone out of my purse and send a quick text to Dakota.

Me: Meet me in the bathroom.

While waiting for her, I debate if Max's interest in me is real or just a product of the games I was playing earlier in the week. Did he come here specifically to crash my date? If jealousy is the only reason Max is here, I don't think I'm interested.

I want him to want me *for me*...not stupid mind games.

A bang on the door has me sighing with relief as I rush to let Dakota in. When Max's broad frame steps into the women's restroom, I turn my back on him and run my hands through my hair.

"I said I needed space," I exclaim, bracing myself on the sink.

"You said you needed to pee. I gave you time to pee."

"What are you doing here, Max?" My eyes find him in the mirror. He's standing next to a women's tampon dispenser and finally looks human enough for my lust-filled brain to clear. "Did you come here to crash my date?"

He stares back at my reflection. "I came here to check on you. You didn't reply to my text."

"I didn't need a ride home. I thought the lack of response would have made that clear."

He tilts his head. "I thought we talked about you not texting me."

"We were referring to Everly, Max...not you!" I turn on my heel to face him.

"Well, let's change that." He steps so close to me and adds, "I want you to text me. I like to know what you're doing."

"My weekend plans are none of your business!" I snap, hating that his heat is causing my nipples to pebble. I cross my arms over my chest.

His eyes narrow imperceptibly. "You always have secrets."

"No, no way. You don't get to gaslight me on this." I thrust my finger into his hard chest. "You rejected me last week. You ran out of my place like you were on fire. Which means you don't get to show up on my date and toss out accusations."

I move to head for the door and get out of the confines of Max's scent, but before I can grab the handle, he hooks my arm and twirls me around to look at him.

"Why are you running from me? I came here for you." He has the nerve to look confused.

"Because I don't see why you're interested now!" I cry as my gaze focuses on his broad chest. His eyes are too probing. Too curious. Too focused. I can't look at him when I add the dark truth that swirls in my belly. "I can't be the type of girl you normally pursue."

His finger crooks under my chin, forcing me to look up at his angry expression. His nostrils flare when he asks, "What does that mean?"

I feign a casual laugh that I don't feel. "You're rich, Max! And you're successful. You can get any girl you want. You probably sleep with tiny supermodels you can toss over your shoulder. That is not me."

"I could toss you over my shoulder, Cassandra."

"And hurt your back in the process," I jibe at myself. Humor is a defense mechanism I've come to rely on my whole life. It gives me power over the narrative of situations, and with power comes confidence. Both of which seem to be eluding me now. With a heavy sigh, I finally say, "I don't want to be a convenience fuck."

My voice cracks at the end, and Max's face contorts with disbelief and another emotion I can't quite put my finger on. *Please, God, don't let it be pity. I couldn't stomach it.* Tears well in my eyes as I fight to shake this ridiculous emotional reaction that's overcoming me.

Why am I losing it right now? He's just a guy!

A loud banging on the door rips me out of my own personal meltdown. "Cozy, are you in there? It's Dakota. I just saw your text!"

I nearly sob with relief as my best friend comes through for me at just the right time. I scramble away from Max and shakily wrench open the door, nearly falling into my friend's embrace.

"We're leaving," I rush out, not waiting for an answer as I grab my friend's hand and drag her behind me.

Dakota hooks her thumb over her shoulder. "Am I drunk, or did Jeff get way hotter?"

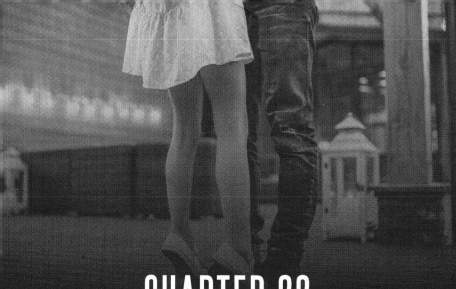

CHAPTER 22

Max

I t's midnight, and I find myself pacing my bedroom and staring at Cassandra's tiny cottage glowing down by the creek like the fucking creep I am. Every once in a while, I see her silhouette move through the pulled blinds, and that's all it takes for my cock to stir in my jeans.

Goddammit, she's completely unmanned me.

What the fuck am I doing? Did I really barge into the bar and expect her to come home with me?

Yes, yes, I did.

Especially when I sat in that bar for over an hour watching her tolerate that douchebag. She so clearly wasn't into him. Her body language was obvious. And he just stared at her like a lost puppy begging for a morsel.

She's too good for him. It's why he got so drunk. He couldn't handle being sober in her presence, and when I saw him make one wrong move, I was done watching.

After he was out of the way, I thought everything would click into place. I thought we'd talk out an arrangement that suited both of our needs, and we would be on our way to bone town. Like another business deal.

Jesus. Bone town? I really have been around Cozy too much.

Then she went and called herself a convenience fuck, and I don't know what happened after that.

When is fucking ever convenient? It's not. It's actually a lot of work. And when you find someone you want to fuck, finding time for that isn't exactly easy either. Especially when she's your kid's nanny and a forbidden fruit that you shouldn't taste, but you just couldn't help yourself.

Fuck.

And all that bullshit she spewed about not being the type I normally fuck? She doesn't know me. And she clearly doesn't know herself.

Does she not see how beautiful she is? How her quiet confidence in those ridiculous tie-dyed crop tops she's always wearing is quite possibly the sexiest thing I've ever seen? Does she not see how the soft curves of her body make it impossible for me to make the right decision here? How can she not grasp what's so fucking obvious?

The lights of her house shut off, and it's like a hardwired switch on my patience.

With a low growl, I slide open the door to my deck and march my ass across the lawn to her tiny house. She's not going to bed. Not until I put those fucked-up thoughts she has out of her mind for good.

I bang loudly on the door and back up to pace in the grass, my chest heaving with all the thoughts running through my body.

It takes her a moment, but finally, a light flicks on inside, and she opens the door with a dejected look.

I fucking hate that look.

"Max, I'm going to bed," she groans, pulling her cotton robe tightly across her breasts as she steps outside and leans against the side of the house. "Let's just forget this horrible evening ever happened."

"I can't forget," I bark, pointing at my head like a lunatic as I continue to pace. "Because I have a daughter. And knowing that she could grow up someday and have fucked-up thoughts about her physical appearance will never be something I'm okay with."

Cassandra's brows knit together. "What?"

"What you said about me throwing you over my shoulder? First of all…I could do that. Feel free to challenge me on that. I love a challenge." I turn on my heel to march the other way. "But second of all, who gives a fuck if I couldn't? Do you think that makes you any less worthy of someone? It doesn't. It's a superficial fucking nothing-burger of a comment. It tells nothing about the person you are or the beauty you possess."

I pause to prop my hands on my hips, hitting her with a lethal glare before I deliver the next bit. Her lips are parted, and her eyes are wide and glistening in the security light as she falls back against the white siding.

She looks like a goddamn angel.

"Third of all, you are not now, nor could you ever be a convenience fuck. In fact, you are the most inconvenient fuck of my life. Which is why I need you to hear the next part."

"There's more?" she gasps, her fingers touching her parted lips.

"A lot more, Cassandra," I growl, my voice echoing off the house as I stalk toward her, slowly registering her body language to make sure I'm not scaring the fuck out of her.

I might be scaring the fuck out of myself.

I'm not sure I've ever spoken like this to a woman before. Not even my ex-wife got under my skin this much.

When I enter her space, I flatten one hand on the siding by her face and use my other to tug at the tie on her waist. Her chest heaves as I pull apart the thin robe to reveal the matching tie-dyed short set she's wearing. It's green, like her eyes. I run my finger along the exposed part of her soft stomach. My cock thickens in my jeans at the memory of my lips on her flesh.

I lean into her neck and inhale deeply, running my nose from her neck to her ear and then her hair. A low grumble vibrates in my chest when that heady scent of coconut hits me.

I have her right where I want her. Placid, responsive, and thankfully quiet for what I'm about to say.

My voice is low and controlled as my breath falls on her ear. "If you think for one fucking second your body isn't everything I want…" My voice catches in my throat as I palm her side, my thumb brushing along her breast as my pulse races in my veins. I take a deep breath to collect myself. "Everything I have been craving…" I blow softly on her collarbone and relish in the shiver I see roll through her body. "And everything I jack off to when I can't sleep at night because you haunt all my waking moments…" My tongue slickens my lips as I pull back to stare hungrily at hers. "Then you're not as smart as you think you are."

In one last ditch effort, I grab her hand and place it on my groin, eliciting a gasp from her perfect, plump lips. Her fingers form around the ridges of my cock, squeezing the firmness of it through my jeans.

Her head falls into my chest as she sags into me, so I dip my head and whisper against her earlobe. "I'm a grown-ass man, and I've never been inspired to give a woman a hickey before. Make no mistake, you aren't a convenience fuck, Cassandra. You are a dream fuck."

Her eyes snap to mine as she releases my dick to grab my neck and haul me down to her. Our mouths fuse, our tongues gliding against each other as my hands roam her supple curves, squeezing and groping as the dam finally breaks inside both of us.

I slip my hands inside her robe and slide my palms down to her ass, hoisting her up into my arms. Her strong legs wrap around me as I carry her through her open door, kicking it closed behind me once we're inside.

This is how I expected the night to end. Her in my arms, my cock nudged firmly into her warm center. If she needs me to tell her she's fucking beautiful every goddamn day to get her to believe it, I'll do it. I'll make it my life's mission to do it. For her and for Everly.

But Everly is the farthest thing from my mind as I make my way over to the ladder that leads up to the loft. I press Cassandra's ass against the rungs and take the opportunity to rip the robe off her body. My lips find her chest as I glide my hands over her delicious legs, my fingers digging greedily into her flesh as her sweet sounds have my cock trying to bust through my jeans. Jesus, I need to be inside her.

My voice is a husky growl against her neck when I say, "I still maintain that I can throw you over my shoulder, but I'm afraid my abilities stop at carrying you up a fucking ladder. Not unless you want to risk breaking my cock in the process."

A high-pitched laugh bursts out of her, and the sexy sound of it lights up my whole fucking body. I actually feel myself smiling like a dope as I pepper kisses against her neck.

Fuck, I've never heard her laugh like that before. It's a good sound.

She slides her hand between our flush bodies and strokes my cock. "A broken dick is no use to me."

"Then get fucking climbing." I nudge her with the topic of conversation, and she bites her lip sexily.

Giggling, she turns to begin her ascent, and I can't help but reach out and smack her ass hard. She yelps and pauses on the ladder as I lift the hem of her shorts up and take a bite out of her juicy ass. God, it's just too irresistible not to taste.

She turns to gaze down at me. Her dark hair brushes her cheekbones. "Do we need to discuss your kink?"

"You first, sweet cheeks." I shoot her a dirty smirk, and her eyes flare with something that intrigues me, but she quickly turns and shimmies the rest of the way up the ladder, leaving me with more fucking questions about this nanny.

When I reach the top, she's perched on the edge of the bed, looking flushed and a little nervous. I stalk over to the reading chair and flick the lamp on to see her better.

Standing over her, I tuck a strand of hair behind her ear. "You okay?"

"Yeah," she answers quickly. "Why wouldn't I be?"

I frown and kneel in front of her, my hands resting gently on her thighs. "We should probably discuss what this is first."

She swallows slowly, her green eyes captivating me. "This is just fun, Max. You don't have to worry."

I eye her seriously. "And you're sure you're good with that?"

"Yes," she says with a laugh and reaches out to begin undoing the buttons on my shirt. "I'm sorry I wigged out at the bar. You just threw me off guard with your stalker vibes."

I grimace at that label because it's scarily accurate. "Yeah, sorry about that. I'm not someone who's ever been good at sharing."

"Such a caveman thing to say." She rolls her eyes as she opens my shirt, lightly scoring her nails down my bare chest and causing my dick to thrust into the fucking bed.

I fight back a moan as I eye the red spot on her chest again. Why does that turn me on so fucking much? I really am a fucking caveman.

Eliminating the space between us, I end this discussion with my tongue down her throat...which she doesn't seem to mind as she groans into my mouth and falls back onto the bed. Her legs wrap tightly around my hips as my lips glide over her neck, collarbone, shoulders, and chest.

"Take this off," I command, yanking at her crop top like the caveman she just called me.

I hold myself over top of her as she wriggles herself out of it. When her breasts are completely exposed to me at last, I think I die a little inside. They are just as beautiful as I imagined. The large, supple mounds of flesh paired with tight, rosy nipples are all mine for the night.

I hold the weight of one in my hands and lower my head to suck the tip into my mouth. She gasps, and her fingers slice into my hair, her nails scoring my scalp in a way that sends a shiver down my spine. Jesus, she feels incredible—soft and pliant beneath my hands. Warm and comforting in a way I've never experienced with other women before.

Her curves will fucking ruin me for other women.

When I finish playing homage to her other breast, I stand and peel my shirt off my shoulders. Cassandra props herself on her elbows and watches me with a hungry look in her eye as I unbutton my jeans and slide them down my legs along with my boxer briefs.

I like how she watches me.

When my cock bobs toward her, she sits up and bites her lip before gripping my length in her hand.

"Fuck," I cry out, my head falling back at the skin-on-skin contact. She pumps me slowly and slides her thumb over my sensitive tip.

Her voice is husky when she says, "I don't want to be weird... but you have a beautiful dick, Max."

My abs contract as I huff out a laugh. I look down at her, and she's smiling up at me with the sexiest smirk I've ever seen. "Nothing weird about facts," I deadpan and wince when she squeezes my dick tighter in her hands, loving that she's not afraid to touch me.

A harsh breath expels from my lungs when she sheaths my cock in her mouth without warning.

Fuck, I wasn't ready.

Stumbling on my feet, I grab a fistful of her hair and ride her as she drags her tongue along the underside of my shaft before sucking the tip with ferocious intensity. A loud sucking sound reverberates in the room when she pops off me, and the cold air hits my sensitive cock.

"Ah," I bark out when she takes me into her mouth so deep, my cock hits the back of her throat. I shudder when I feel her gag reflex, and my hips involuntarily buck forward. I have to will myself not to fuck her mouth as she bobs eagerly on my dick, tapping the back of her throat over and over with a strong finishing suck on each glide.

My control is waning, so I quickly tug her off my dick and take a step back to dig into my jeans for my wallet.

"What's wrong?" she asks, sounding out of breath.

"Nothing." My eyes stare at her tits.

"Why'd you make me stop then?" I hear the slight worry in her voice as if she did something wrong.

"Because I can't fucking control myself when you suck me like that." My voice is guttural, and I don't mean it to be an insult, so I pause and make eye contact with her. "You're too good."

A pleased smirk teases her swollen lips as I find a condom and roll it on. She shimmies out of her shorts, and I take a moment to relish her naked body perched on the edge of the bed. It's just...perfect.

I drop between her legs and spread her thighs apart. "Cassandra, you have...a beautiful body."

She scoffs and playfully shoves me. "Oh, my God, stop."

"Never," I state, my eyes roving over every inch—every peak, every valley, every soft corner, every dimple. Cassandra's curves are fucking luxury. It's like I've been dining on cheese and crackers my whole life, and now I'm being treated to a five-course fucking feast.

My cock pulses with a need to claim her body while I hungrily growl against her chest, "How have I kept my hands off you this long, sweet cheeks?"

"Well, I am the nanny," she deadpans, and those sinful words make my balls ache in the most devious way. This is so naughty and wrong, but it's all of that that makes it feel *so fucking right.*

My hands run up her calves, palming the flesh of her thighs when I reach them. The way her body flexes from my touch ratchets my heartbeat further. I can see her arousal with my face level with her pussy, and I grunt like a fucking animal, knowing I'm the one who's turned her on.

"We better make this sin worth it then." I dip my head to suck the inside of her leg and glance up to find her lips slightly parted, reminding me of where my cock was mere moments ago, snapping the little control I have left.

She lets out a yelp of surprise as I bite down hungrily before shoving her backward to bury my face between her legs. The moment my tongue spears her sex, my mouth is flooded with her sweetness. I groan in satisfaction, pulling her thighs up around my shoulders so I can work her over deeper.

I flatten my tongue and drag it slowly along the length of her center, growling deep into her folds as she coats my chin. She tastes like pineapple and fucking sex, and my dick throbs in wanting agony.

She covers her face with her hands and moans, "Oh, my God."

My spine tingles, watching her stomach contract each time I swipe my tongue over her clit. The rise and fall of her breasts aren't enough. I need to see her. I need her to see me. I stop my work for a second and squeeze her hips. "You gotta watch me, sweet cheeks. Watch me fuck you with my tongue."

Her head lifts as she gazes down at me with her lips parted and eyes full of desire. Slowly, I raise a finger to her mouth and love how she knows exactly what I want from her, sucking my digit past the knuckle, flicking her tongue over the tip as if it's my cock.

I begin to pull out and she nips me, causing my cock to flex heavily between her legs. She watches as I lower my hand to her center once more.

I plunge a finger into her wet pussy, my forearm flexing as I pump into her, staring at her wet lower lips with undiluted lust. I dip my head to suck on her clit, my tongue laving aggressively at the tight bundle of nerves as her ass rises off the bed. Her thighs tighten around my ears and muffle her sexy noises.

She needs to come. I need her to come. Vigorously, I attack her slit while fucking her with my finger, feeling her body tighten as she gets closer.

I glance up to see that her head has fallen back again. That will not do. I reach up and tweak one of her nipples. "Eyes on me."

She looks down at me again as I thrust a second finger inside her and crook my digits upward to stroke her G-spot. She damn near levitates off the bed as she slices her hands into my hair, telling me without words not to stop.

"Max," she breathes my name out with a sharp cry as her legs begin to quake.

"Watch yourself come on my hand," I groan, nearly coming undone as I start finger-fucking her faster and faster. Her hips grind into me as I dip my head and flick my tongue in circles over her nub, staring up at her the whole time.

In seconds, her pussy clenches around me as she lets out a soundless scream, her face contorting in ecstasy as her body shudders on the bed.

"Fuck, Cassandra," I growl, my fingers feeling like they're trapped in a vise grip as I pull them out of her.

"Jesus." She sighs, her body going limp.

A better man would give her a moment to recover.

Tonight, I am not that man.

I stand and hook her legs over my arms, my fingers digging into her delicious ass as I lift her up and press my cock against her dripping center.

"You ready?" I ask as my eyes connect with hers again.

She nods and grabs my sheathed dick to position it just in time for me to plunge deep inside her. My body freezes at the tightness, and I bite my tongue to stop myself from roaring like a fucking psycho. I'm not going to last long after watching her come and feeling her still pulsating around my cock.

"Holy shit, you feel amazing," I grind out, already feeling the build in my balls as I pull back and thrust harshly forward again, slapping them against her supple ass.

She shrieks in surprise as I watch her tits bounce each time I slam into her. "Fuck, Max...I'm so sensitive still." She struggles to talk as I pound into her, chasing my orgasm as she begins to wind tightly beneath me.

She fists her hands in the comforter, trying to hold on as she slides up the bed each time I bottom out in her. Her eyes close as she arches up to meet me each time I enter her.

"You have to look at me, Cassandra," I bark, my patience wearing thin. "It's nonnegotiable. I need your eyes on me. You got it?"

Her green eyes snap open, captivating me as her brows knit together. She nods in understanding, her hand reaching up to stroke my jaw. "Eyes on you."

"Good girl." I nip at her thumb and, with renewed energy, begin pumping into her, watching her as she reacts to every thrust, every grip, every sound exchanged between us. Her eyes never leave mine, and the security I feel in watching her pleasure is enough to have me come undone in record time.

Not the good kind of record.

But a record, nonetheless.

CHAPTER 23

Cozy

My breath is heavy as my body pulses back and forth, rocking into the mattress as my consciousness fights with my subconsciousness. Awake or asleep? Awake or asleep? Are you in, or are you out?

My thighs squeeze together, desperate for release as I grind against something, my pelvis twisting and swirling like a ship caught in a vicious storm. My pace quickens as I pump faster and faster, feeling my heart rate increase with every moment of blissful unconsciousness. A moan escapes my lips as liquid heat flushes over my body, effectively yanking me out of my dream-like state.

My eyes crack open, squinting against the brightness of my tiny cabin as sunlight pours in through the upper windows. I hear the faint sounds of birds chirping outside, but they are nothing compared to the blood rushing in my ears as the heady aftershock of my release topples over me.

Fighting to catch my breath, I notice a blanket of heat pressed up behind me and glance down to see strong, masculine fingers clutching my breast and rolling my nipple delicately. A hard thickness pumps into my backside, over and over, keeping me on that glorious rocking ship.

"Did you just—" Max's hoarse voice croaks into my ear.

"Come in my sleep?" I finish his sentence on a wobbly sigh. "Yes, I think I did."

"Jesus," he growls, his hot breath on my naked shoulder as he thrusts against me once more.

"Was I..." I pause, feeling a slight tinge of humiliation poke holes in my post-coital bliss.

"Fucking the bed?" he finishes my sentence this time. "Yes...but I like to think I helped."

I cover my face and groan.

"No need to be embarrassed," Max's growly voice murmurs in my ear. "I woke up hard as stone and started humping your ass like a sex-starved teenager."

"Oh," I reply dumbly as his hand releases my breast to wrap tightly around my waist.

"I can't seem to stop getting hard around you," he adds as he continues to slide his silky erection against me.

I blink back my shock because I can't imagine the position I am currently in is all that alluring. Truly, for a female, side laying is savage. My left breast is currently working to swallow my right breast, and my FUPA—fat upper pussy area—is doing its best to fuck the mattress as well. Gravity is a foe for plus-sized girls, not a friend.

Max's cock wedges between my thighs, and he thrusts again.

He clearly doesn't mind the lack of gap.

That would be a funny graphic tee for Dakota's store. Print the London Underground circle brand on there and below it say: *Mind the Lack of Gap.*

I tug my lip into my mouth and recall the insanely wonderful things Max said last night to reassure me he liked what he saw.

"If you think for one fucking second your body isn't everything I want...everything I have been craving...and everything I jack off to when I can't sleep at night because you haunt all my waking moments... then you're not as smart as you think you are."

It was a run-on sentence to be sure, but it got the job done. My libido was like… *"Thank you, sir, may I have another?"*

And what's crazy is, he delivered!

"Make no mistake, you aren't a convenience fuck, Cassandra. You are a dream fuck."

Like seriously. Max Fletcher has *game*. I don't care if he did it just to get in my pants. I will engrave those words on my tombstone when I die.

RIP
Cozy Barlow
Dead From a Good Dickin'

Max's husky voice tears me out of my dick death musings when he says, "After my quick performance last night, I am putting in my formal request for a redo."

"A redo?" I repeat, my brow furrowed as I stare forward at the shiplap walls. "I'm pretty sure I had two orgasms last night."

He growls and nips my shoulder. "I can do better."

"Such an overachiever." I giggle and then frown when I feel the loss of his body heat as he shifts off the bed.

I roll onto my back to become besties with gravity again and tuck the sheet around my body as I savor the view of a bare ass Max walking around the bed. Seriously, zero dad bod situation happening here, and I need to mentally catalog every bit of this view to keep me warm on those cold winter nights.

His ass cheek flexes as he hunches over to pick his wallet up off the floor and dig out a condom.

"Do you just…have those condoms in there all the time?" I ask as he holds a foil packet in his fingers. He's probably a guy who gets so many girls that he has to always be prepared.

"No," he replies curtly.

My brow furrows. "So what…did you just put them in there before you knocked on my door last night? That's kind of bold, isn't it?"

His blue eyes pin me to the bed and darken. "I put them in

there before I went to the bar. I had high expectations for my stalker mission."

"Clearly." I pull the sheet up over my mouth to hide my embarrassingly girlie smile.

He rejoins me on the bed and drapes the sheet over his waist, looking ridiculously hot. Like honestly, his dirty-blond hair is rumpled perfectly, his faint abs on full display. Even his dime-sized nipples are perfect.

Who has perfect nipples?

Mine are more salami-sized and only hot when they're hard. *Speaking of which*...I stealthily slip my hand under the sheet and give my nipples a quick pinch to ensure they're looking good for mixed company. My FUPA, ratty hair, and smeared makeup are a lost cause, but my nipples must triumph and carry the team.

Lifting my gaze from his pecs back to his face, I add, "I don't know if I should be more concerned with your stalker tendencies or the fact that I like them."

His eyes dance with mirth. "Is it stalking if you like it?"

I shrug and chew my lip thoughtfully, marveling over this whole situation. Which...what is this exactly? I mean, I know it's casual. We discussed that last night before we got naked. But...is this it? One and done and we never speak of it again?

Honestly, I didn't even expect him to spend the night. After he rocketed me off for my second orgasm, the only thing I had strength for was crawling under the covers and passing out. I think I assumed he'd sneak out early with one of those awkward...good game knuckle bumps. Yet here he is...looking like a real-life Ken doll in my tiny house. Well, his tiny house.

"What's the plan here exactly?" I ask, hating to pop this bubble of sexiness but knowing that Everly will probably be home soon, and we need to get this sorted out.

"I thought it was obvious." A sexy smirk spreads across Max's face as he uses his teeth to rip open the condom.

Okay, now he's just being obnoxious with the hotness. Like, honestly...I'm going to put a paper bag over his head if he keeps looking at me like that.

Jesus...did I just unlock another kink?

I shake that dirty thought out of my lust-filled brain. "Is this just a one-night stand with a late checkout?"

His amused smile is adorable. "Sure." He bites his lip as his hands slip under the sheet with the condom.

God, why is he so casual? Where's the CEO bossy single dad who looks insulted by my matching tie-dyed sets? Ugh, he probably does this all the time. I seriously need to be cooler than what I'm being.

"Cool, so on Monday, it's back to business as usual...?" My voice trails off as my eyes watch the motions going on beneath the sheets.

"Sounds perfect."

A faint snap of an effectively placed condom is like a starting gun and the bed dips as Max crawls over top of me, positioning himself between my legs.

"Oh...sorry for marking you again," he murmurs as he presses his lips gently on my breasts.

"Another one? Where?" I look down at my chest and only see the one spot that's nearly gone now.

He shoots me a rueful grin. "Your ass has a pretty nasty bite mark."

"Were you like...looking at my ass while I was sleeping?"

"It's a great ass," he replies with a wink before resuming his assault on my breasts.

I shake my head, fighting the urge to think he's a creep while also feeling touched that he called my ass great. It's a strange mental cocktail I should probably unpack with a therapist someday.

"Okay..." I moan loudly as Max thrusts himself deep inside me without warning. My head falls back onto the pillow, and I close my eyes as my body adjusts to his size.

He presses a soft kiss to my lips and mumbles, "Eyes on me, sweet cheeks."

That he demands I watch him during sex is probably another thing that needs to be unpacked, but I'll ponder over that after this late checkout.

CHAPTER 24

Cozy

My breath trembles as I trudge across the long stretch of lawn up
to the Fletchpad on Monday morning. I should really stop calling it the Fletchpad. That label gives off bachelor pad vibes, and
it most certainly is not a bachelor pad. It has a library…with a ladder! Not to mention a millionaire with a beautiful dick.

Okay, focus, Cozy. It's Monday morning, the start of another
week of being the GOAT summer nanny. You're going to play it totally cool. Totally chill. Like you have sex with hot millionaires with
pretty penises who have veins in places you didn't know men's bodies
could display veins every weekend. This is just a typical workweek.
You need to completely forget the fact that you fucked your boss on
Saturday night and again on Sunday.

Honestly…I didn't see that morning session coming.

When he said he wanted a redo, he wasn't kidding. We were
both sweating our asses off by the end of it. And somewhere in the
middle of it, he put a pillow under my ass, and when I tell you that

That's right…Max Fletcher gave me four orgasms this weekend. Not that I'm counting because I get orgasms from millionaires all the time.

And that looking thing he makes me do during sex?

"Eyes on me."

It is the most intimate thing I've ever done with a guy. Even more intimate than ya know…just letting him put his dick inside me.

There's an erotic ridiculousness to watching a man fuck you. Like…his sex face is kind of scary…but kind of awesome. Like a feral animal that you want to attack you.

I have no idea what my sex face looks like. I'm going to take a wild guess and say, not good. Probably a cross between a screaming banshee and a ram in heat.

Male sheep do this creepy upper lip curl whenever the female sheep want to breed. It's so gross. My sister and I used to imitate the freaky expression and chase each other around the barn. God, that was such a weird life. I loved it, but I prefer to visit it now, instead of live in it.

I could get used to the millionaire life real quick. I know I'm not in the Fletchpad, but the tiny house gives me a taste of luxury living, and I have to say…I'm a fan. If only a person didn't have to sell their soul to achieve this kind of success.

Steeling myself, I walk in the slider off the living room, the familiar scent of Max and Everly's home like a warm hug after a long day. It's almost six o'clock, so I tuck my Kindle under my arm and tiptoe over to the couch to resume my usual waiting for Everly to wake up pose.

The click of men's shoes has the hair on the back of my neck standing up. "Morning," Max's deep voice says from behind me.

I turn to see him in the kitchen pouring himself a cup of coffee. He usually doesn't have coffee here. He usually sprints out the door as soon as he lays eyes on me.

"Morning," I reply, waving my Kindle at him and then facing forward again. *Nice move, Casual Cozy.*

Max's footfalls approach, and I look up as he rounds the couch and lowers a mug of coffee to me. "What's this?" I ask, shivering at the smell of his cologne that's been freshly applied this morning.

Note to self…never wash tiny house sheets.

"Coffee," Max answers, straightening his long black tie over his white button-down and charcoal suit.

I look inside the cup and see that it has creamer. "Did you—?"

"Is that not how you take your coffee?" His brows pinch together, and he points up to the second level. "Everly said that vanilla creamer in the refrigerator was yours."

My lips part with a silent…*holy fucking shit, are you serious?* Instead, I clear my throat and respond, "Yeah…this is how I take my coffee. Thank you." I was going for cool as a cucumber, but I fear I might have given off an air of regal Queen of England at teatime vibes. Hopefully, he didn't notice.

He slides his hands into his pockets, an amused look on his face as he stares down at me.

Is he waiting for me to take a sip?

He is…he's waiting.

My eyes widen, and I hurriedly jostle the mug up to my lips, taking an inelegant slurp that I swear echoes off the walls. I smile up at him. "Tastes great."

"Good." He smiles and continues standing there.

Jesus, now what? My tongue darts out to wet my lips. "Are you going to the office today?"

"Yes." He tilts his head, his eyes narrowing imperceptibly at me.

"Cool, cool." I chew my lip nervously. "What did you and Everly do yesterday? I didn't see much of you two."

"Oh, we went to my parents' house for a visit. We often go there on Sundays if we're in town."

I nod and pick at a chunk of flesh I've broken loose on my lip. "I did nothing like usual! I'm getting really good at it." I laugh a bit too loudly and then flinch.

The sexy smirk on his face is completely disarming. I open my mouth to say more, but then my phone begins vibrating on the sofa. My face falls when I see my sister's name on the screen.

"It's my sister!" I hiss, setting the cup down and staring at the phone like it's going to catch fire at any moment.

Max frowns. "Rebecca?"

"Yeah, that's the only sister I have!" I snipe, shooting daggers at him for being so dense because seriously, this is bad news! "What do you think she wants?"

Max leans forward with a serious look and dips his voice low to say, "Oh, I emailed and told her we had sex this weekend."

Chills erupt over my body.

His straight face cracks into a broad smile. "Cassandra, I'm kidding. I have no idea what she wants. Just answer the phone and act normal."

"Act normal," I repeat in a mocking tone as I stand to stare down at my vibrating phone. Seriously, why does it have to be vibrating? I feel attacked. Like the universe is mocking me along with Max.

"She totally knows," I croak nervously.

"How could she know?"

"'Cuz I'm like a ram at mating season!" I exclaim with wide, manic eyes. "She can smell that I've had sex!"

Okay, that was maybe dramatic, but seriously, Rebecca has a weird big sister radar that just always seems to know when something insane is happening in my life and she needs to call to insert her unrequested opinion.

"What are you talking about?" Max's shoulders shake as he silently laughs at me while rubbing his warm hand up and down my arm, slightly disarming me. Does he realize he's touching me so... familiarly? I mean, it feels nice, but...what if my sister can see us? "You're freaking out over nothing. She's probably just calling to check in."

I nod and rub my lips together aggressively. The vibrating phone triggers other vibrator memories, so I need to get my shit together and pick up the call.

I crack my neck and swipe the screen to answer. "Hello, this is Cozy Cassie, nanny extraordinaire."

Max's lower lip juts off to the side as he slashes his hand across his neck, silently telling me to cool it.

"Cozy?" Rebecca's voice breaks into the line. "Why are you answering your phone like that? You sound stupid."

I clear my throat and try to chill out. "Because I'm doing super good at my job."

"That's what I hear," Rebecca replies smoothly. "Despite the way you just answered your phone."

"Come again?" I inquire, my head jerking back.

"Max Fletcher emailed me with a glowing review of you so far."

My eyes snap to Max, who's watching me with a heated look. A look that makes me feel like he's seen me naked. "What did he say?"

"He said he's never seen his daughter happier."

Chills erupt over my entire body as a knot forms in my throat. My eyes hold his as I say, "He said that?"

"Yes, that's what his email said. He also said that I should consider requiring my nannies to have lifeguarding experience. What's that all about? He didn't elaborate."

My lips purse together as I turn away from Max to focus on my response. "We had a little incident. Not with his daughter, just me. I was fine, though. Crisis averted."

Rebecca sighs that big sister sigh into the line. "Just be careful, okay? Be responsible."

"Yes, Bec, I know." I pause for a moment before whispering under my breath, "When did he send that email?"

"Hmm, let me look." I hear clicking through the line, and then she replies, "Early last week. Why, did something bad happen since then I need to know about?"

"No, Becca," I answer quickly, the smile on my face feeling damn near permanent. Something about Max saying all that before we slept together makes it feel that much more real.

"Everything else with you good?" she chirps lightly, and I can hear the clicking of her keyboard in the background again. "Anything personal to report?"

Oh, sis…if only you knew. "Nothing of interest. Does Jacob miss me yet? I could come over some night this week and play gin rummy with him again."

"Jacob does not miss you, Cozy," Rebecca drones. "You've only been gone a few weeks."

My lips smush off to the side. "Well…tell him to call me if he gets bored watching *Housewives* with you."

"Bye, Cozy."

"Bye, Bec."

I end the call with a smile, feeling like I won some major points with my sister for once. When I look up to thank Max for the email, I notice he's frowning at me.

"Who's Jacob?" he asks, walking toward me with his brow furrowed, looking strangely like a lion approaching his prey.

"My sister's husband."

Max stops walking. "You play cards with him?"

"Yeah." I shrug, walking over to the sofa to resume my position. "I lived with them before I moved here, so we became card buddies."

"Huh," Max huffs, eyeing me curiously. "Have you always lived with your sister?"

"God, no!" I exclaim with a snort. "She barely tolerates me. I was there six months and totally outstayed my welcome."

"Where did you live before that?" he inquires, his eyes doing that probing thing again that makes me shiver.

I shake my head and shrug again. "Just…an apartment."

"Where?" Max asks, not letting up. "I might own the building."

I bark out an unattractive laugh. "You didn't own this building…trust me."

Max eyes me harshly. "Why won't you tell me where you lived?"

"Why do you need to know?" I snap back, holding his gaze equally harsh.

"Daddy! You're still here!" Everly's voice peals as she pads barefoot down the spindle staircase. Her feet thud across the hardwood before she launches herself into his arms. "Are you working from home again this week?"

"No, Everly…I'm just…running late." His head twitches like he's just realized what time it is. He gives Everly a tight squeeze and adds, "But I'm glad I got a hug before I left."

"Me too! Are you sure you can't stay for breakfast? I taught Cozy how to make pancakes."

"Did you?" he says with a laugh. "I'm afraid I don't have time. But you two have fun today."

He sets Everly down and presses a kiss to the top of her head. His eyes find mine for a split second before the muscle in his jaw tics, and he makes his way out of the house.

Everly flops down on the couch beside me and immediately nuzzles herself under my arm. "What are we going to do today, Cozy?"

"Oh," I gasp and turn wide eyes to Everly. "I have a really fun activity planned for us today."

"What?" she squeals, turning on her side to look at me with all the childhood enthusiasm a kid can muster at six thirty in the morning.

"Today, we're going to practice the art…of sitting."

Everly's trill of laughter fills the house as she falls into my lap and makes herself comfortable. She's going to be good at this, I can tell.

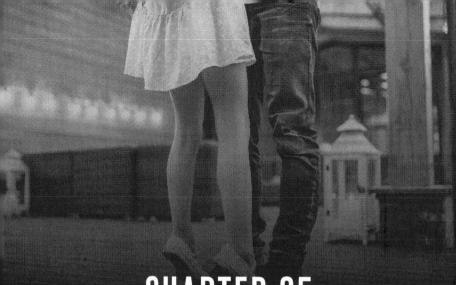

CHAPTER 25

Max

My cell phone rings as I sit on a Zoom call for a bakery franchise branch we're opening in Colorado Springs. I see the name Kate flash on the screen. Knowing the leader on this account can handle this meeting, I click off my camera and mute my mic to answer the call.

"I'm just curious enough to still accept your calls, Kate Smith," I say with a smile I hope she can hear.

"Aw, Max…don't you know I'm like a ball-obsessed rat terrier? If you just keep chucking balls at my face, I'll eventually leave you alone."

"That's…an interesting analogy."

"I'm a writer, Max," she deadpans.

Chuckling, I ask, "What can I do for you, Kate?"

"Can I get Cozy's phone number? Your nanny?"

"Um…sure." I frown curiously. "Do you need a sitter for Tucker? I'm not sure she really does babysitting gigs, but I suppose you can ask her."

"No, we don't need a sitter. I want to commission her to make me some charcuterie boards."

"Oh." My brows lift in surprise. "How many are you thinking?"

"Hopefully tons," Kate replies excitedly. "I have this big idea that I could actually use your advice on since you're a man about town."

"Okay…"

"I want to open a bookstore where we sell unique book boxes to readers. They'll include signed books and some unique gift items, like a mini charcuterie board that's themed with the book, some swag, and like…a T-shirt or something. I also want to get Norah and the bakery involved. But all the proceeds will go to charity. I know you're on the board of Rainbow Project, so I figured you could give me some tips on setting up a 501c? Maybe get me in touch with your lawyer?"

"Yeah, I could definitely help you out with this. This sounds really cool, Kate," I state seriously. She's always such a jokester, but this shows a whole new side to her.

"Thanks, I have a whole mission statement and a business plan… maybe we could meet at Norah's bakery sometime this week and go over it?"

"Absolutely. I'll have Marcia check my schedule and text you some times that work for me."

"Excellent!" Kate peals excitedly. "And text me Cozy's number."

"I will for sure. I can't imagine she wouldn't be up for this. She seems to love making those boards."

"That's good to hear because if this takes off like I think it could, I might have a full-time job offer for her."

"Really?" I tug my tie and consider that concept.

"Yeah, but don't worry, nothing will get going until well after the summer, and your ex-wife is back. I promise I won't steal Cozy from you. She'll be totally done with you before we're ready to launch."

After I end the call with Kate, I can't help but marvel over the fact that nearly a month of summer has already passed. It's shocking how quickly I've gotten used to having Cassandra and Everly at home every day. The thought of both of them leaving at the end of summer is…depressing.

A notification pings on my phone, and I see a photo of Everly lying out on one of the pool chairs with green muck on her face. She has her hands propped behind her head and a goofy smile on her face.

Cassandra: Rise and grind, baby. The Sea Monster has shown her true colors. Next stop...she's going to pumice my feet.

Me: I don't know what that is, but it sounds dirty.

Cassandra: The sexy dirty or the actual dirty?

Me: Yes to both.

Cassandra: And another kink is unlocked for the Zaddy.

Me: Zaddy?

Cassandra: Pretend you never read that.

Me: Too late. I googled.

Cassandra: Please tell me you're joking.

Me: It says a wealthy, handsome, older male. I'm not that much older than you.

Cassandra: It's the gray hairs in your scruff.

Me: I have grays?

Cassandra: Just a few. Don't worry, they blend in with the blond. And they look good! Sexy. Distinguished. Total Zaddy vibes.

Me: I'm sending screenshots of this conversation to your sister.

Cassandra: You're a mean Zaddy!

I'm smiling at my phone like a love-sick puppy when I hear my colleague calling out my name repeatedly through my computer speaker. "Max, are you there? The client has a question for you. Max?"

Blowing out a huge breath, I smooth my tie down to compose myself before flipping my camera back on and unmuting my mic. Zaddy or not, I have a company to run.

CHAPTER 26

Cozy

"Hello?" Dakota's groggy voice mumbles into the phone line. I glance at the clock and cringe when I see it's five thirty in the morning.

"Dakota," I hiss, needing her to wake the hell up and match my energy…which is acting like I'm on my tenth cup of coffee when in fact I haven't had a sip. "Do you remember that 90s movie with Alicia Silverstone and Cary Elwes? It's called *The Crush*. He's a writer and moves into their guesthouse, and the teen daughter becomes obsessed with him, builds a shrine of him, and like…tries to kill his girlfriend with a swarm of bees in a dark room?"

"Yeah."

"I'm Alicia Silverstone's character." My voice cracks as I jam my hand through my bedhead. "I'm currently up in my loft bedroom gaping out the window like a pervert watching Max swim laps in the pool. It's still kind of dark out, but I can see him, Dakota. I am officially the stalker in this situation now."

The sound of muffling breaks through the phone before Dakota yawns loudly. "First of all, if anything, you're Alicia Silverstone in that babysitter movie. Remember she has like two teenage boys going after her plus the dad? God, that movie was dirty as hell. Your parents' old VHS collection probably should have been locked away." She giggles sleepily.

I duck down when I see Max hoisting himself out of the pool. The sun is starting to peek through the trees, so I get a nice golden view of him drying off. He turns his back to me, and I notice his swim trunks are riding so low that the very top of his ass crack is showing, and I can see his tan line. Seriously, now a plumber's ass is hot? *Another kink unlocked.*

"So if I'm the Alicia Silverstone babysitter, what does that mean? He's the dirty one, not me?" I ask, still feeling desperate to find some semblance of comfort in this painful situation.

"Oh, you're both dirty, for sure."

I groan, "Why did we think it was a good idea for me to hook up with my boss again?"

"Because you're not a teenage nut job, Cozy. You're a grown woman, and Max is hot. You would hate yourself if you didn't seize the day and bag the Zaddy. I'm fucking proud of you."

My lips buzz with yet another heavy breath. Been doing a lot of heavy breathing these days. And unfortunately, Dakota's pride does nothing to quell the anxiety still swirling in my tummy. I thought the sexual tension would dissipate after we hooked up. But that Zaddy asshole has made me coffee three mornings in a freaking row. Three! And you know what? There is something intensely erotic about having a man in a suit hand you a cup of coffee. Starbucks needs to change their employee uniforms immediately.

Okay, my kink counts are out of fucking control now.

Not to mention Max's kinks! Biting, hickeys, intense eye contact. It's a lot. We are a lot. I haven't even needed to pick up my Mercedes Lee Loveletter books this week because I am living in some sort of Loveletter fantasy.

Even my text exchanges with Max are like…not PG rated anymore.

Me: Fair warning…Everly and I have been tie-dying today, and she may have snuck into your closet and transformed a few of your white T-shirts.

Max: Oh, boy.

Me: Yeah, also…your closet is like straight out of a Mercedes Lee Loveletter novel. I may have drooled a little while walking around and fondling your things.

Max: One of these days, you'll have to tell me what it is you love about Kate's books.

Me: Hiding eyes emoji. That would not be an appropriate conversation to have with my boss.

Max: I think we're far past the point of appropriate, don't you, Cassandra?

My brain rips out of my mental musings to ask Dakota, "Why are both movie references we're talking about for my life story cheesy psychological thrillers instead of sweet, romantic comedies?" My hand grows sweaty as I clutch my phone like it's my lifeline.

"Because you're you, Cozy. And it simply would not be on brand for you to identify with traditional," Dakota replies simply.

"Fair point."

"Just chill out, okay? Maybe go visit your parents tonight. Get out of that tiny house of sexual memories and breathe in the fresh country air."

"That's a good idea," I respond crisply because it totally still smells like Max in here. "Nothing like a hardy discussion about my future with my mother to bring me back to reality."

"Mmmkay, Bestie. I'm going back to sleep now," she coos into the line and doesn't even wait for me to say goodbye before hanging up.

I feel rejected, and the sun isn't even up yet. Wish I could say the same for my libido.

That evening, when the familiar sight of my family's big red barn comes into view, I feel a modicum of relief as I pull into the large circle driveway to park. Leaving my keys in the ignition, I trudge my way up to the classic white, two-story home.

Both my parents have full-time jobs and use their hobby farm as supplemental income. They raise lambs and sell the babies to young kids in 4-H. Some even keep their animals out here and come out to feed them and work with them every day to prepare them for the fair. It's a decent side hustle for my parents, so I think they'll do it as long as they're physically able.

We didn't grow up with a lot of money, and I remember as a kid being wildly jealous of my classmates who wore name-brand clothes. For Christmas one year, I got an Under Armor hoodie from my grandparents, and I wore that thing until it was practically see-through because it was the nicest thing I owned.

Which is why I had such strong ambition when it came to my studies. I was certain that if I got good grades and took all the right college classes, then I could find an amazing job, be rich, happy, and have everything my heart ever desired.

Boy was I so very wrong.

"Hey, Cassie!" my mom, Sheryl, calls out from the front door as I walk up to the wraparound porch.

She opens her arms for a hug, and I sink into her like a warm blanket. My mom and I have similar builds of big chest and curves, but my dark hair and fair complexion come directly from my dad.

"Come on in. Dad just got in from doing chores." She steps back and holds the door open.

When I walk in, my dad is just finishing washing his hands at the kitchen sink when he turns to me for a hug. "Good to see you, turbo," my dad, Kurtis, says, squeezing me firmly. He's called me turbo ever since I got my license. Said I kicked rocks every time I peeled out of our gravel driveway to go to school.

"You're staying for supper, right?" Mom asks, checking what looks like a pot roast in the oven.

"Yes, definitely," I reply, sitting down at the table with Dad. "It smells great."

"How's the new job?" Dad inquires, his eyes crinkling with the big smile on his face.

"It's good…the kid is so sweet."

"Everly is her name, right?" Mom confirms, tossing the potholder on the counter before coming over to join us.

"Yes. She's eleven, so it's super easy. Honestly, she can take care of herself mostly, but she's at that age where she's not quite old enough to be home alone all summer. So I feel more like a buddy than a nanny."

"I can see that," Mom says, her brow furrowing as she watches me. "Does it pay well?"

"Yeah, it's good," I answer quickly.

"But it's only for the summer?"

"Yes."

"And what will you do after that?" she pries, and I feel a bit like I'm being interviewed for a job instead of reconnecting with my parents.

I shrug noncommittally, not prepared to tell them about the odd call I got from Kate, aka Mercedes, yesterday. I'm still not sure how I feel about that whole idea she pitched me, and until I do, I don't need my parents' opinion on the matter.

My mom sighs heavily. "All that education and you're just… nannying."

"I'm taking some time, Mom," I say for the hundredth time.

"While eating away at your savings," she replies quickly. "Your student loans are going to dry up your pot pretty quick, and then what will you do?"

"Sheryl…" my dad warns.

"Kurtis, she needs to hear this," Mom snaps, turning her gaze from me to him. "It's been seven months now. She's healthy, and she needs to find a real job to make some real money."

"Mom, I'm fully aware of my financial status," I respond tersely, my anxiety bubbling up with every word that comes out of her mouth. "You don't need to worry about me, okay?"

"That's impossible," she says. "I will worry about you and Rebecca until I'm cold in the ground. That's what parents do forever. Your age has nothing to do with it." She inhales a deep breath and presses her fist to her lips. "Mothers worry, Cassie. Especially after one gets a call like I did last year that her young, healthy, seemingly thriving daughter was in the hospital."

My eyes sting at the tormented look on her face. I hate that my mom had to get that call, and I hate that I didn't see the signs to prevent myself from getting to that level.

I slide my hand across the table to hold hers. "Mom, I'm figuring out my next step, all right? This isn't forever. It's just for now. But I'm okay, I promise." I lean my head down to capture her eyes with mine. "Look at me. Don't I look happy?"

"You do." The corner of her mouth quirks up into a soft smile as she reaches out to stroke my face. "Like the old Cozy Cassie. You even look like you've gotten some sun this summer."

I smile, grateful the conversation is calming down. "Well, Max has a pool."

"Who is Max?" Dad asks curiously.

"Um…the dad," I reply, feeling my cheeks flush under my parents' watchful eyes. I tuck my hair behind my ears and stare down at my hands on the table.

"Is he a good guy?" Dad inquires, and I can feel his papa bear energy flare up. He always was so protective of Becca and me. Similar to how Max is with Everly.

"He is a good guy," I answer, feeling those annoying butterflies take flight in my belly as I picture him with Everly at the kitchen counter. "I expected him to be very different, like a lot of the rich CEOs I came across in Denver. You know…always traveling, barely present in their children's lives, egos bigger than the Rockies. But he's not like that…he's got better balance, it seems."

My brow furrows at this realization I haven't really given Max proper credit for. Yes, he works nearly twelve-hour days, but when he's home with Everly, he seems completely focused on her. And I haven't seen him go into the office once on the weekends so far, which, for the CEO of a company, that seems almost unheard of.

My mother's voice chirps in next, "Rebecca said he's a bigwig in Boulder. Maybe you could find a job at his company when the summer ends?"

And we're back to our regularly scheduled programming!

My parents…God bless them, but they just can't quite wrap their heads around my new outlook on life. They are typical middle-class people who have saved for every treasure in their lives and never gone a day without working. And I love them for that. Their hard work set me up to have the privilege of taking some time for myself.

And maybe if I had chosen a different career path, hell, even a different company, things wouldn't have gone so sideways for me. All I know is that I'm going to be a lot more careful about my next career choice. And I'm going to know what I'm getting into before I jump into the deep end. Or get yanked in.

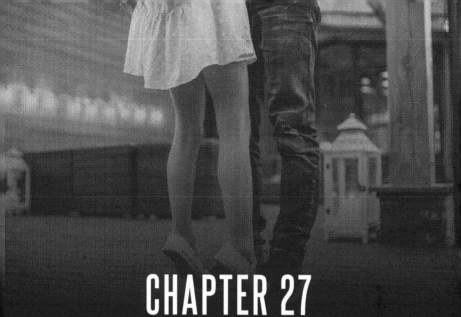

CHAPTER 27

MAX

It's late Friday night when I hear the faint buzz of a sander running in the garage. Everly is in her pajamas and watching a movie in the basement, finally seeming to be in better spirits after we talked at dinner. Apparently, today wasn't the best for her, but she assured me nothing was wrong, just an off day, so it makes me think Cassandra's texts she sent me earlier might be right.

> Cassandra: Tough day today. ☹ Everly cried a lot after she hung up with her mom and just couldn't seem to shake the emotions away all day. I even tried to do a dance party with her on the deck, and she wasn't in the mood.

> Me: What can I do to help?

> Cassandra: Ice cream always helps me when I'm feeling blue.

> Me: I'll bring it home when I'm done at the office. You think she's just homesick for her mom?

> Cassandra: Yeah, I'm sure that's part of it. I also think it could

172 AMY DAWS

be hormones. I'm not a mother, but I'm a woman, and when she broke down crying because she misspelled a word on her book report, I knew it wasn't just missing her mom.

Me: Maybe a quiet night at home tonight?

Cassandra: Definitely. And perhaps some screen time. I know you try to limit her, but she's a young woman whose body could be changing. It's a lot to think about, and sometimes the escape of a good movie helps calm the nerves.

Me: For once, I agree with you, Cassandra.

Cassandra: It's about time. ☺

Me: Thank you for letting me know.

Cassandra: Always. XoXo

I head downstairs and find Everly still engrossed in her movie. Her eyes look bright and happy as she offers me a quick smile, so I leave her to continue watching some young Lindsay Lohan film in peace.

I walk through the kitchen toward my bedroom but pause when I reach the door that leads into the garage. I should really talk to Cassandra. This is the first day that Everly has struggled since she started, and I want her to know that I appreciate her comforting my kid.

Plus, I haven't had time to really talk to her all week. She seems jumpy every time I bring her a cup of coffee, and I'm not trying to freak her out. I'm just trying to show her that she's appreciated. And she is. Today she sent a photo of Everly cuddled into her chest. Her eyes were red, and her smile was kind of sad, but I still saved the damn thing to my phone because she was cared for. That's not something I take lightly.

I make my way out to the workshop and find Cassandra hunched over a long piece of wood clipped to a sawhorse. She's running a handheld sander over it and my eyes can't help but slide over her curves. They are still just as alluring as they've always been. I wonder if my teeth marks are still on her ass?

My dick reacts to that errant thought almost immediately, pressing against the zipper of my jeans. It's interesting because with most women I hook up with, the attraction fades almost instantly after we sleep together. But with Cassandra, I didn't want to leave her bed the next day. When my brother texted me to ask what time to bring Everly home, I nearly begged him to keep her one more night so I could continue the fuck-a-thon with the nanny.

God, I'm fucked up.

And I will not allow sex to be a priority over time with my child, no matter how mind-blowing it is.

"Oh hey," Cassandra says, jumping when she spots me leering at her from the doorway of her shop. "Didn't hear you come in."

She shuts her sander off and pops out her earbuds before pushing her goggles on top of her head. She's wearing that backward green hat again, and I swear to fuck, it's the sexiest thing I've ever seen her in. *And I've seen her naked.*

"How's Everly?" she asks immediately, and it just somehow makes her even more attractive.

"She's good. Watching some Lindsay Lohan movie downstairs," I reply, making my way over to what she's working on.

"Which one?"

"She's young in the movie and has a horrible British accent."

"*Parent Trap!*" Cassandra exclaims excitedly. "I loved that movie as a kid. You know I thought Lindsay Lohan really had a twin sister. My sister told me the twin hated the fame they got from the movie and went into hiding. Thought that was dead-ass facts until like two years ago."

"Seriously?" I stare back, waiting for the punchline that doesn't come.

"Yeah, I'm not proud." Her lips purse as she removes her leather apron to yank on her top to cool herself down. I have to fight my eyes from ogling her chest as she adds, "Anyway, did she enjoy the five kinds of ice cream you came home with?"

Cassandra's taunting expression is something I would really like to kiss off her face. How is she mocking me for buying too much ice cream when she literally just told me she thought Lindsay Lohan was a twin until recently?

I shrug and run a hand through my hair. "I maybe went a little overboard on flavor selection."

"You think?" She giggles.

I pin her with a heated look. "I'm an overachiever when I want to be." She bites her lip, causing me to bite mine as well, and it suddenly feels very hot in here. I pause before adding, "I just wanted to stop in here to say thanks again for today. She's had issues with anxiety in the past, and it's usually something she wants her mom for, but she seemed really comforted by you. That means a lot."

"Oh, anytime." Cassandra gestures to her body playfully. "It's hard work being a female and constantly trying to fuck the patriarchy."

I chuckle and divert my attention from her body to the board she's working on. "What's this piece for?" I ask, reaching out to feel the misshapen hunk of wood on her sawhorse. "Is this something for that thing Kate called to talk to me about? Her book box thing? I hope it was okay I gave her your number."

Cassandra's brow furrows as she shrugs her shoulders. "Oh yeah, that was fine. I don't know what the plan is with all of that yet. It seems like a big undertaking."

"For you or for her?"

"Um…well, her definitely. And me? I never considered starting a business out of this hobby of making charcuterie boards," she stammers, nervously rubbing her forehead.

I watch her curiously. "Isn't that kind of the dream for most people? Make a career out of something you love to do?"

Cassandra hesitates before speaking, clearly weighing her words. "But is it good to monetize things we love? We might risk not loving it if we start to put deadlines and money labels on it."

"I don't think Kate would feel that way about her books," I reply, hating the way Cassandra's body language has shifted. She's getting closed off and twitchy, which is an odd reaction when we're talking about something she enjoys.

Cassandra's brows lift knowingly. "That's true. I'm just currently subscribed to the anti-hustle culture, so it's just a lot for me to consider."

I shoot her a teasing wink and lean in to whisper, "Heaven forbid you abandon your willy-nilly lifestyle and do *more* instead of *less* for once."

Her jaw falls open as she hits me with a positively lethal gaze that excites the fuck out of me. "I'm no stranger to doing more, don't you worry. I am just currently choosing to make *life* my main hustle and my nanny job my side hustle. That's how you embrace the soft life, and nothing is wrong with that."

"Mmmkay." I click my tongue as she huffs indignantly. It's fun to get a rise out of her, but I know how she gets when I start asking too many personal questions, so I turn back to the mess on the counter. "You still haven't told me what you're making with all these wood chunks."

Her face instantly brightens. "Oh…I found these great pieces of driftwood down by the creek this week so I'm prepping them to scatter in a square mold and fill the gaps with epoxy. Everly picked out this great teal pigment that will look amazing."

"Have you worked with epoxy before?" I ask, mildly impressed. She acts like she doesn't have ambition, but it's total bullshit. This woman has hard work ingrained in her.

"The magic of YouTube is very helpful for DIYers." She waggles her eyebrows excitedly and moves over to the counter, where several other pieces sit next to a metal chisel. "I have to gouge out the old bark from the pits first or the sealer won't adhere." She holds the chisel out to me. "You should try it. It's freakishly satisfying."

"Okay." I laugh and step forward, taking the tool from her hands and pushing the edge down into the hole.

"If you go at it from this angle." She presses her tits against my arm as she reaches around me to demonstrate. The scent of coconut lotion, perfume, whatever the fuck she wears mixed with sawdust has my eyes closing involuntarily.

Fuuuck, she smells incredible.

She holds my hand as she shows me how to work the bark out, and I realize we're having a bit of a Patrick Swayze and Demi Moore

Ghost moment. I turn my head toward her and shoot her a smirk. "Most men would be emasculated by this. But considering my ex left me for another woman, it's safe to say I have no problem with this role reversal."

Her breasts move against me with her soft laughter—a hint of mischief dancing in her eyes. "I'd take it either way."

My cock grows hard at the wickedness in her words. It's not a direct come on. It's somewhere in the gray area. Then again, so was my comment. There are a lot of blurred lines here, and I'm getting kind of tired of not seeing clearly with Cassandra. And the silence that descends after her comment feels crystal fucking clear.

Cozy

I realize belatedly that my breasts are pressed firmly against my boss's arm. That sculpted arm that I can feel the muscles of through his thin T-shirt. The quietness in the room is deafening as Max pauses work on the driftwood and stares at my lips.

The heat in his eyes makes my stomach tighten, and my yoga shorts suddenly feel too snug, while my breasts practically grow a whole cup size inside my thin gray camisole. I'm not dressed properly for Max Fletcher to be looking at me like *that*.

I squeeze my eyes shut and force myself to swallow, hoping it will somehow eliminate the need pulsating between my legs. It's inappropriate. Everly is awake inside. She could come out here any minute, and she doesn't need to see me looking at her dad like this.

Or her dad looking at me like that.

Because he's the one who started this. Whatever this is.

Max sets down the wood chisel and licks his lips, dragging his lower lip through his teeth before releasing it. His eyes do that color shift thing again, darkening as if revealing the direction of his thoughts. He turns so he's facing me, one hand splayed out on the counter as he invades my personal space with that stupid mafia man scent of his.

He reaches out a finger and wipes at something on my face. Maybe dust, maybe dirt. Could be sweat. Honestly, I've been out here for a while, and I'm a hot mess.

He pauses for a moment before the back of his finger glides along my jawline and down my neck to trace the ridge of my collarbone. Goose bumps erupt over my body, causing my nipples to tighten under my thin bralette. The way his nostrils flare as he watches my chest heave is damn near carnal. Warmth rushes in my chest as his hand glides down over the swell of my breast. The mark on my chest is gone now and I swear I see a flicker of disappointment in his eyes as he notices that fact.

"I don't know what you're doing to me," he rasps, his fingertips hovering over my flesh like he wants to pull away but can't find the strength.

"What do you mean?" My voice is breathy and embarrassing, but he doesn't seem to notice.

His Adam's apple slides down his throat as he forms his hand over my breast and squeezes gently. "I can't seem to control myself around you." His eyes are devastating when he looks back up at me.

I arch into his touch, damn near panting for him to grip harder. To press into me, to bend me over this sawhorse and fuck me from behind.

I have spent the past week replaying what his body feels like against mine, and I am unwell from it. He has haunted all my waking moments, and the only thing that could make this ache in my body go away is for him to finish what he's starting.

My pulse quickens as he towers over me, his eyes gripping mine in a chokehold I don't want to be released from. The loud inhale and exhale of our breaths is all the soundtrack I need to reply, "What are you going to do about it?"

His head jerks at my response, his jaw muscle twitching violently as he turns away and debates. Finally, I hear him moan, "Fuck," under his breath before he grabs my face and seals his lips over mine.

The heat of his tongue swirls into my mouth and is like a salve to a wound that was aching all over my body as I wrap my arms around his hips and hold on for dear life.

How long have I wanted to kiss this man again? Days? Weeks? Since the first moment I stepped into that boardroom for my interview? It has to be longer than this moment because the ecstasy of relief I feel flush against him again is like nothing I've ever felt before.

He shifts to pin my back against the worktable, and I hear the clatter of tools fall to the floor beside us as his grip leaves my face and slides down to my waist. He steels his hands under the fabric of my top to my breasts, squeezing them harshly in his large hands. It's a punishing grip, his body clearly overcome by the sexual frustration just like mine.

The delicious pain of his assault causes me to whimper into his lips as slickness grows between my legs. My tongue fights to keep up with his as he consumes me, swallowing up every moan, groan, and gasp that slips out of me.

"Fuck," he grunts again, breaking our kiss to turn me around. He presses my front up against the worktable and folds over me to grind the ridge of his hard cock into my ass. My hands spread out to brace myself as our bodies roll into one another, my fantasy very nearly becoming a reality.

My clit throbs as I feel my panties grow wetter with every thrust of his hips. This isn't enough. I want him in me, I want him on me, I want him tasting me. I want to taste him. I want to break myself into multiple pieces so that every fucking part of this can be happening to me all at the same exact second.

I yank his hand off my hip to guide him to my center. He rubs me through my shorts, and the fabric dampens with my arousal as I ride him, my pelvis fucking his firm strokes.

Groaning loudly, he presses his head onto my back and bows over me, blanketing my body with his heat as he continues to dry hump me. The naughty, illicit nature of what we're doing fully clothed somehow feels hotter than being stripped naked and fucking on the sawhorse.

A tiny yelp escapes my lips when I feel him bite down on my shoulder, and it's as if that noise shocks him back to reality because he pulls his hand away and backs up.

"Fuck," he growls and shoves both hands through his hair. "Shit, I bit you again."

"It's okay," I exhale with a laugh, glancing at the tender area that's reddening already.

I feel the loss of his warmth as he puts more space between us and begins pacing by the sawhorse, his erection painfully obvious. "Jesus…Everly is still awake. She could have walked in."

I fight to catch my breath, straightening my tank top back to its rightful position before crossing my arms over my nipples. "I'm sorry. I don't know what happened."

"You happened," he snaps back at me, his face looking almost angry.

"You think this is my fault?" I exclaim, my state of arousal being doused rather quickly. "I'm pretty sure you touched me first."

"That was after you fucking ghosted me," he stammers, looking more unraveled than I've ever seen him.

My face twists up in confusion. "I didn't ghost you! I've been talking to you all day."

"Not that kind of ghost, you like…Patrick Swayze'd me." He gesticulates with his hands like he's wrapping around someone at a pottery cauldron.

I huff out a noise of annoyance. "You can't turn a person into a verb."

"You are all fucking verb, Cassandra." He begins pacing again, his breath hitching in his chest as he points between us. "This isn't working."

My chest contracts with the ominous words he's just uttered. I press my hand to my heart in a feeble attempt to calm down the dread that washes over me at where I think this is going. I try not to cry when I ask, "Do you want me to quit?"

Max stops, and a vein in his forehead pulses angrily as he gapes back at me. "No! Fuck…I can't lose—Everly can't lose you," he thunders.

My brow furrows with stubbornness. "Well good because I'm not going to quit."

"But this tension is…impossible." He exhales heavily, and his shoulders drop. "We can't lose control like this again, especially when Everly is around."

"I agree." I swallow the thickness in my throat and try not to show my disappointment. "We can't let it happen again."

"Or…" Max starts, rubbing the back of his neck, clearly deep in thought. His eyes glance at me nervously. "What if we do let it happen again? What if we let it happen as much as we need it to? What if we just…bang it out?"

"Bang it out?" I repeat, my libido popping back up out of nowhere like a wanton hussy.

Max shrugs. "Yeah, so we just keep doing this but maybe with some specific rules that we both agree to so there's some structure and order to it."

I pause to consider this. "Like, do you want me to sign a contract?"

"Jesus, no! What the fuck?" He looks angry again.

"Sorry…I was just thinking a Christian Grey moment and my imagination got carried away."

"Clearly."

I chew my lip nervously.

"Is that a kink we need to discuss?" he asks, his eyes watching me carefully.

"BDSM? Oh, my God, no!" All the blood rushes to my cheeks as my choking fantasy silently breaks into the party to say *heeeeeyyyy girl.*

"Okay then." He looks relieved.

Silence descends again before I offer, "Okay, so we're going to bang it out with rules…what kind of rules are we talking about?"

He nods, his brow furrowed deep in thought. "No hookups while Everly is awake."

"Obviously," I reply with a laugh and then wince because it's literally what we just did.

"No…hooking up in the house," Max says. "I think the main house needs to be a boundary so we should do it at yours every time."

"That's a good one." I nod seriously, realizing that my tiny house has just been re-labeled as a sex house, and I'm not mad about that. I add to that rule, "And no sleepovers."

"Really?" Max frowns at me.

"Well, it's not like we can just leave Everly sleeping alone in the Fletchpad all night."

"Oh, right, of course." Max shakes his head as if he can't believe that thought never occurred to him. "And I'll be sure to turn the alert on for the security camera in her room when I come over, so I'll be notified right away if she gets up."

"There's a camera in her room?"

Max stares at me like I'm a moron. "There are cameras all over the house, Cassandra."

"Where?"

Max points at a round thing in the corner.

"I thought those were fire alarms!"

He shakes his head.

"Oh, my God, so you've like…seen everything me and Everly do all day long?"

He shrugs, and I see a small smile tease the corner of his mouth.

"What the hell!" I exclaim as a powerful mixture of rage and humiliation swirl in my belly. "That would have been something nice to know a month ago. God…so you've seen—"

"The dance parties? Yes, I've seen them." He pins me with his eyes as a smug grin tugs on his lips.

"And the—"

"The time you slipped on the floor in your swimsuit when you ran inside to grab drinks for you and Everly? Yeah, I saw it." His smile spreads fuller now, revealing his perfect white teeth as he takes a step toward me.

I slice a hand through my hair, absolutely shocked that he has been keeping tabs on me for a month. Have I picked my nose? Removed a wedgy? The horror! "Jesus, Mary, and Joseph!"

"I don't watch everything…just the clips that record movement for more than sixty seconds. And once I started trusting you, I quit watching mostly." His smile is replaced with chagrin as he fails to quell the anxiety roaring through my body.

"Oh, thanks for that." I groan in mortification at the things he might have seen. "This is some messed-up nanny-cam stalker bull-shit. Like honestly, I don't know if you are mentally well, Max." Let's face it, we're both fucked up because as much as it horrifies me to think about what he could have seen...I'm also oddly aroused by the stalker vibes. But only a little...

He scoffs and shakes his head. "Cassandra, I'm wealthy and have a large house. Did you really think I wouldn't have security cameras?"

He makes a good point.

I shake my head and get back to the task at hand. "Okay, so late-night hookups only, no bangers in the Fletchpad, no sleepovers, and...what else? Did we miss anything?"

Max's jaw muscle tics again, indicating we very much missed something. He props himself on the sawhorse and crosses his arms over his chest. "If we do this, it's just us, right? You're not going to go stroke some other dude's eyebrows at a bar this weekend?"

My jaw drops. "It was one time! I just wanted to see how they felt!"

His eyes dance with mirth. Sexy mirth. The sexiest of all the mirths. "You didn't answer the question," he presses, his eyes captivating me.

I lick my lips and struggle not to smile back at him. "Luckily, you have a very nice quizzical brow, so I think my brow fondling needs will be fully satisfied."

"Fucking right they will," Max all but growls, giving me a glimpse of that alpha male energy as he obviously struggles to stay on his side of the room.

My stomach swirls with desire as I realize this is really happening. I'm going to get to sleep with this tall, sexy drink of a man again. And my daydreaming fantasies will multiply!

I realize this is some sort of nannies with benefits situation that could likely turn into a complete disaster, but considering I'm not here for that much longer, I think we can make this work. We're mature enough to handle this.

I purse my lips as I eye Max seriously. "Can the last rule be that no matter what happens between us, it doesn't affect me being Everly's nanny? I like her too much to let drama between us push me out of her life. If things go sideways, you'll have to fire me because I'm not going to quit on her."

Max's face grows pensive as he stares back at me. "I'm not firing you, Cozy."

His use of my nickname sends a rush through my body, and I steel myself to nod woodenly. "Okay then."

"Okay then," Max adds sexily.

"We have a deal." I smirk and step forward to hold my hand out to his.

He stalks toward me, wafting me in his delicious scent as he takes my hand in his. My smile falters the instant I feel the heat of his palm against mine. Max's eyes flick down to my lips, and his nostrils flare, clearly feeling the current of electricity coursing between us.

"I'll see you later tonight," his voice growls with wicked promise before he finally lets go of me.

I nod and swallow thickly, watching him take measured steps backward before retreating into the house.

This is going to be interesting.

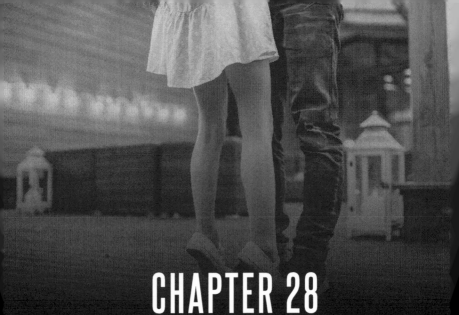

CHAPTER 28

Max

The summer night air is crisp as I make my way across the grass at ten o'clock. Everly is fast asleep, finally. I know because I checked her camera on my phone about a hundred times before locking the house up to run across my lawn like a sex-starved teenager.

This feels irresponsible and childish as hell. But Everly is eleven. She's not some toddler I'm leaving in a crib. If she wakes up looking for me, my phone will ping, and I'll get dressed quicker than she can climb down the winding staircase. And hell, I'm still on the property. It's not like I'm abandoning her to have casual sex with her nanny.

Except that I am.

But fuck it, this is more fun than I've allowed myself to have in years. Hell, my normal routine when Everly is at my house is to work for hours at my desk after she's asleep. I usually have loads to catch up on just from taking time away from work to give her my focus, so I don't fully have time for this.

But for once, I'm putting my needs ahead of work because I'm living on borrowed time. Once I partner with All-Out, my life is going to change drastically. This will probably be my last fling with a woman before my company explodes. I'm not going to feel bad about this, no matter how fucked up it is.

My cock thickens in my jeans, liking where my mind is going.

I have never met a woman I've struggled to keep my hands off of the way I have with Cassandra. Hopefully, banging it out will snuff out this insane allure she carries. And hell, she wanted a summer fling. Nothing says summer fling like fucking your boss when you're off the clock.

I stand in front of her door and check my phone one last time before knocking. No turning back now, Max. You're all in.

Cozy

"Hey there. How was the rest of your evening?" I croak when I open my front door, and Max walks in, wafting me in his freshly showered scent.

"Take off your clothes," he says, peeling his shirt over his head and tossing it to the floor. His eyes are wide and a bit crazed.

"What's the rush?" I ask, walking backward toward my sofa as he stalks toward me.

"The rush is that I had to take an ice-cold shower after our little garage moment so that I could be a semi-decent father and put my kid to bed. Now she's asleep, the security camera is on, and I don't want to be a semi-decent father anymore."

My lips purse together with a poorly concealed smirk as I perch on the arm of the couch. "Do you want to be a Zaddy?"

Max stops in front of me, the heated look in his eyes replaced with genuine confusion. "What is this Zaddy obsession you have?"

I giggle and shake my head. "It helps if you wrinkle your nose when you say it."

He stares at me like I'm an idiot. I totally am.

"Come on...try it." I nod my head toward him and know there is no way in a million fucking years that millionaire Max Fletcher will concede to me on this.

He licks his lips and tilts his head before lowering both hands onto the arm of the sofa, caging me in. He inhales deeply, dragging his nose along my neckline before locking his eyes on mine. His nose scrunches up, and he growls, "Zaddy."

I fall backward onto the couch in a fit of giggles, curling my legs up into my chest. "I can't believe you actually did it."

He watches me with a smile and it's quite possibly the hottest he's ever looked. "You're seriously weird."

"I know." I sigh happily. Jesus, I am happy. And we haven't even had sex yet.

Max pulls his phone out of his jeans and checks it briefly before setting it on the end table. "Now are you going to be a good girl and take your clothes off like I told you to?"

He begins removing his jeans, so I eagerly scramble up off the couch and ditch my cotton robe and the pajamas that I took way too long to pick out. It's a matching satin short set that makes my tits look good, and Max barely even notices it.

However, once I'm completely naked, the look in his gaze *is a thousand times better.*

Honestly, the past week, I had been fighting with my inner self that all those wonderful things he said about my body were just to get me into bed. A man like Max Fletcher couldn't possibly be *that* attracted to a girl who shops in the plus-sized section of a department store.

Not that I hate my body. I don't! Yes, I have stretch marks around my hips and breasts, and yes, my tummy is soft and jiggles when I move, and lord knows my ass and thighs have a plethora of dimples.

But for the most part, I can look in the mirror and like what I see. I see someone who has learned how to enjoy life outside the confines of society's standard of beauty. I see someone who enjoys eating healthy and indulging when she wants to. I see curves and balance. I see a body that bounced back from a horrific experience that nearly killed her.

This is my body, and I love it.

And when Max stands gloriously naked before me and drags his fingers up my arms to cup my face and kiss me reverently, swirling away any shred of doubt left inside me, I decide right then and there to allow myself to believe that a man like Max could love my body too.

"See that?" Max turns me in his arms to press his warmth to my back as he points at the mirror mounted on the far wall. His body is tall and sculpted behind mine that's rounded and soft.

"Yes," I gasp as his hand reaches around to tug gently on the bud of my nipple.

His whiskers tease the shell of my ear as he murmurs, "You're going to watch me fuck you from behind and I want you to never take your eyes off me, got it?"

I inhale a shaky breath and nod a bit too enthusiastically as my dark hair falls into my face. I demurely tuck it behind my ears and watch him over my shoulder as he pulls a condom out of his wallet and sheathes himself.

Big, long, beautiful dick.

He grips my waist and positions me over the arm of the sofa, giving my ass a playful smack before greedily palming it as he bends me over.

"I thought you weren't Christian Grey," I tease jokingly, staring at his sexy body in the mirror.

"I'm not," he growls, gripping his cock and sliding his tip along my dripping wet center. It's been wet since I left the workshop, and I swear it grows wetter every time he looks at me. "I'm Max Fletcher, and you can feel very free to scream that whenever you want, sweet cheeks."

Without warning, he plunges deep inside me, and I cry out, my eyes struggling to stay open as I watch his abs contract as he pushes in to the hilt.

"Fuuuuck," he groans and flinches as he pulls out and thrusts back in. "Every time, you're so wet for me, Cassandra."

"Yes," I moan, my fingers digging into the couch cushion as I arch my spine and press back into him. My clit throbs between my thighs.

He slams into me again, his eyes watching me hungrily in the mirror. "Do you like watching me fuck you?"

I whimper out a strangled *uhh-huhh* before he picks up speed and begins pistoning into me at a rapid speed, grinding my clit against the sofa in a way that makes it damn near impossible to hold my head up. Holy shit, how can I watch him when everything in my body feels like it's going to explode?

"Eyes on me always, sweet cheeks," he instructs, bending over and sliding his hand up my chest to pull me upright. He gently grips my neck to force me to look at our reflection in the mirror.

"Oh, my God, Max," I exclaim, overcome by the image of his large hand on my neck, holding me in place as he arches his cock up into me.

Fireworks fill my vision as my orgasm hits me out of nowhere.

Jesus, I think I just came off our reflection alone.

"Fuck," Max barks, clearly caught off guard by my climax as well. He lowers me back over the arm of the couch and jackhammers inside me a few more times before calling out my name and finding his own release.

When he's done, I allow my head to fall onto the cushion, and he falls over the top of me, both of our bodies slick with sweat as we struggle to catch our breaths.

"That was faster than I planned…again," Max says with a huff.

I smile into the cushion and peel a strand of my hair out of my mouth. "The beauty of this arrangement is that there's always next time."

Max laughs and presses his lips onto my shoulder blade, sucking a spot softly before extracting himself from my body. He walks bare-assed down the hall to the bathroom and sets about his business as I heave myself off the couch and shakily slip into my robe.

When he comes back out, he's got a seriously sexy smile on his face as he slips back into his black boxer briefs and stands before me like a Calvin Klein model.

I drop down onto the sofa and watch him curiously as he pulls his jeans up over his hips and leaves them unbuttoned.

"Hey, if we're going to be doing this on a semi-regular basis, then I have to ask…what's with your eye contact thing?" My eyes narrow to see what his body language does.

He sighs heavily and pauses his pursuit of putting on his T-shirt. "Uh…no, I'm not going there."

"Why not?" I ask, feeling offended.

"Because it's personal."

"What do you think what we just did was?" I snap, not willing to let this one go. If he can be a nosy asshole, so can I. He checks his phone for a moment, and I fear he's going to leave without telling me, so I offer, "If I tell you mine, will you tell me yours?"

His eyes lift to mine, looking mildly intrigued. He clicks his tongue with a teasing smirk. "Depends how good yours is."

I lick my lips and feel my cheeks heat.

"Shit, it is good," he says with a dirty smirk and comes over to join me on the couch in all his shirtless, unbuckled jeans glory.

Honestly, the way his abdomen looks when he sits down is insane. His abs just sort of stack on top of each other and look good enough to eat. Though truthfully, Max would look just as hot with a dad bod.

"Come on, I'm waiting…" he pries, his eyes looking younger by the second.

I roll my eyes. "Fine, you want to know my kink?" I hesitate, chewing on my lip nervously as his eyes burn into me. "I'm intrigued by the idea of a little…light choking."

Max's eyes bulge. "Choking?"

"Not like…breath play, where you make me pass out and bring me back to life. Just like…" I grab his hand and hold it to my neck. His fingers curl around my flesh gently as he embraces me. "Just like…a claiming."

He bites his lip and eyes me sensually. "What do you like about it?"

I shiver at his wicked tone. "Just the idea of a man's masculine hand wrapped around the most tender part of a woman's body. A neckline is very elegant, don't you think?"

He releases my neck and nuzzles into me, sniffing deeply before pulling back and replying reverently, "Fuck yes."

I smile, pleased at his reaction to my freaky side. "So the thought of you gripping it fiercely and trusting you'll protect me…" I wet my lips and shudder. "It's hot."

His eyes heat with desire as he watches me for a moment, so I nudge him in the abs. "Now, come on, tell me yours, Mr. Eye Contact."

He sighs dramatically and turns to face forward, slumping in the couch as he rubs his hand over his head. "Jessica never looked at me during sex."

My brow furrows. "What?"

He looks defeated as he lays his head back on the couch and stares up at the ceiling. "Jess never made eye contact with me all the times we were intimate. It should have been a sign."

"A sign that she was a lesbian?" I ask, filling in the blanks.

He shrugs. "Yeah."

I take a moment to absorb that train of thought. Could there be any truth to it? I guess only Jessica would know that. My voice is thoughtful when I inquire, "So now you think any woman who doesn't gaze into your stunning indigo eyes as you rock her fucking world could possibly be into women?"

"My eyes are blue," he replies, avoiding the question.

"They are a lot more than blue, Max," I respond seriously, and he turns to look at me with a vulnerability in his gaze that I've never seen before. I reach out and slide my fingertip over his furrowed brow line, and his eyes flutter closed as I skate my touch over his eyelids. "It depends on what you're wearing, but sometimes they look dark purple…like when you're by the pool. Everly's manage to look bluer in the water, but yours pull something else. And I swear when you're aroused…they darken to damn near navy."

When he opens his eyes to look at me again, the roaring fire in the depths of them has my stomach doing an entire gymnastics routine.

My breath catches in my chest, and an idea comes to mind. "I want to try something," I state, un-threading the sash on my robe while feeling his gaze on me. Swallowing the nervous knot in my throat, I tie the robe tie around my eyes.

"What are you doing?" His voice is a deep, husky rasp.

"Give me your hand," I command, and when I feel his large warm palm against mine, I scooch down in my seat and lay my head on the back of the sofa.

Guiding him between my legs, I press his fingers against my center. A strangled grunt emits from him as he pushes one finger inside me.

"What do you feel?" I ask, my pelvis thrusting up to meet his finger as he pulls it out and swirls it around my clit.

"You're wet as always."

I smile knowingly. "I don't have to look at you to know it's you causing my body to react like this."

He thrusts a second finger inside me, and I cry out at the invasion. I'm tender down there from our couch fuck, but the pain is delicious in some ways. Like scratching a bug bite you know you shouldn't scratch.

"Just feeling your body heat, Max, and smelling that crazy hot cologne you wear is all I need to—"

Max has taken over now, his fingers thrusting quickly inside me as he shifts off the couch to the space between my legs. He pulls his fingers out to put my legs on his shoulders, and I cry out again when his whiskers brush against my inner thigh.

"Max!" I exclaim when his tongue swirls along my bundle of nerves, his hot breath blowing against my damp thighs. He teases me mercilessly as my hands score through his hair and my hips pump up into his face, begging for more.

I struggle not to rip the robe sash off my eyes because I'm sure he looks incredibly sexy between my legs right now. But he needs to know that it's him turning me on whether I can look at him or not.

Max sucks hard and bites down lightly, and the sudden sharp strum causes a wave of pressure to explode between my thighs. I scream loudly, my legs squeezing around his head as my fingers pull on his hair, my climax taking over all my wits.

When I finally peel myself off the ceiling, I can hear Max chuckling from his position between my legs. Blindfold still intact, I slide off the sofa like jelly onto his lap before he pulls the blindfold off to see the blissed-out, drugged-out expression all over my face.

His lips glisten with my arousal as he murmurs sexily, "You missed a good show."

I smile dreamily. "I don't need to watch you to know that I want you, Max."

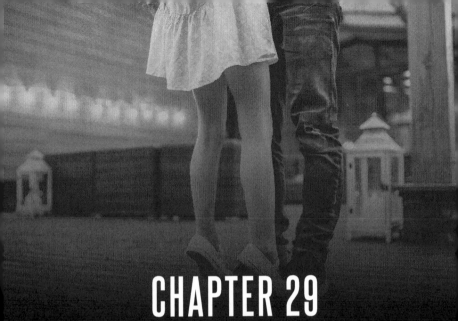

CHAPTER 29

Max

Well…*that escalated quickly,* I think to myself as I brush my teeth on Monday morning. I didn't fully expect to sleep with Cassandra again last night, but when she texted saying she had a leaky faucet and wondered if I could come take a look, I didn't question the matter.

Spoiler alert…her faucet was fine.

So was her shower, by the way. Props to me for springing for the rainfall showerhead in the tiny house. I was able to enjoy every bare inch of Cassandra's body and keep us both warm under the hot water at the same time.

Except for that one moment when a notification went off on my phone and I had to dart out of the shower to check it, only to see a text from my mother. I seriously need to change the notification sound on my security system to prevent that from happening again.

But regardless, I was glad she texted. Saturday night, it took every bit of my strength not to go knocking on her door again. I submerged myself with work, poring over documents I finally received from

All-Out and doing my best to stop myself from staring down at her place every time I looked out my bedroom window.

Jesus, I really am a stalker.

Cassandra didn't look like she was home, which is probably why I was so fixated. She told me in the shower that she spent Saturday night at her sister's house for dinner, and the level of relief I felt knowing she didn't go to a bar was a little alarming. I never really considered myself a jealous person. Yeah, I had issues watching Jessica move on with another woman, but I wasn't jealous. I was just adjusting to the idea that we wouldn't be a family anymore.

It was hard to watch the woman I was with all through college and had a child with right after we graduated turn into someone completely different. Yeah, she was still the woman I fell in love with, but it was impossible for me not to wonder if it was the real her that I loved…or the version of herself she thought society wanted her to be.

Those were the thoughts that consumed me after she sent me a bunch of articles about compulsory heterosexuality, which is something she identified with. It's the theory that heterosexuality is assumed and semi-enforced upon women by a patriarchal and heteronormative society. Basically, society only fed her straight culture, and until she was comfortable enough to go against the supposed "norm," she couldn't truly identify with her sexuality.

It all made sense to me, and frankly, opened my eyes up to ideas I had never considered. Not that my opinion on her sexuality really mattered. It was Jess's journey, and I was happy for her to finally speak her truth. I was even happy when she married Kailey only two years after we divorced. I attended the wedding.

But Jessica's coming out changed me as well. It made me more guarded and less of a believer in love. I stopped seeking out meaningful relationships and focused on being a dad and growing my company. Honestly, having split custody with Everly meant that I could obsess over my work when Everly wasn't with me. I hate to say my divorce helped my business flourish, but it did. If we had been a traditional happy family all living under one roof, I wouldn't have dedicated the time I did to my company to bring it to the next level.

It's wild how my ex-wife's sexuality changed the course of my entire future. Now I'm on the brink of leveling up my company once again, yet here I sit, brushing my teeth and thinking about the nanny.

I need to get this jealousy in check and keep my eye on the prize. Cassandra and I are just having fun. My priorities are still Everly and Fletcher Industries. I have no room in my life for anything else. The sooner I bang it out with Cassandra, the better.

I'm shocked when I come out of my bedroom to find Everly seated at the kitchen island with Cassandra. They both have halos of gold around them as the rising sun pours in through the windows. Cassandra is blowing on Everly's bowl of oatmeal, and the view of the two of them laughing together gives my heart a strange jolt of contentment.

"Morning, Dad!" Everly says when she sees me standing there, watching them like a freak. "I'm up early today."

"Yes, you are." I laugh and walk over to press a kiss on the top of her head. She smiles and nuzzles into me before my eyes find Cassandra's over top of Everly.

"Morning," she greets, and the flush in her cheeks causes my muscles to tighten.

"Good morning," I reply, a bit too crisply.

She looks amused as she walks over to the coffeemaker to pour herself a cup. I head over to the refrigerator to grab my protein shake, and when I turn around, I nearly barrel into her.

"Sorry!" she apologizes, holding her hands up and backing away.

"I'm sorry," I mumble and then quickly turn back into the fridge. "Here."

I thrust her coffee creamer into her hands, and her fingers brush mine as she takes it from me, causing the silvery feeling to sizzle up my arm. She murmurs, "Thanks," and bites her lip nervously.

I would like to bite that fucking lip.

Clearing my throat, I bring my protein shake over to the island across from my daughter who I really should be focusing on right now. "What are your plans today?" I ask because it's a reflex and maybe slightly because it gets a rise out of the nanny every time I ask it.

"Zero plans, Dad." Everly rolls her eyes and glances at Cassandra like they're sharing an inside joke about me.

"Not getting bored?" I tilt my head and eye my daughter.

Everly's brows furrow. "Um…obviously not. Plus, it's book club week, so Cozy and me have a shar-kootey board to shop for. She's the cool nanny at my club."

"Is she?" I turn my eyes to Cassandra, who looks decidedly embarrassed. "Why is that exactly? I mean, other than the obvious?"

"Because she brings the best snacks," Everly answers and scoops up a big bite of oatmeal. "You should have seen the kids eating the last board we brought. They were savages!"

I laugh and take a sip of my drink. "Well, I don't want to get in the way. I'll see you later, kid."

I walk around the kitchen island to give Everly a kiss on the temple, and when I turn to walk out, the back of my hand brushes the back of Cassandra's. The urge I have to grip her wrist and plant a goodbye kiss on her lips is a troubling thought that consumes me at the office all day.

CHAPTER 30

Cozy

"These are going to look so cool, Dakota!" Everly peals as she bags up a soaked and freshly dyed T-shirt into a gallon ziplock baggie. "Thank you for helping me make these for my friends!"

Dakota smiles and zips the baggie closed. "My pleasure, Everly. The Book Sitters Club is a sweet book club name. It belongs on matching T-shirts."

I smile from the front desk of Dakota's graphic tee shop as Everly starts on the second T-shirt. "Only thirteen more to go." I scrunch my nose up, knowing Everly has her work cut out for her.

"I'm good…I got this!" Everly says, turning another squirt bottle of dye upside down to douse the next tee.

"I'll go grab the other dye bottles in case you run out," Dakota tells her, pulling her gloves off and making her way to the back of the store.

My phone pings with a notification, so I pull it out and see a message from Max.

Max: New rule. You can no longer step foot in my kitchen

Max: You need to stay on the other side of the kitchen island in the mornings.

Me: How am I supposed to make my coffee?

Max: Make it after I leave or wait until I make it for you. I can't keep bumping into you in the dark kitchen with your sexy sleepy eyes every morning. It's becoming a problem.

Me: That is such a caveman thing to say.

Max: I've been driving to the office hard every day this week. The new rule stands.

Me: Well then, I get a new rule too.

Max: Hit me.

Me: You need to have your tie tied before you come out of your bedroom.

Max: Seriously?

Me: Yes. I'm two seconds away from grabbing onto it and dragging you into me.

Max: That sounds like a "you" problem.

Me: Tie your tie, and no one gets hurt.

Max: Fine. I'll have Marcia fax you the updated list of rules.

Me: Nobody faxes anymore, Zaddy.

I'm smiling like a loon when I look up to see Dakota propped on the counter directly across from me, eyeing me with a knowing smirk. I glance past her to see that Everly is humming to herself as she continues her tie-dye work. I snap a quick pic.

"Have something you'd like to share with the class?" I state coyly before shooting the picture off to Max.

Dakota's voice is low enough Everly can't hear when she says,

"What could I possibly have to say about my best friend bagging a Zaddy?"

I giggle and shake my head, instantly picturing Max when he said Zaddy back to me. God, I love that he wasn't too cool to say it. "Wonders never cease."

"Oh, I didn't wonder," she corrects. "I knew the minute I picked you up at his house that this wouldn't be a clean summer."

"How did you know?"

She sighs. "I'm a Zaddy whisperer."

"Shut up." I bark out a laugh and then lower my voice so Everly can't overhear. "Seriously, this week…he's come over like five times."

Dakota's eyes widen. "That's a lot of *coming*."

"Shhh." I press my finger to my lips and feel my cheeks burning. "I didn't expect it to feel so…natural."

"Yeah?"

"Yeah, he's…" I close my eyes and shake my head. "So good."

"Details, whore." Dakota eyes me like a seagull on a beach looking for food.

"Not now." I glance over at Everly whose tongue is sticking out of her mouth as she struggles to seal the ziplock bag. "Drinks this weekend maybe?"

"It's a date."

I nod, pleased that we've made plans. "I need to act like I still have a life outside of him. I don't want to freak him out like I'm catching feelings."

"Are you?"

"No," I reply quickly. "I mean, I like him, but he keeps mentioning this big corporate merger coming up in a couple of months, and I seriously try to tune him out every time he talks about it just so I don't have a panic attack. But it sounds like his business is going to be giant after that, which isn't my gig. I know that corporate grind world, and I want nothing to do with it."

Dakota nods thoughtfully for a moment before asking, "Have you given any more thought to Kate's business proposition?"

I exhale heavily. "I'm sure I should say yes, but I'd need to figure out where I'm living after this summer before I can fully commit. I have to make these penis-shaped boards somewhere."

Dakota laughs. "I freaking love this idea. I don't even read her books, but I want one of these book boxes. I mean...a cocktuterie board with a dirty novel? How fun is that?"

Very fun. And I can think of the perfect cock model for a sample board.

I shake away that dirty thought and add, "Well, I'm glad you're into it because I gave her your number to talk about T-shirts."

"Seriously?" Dakota peals excitedly.

I nod, and she reaches out to give me a high five. "Hells yes! Look at us...a couple of independent business owners fucking the patriarchy one graphic tee and wang board at a time."

"What are you guys talking about?" Everly calls over her shoulder to us.

"Fucking the patriarchy!" Dakota replies with a cheer and then looks back at me. "P.S. I want a kid I can swear in front of and have her be behaved enough to know not to repeat it. That's like...the cutest party trick ever."

I prop my head on my hand and smile proudly at my charge. "Yeah...she's pretty awesome."

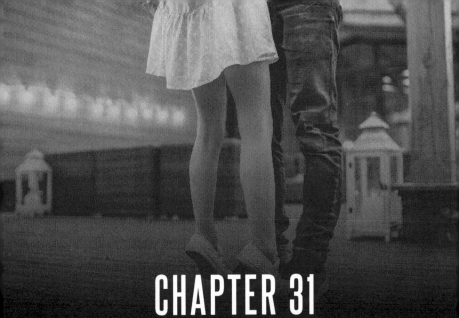

CHAPTER 31

Max

"Max, hey...I'm glad I caught you." Jessica's voice fills my SUV through the Bluetooth connection as I drive home on Friday. "Is now an okay time to talk?"

"Yes, I'm on my way home, so I'm free."

There's a slight pause. "Isn't it only five o'clock there?"

"Yes," I reply, glancing at the clock. "What time is it in Bulgaria? It's got to be late."

"Early actually. We've been shooting nights this week. I have to set an alarm to wake up for my daily phone calls with Everly."

"Yikes, sounds tiring."

"It is, but I'm still trying to wrap my brain around you going home at five on a Friday. You never picked up Everly before six o'clock."

I frown at the subtext to that text. "I was never late, though."

"No, you certainly weren't." She clears her throat, and I hate that even after a decade, I know Jessica's judgmental voice. "Anyway, I just wanted to tell you that I think that nanny you found is incredible. I finally got to talk to her for a bit yesterday, and she is lovely."

My eyes widen at her remark. Not that I don't think it's true, but I'm just shocked to hear Jessica say it. Jessica and Cassandra couldn't be more opposite. Where Cassandra is relaxed and go with the flow, Jess is organized and scheduled. Jessica probably would have had a stroke if she'd been at that interview with Everly and me. This is definitely unexpected.

"And it got me thinking..." Jess continues. "Maybe Everly doesn't need to be doing all the activities we have her in. I don't know if it's because I see her through a video phone screen every day, and it's giving me a bird's-eye perspective, but I swear I'm seeing a transformation in Everly these past few weeks. That anxiety she used to have is practically gone."

"Well, she had that one bad day," I offer, my brow furrowed as I recall Everly's tear-soaked cheeks when I walked in the door with all the ice cream.

"Yeah...I meant to call and talk to you about that. I think that was my fault. I started talking to Everly about gymnastics because they want us to sign up soon, and she sort of flipped out on me. I tried to calm her down, but she was definitely triggered."

My jaw clenches at the irritation over not knowing that that was what caused Everly's bad day. "You should have told me, Jess."

"I know, Max. I'm sorry. I've been a little busy over here."

I roll my eyes and bite my tongue because what does she think it's like back here? Knowing that's not a conversation I need to have with her, I ask, "So what are you thinking then?"

"I'm thinking we take a page out of Cozy's book and let Everly tell us what she wants to do when the school year starts up. We've raised a good kid. Maybe it's time to let her show us how she wants to live her life."

"I think that sounds like a great plan," I reply instantly, grateful that after a decade of co-parenting, Jessica and I are still mostly on the same page when it comes to Everly.

However, I don't think I ever would have predicted both of our points of view to align with a nanny who said, *Why do more when you can do less?* But this feels right for Everly.

Jess and I end the call on a positive note, and it's just after five by the time I walk into the kitchen. I instantly feel lighter as the scent and comfort of home invade all my senses. I search for my kid and spot both her and Cassandra outside on a blanket.

They're lying on their tummies with their feet pointing at the sky and making what looks to be some friendship bracelets. My chest expands at the picture-perfect moment. Seeing those two has become a familiar sight for me the past five weeks. One I will miss when the summer ends.

I drape my jacket over a barstool before opening the slider to the deck. Everly's head pops up when she hears my footsteps.

"Dad!" She rushes up the deck steps and barrels into my stomach, wrapping her hands around my hips. "Can I please, please, please, *pleeease* have Claire come for a sleepover tonight?"

"Claire?" I ask, frowning over at Cassandra. "Lynsey's niece?"

"Yes!" Everly exclaims. "We were chatting on kids messenger, and I think it would be so much fun to have her here. Can I please?"

She holds her hands up in prayer and gives me those puppy dog eyes that I can never say no to. "Sure, it's fine by me."

"Yes!" She thrusts her fists up into the air. "Okay, second question…"

"Oh, God," I groan and begin to undo my tie, knowing the next request is going to be the tough one. Everly always buries the lead.

"Can we do the sleepover in the tiny house? Cozy said she didn't mind. And I love sleeping in the loft. It feels like camping."

"Spoken like someone who's never camped," I retort, shaking my head adamantly. "That is Cassandra's home. You cannot use it like it's a playhouse."

"But she said she didn't mind!" Everly whines and looks backward. "Right, Cozy?"

Cassandra shoots me a guilty look as she slides her hands into her pockets. "I really don't mind. I washed the sheets today and everything but it's obviously your call."

"Please, Dad?" Everly whines again, tugging on the tails of my tie.

I sigh heavily and look at Cassandra. "Are you completely sure? This is one request I have no problem saying no to."

"It's fine." Cassandra waves her off. "I'll go stay at my sister's or Dakota's."

My brow furrows at that reply before Everly says, "Or you can sleep in my bed!"

Or she could sleep in my bed, I growl inwardly like a fucking psychopathic papa bear. I clear my throat and shake that thought away. "We'll figure out the sleeping arrangements for everybody later. Let's call Claire's parents first, okay?"

Everly whoops with joy, and I do my best not to think too much about my decision to break my rule about no sleepovers with women in my house.

Cozy

"Claire will be here within the hour," Max calls up the spiral staircase to Everly, who squeals with delight.

"I'm packing my overnight bag for the tiny house," she yells down. "This sleepover is going to be GOAT!"

Max turns his sexy, confused face to me.

"Greatest of all time," I translate with a laugh because he doesn't remember from the last time we explained it to him. He's such a cute grump sometimes.

"I'm going to cancel Michael tonight and just order pizza," Max grumbles, pulling his phone out to text his chef. He looks stressed. An eleven-year-old having a friend sleepover has ruffled him. It's adorable.

"Ask him if he has any cookie dough first," I offer helpfully. "The girls could make the cookies without the mess of making the dough."

Max wags his finger at me. "Genius."

"This is why you pay me the big bucks." I laugh and then cringe because the fact that Max is still putting deposits into my checking account every week feels kind of weird now that we're sleeping together.

"That and because you keep my kid alive," he responds like he's reading my mind.

After a moment, he sets his phone down and looks around. "Pizza and cookie dough ordered. What else do I need to do for this?"

"Everly's really never had a sleepover here before?" I ask, thinking about how I unintentionally planted this seed in her head when I told her a story about Dakota and me having a sleepover in a graveyard once. Not one of my finest nanny moments, but Max doesn't need to hear about that.

He shakes his head and leans down on the counter, giving me an eye-level view of his devastatingly handsome face. It's inhuman. He should be studied in a museum.

"I've always been very possessive of my time with Everly. Getting her a few times a month feels like nothing in the grand scheme of things, so the last thing I would want to do is share her with her friends."

I nod slowly. "I guess I can understand that."

Max gets a pensive look in his eye. "Though I'm starting to realize that giving her a bit of freedom is nice too. It's been good seeing her relax this summer and just do normal kid stuff. Jess even called me today to tell me that she thinks Everly is really happy. She said it's thanks to you."

My head jerks back at that shocking remark that just tumbled out of Max's lips out of nowhere. It's like he's talking about the weather and not telling me that I not only made his kid happy but earned the approval of his ex. I don't know why it feels important for Jess to like me exactly, but it does.

"Jessica said that?" I croak, my eyes stinging around the edges.

"Yes, she did." Max hits me with a meaningful look. "And she's right. I see it too."

And the hits just keep on coming.

"You do?" My traitorous eyes glaze over with tears.

"Yes, Cassandra." Max's brow furrows as his eyes do that crazy darkening thing again. "You're incredible with Everly. You're incredible with everyone. You have this strange way of just allowing people to be themselves. It's very...irritating."

He winks playfully, and I garble out a laugh, grateful for the light jab at the end. This moment was getting too heavy, and I'm not about to start blubbering at Max's fancy kitchen island.

I swallow down my emotions and embrace that sexy look in his eye with my own flirtatious response. "Sometimes less is more. Maybe you should embrace the slow livin' lifestyle too?"

"There are some things I like to take my time with," Max murmurs a sexy noise as his eyes drop to my lips. I inhale a deep breath because I've seen that look before. I make that look at him when he does what he's doing right now and breaks one of the rules by wearing his tie loose around his neck. It's ungodly sexy.

"She's here!" Everly peals from somewhere upstairs, causing Max and me to rip apart like someone threw firecrackers between us. She clunks down the spiral staircase, her bag whacking the metal spindles every step she takes. She smiles brightly at her dad and me. "She's here, you guys!"

"Go out and greet her," I reply with a laugh.

She drops her bag with a loud thud and turns on her heel to run out the front door. I wave a hand over my face, my cheeks feeling like they're on fire as I turn on my heel to face Max.

I hook a thumb toward the slider. "I'm going to go out and pack a bag of my own, and then I'll get out of here," I say, realizing that I've been lingering in Max's kitchen for far longer than I normally do after he gets home at night.

"What are you talking about?" Max's brow furrows as he walks around the island to stand in front of me.

"I'm going to leave," I explain, staring up at him as he bows over me, exuding all his masculine energy that I want to make a blanket out of. "I don't mind going to my sister's. My brother-in-law totally misses me."

"Cassandra," Max snaps as he reaches up to cup my chin. His face is deathly serious when he adds one of the sexiest four-letter words I never thought of. "Stay."

Tingles erupt over my entire body at the *"I dare you to move"* expression on his face. My voice is weak when I rasp, "But...our rules."

"Fuck the rules," he murmurs, his voice guttural as he brushes his thumb over my lower lip, causing my entire body to sway. "Stay the night."

My chest inflates with anxiety, desire, nerves, and a million other emotions that I can't put a name to because Max is looking at me like he's seen me naked…because he has.

"Are you sure Everly won't think it's weird?" My eyes dart to the door as I hear voices outside.

"You can stay in her bed," Max replies with a heated look in his eyes as he releases my chin. "After you stay in mine."

The boyish wink he shoots me before casually walking outside to greet Claire at the door is literally panty-melting.

My panties…are gone.

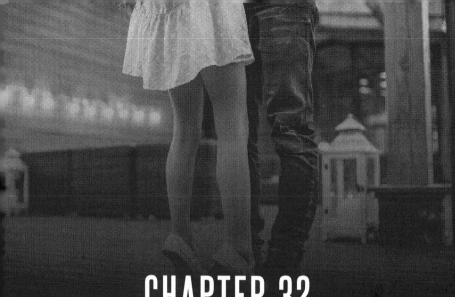

CHAPTER 32

Max

"This feels weird," Cassandra squeals from her spot on the sofa in my living room. She's curled up under a blanket, her dark hair in a tiny bun, and she looks as good as ever in her loungewear as she does in her going out wear.

"Why weird?" I ask, walking over to refill her wineglass with more red. I set it down on the end table beside her, deliberately brushing my body along hers as I reach for my glass of whiskey.

"Because I'm in the Fletchpad," she exclaims dramatically before taking a sip of her wine.

"Would you stop saying Fletchpad?" I laugh, flopping down next to her anxiously curled-up body. "It sounds like a fucking frat house. I prefer to block out my college years, thank you very much."

Her cheeks flush as she stares hungrily at me. "If this was a frat house, I would totally let you do me on your loft."

My brows lift with interest at that very pleasant mental image she's just summoned. I drape my arm over the back of the sofa and

"I am," she responds, her green eyes wide and wary. "Your daughter is right outside."

She points toward the tiny house, and I look over my shoulder to see the reading lamp in the loft area glowing in the window. I got them settled for bed with a movie on Everly's iPad an hour ago, and they both looked exhausted when I just checked on them. "I'm telling you...they're seconds away from passing out."

Cassandra shakes her head and takes a large drink of her wine. "But it feels like that's Mom and Dad out there, and I'm in here making out with my boyfriend and could be caught at any moment."

"Boyfriend?" I can't help the smirk that lifts the side of my face. Why am I smirking at the boyfriend label?

She rolls her eyes and pokes me in the chest. "You know what I mean."

I lick my lips and lean in close. "I might need a demonstration about the making-out part."

"No freaking way!" She pushes me back with her foot in a really inelegant way that only Cassandra could make look cute. "I'm not letting your kid catch us being inappropriate on the couch. Everly and I do a lot of artful sitting here. We will not defile this sacred space with your wicked Zaddy ideas."

My brows lift at that accusation. "First of all, you brought up the making-out thing, so that's your wicked idea. Second of all, I have the security cameras all on, so as soon as they hit the pool deck, my phone will ping."

She chews on her thumb nervously. "Are you sure?"

"Put that wine down and get the fuck over here, Cozy," I demand. Apparently, all she needed was a command to finally get with the program.

She sets her wine down and leans over to kiss me. It's not nearly enough, so I reach under her arms and pull her over to straddle my lap. My cock grows as her soft breasts press against my chest. She thrusts her hips over my groin, and I growl into her lips.

"Fuck, I love your body," I grunt, grabbing her ass harshly in my hands and thrusting upward.

"You do?" she gasps as she grinds over my lap.

"Fuck yes." I reach up and unzip her hoodie, revealing her sports bra-covered breasts smashed together like art. "And if it wasn't totally fucking weird, I would pepper your tits with hickeys right now."

"Please don't." She sighs, combing her fingers through my hair and gripping it to yank my face back. "I have to wear swimsuits around your kid."

"Lucky kid." I smirk before leaning in to slide my tongue up her neck, inhaling her intoxicating scent. "Fine, no more hickeys."

My hand glides up her chest to her neck as I hold her in place to kiss her lips. I've learned quickly what she likes about this. It's the moment of control, that moment when she gasps out the release of power and gives it to me to control her.

It's fucking hot.

It's too hot.

I need to get her off this fucking couch. *Now.*

"We have to get out of here." I shift so she's off my lap, my cock feeling like it's going to rip through my jeans any second.

She sits on the couch, looking like a sack of tossed potatoes, so I reach my hand out to her to help her up. As soon as she's standing, I bend over and press my shoulder into her torso before standing back up.

She cries out loudly. "You did not just throw me over your shoulder! Put me down!"

"I told you not to challenge me, sweet cheeks." I give her ass a hearty smack and squeeze as I walk through the kitchen and into my bedroom.

Kicking the door closed behind me, I toss her onto the bed and relish the view of her in my space. I don't fucking hate it. In fact, I kind of like it. And I especially like that I didn't have to climb a ladder to get her horizontal.

She looks dazed as her eyes adjust to the dim lamps glowing on the bedside tables. I pull my shirt off over my head when a horrible thought occurs to me.

"Fuck…I'm out of condoms."

"What?" she chirps, propping herself up on her elbows.

I shake my head, irritated by myself. "I was going to stop for them on the way home, and Jess called, and I got distracted."

"Oh," Cassandra responds with a heavy sigh, her eyes glancing down to my cock bulging in my jeans. The sex eyes she's giving me are not helpful.

I sigh and run my hands through my hair, aching to be inside her and cursing myself for being such a fucking moron. I look down at her with a pleading look. "If you stay here for the girls, I'll go run to the store." I adjust myself, willing my erection to go down so I can be seen in public.

Cassandra's voice interrupts my efforts as she softly says, "I'm on the pill."

My cock roars back to life as my gaze snaps to her. "You'd be okay going without?"

"When's the last time you were tested?" She eyes me thoughtfully.

I have to shake the thought of going bare out of my head to think seriously. "Probably at my physical like six months ago."

"Have you slept with anyone between now and then?"

"No," I reply instantly. "But I also have never gone without a condom before." And it's true. Everly was conceived from a broken condom, and even after she was born, my ex was insistent on me wearing one while she went on birth control.

Her lips part as she adds, "I haven't either."

My mind rumbles with this possibility as I sit down on the bed beside her. We need to be responsible about this. Cover all our bases. "When was your last partner?"

She laughs and flops back to cover her face with her hands.

"Hey," I tut, leaning down next to her to pull her arms down. "Eyes on me, remember?"

She bites her lip nervously, her emerald eyes vulnerable when they find mine. "Like a year, probably."

"Jesus."

"Yeah." She inhales deeply. "There was this guy from my job in Denver, but it was a long time ago now."

"Denver?" I can't help but ask, bracing myself for her to shut me down like she always does when I ask about her past.

She smiles and strokes my eyebrow. "My old corporate job."

My head jerks. "You had a job in corporate?"

"Yes." She frowns, and her eyes turn pensive. "But I really don't like to talk about it."

"Why not?" I inquire, splaying my hand over her waist, patiently waiting for whatever morsel of her past she's willing to offer me.

She gets a sad look in her eyes and turns to stare up at the ceiling. "Because I didn't leave on good terms, and it's why I moved back home to Boulder."

My mind whirls with these new puzzle pieces clicking into place. She had a job in corporate that she left on bad terms. What the hell happened? I can't imagine Cassandra quitting any job unprofessionally. The few times we've discussed her performance here, she always seems oddly professional, despite her willy-nilly outlook on life.

A lot of things are making so much more sense now.

"I needed a big change," she adds, turning back to face me. "A re-set."

"Like a nannying job," I offer, staring down at her thoughtfully. Her life philosophy, her casual laissez-faire attitude. Her intense commitment to making no plans. Her resistance to committing to the charcuterie business with Kate.

She's not lazy...she's recovering. From what exactly, I don't know. I open my mouth to ask her more questions, but she rolls toward me and places her hand on the ridge of my cock.

Her lips press against my chest as she murmurs, "Anyway...I'm clean. You're clean. Let's get back to banging it out."

She pushes me onto my back and crawls on top, giving me a perfect view of her as she peels off her hoodie and sports bra. Her breasts fall toward me, and I can't help but reach up and grope them, all thoughts of Cassandra and her past life vanishing in the presence of these sexy things in front of me.

I sit up and wrap my arms around her, sucking her nipple into my mouth as she combs her fingers through my hair.

Fuck, I love when she does that.

We ditch the rest of our clothes and slip under the covers before she returns to her position on top. She grips my bare shaft and holds me to her wet center.

I feel like I'm going to fucking blow it already.

"You sure?" I ask, staring up at the most beautiful woman I've ever seen.

Her answer is to slowly sink down on top of me, and the audible groan that erupts out of my mouth makes me really fucking glad my kid isn't in the house right now.

"Fuck, Cassandra, you feel so fucking good," I growl, my hands sliding up her legs and gripping her ass firmly as she stills on top of me.

"Oh, my God, Max," she moans out a high-pitched cry and throws her head back. Her hands are in her hair as she begins to move on top of me, riding my cock like a goddamn wet dream.

Her eyes aren't on me.

But her sweet, soaking wet pussy is on me as it grips my shaft with every grind of her hips. I force myself to ignore the fucked-up thoughts that invade my mind. Thoughts where I doubt she's into me or that I'm enough to satisfy her.

Cassandra wants me. Her body feels like it was made for me. Every curve, every dimple, every soft and firm part of her feels like it was made for my hands and my mouth. I crave her on a carnal level. And having her bare like this just further stokes my desire to devour her. This attraction isn't one-sided. She's here with me—no question.

She jerks forward as I grip her hips and thrust up into her, stroking her G-spot harder so we can come together. Her hands rest on my chest as her haunted eyes find mine. The erotic look of pure fucking euphoria on her face is enough to have me come apart.

I wrap a hand around her waist and hold her as I flip us over. She gasps when I grab her wrists and press them hard into the mattress above her head. I lower my lips to her neck and suck softly on her flesh, inhaling her scent as I chase her to the finish line.

Just as her center begins to grip me, she yanks her hands free and wraps them around my face. She pulls me away from her neck to look at her.

"Eyes on me," she rasps, and hearing my words echoed from her lips as her orgasm begins squeezing my cock has me joining her in unison while our gazes hold each other.

The connection I feel with her, the connection I see reflecting in her eyes as I fill her with my release and no barrier between us… is unlike anything I've ever experienced before.

CHAPTER 33

Cozy

Max's head rests on my belly as I play with the strands of his hair. He always gets this drugged look in his eyes when I mess with it. I fear I may be slightly addicted to that face.

We're spread out naked on his bed, blankets and sheets strewn all over. I can't help but smile when I realize that this is the most comfortable I've ever felt with a man physically. Which is an odd thing to realize with someone you're just "banging it out" with.

With past men, I had to remind myself to be confident because I knew that was what men liked. But with Max, it has come naturally. Maybe because I was too shocked when it started to give myself time to be self-conscious. Or maybe it's the way he praises my body when we're intimate or how his eyes rove over me like he's committing every inch of me to memory the way I do to him.

It could be any one of those things.

"Can I ask you a personal question?" I ask, my head propped on his upholstered headboard as I look down at him.

"I'm going to need a sandwich before I can go again," he mu

"Not that." I tug his hair gently and look up around his bedroom. "Did you live here with Jessica before the divorce?"

Max's brow furrows as his glazed eyes turn to me. "No...why?"

I shrug. "Just curious."

He closes his eyes as he adds, "I've never brought a woman in this house before actually...ouch," he snaps, and I realize belatedly that I'm pulling his hair.

"Sorry!" I release his locks and stare down at him with my eyes bugging out of my head. "You've never brought a woman here?"

"No," Max says simply, moving off my stomach to rub his head. He lies on the pillow next to me, his bicep flexing as he props a hand behind his head. "I go to their place, or I get a hotel room."

I turn on my side and pull the sheet up over us so I can focus on this very shocking admission. "Even on the weeks when Everly is at her mom's?"

His perfect profile nods in confirmation.

"That's messed up, Max."

"Why?" he asks with a laugh, turning to look at me with that boyish grin that gives me butterflies.

"Because you're in your mid-thirties." I shake my head to refocus. "Why don't you bring women here?"

He licks his lips and looks around the room with a thoughtful expression. "Because I bought this home for Everly and me, and since I never date anyone seriously, why would I bring them into this world?"

I take a moment to consider this. He's shown over and over how much his daughter means to him. How he rearranges his life to make sure she knows he loves her. It's crazy to think he's never wanted a partner to be a part of all that.

"You've been divorced for years, though." I watch him carefully. "There's never been anyone special in all that time?"

"No," he replies simply as his chest rises and falls with a deep breath.

"Did you love Everly's mom?" I ask, wondering if he's still completely heartbroken over losing her.

His jaw muscle tics before he answers, "I thought I did at the time."

My brow furrows. "Then why wouldn't you want to find that again?"

He turns on his side to face me, and there's a distinct look of resignation on his face as he rests his hand on my hip. "I had trouble trusting women after Jess came out to me. I know it's her story and her truth, and I'm happy she's happy now. But things about our life together have this strange cloud over them after she told me the truth."

"Like what?" I chew my lip nervously as I clutch the edge of the sheet tightly in my hands.

His eyes are tight and pensive. "Honestly, every memory. Our entire relationship in college, the moment we found out she was pregnant. The day I proposed. It was at our college graduation. She was four months pregnant by then, but I'd planned to propose to her that day even before we found out about the baby."

My lips curve down into a sad smile. I can't really picture Max as a public display of affection sort of guy. He seems too buttoned up and focused to do anything in front of a bunch of people.

"We were both in our cap and gown. I thought it was so special. But now it's all clouded over along with our wedding day and even Everly's birth."

"In what way is it clouded?" I inquire, my stomach twisting into knots over him reliving some of the best moments of a family's life and not seeing any of the joy in it.

"It's clouded because I was so fucking happy and in love, and I thought I had a partner who was sharing in all that with me, but I didn't. In fact, Jessica was in hell fighting against her true self with me and faking every moment we spent together. Is it *really* love if someone didn't ever fully love you back?"

My breath catches in my throat at hearing the pain in his voice as he confesses the true depth of what their relationship was. He was living his dream with the woman he loved, and he believed she was putting on a show for him. What an awful feeling.

My chin trembles at that image. "Is that really how she felt?

Have you asked her that?" I can't cover up the emotion that cracks through my voice as I reach for his hand gripping my hip.

"We've discussed a lot of things. And I've even spoken to a therapist." He exhales heavily, his eyes haunted as he turns away from me to stare up at the ceiling. "And that's the fucked-up part. I've read lots of books and broadened my sights, so I *know* that what Jess dealt with is far bigger than what I had to deal with. But that doesn't change the fact that what I thought were the best years of my life were all a lie. That's why I don't do relationships. I don't want to put myself in the position to be blindsided again. I was in love with someone only to find out they weren't in love with me that whole time—at least not in a meaningful, all-consuming kind of way. It gives a guy a healthy dose of inferiority complex."

I inhale sharply at that label. How the hell could Max Fletcher, this beautiful specimen of a man in front of me, ever suffer from an inferiority complex?

"That complex is why I focused so intently on growing my business when I was younger. At least there's no heartbreak in business. The risks are purely financial, which I can stomach a lot easier than emotional. Especially when I already have something in my life that fulfills me in all the emotional ways I never imagined."

"Everly," I finish his thought, a knot forming in my throat over the image of this strong, virile man who has the success anyone would ever dream of, but in reality, he's broken on a fundamental level, only allowing the love of his daughter into his life as a form of protection.

"She's my world." Max's voice cracks at the end, and I think my heart stops at the pain in his eyes. He clears his throat and adds, "She chases all my clouds away. What more do I need in life?"

CHAPTER 34

Cozy

The faint sound of birds chirping rouse me from the hardest I've slept in months. My eyes pry open as sunlight pours in through the parted blinds in Max's bedroom. I come to, my brow furrowed as I realize I spent the night here last night.

"Shit," I whisper to myself and look down to find Max's arm banded firmly around me. His hot body is pressed up behind me, and the steady rise and fall of his chest indicates he's still asleep.

Jesus…apparently epic sex and a big heart-to-heart knocked us both out. I had every intention of going up to the guest bedroom. But Max's warm chest felt so good under my cheek. And the way he played with my hair after I slung all those heavy questions at him made it impossible for me to leave.

God, this man has such power over me. I don't even know how to understand it. The realization that he's not just an uptight boss makes him so much hotter than he was twenty-four hours ago. Is it the broken man thing that's turning me on? I don't need a broken man. I'm broken enough my damn self.

Plus, I'm not sure Max is truly broken. He's more just stubborn. He's choosing to live a certain way because he thinks that's all he will need in life. But Everly will reach an age when she doesn't need him as much anymore, and he'll want someone to share that vacancy in his life with.

He shifts behind me, and a soft gasp escapes my lips when I feel his rock-hard erection digging into my back. Like seriously, how do men sleep through this level of a boner? Surely, it's painful.

Glancing at the clock, I see it's still barely six, so we should have plenty of time to fool around before the girls wake up.

I slip my hand under the blanket and reach behind me. He stirs when my fingers wrap around his long shaft. His groin mindlessly rocks into my ass as he squeezes me tighter around the waist. His strong arm banded around my waist is fucking delightful, but I will not be distracted.

I turn over and slide myself under the covers to give Max a wake-up call he certainly earned after last night.

"Fuck." His harsh morning voice croaks when I pull him into my mouth, tasting the salty pre-come and moaning around his silky hard flesh.

"Cassandra," he groans my name as I fist his base and slide my lips over his cock, feeling electrified every time his hips jerk. "God, Cassandra."

The sound of my name on his lips warms the blood in my veins. Before I came into this house, I never liked my first name. It always felt like it was meant for someone more elegant and mature than me.

But when Max says it like he just did, *God, do I become a Cassandra.*

I pull him into the back of my throat and hear a faint notification buzz on his phone. I pause my best work to listen and gasp literally around Max's dick when I hear Everly's faint voice chirp, "Let's go see what my dad will make us for breakfast!"

"Is that the camera? Is Everly coming inside?" The pitter-patter of rapid footsteps in the house has me flinging back the blanket. "Did you lock the door?" I whisper-shout, my entire body tense with terror.

Max's half hooded eyes pop open. "Shit."

Hide...I need to hide!

The two pairs of feet close in on us at rapid speed as I throw

myself off the far side of the bed, my kneecap making a really horrifying thump as it smashes into the hardwood floor along with the
duvet that I took with me. Max scrambles for the sheet to cover himself as I bite my lip and grab my knee, screaming in silent agony. Are
his floors really just wood? It felt like concrete or boulders! Or perhaps a bed of nails!

"Daddy, Claire and I are hungry," Everly's voice says as she enters
the room sounding like she's been up for hours. "We want pancakes."

"Pancakes?" Max repeats, sounding far calmer than he deserves,
considering his cock is probably still covered in my saliva. He coughs
loudly, and I hear the rustling of sheets. "I can probably manage
pancakes."

"Where's your dad's shirt?" Claire giggles, and my eyes widen.

"My dad never wears a shirt to bed," Everly answers with a click
of her tongue. "Does your dad wear a shirt?"

"Yes, but my dad's belly doesn't look like your dad's belly. It's
hairy."

"Ew!" Everly peals.

"Okay, how about the two of you give me some privacy, and I'll
be right out to help you." Max has his dad voice on. Good move.

"Let's go wake up Cozy next!" Everly cries excitedly.

"Um…" Max blurts out a noise that barely sounds human. "She
um…went for a run."

Fuck, Max! Everly is going to see right through that!

"Cozy doesn't run," Everly states knowingly. *I'm equal parts
touched and annoyed that she knows me so well.*

"She, um…went for a breakfast run, I mean." *Nice save, Max.* "I'll
call her to see if she can pick us up some pancakes."

The two girls cheer, and I hear their feet thump loudly as they
take off, leaving the door wide open. *Bless their little hearts.*

Max wraps the sheet around his waist and pads barefoot over
to the door, and I hear the merciful click of a lock before I emerge
from my duvet nest of anguish. I flop my hands on the side of the
bed and blow a chunk of hair out of my face. "We might need Dr.
Josh to make a house call."

Max

Cassandra is icing her knee at the breakfast table while Everly and Claire hit her with a million questions about how she hurt herself on her breakfast "run."

"So there was a bird?" Everly asks again.

"Yes."

"And a dog?" Claire chimes in next.

Cassandra nods gravely. "Yes."

"And they ran into each other before they ran into you?" Everly looks dubious. I can't blame her. I think there was a wizard in the story at one point, but Cassandra realized her error in judgment and changed wizard to whizzing. It got really messy after that.

"Are you sure the dog didn't attack the bird?" Claire inquires, licking syrup off her fingers. "My dog loves to chase birds. One time he killed one. Ripped its head right off and dropped it on my mom's good rug."

"You have a dog?" Everly gasps, and I feel mildly concerned that she just skipped over the head ripping part of the story. "My grand-parents have a dog."

"Yes, his name is Rufus. He eats his own poop."

"Ew!" They giggle together and begin talking about dogs and poop, giving Cassandra a much-needed reprieve from her epic tale of wizards, birds, and dogs.

I mouth a quick, "I'm sorry," to her for the tenth time. I cannot believe I didn't lock the door. It didn't even occur to me last night. I suppose because it's never been something I had to get in the habit of doing.

And honestly, after unloading on her a decade's worth of baggage, I must have been too exhausted to even consider it. Jesus, that was a lot more than I intended to share with her. Hell, I think it was more than I said to my fucking therapist after a month's worth of sessions.

Cassandra has this way of disarming me a lot. I thought banging it out would help with that, but I fear it's just making it worse. She's getting under my skin, and I'm not sure what I think about that.

The girls put their plates in the sink and go outside to play, giving Cassandra and me some privacy at last. I walk over to her and set my phone down on the table beside her, so my hands are free to inspect her knee. I grab her by the ankle and sit down on the chair that her leg is propped up, placing her foot in my lap. Pulling the ice off, I wince when I see a decent bruise forming already.

"Yikes. That's going to leave a mark."

"At least this mark was self-inflicted," she murmurs, trying to look angry but failing miserably.

"You want me to call Josh?" I look up and watch her carefully.

"No," she replies with a laugh. "Farm girl, remember?"

"How could I forget?" My hand lingers on her leg, and I have to fight the urge to slide my palm up between her thighs. Her breath hitches, clearly picking up what I'm putting down, but our dirty thoughts are interrupted when my phone pings with a notification.

Cassandra grabs it and slides it over to me while glancing at the screen. "Who's Henley?"

A wave of adrenaline rushes through my body. "Fuck."

"What?" Cassandra asks, her eyes darting down to the phone with a frown.

I open the text and see a photo of Henley in a dress. The caption asks, *Will this do?*

I turn my phone over and run my hand through my hair, ruffling it on the top as I try to figure out what the fuck to do about this situation.

"Max, you're scaring me." Cassandra's voice is charged with anxiety.

I flatten my hand on the table. "There's nothing to be scared about...I just fucked up."

"Fucked up how?" she presses, pulling her leg off my lap as if sensing what's coming.

I can talk my way out of this. I can explain the situation and make her see reason. This doesn't have to be a thing.

Turning to face Cassandra, I spread my legs out to straddle hers as I hit her with a serious look. "I invited Henley to be my plus-one at this charity event in Denver happening in a couple of weeks. This was before you and I started…banging it out." That phrase suddenly feels painfully juvenile. "I'd completely forgotten about the event altogether, let alone the fact that I invited Henley."

Cassandra blinks back at me curiously. "Who is she?"

"She's…" *Shit, how do I say this?* "Someone I see in Aspen when I'm there."

"Like a fuck buddy?" Cassandra asks what I can't admit. I nod woodenly, and she huffs out a dry laugh. "For a guy who doesn't do relationships, that's scarily close to one."

"Cozy," I state.

"Don't Cozy me," she snaps petulantly. "Did you invite her after you kissed me?"

My brow furrows. "I might have."

She licks her lips and nods, her jaw taut with irritation. "It's fine… you two should go."

"I don't want to go." My tone is sharper than I intended, but I'm irritated by her cold, calculated stare. That's not how Cassandra is with me. Ever. "I'm on the board, so I have to go."

"Who's watching Everly?" She smiles at me, and it's so fucking fake, it makes me feel ill inside.

I sigh heavily. "She'll stay the night with my parents."

"Great," she replies crisply. "I can cover the rest of the time if you want to make a weekend out of it. It's no problem."

She moves to get up and stumbles, so I stand and brace my hands on her waist, feeling her body shudder at my touch. And not the good kind of shudder. "Cassandra, what are you doing?"

"Nothing, Max," she peals in a saccharinely sweet tone, squirming out of my embrace. "I'm just going home…er…back to the tiny house. I shouldn't be in here anymore anyway. It's the weekend."

My chest puffs out as I stare down at her. "Don't do that."

"I'm not doing anything." She laughs, hobbling away from me. "We banged it out, and we're good to get back to our lives. I'm going out with Dakota tonight anyway, so this works out just fine."

My hands turn to fists at my sides. "You're going out?"

"I made plans with her earlier this week." She shrugs dismissively.

My teeth crack inside my mouth. This is the first time that Cassandra acting her age has irritated me this much. Haven't we moved past that point by now? My voice is gravelly when I ask, "Seriously? That's how it's going to be?"

She stops at the sliding glass door and turns to look at me with an annoying shrug. "Max…we both knew what this was. I don't know why we're acting like this wasn't a part of the plan." She opens the door and heads outside, and for the first time, I don't stare at her ass as she walks away.

I stare at the floor.

Pissed the fuck off.

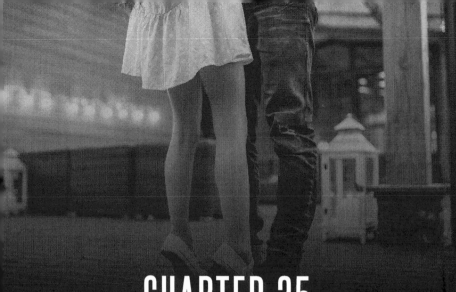

CHAPTER 35

Max

"Dad, what's the matter?" Everly says, flopping down on the sofa beside me. I shake my head and turn to look at my kid whose blue eyes are wide and worried about me.

It's Sunday night, and she's fresh out of the shower. Her blond hair is still damp and soaking the top of her summer vibes night shirt.

My daughter just caught me staring out the back slider like a stalker, looking for any sign of life from Cassandra instead of reading the damn book that's open in my hands. I've been unstealthily staring at her tiny house since she left yesterday and never returned.

Her lights are on, so she came home at some point this evening, but I don't know when. A part of me wants to march down there after Everly goes to bed and demand to talk about what happened yesterday. But another part of me, the louder part, has been trying to figure out what the hell to do about this situation.

The situation of not wanting to be done with whatever the hell it is we're doing with each other. We certainly aren't just banging it out anymore, that's for damn sure.

I steel myself to give my kid an easy smile that I know doesn't reach my eyes. "Nothing is wrong, kid. Why would you say that?"

Everly's head tilts as she watches me curiously. "Because you look sad."

"Why would I be sad?" I ask, my voice rising in pitch a bit too much.

"Because last night you didn't talk much at dinner, and you always talk a lot to me at dinner time."

My jaw clenches when I realize that I let my fight with Cassandra affect my time with Everly. This is exactly why I shouldn't do relationships. This shit right here. This should be all the sign I need to be done with all of that. Clean break. The end.

"I'm sorry, Everly," I reply, tucking a damp strand of hair behind her head. "I was distracted, but I won't let it happen again."

Everly's face looks bothered by my response instead of comforted. "Dad, you don't have to be perfect for me, you know."

"What are you talking about?" I inquire, frowning curiously at her.

"It's okay for you to be sad sometimes." She shrugs her tiny shoulders. "I get sad sometimes, and you still love me, right?"

"Of course I do," I answer instantly.

"So it's okay to be sad," she confirms. "Cozy says crying cleanses the soul. I think it would be good for you to cry."

My knee-jerk reaction is to ask her if Cassandra has been crying, but I pause that train of thought because my kid is talking about me. "Do you think my soul needs cleansing?" I ask, half horrified I repeated those crazy words, half desperate to know the answer from my eleven-year-old.

Everly looks down and murmurs, "Kind of."

"Why?" I lift her chin to see her face when she answers me.

"Because you're so lonely, Dad," she says, her voice soft and sensitive. "I think you've been so lonely for so long that you don't know how to be un-lonely anymore, and that's why you can't find a nice girl."

I laugh at her sweet concern. "What if you're the only nice girl I want to care about?"

"Dad." Everly sighs heavily and rests her head on the couch as she looks at me. "I don't want to be the only one to worry about you."

Fucking hell, my daughter just cut right through my heart. I stare back at her grave face and find her completely serious right now. "You worry about me?" I ask, bracing myself for the answer.

"I worry about you all the time," Everly replies simply. "I hate when I leave you to go to Mom's and have to leave you here all by yourself."

"Hey…you don't need to worry about me," I assure her and reach out to hold the back of her hand. "I'm a grown-up. I'm okay. Plus, I have friends. Your crazy uncles. Grandma and Grandpa."

"But you don't have a Kailey," Everly says, referring to Jessica's wife. "Or someone to give you a hug…like this."

Everly crawls over to me and wraps her bony arms around my neck and squeezes me. My body sags in her tiny frame as I wrap around her and press a hand onto her damp hair and inhale the scent of her shampoo. She used to smell like a baby. Now she smells like strawberries, and I hate it. I wish I could rewind time and make her a toddler again, not an almost teenager sitting on the couch having a mature conversation about emotions with her father.

Dammit, how did time fly by so quick?

She pulls away, and my eyes sting when I ask, "Why do you think I need someone to hug?"

She lifts her shoulders. "Hugging is probably better for the soul than crying. But I'd have to ask Cozy about that to be sure."

Her face is the picture of innocence as she looks up at me with those baby-blue eyes that aren't so babyish anymore. They hold empathy and intelligence in them. A maturity that I don't think I give her enough credit for.

I chuck her chin gently. "Is it so bad that I spent the past few years just focusing on hugging you? Our time together hasn't been so bad, has it?"

She sighs and leans her head on my arm. "No, but I'm getting older now, Dad. I don't need so many hugs."

"Don't say that," I croak, my voice catching in my throat as I wrap my arm around her and hug her to my chest. "Please, kid…

promise me you'll always need a hug from your dad. I'm not ready to be done with the hugging."

"Okay, okay," she squeals as I squeeze her a bit too tight and press a kiss into her damp hair. I relax my grip and let her breathe again just in time to say, "I still think now would be a perfect time for you to get a girlfriend."

"Why? You and Hilow want to double date?" I deadpan.

"Daaad," she groans with embarrassment, and I smile for the first time since Cassandra left my house yesterday morning.

"You know what's better than hugging?" I ask, moving up off the couch and dragging my daughter with me. "Dancing."

"Here?" She looks around, looking shy all of the sudden.

"Come on, I've seen you do it with Cassandra." I laugh and tell Alexa to play "My Girl by the Temptations". The punchy music wafts through the house sound system as I point to my feet. "Stand on my feet like you used to when you were little. That would make me really happy."

She rolls her eyes like I'm a big dork but does it anyways as I wrap one arm around her back and hold her hand out with the other. I move us around the living room, relishing in her giggles. This is time I need to cherish with my daughter who's growing up way too fast.

I don't know what I'm going to do about the nanny who has somehow managed to turn my world upside down. But I know I'm not going to sit here and be sad in front of my kid anymore.

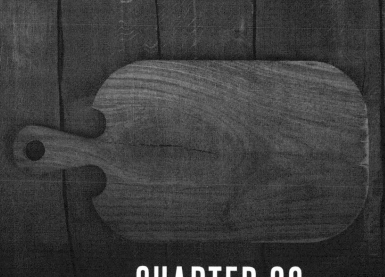

CHAPTER 36

Cozy

"Cozy, is it okay if we read for a bit before we swim?" Everly asks as I rub sunscreen on her back, careful to avoid her adorable little tankini with flowers all over it. "I want to get sweaty before I dive in."

"That sounds like a fabulous idea. Plus, your sunscreen needs to dry anyway," I reply, wiping my hands off on the towel before grabbing my Kindle out of my tote bag. It's another one of Everly's and my pool days, but this one is going to be a little different than all the others. "We have some time to relax before the guy gets here anyway."

"Perfect." Everly settles in the chair beside me, and I pop open a new dark mafia romance on my Kindle when a notification pings on my phone.

Dakota: Well? How was it this morning?

Me: Fine. He ran out of the house right when I walked in. So it's back to Awkward City just like that.

Dakota: You only have yourself to blame.

Me: I know. But it's for the best. He lives a life I am not interested in being a part of. Better to end it before I start catching feelings.

Dakota: Mmmkay. ;)

I'm staring down at my phone, trying to figure out what Dakota means with that winky face when Everly shakes my shoulder. "Cozy, he's here!"

"He is?" I jerk my head around and spot a young guy who looks fresh out of high school strolling into the backyard dressed in red swim trunks and a white T-shirt with the sleeves cut out all the way to the bottom hem. Honestly, it's a pointless shirt, but the kid can pull it off.

I wave him over. "Heyo!"

"Are you Cozy?" he asks, pulling his hat down over his shaggy brown hair to block the blistering afternoon sun.

"Yes, you're Ryne, right? It is Ryne, not Ryan?" I reach out, and he looks confused when I shake his hand.

"Yeah, Ryne."

"That's a cool name."

He shoots me a crooked smile and nods. "It used to be Ryan, but Ryne has more swagger, don't you think?"

My lips thin as I try not to laugh. "Totally. Anyway…thank you for coming."

"No sweat. I love the private gigs." He pulls his sunglasses off and looks over at Everly. "You ready to learn how to swim, little one?"

A peal of laughter erupts out of Everly as she leans against me for balance. Ryne looks confused.

"Sorry, I thought I explained on the phone. The lesson isn't for her. It's for me."

"You?"

"Yeah," I reply, and Everly holds my hand in solidarity. "I, um… don't know how to swim, and this one is a fish. I would love to just learn the basics so I can be a better nanny."

"Nanny?" Ryne looks me up and down, clearly assessing my age. "You're not this one's mom?"

"No." My lip pops out into a childish pout. I would have had to be a teen mom to be Everly's mother, thank you very much…*Ryne.* "Can you just do the swimming lesson?"

A slow smile spreads across Ryne's face. "Bet! Let's get started."

Over an hour later, Everly is cheering me on from the side of the pool as I stand on the edge of the diving board hunched over with my hands pointed down at the water. The board dips when Ryne's weight comes out to join me.

"You need to have your arms up over your ears." He reaches around me to adjust my arms to the proper place. His hands linger on my waist for a moment, and I cringe at the close contact. Ryne's honestly a great swim instructor, but this is maybe a bit too hands-on.

"I think I got it," I announce, shaking him off.

"All right, Cozy…let's see your dive."

He steps back, and I roll forward, plunging hands first into the water. That one felt good! I've been belly flopping for the better part of twenty minutes, and that was the first dive that didn't sting!

I practice the breaststroke up to the surface because that was also one of the lessons Ryne taught me. When I wipe the water out of my eyes, my face falls when I see a suited figure standing at the side of the pool.

"Daddy!" Everly peals, running over to embrace Max. She leaves a wet Everly imprint on his perfectly tailored suit, and he can't even crack her a pleasant smile.

"What are you doing home already?" she asks, holding his hand.

Max's face is twitchy as he tries to smile down at her. "Oh, I had some things here to take care of, so I got off work early. Why don't you go inside and get changed and you and me can go get some ice cream when I'm done here."

"OMG, bet!" Everly says, repeating Ryne's youthful term of "let's do it" and takes off toward the house, and I do my best to swim with my newly learned crawl stroke over to the steps. When I climb out, Max is there to greet me with a towel.

"Mind telling me what's going on?" he seethes, his nostrils flaring angrily.

I wipe my face off, certain my makeup is running all over. I wasn't worried about it when it was just Everly and Ryne…but my hot boss that I just had condomless sex with a few days ago…I am suddenly acutely aware of my entire appearance.

I huddle under the towel at Max's lethal eyes. "Ryne's a swim instructor my sister recommended. Today was my first lesson."

"You think you should do a swim lesson when you're on the clock?" Max snaps.

My head jerks at his comment that was made to make me feel like his employee, not the woman he just had sex with less than seventy-two hours ago. Guess we really are done banging it out then. Which means I don't need to stand for his shit right now.

I square my shoulders and try to stand straight. "Considering he's a trained lifeguard, I can't honestly see how you'd be upset about this. If anything, Everly is safer when he's here."

"Why didn't you mention it to me?"

I shrug and puff out my lips. "I guess I forgot."

"You forgot?" Max laughs and shakes his head. "That's really convenient."

"What do you mean?"

"Is this tit for tat?" Max hisses, his head dipping so he's inches away from my face. "I did something bad so now you do too?"

"No…Max, Jesus!" I snap, realizing we're not just acting like a boss and employee anymore. "I swear this was a coincidence."

He stands back up and nods aggressively. "It's no coincidence that his hands were fucking all over you," he spits out, and it's then that I realize why he's so angry.

"Are you jealous?"

"Don't be ridiculous." Max licks his lips, and his eyes move past me to follow Ryne, who is slowly approaching. He practically snarls at the guy, "You can go now."

"She paid for ninety minutes." Ryne is unfazed by the suited caveman beside me.

"Go home, Ryan," Max seethes, and the vein in his forehead bulges angrily.

"It's Ryne," Ryne says, his voice so chill and completely unaware of the situation before him. *Brave, brave stupid boy.*

Max's forehead lines stack on top of each other. "What?"

"My name...it's Ryne."

"Like...watermelon rind?" Max does not look interested, but that was an interesting way to confirm his name pronunciation that I had not considered earlier.

"No...there's no D at the end." Ryne pinches his fingers out in front of him like he's pulling on a line. "Just...Ryne."

A deep growl rumbles under Max's breath, and I grab his arm and pull him behind toward the tiny house. "Thanks again for coming, Ryne. You were very helpful." *Translation: Run, Ryne!*

I hate that my knee still hurts enough that I can't stomp my way across the lawn without a limp in my gait, making me that much more irritated with Max each step.

"I'll see you same time next week," he calls back down.

Max barks out a laugh at those words, and I smile noncommittally and wave Ryne off. Finally, I reach my tiny house and shove Max inside.

When I have his explosive rage contained inside the white shiplap, I unleash on him. "What the hell is the matter with you?"

His dark blue eyes turn to saucers. "Me? You think something is wrong with me? I pull up the pool security camera and see some fucking asshole groping you, and you think *I'm* the problem?"

"He wasn't groping me."

"Cassandra," Max growls, turning me around and standing behind me. "What do you call this?"

He presses his warm body into mine and slides his hands down to where Ryne's were earlier. He pulls me back into his groin, and the instant zing of desire between my legs has me yanking away from him. "I promise you, it didn't feel like *that*."

"What did it feel like?"

"With him, it felt like nothing!" I exclaim, shaking away the thought of Ryne touching me. "Like a swim instructor teaching me a lesson."

"If you say so," Max huffs, pulling his tie loose so it's dangling around the lapels of his dress shirt.

My breath falters at the sight of him all out of breath, red-faced, and looking like he's about to burst out of his suit any second. It's too much. It's all too much. Especially because I know what we have is over, and we're done with this part of our relationship.

"You should leave," I croak as an ache blooms in my chest and my fingers itch to reach out and touch him.

Max's face falls as if my words have snapped him out of his jealous fit. "Fuck, Cassandra, I'm sorry. I just freaked out when I saw the—"

I hold my hand up to stop him from embracing me. "I'm not kicking you out because of your fit. You need to leave because you just undid your tie, and I know we don't have rules anymore, but it's too much." I try to block out the image of him with those top two buttons undone, revealing a few inches of his sculpted chest. My body vibrates like a feral animal ready to attack.

Dammit, we didn't bang it out enough. Not even close. Why did I have to throw such a tantrum on Saturday?

His eyes are intense and probing when he asks, "Do you really want me to leave?"

I struggle to breathe as I glance up at the house, desperate for an excuse. "Everly is going to come out for ice cream soon." *Translation: If you stay, I'm going to rip that shirt off you and give you a hickey for once.*

Max's chest heaves with a deep breath as if he knows what my thoughts are. He wants to fuck around and find out.

I turn on my heel, willing myself not to give in to this ridiculous attraction I have to this man.

His footsteps come closer, and his breath is hot on my bare shoulder when he utters in a threatening tone, "I'll leave on one condition."

"What?" I nearly pant as painful goose bumps erupt over my whole body.

His voice is deep with determination when he adds, "You go out on a date with me tomorrow night."

"What?" I blurt inelegantly as the sexy moment between us feels popped by this ridiculous request that must be a joke.

I turn around with a laugh only to find him staring back at me with zero humor on his face. He takes a step closer and looms over me. "You are right. We're done banging it out, Cassandra. I want a fucking date."

His scent wafts over me, and I find it hard to think straight. "But you don't do relationships."

"And you just wanted a summer fling," he quips, his eyes dropping to my lips. "I said fuck the rules this weekend, and I meant it. We can make our own rules."

My stomach swirls with anxiety and arousal, and it's a heady combination that makes my knees wobble. He wants a date? With me? That's far different than casual sex. What's changed for him? What's changed for me? Nothing. Except the thought of him taking someone else to that event nearly crushed me. And then there's the fact that he had a meltdown over a college-aged swim instructor five minutes ago.

God, we're a mess.

"Max, I don't want this to be like that night you came to the bar," I state, steeling myself to be firm. "Getting jealous of each other is not what dating is. We're acting like children."

"This will be different." He reaches up and brushes his thumb along my jawline. The tender embrace is so mind-altering, I see stars for a second. "Dating means I don't have to be jealous of anyone who talks to you because I know it'll be my cock buried inside you and your lips screaming my name at the end of every night."

A whimper escapes my mouth as I fall into his touch. "I think what you just described is a bit more serious than dating."

The corner of his mouth tips up into a sexy smirk. "We'll figure it out as we go, but I'm done acting like I'm not obsessed with everything about you. I want more than just fucking. I want *you*." I'm pretty sure I'm nodding my head in agreement because he leans in and presses a kiss to my forehead before adding, "Be ready at six tomorrow night, sweet cheeks."

I nearly fall forward when he takes off in search of Everly. Like a madwoman, I rush over and lock my door to prevent myself from doing something crazy. Like chasing after him and asking to go for ice cream with him and Everly.

He wants to date me. He's obsessed with me. He...wants me.

And I want him.

But I can't get ahead of myself. This is just a date. We aren't some happy family. I'm still the nanny, and he's still the millionaire. We're not a Hallmark movie with a happily ever after. If so, I would need to change that channel immediately because there's no way I'm ready for all that.

CHAPTER 37

Max

"What are we doing here?" Cassandra asks as the driver I booked drops us off on the tarmac.

"Going on our date," I reply simply as I hop out of the car and walk around to open her door.

She remains in her seat and stares up at me with an almost angry glower. "Where is our date, Max?"

"Don't get too excited. We're just going to Aspen." I reach down for her hand, which she thankfully gives me.

"We're flying to Aspen?"

I nod and take in her appearance one more time. She's wearing these sexy tattered jeans and an off-the-shoulder red top that exposes her neck, collarbone, and shoulders. I'm practically salivating to mark her, and I wonder for the hundredth time why I'm so obsessed with leaving hickeys on this woman.

"Flying is faster than driving," I respond with a wink as I walk her over to the jet. When I suggested a date yesterday, she probably expected dinner and a movie. But considering I rubbed my cum over her clit four days ago because I liked the look of my release on her cunt, I figured this upgrade wouldn't be an issue.

Cassandra will learn quickly that I've always been an overachiever.

My hands linger on Cassandra's hips as she climbs the stairs into the eight-seater plane. She stops in the plush aisle and turns with wide eyes and ruby red lips that I really want to suck and fuck. "Is this your plane? Or did you like...book it special for this?"

My shoulders shake with silent laughter. "It's my company's plane. We use it for work mostly, but Everly and I take it to Aspen a lot on my weekends with her."

"Eleven-year-olds on private jets...makes perfect sense," Cassandra tuts and then turns and points at the white leather seats. "Where do I sit?"

"Wherever you like," I reply with a grin.

She finds a seat she deems worthy, so I take the one opposite her so we're facing each other. The flight attendant delivers a champagne to Cassandra and a whiskey to me.

Her sexy green eyes narrow on me over the top of the bubbling flute. "This is a really solid flex, Max. I bet you're really pleased with yourself, aren't you?"

I laugh and drag my thumb over my lip. "I'm getting hard just watching you freak out."

"Such a perv," she exclaims with a delightful smile. She looks around the cabin and frowns, her mind clearly moving faster than the plane. "But seriously, we're coming back tonight, right? I didn't pack a bag."

"Don't worry about it." I sit back in my seat and shrug.

Her face grows serious. "Max...what do you mean? What about Everly?"

"She's with Wyatt so she'll be feeding the goat in the morning. Don't stress. We'll be back before he brings her home tomorrow."

"Tomorrow." Cassandra exhales through her nose as the pilot indicates we're getting ready for takeoff. "This is ridiculous. This isn't what real people do on dates."

"I told you we're making our own rules." I take a sip of my whiskey and wonder when I'll stop smiling tonight.

This date is a much better soul cleanser than crying. I would inform Everly of that fact if I decided this was something my daughter should know about yet…which I don't. Way too soon for that kind of talk.

For now, I'm just trying to reclaim control of this situation between Cassandra and me. Her walking out of my house this past weekend was not an image I'd like a replay of. Therefore, amending the terms of our agreement into dating seemed like the most reasonable next step. I am a businessman after all. If I find something I want, I will figure out a way to possess it.

And I can't wait to possess Cassandra tonight in my Aspen home.

When we reach our altitude, I nudge her leg with my foot to turn her attention from the window to me. "Tell me about your best first date."

Her brows pinch. "So you can feel superior that you've already topped it with a private jet?"

I shake my head slowly. "I know it will take a lot more than this to woo you, Cozy."

Her eyes flash with intrigue. "Why do you randomly call me Cozy sometimes? You almost always call me Cassandra, but you've let Cozy slip a handful of times, and I can't figure out why."

I inhale deeply and give it some thought before I answer. "I only use Cozy when I feel really comfortable with you."

A look of disappointment flits across her face. "So then all the other times, you feel uncomfortable around me?"

I lean forward and slip my hand through the large hole on her knee, my fingers teasing her flesh as I pin her with a serious look. "Yes, Cassandra. You make me uncomfortable nearly every minute of every day since I met you. And I have discovered that I like feeling uncomfortable."

Her cheeks flush a ruddy color as she pulls her lower lip between her teeth. "Okay then."

"What about you? Do I make you uncomfortable?" I wait with bated breath because Cassandra hides her cards a lot, and this is the most unarmed I think I've ever seen her.

She licks her lips, and a tender smile lightens her face. "Not un-comfortable…just scared."

"Scared of what?" I ask, frowning.

"For you to be too good to be true."

She takes a nervous sip of her drink, and if I wasn't trying to woo this woman, I'd be making her a member of the mile-high club right fucking now to put those fears to bed. But we have a long night ahead of us. And I intend to put those fears to bed in ways other than sexual. At least for now.

We touch down in Aspen, and Cassandra is decidedly more re-laxed after the two glasses of champagne during the short flight. I open the door to usher her into the black SUV I rented, and she gig-gles when I slip into the driver's seat.

"What's so funny?"

"Oh…just that I'm having an Anastasia Steele moment, and I'm wearing jeans with holes all over them instead of something sleek and sophisticated like Christian Grey's girlfriend would wear."

"I like your jeans," I murmur, leaning across the console to wrap my hand around her thigh. She looks young and casual, and she re-minds me that I'm more than just a dad and a boss. It feels like it's been ages since I've considered that concept.

I press a soft kiss to her lips, dragging my nose down to her neck and inhaling that coconut smell of hers like it's my last breath. She whimpers slightly, and it takes all the strength I have to pull away from her and drive.

"Where are we going now?" she asks with sexy eyes that tell me exactly where she'd like to go.

I smirk. "You'll see."

Our sexual tension is palpable as we drive into downtown Aspen, where many high-end luxury shops are located. I don't spend a lot of time shopping in Aspen. I'm usually here for business or with Everly, and in that case, we do more skiing and hiking than anything else.

Henley is obviously someone I would see when I was here for business only. My visits with her were almost business in nature, which is harsh to admit, I realize. But she seemed happy with that arrangement as well. It's shocking how quickly I started breaking all my rules for Cassandra.

Once I find a parking spot in front of our destination, I open Cassandra's door, and her eyes are wide when she sees where we've stopped.

"This isn't where we're going, is it?" she inquires, pointing at the shop's sleek storefront.

I nod and smile, grabbing her hand when she's out of the car. "Yeah, we're going here."

She frowns. "I know the designer who owns this shop. Her name is Tatianna Ashley. She works with Dakota's T-shirt shop."

"I know," I reply with a smirk and begin to pull her toward the door.

"How do you know?" Cassandra asks, stopping me with a firm tug on my hand.

I turn and hit her with an easy shrug. "Because I asked Dakota."

"Asked Dakota what?"

"Where you like to shop."

Just then, the front door of the shop opens, and a short woman with bright pink hair pops her head out. "This must be Cinderella!"

I smile and nod while having to drag a very reluctant and confused Cassandra toward the door. We step inside the plush showroom with a limited number of items on display. This definitely isn't a shop-in-the-store type of business. This is a by-appointment-only business…which explains why Dakota had to make some calls for me.

"You must be Cozy!" Tatianna pulls Cassandra in for a hug. "Dakota has told me so much about you. I feel like I know you already with how much she talks about you. I scored one of your charcuterie boards like a month ago from her. I'm obsessed!"

"You did?" Cassandra seems star-struck. It's adorable.

Tatianna turns toward me with a smile. "Tell me about the event. I know it's an LGBTQ+ charity, so I've pulled some pieces, but it'll help my girls and me if we know the theme."

"Actually…can you give us a moment, Tatianna?" I request, feeling anxiety prickle this sexy bubble I've been living in for the past hour with Cassandra. "I just need to have a quick chat with Cassandra, and we'll be right with you."

"No problem! Now that I've seen her body in person, I have some more things I want her to try," she exclaims and then turns to tell her two staff members who slip into stride with her as they head toward the back of the shop, out of sight.

Cassandra's green eyes are saucers as she yanks me to her. "Max, what the hell is going on?"

I rub her arm reassuringly because she looks like she's going to faint. "I stopped at Dakota's shop earlier today to ask her for some ideas about a date for you and me."

"Yeah…"

"And I told her about the charity gala."

Cassandra's eyes furrow instantly. We haven't revisited that awkward topic since it popped up this past weekend and I can tell by the light dimming in Cassandra's eyes, she's not enjoying the reminder.

"Listen, I talked to Henley, the woman who was going to accompany me to the event, and I told her that I was seeing someone seriously and I didn't think it was appropriate for her to go with me anymore."

"You did?"

"Yes. She completely understood." I inhale deeply and step forward, ready to bring out the big guns to close this deal.

"Cassandra, I want you to come with me to the charity gala next week. It's an important event for me. The Rainbow Project is a college scholarship program for LGBTQ+ kids. I'm on the board, not because I have to be, but because I want to be. Everly is the daughter of a lesbian mother and stepdaughter of a pansexual mother. This community will always be a part of her life and, therefore, my life. It's important to me to use the success and influence I've found in business to help kids in that community find their place in this world. I would love to show you that part of my life."

Cassandra's chest rises and falls as she stares back at me completely gobsmacked. I knew she wouldn't say yes to coming next weekend if I didn't ask her in a big way. She has to understand she's not second choice. That's why I stopped at her best friend's shop downtown for advice. I thought if I took her shopping for a dress, she'd have no reason to say no. When Dakota said Cassandra loved this designer in Aspen, my home away from home, dinner and a movie suddenly got an upgrade.

Hopefully only making it harder for her to say no to me.

"Will you please let me buy you a dress tonight and come with me next Saturday?" I ask, feeling strangely vulnerable for the first time all night.

Suddenly, the private jet and the grand gesture of taking her to a designer for a dress seems like total fucking overkill for a first date. What if she says no, and this was all for nothing? What if we have to ride back on that plane together in awkward silence because Cassandra has made it clear to me in the past that she doesn't care about material things? *Fuck...I might have just blown it.*

My mind is thwarted when Cassandra throws herself into my arms and seals her lips over mine. Her hands band tightly around my neck as I hug her to me, and our lips tangle together. The kiss is so feverish, I wonder briefly if the noises I hear are coming from her or from me.

Finally, she pulls back and laughs. "You really are a decent human, aren't you?"

I laugh and shake my head. "Does that mean you'll come?"

"God, yes. What do I have to wear?"

I shrug and stare at her lips. "A dress with nothing underneath if it's up to me."

She pats her hands on my chest. "Spoken like a man who's never come across Spanx before."

"Like spankings? Another kink unlocked, Cozy?" I waggle my eyebrows sexily at her, and she laughs. I don't get it.

CHAPTER 38

Cozy

It's impossible to wipe the smile off my face at the fancy restaurant Max takes me to after we finish shopping. One would think I'd be stressing over the fact that I am completely underdressed for the vibe here, but after the incredible shopping experience I just had, nothing will bring me down.

Dress after dress that Tatianna brought me zipped right up. I was able to walk out and model some of the pieces for Max and had a total *Cinderella* with her Fairy Godmother moment.

As a bigger girl, that makeover scene you see in the movies is never something I've been able to picture for myself. Hollywood has gifted that story arc to the size two girls who can fit into items straight off the rack.

A shopping spree for girls with curves is more like an Olympic sport you have to train for your whole life.

First, you have to find the limited shops that carry your sizes. Then there's the squeezing, the yanking, and the crushing disappointment that overwhelms you when something you try on doesn't button up or accentuates all your worst features. Shopping for bigger girls s something you need to be in peak physical and mental condition for. You have to tell yourself that just because this looks bad doesn't mean *you* look bad. This just isn't the style for you. Keep looking. You'll find something that will make you feel beautiful.

And honestly, shopping for smaller-sized people isn't easy either. Everyone has flaws they see in themselves, no matter what size they wear. Just because a person's pant size is in the single digits and mine are in the double doesn't make her immune to misery in a dressing room. That is a one-size-fits-all sort of pain.

Which is why that makeover scene in a movie makes girls of all sizes swoon hard. We all want to experience that moment when a dress doesn't just make us feel beautiful but it makes us feel desired.

Confidence is a game I can play on my own. I've gotten pretty good at it, as a matter of fact. But that moment when you put on a pretty dress and a man looks at you like you're the most beautiful thing in the world…fat or thin—that's a game that requires two players.

And Max played his part like a king.

As Max samples the red wine the sommelier suggested we order with our steaks, I stare at him like my own personal meal. He is nothing like the countless CEOs I came across during my time in the corporate world. How has he managed to stay so sane with all this success he's found? He literally just flew me here on a private jet, bought me a dress that will be delivered to his Aspen home by morning time, and he's not checked his phone once since we arrived at this restaurant.

Is he really even human?

"You look like you're having loads of dirty thoughts," Max says, his indigo eyes narrowing wickedly as he swirls the freshly poured red wine in his glass.

I lick my lips and lean forward, lifting up my own glass. "How can you tell?"

His heated eyes rove over my face, causing me to flush. "You have a facial tell."

"I do not." I laugh, feeling butterflies erupt in my belly at the sexy, happy look on his face. Am I really what puts that there?

The alluring muscle in his jaw shifts as he smirks. "Your nose gets red when you're thinking about sex."

Instantly my hand touches the tip of my nose that feels surprisingly hot. "Does it really?"

He takes a sip of his wine and quirks a brow. "Were you thinking about sex a moment ago?"

"More or less," I answer with a grin and cover my face with my napkin.

He winks. "You have a tell, sweet cheeks."

My body curls in on itself when I think of all the times I've had dirty thoughts around him. It was before we ever kissed...well before we started hooking up. Did he know every time? Did he know during my interview?

"What's your tell?" I watch him curiously, his gaze fixed on me in a way that makes me feel completely naked.

"Mine is a bit more obvious." He waggles his eyebrows lasciviously and holds his hand out to me. "Give me your hand, I'll let you feel it."

"Such a pervert," I exclaim, and his wolfish grin is panty-melting.

"It takes one to know one," he volleys back.

He's not wrong.

I chew my lip and sip my wine, musing a bit before asking, "How do you make it look so easy?"

"What?" He sets his glass down and gives me his undivided attention.

"Life," I reply simply. "You seem to have such incredible balance. Everly, work, friends, family. You literally do it all, and now you've whisked me away to Aspen on a moment's notice without even breaking a sweat. What is your secret?"

Max's face grows serious as his jaw slides back and forth. "If it looks like I'm not sweating, it's because I have an army of people who are wiping my face."

I set my glass down as I notice the obvious shift in his expression. Gone is that boyish, sexy smirk that makes me feel like a schoolgirl. In an instant, Max has transformed into that powerful, smoldering

CEO who makes me feel terrified in the best way possible. It's an odd thing for me to be so attracted to, considering my past.

Max's voice is guttural when he adds, "I wouldn't have achieved a thing in my life if it weren't for the constant support of my family, friends, and staff. Hell, I don't even know when my next dentist appointment is. Marcia has to tell me. Bettina runs my home. Michael does all the cooking. I pay a lot of people to help me with many things. It takes structure and order for me to thrive and achieve this balance."

I nod slowly, insecurity spreading through my body because I tried to do what Max is doing and failed…miserably. Once upon a time, I had big dreams and huge ambitions. I thrived off the buzz of being busy because I thought I was destined to be someone important.

If only I'd done better and been capable of more.

"What are you thinking about?" Max asks, doing that mind reading thing again. Though this time, I'm certain my nose isn't red.

"I wasn't always like this," I offer softly, feeling my chin tremble as I reach out and pick up my wineglass for a fortifying drink, trying not to let my hands shake.

"Not always like what?"

"Miss Willy-Nilly," I reply with a laugh and exhale heavily as nerves swirl in my belly. "Miss Why Do More When You Can Do Less."

I wave my hands out like a circus monkey, but Max doesn't laugh like I think he's going to. He just watches me quietly, waiting for me to continue.

I don't know why I feel compelled to tell him all this now. We're having such a nice time, and this will certainly overshadow the *Cinderella* vibe of the day. But it feels important somehow. I want Max to understand how I became who I am. Especially if we're going to have a chance at truly being together.

I take one more tremulous drink of my wine, using my left hand to ensure myself that I am okay now. I am healed. I feel Max's eyes on me the entire time as I steel myself to say, "You know how I told you originally that I worked on those charcuterie boards as a form of therapy?"

"Yes," Max answers, his brow furrowed curiously.

"Well, I let you believe that it was mental therapy, but in reality, it was physical therapy." My heart pounds at the memory of those awful couple of months when my body didn't feel like my body. It was like an alien had taken over my left hand and would do whatever it wanted instead of what I wanted. It took nearly three months for me to get it to a place where I could feel secure in its movements. I inhale a deep breath before stating the truth out loud, "I had a stress-induced stroke at Christmas time last year that paralyzed my left arm."

"Are you serious, Cassandra?" Max snaps, shoving his wine aside and leaning across the table. His eyes are the most severe I've ever seen them, and I feel slightly terrified at the reality of my truth being displayed back to me. "An actual stroke?"

I nod and force myself not to cry. "It's rare at my age, but it can happen. It happened at my corporate job that I mentioned to you."

His eyes swim with fear as he watches me, barely even taking a breath as he inquires, "Jesus Christ, what happened?"

"Stress," I respond with a garbled laugh that feels pathetic. "Loads and loads of stress."

"What did you do at your last job? What was your position?" Max asks, his face taut with shock.

I sigh heavily, feeling horrified at the thought of recounting everything but knowing that he needs to hear it all to get the big picture. I inhale deeply and force myself to be professional. "I was in asset management, managing a large portfolio of industrial and commercial buildings scattered throughout the United States. I started right out of college, so I was only nineteen in the beginning, but I was twenty-five when I finally hit my breaking point, so I had been there for six years."

Max nods knowingly, likely very familiar with the corporate hustle and bustle. He has a company jet after all, something I would have appreciated instead of taking commercial flights four out of seven days a week every single week.

"When I originally started with the company, it was new and very entrepreneurial. Everyone wore a lot of hats. I was always someone who picked things up quickly, so I was given a lot of responsibilities that I was never really qualified for, but I liked it. It forced me to learn and grow quickly, which felt good at the time because I was so young. Plus, I've always liked a challenge, like you."

I offer a wobbly smile to Max, hoping he can see a glimpse of himself in me. Like somehow, I need him to see my potential, which is insane because I want nothing to do with corporate life anymore.

"My coworkers were all young, not as young as me, but it was definitely a work hard, play hard environment. I was always kind of a quirky book nerd in school and wasn't super social unless forced, and given that this was a small company, and we were together a lot, all my coworkers became my close friends. They would sneak me into bars at nights and on the weekends. I even dated a guy there semi-seriously. It was nice.

"The company I worked for always ran lean. They were all about making as much money as possible and doing it with the least amount of people, often forcing me to do jobs that weren't a part of my job description. If you complained or requested more money, they basically told you that if you think you are worth more, then go out and look for another job."

"Such bullshit," Max interjects, shaking his head in disappointment. "A company should always know the value of their employees. That's what annual reviews are for. Did they do those?"

"No," I reply with a laugh, picturing my old boss sneering at me when I proposed a schedule of performance reviews for the staff. If I scheduled everything out, I thought it would help him say yes. It didn't. It was a complete and utter waste of time.

"I didn't grow up with a lot of money, so what I was earning seemed like more than I ever dreamed I could make," I add, recalling the proud look on my parents' faces when I told them what my signing bonus was. "So even though I thought I was worth more, I still didn't think I could start over somewhere and make as much. Not to mention, I was so busy that I had no time to job hunt, let alone update my résumé."

I pause and take another sip of my wine, feeling my body resist the emotions that place elicits, but knowing I want to power through this. I have to.

"My mental health really took a toll about a year ago when the company started to grow. They wanted to stay lean still but operate like a big corporation. So a lot more protocols, more reporting, more steps to basically everything, which meant even more work. I had to run every little thing by our CEO. He was busy and didn't get back to me quickly, and then things wouldn't get done, and I'd be blamed for it. I started to feel like I wasn't even doing the job I was hired for, and I began questioning my ability and my purpose for even being there."

My eyes well with tears, but now that I've started, I can't seem to stop. "I questioned everything about myself…even down to the clothes I wore to work every day. I had zero confidence. I wasn't eating. I was miserable all the time. But I kept showing up every day because all my 'friends' were there, and it felt like we were all in this together.

"I started having anxiety attacks where I couldn't see. I'd wake up in the middle of the night after having another nightmare about work, and there would be black spots in my vision. The first time, I called 911 because I didn't know what was happening. The doctors got me on some meds that helped, but it didn't take away the stress I was still under."

Max stares back at me with so much compassion that I'm not sure I can look at him for the next bit, so I decide to stare at my glass of wine.

"On Christmas Eve this past year, I was supposed to be driving home to be with my family. Instead, I was in the office working late with about eight other people trying to fix a huge mistake someone made. People were tired and cranky…everyone was pointing fingers at everyone.

"Then all of a sudden, I couldn't feel the left side of my face. My arm felt really heavy, like I couldn't lift it, and I opened my mouth to ask for water, and I couldn't even understand what I was saying…I was just mumbling incoherent gibberish. It was weird because I could tell I wasn't making sense, but I couldn't make my brain fix the issue. The last thing I remember is everyone gaping at me as I fell to the ground."

"Fucking hell." Max reaches out to grab my hand splayed out on the table, but I pull away and cross my arms over my chest. I know his affection will make me break down, and I really don't want to be the girl in ripped-up jeans crying in the middle of a fancy restaurant.

"My next memory was waking up in a hospital with a tube down my throat and my mother sobbing in the chair beside me."

"Cassandra." Max whispers my name so reverently that it causes tears in my eyes.

"The doctors said neuro stuff was all miraculously okay, but they weren't sure if I would regain full function of my left arm."

"Fuck." Max's pained voice is crushing to hear. It reminds me of my family's tone as they huddled around me in the hospital bed, waiting for me to recover. His tone is thick when he adds, "I'm so sorry that all happened to you."

I nod slowly. "I was in the hospital for a week and physical therapy care facility for two weeks after. I came home to do outpatient therapy, and it was my dad's idea that I start doing some woodworking to improve my fine motor skills. Which…as you can probably tell, worked because I gained back the full function of my left arm. I guess I defied the odds."

The corner of Max's mouth tips up into a smile, but it's a sad smile. One that doesn't reach his eyes. "You said you left that job on bad terms…"

"Yeah…I haven't even got to the bad terms part yet." I inhale and shake my head, feeling the weight of those six years like a fucking storm cloud hovering over me. "The thing that really sealed the deal about me leaving that job wasn't the stroke. It was the fact that none of my coworkers came to visit me in the hospital. Not one. I'd watch the door every day for people who I considered family for most of my adult life to check in on me, and no one ever did. My sister showed up, my parents did. Hell, even Dakota did once I let my mom tell her what happened to me. But none of the people who I spent endless hours with ever stopped by."

"What about the boyfriend you mentioned?" Max asks, his face taut with poorly concealed rage.

"He texted me once." I laugh, and it hurts. "We'd broken up several months before the incident, and he was with someone new. My boss emailed me about disability leave, but that was pretty much the extent of his communication with me."

A look of disgust mars Max's handsome face. "What company was this? Who was your boss?"

"It doesn't matter," I respond quickly, shuddering at the thought of even saying his name aloud. "I never stepped foot back in that building, and I never will. All that work, all that commitment to a company that didn't care about me when I literally almost died in front of them makes me sick to my stomach. I never even went back to my apartment in Denver. As soon as I was released from the care facility, I went straight home to Boulder and moved in with my sister because I couldn't handle my mom's hovering and worrying. I hired a company to pack up my entire apartment. Most of my boxes are still in storage because I'm terrified if I open them up, there will be something that triggers a panic attack or worse, another stroke. I was twenty-five years old and had a stress-induced stroke at my job. How embarrassing is that?"

"It's not embarrassing," Max replies softly, reaching out and grabbing my hand firmly.

"It is, though, because I couldn't handle the stress like everyone else." *Like you*, I want to say, but I don't. "I'm a total failure."

"You're not a failure, Cassandra," Max nearly growls. "You can't control what happened to you any more than I can control having my wife leave me. It's just a part of our past lives that we have to navigate our way through."

"I know, but you've accomplished so much despite your past life. I was a twentysomething with no responsibilities other than my job, and it nearly killed me. How are you so much better at this than me?"

"I'm not," Max snaps, his eyes boring into me. "We just handle stress differently. I mean…hell…I may have accomplished a lot, but I spent nearly a decade of my life devoid of any real romantic relationship. My eleven-year-old told me this weekend that she worries about me constantly. You think I'm not fucking up? Trust me, Cozy. I fuck up plenty."

He exhales heavily and sits back in his seat, thrusting a frustrated hand through his hair. "What happened to you is the result of employee neglect from a shitty corporation and vile boss. You're lucky to be alive." His voice cracks, and my eyes instantly fill with tears at the stricken look on his face.

I hold my hand out to his again, and he calms down to lean forward and twine his fingers through mine. I'm suddenly struck with the very real possibility that I might not have lived to experience this feeling with this man at this moment because of that stroke.

That reality affects me far more than I'm ready to admit.

I cup my hand over his. "I know that now, Max. I realize that my body just isn't built for that kind of high-pressure work environment. That's why I've spent the past seven months living life by my own rules and no one else's—except for our bang it out rules, of course." I laugh and swipe at an errant tear that slides down my face. "I've been calling these past seven months my Great Defrost."

Max doesn't smile back at me as his Adam's apple slides down his throat. "So are you defrosted yet? How is your health now? Really."

"I can safely confirm that I am the picture of health." I sit up straight and give him a cheesy smile before morphing into a genuine one. "Honestly, I feel better and happier than I have in years. Very warm and cozy."

Max's brooding eyes soften and crinkle around the edges. His voice is seductive when he asks, "Do I get to take any credit for that happiness?"

I bite my lip nervously. "Yes, Max. Against all odds…I'm afraid you do."

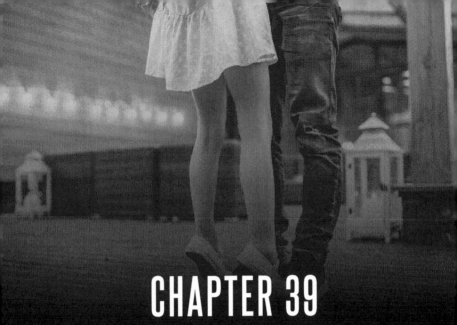

CHAPTER 39

Max

"Let me try this whiskey of yours," Cassandra says, standing between my legs as I sit on top of the kitchen counter in my Aspen house. Her hands slide up and down my thighs, making the constant state of my dick's arousal more painful by the second.

I growl and kiss her neck, enjoying the view of her in my home. She's barefoot and sexy as fuck, with her lips raw from the make-out session we had in the game room. I wanted to strip her naked and take her on the pool table, but she demanded we finish the tour.

Such a sexy, bossy nanny.

A bossy nanny who is so much more than a nanny. I fucking knew there was more to Cassandra than meets the eye. Her determination to play life casually always felt like a cover for something. But what she told me was ten times worse than I could ever imagine.

I'm going to get the name of that company out of her one of these days. This isn't something I can just let go of. But for now for tonight, I will savor the person she has become and appreciate her vulnerability that was long overdue.

Admittedly, I struggle to picture this corporate grind person she used to be. Dressed in business suits and hopping on commercial flights every single week isn't her. The woman in my arms right now, grabbing my drink and wrinkling her nose as she smells it, feels like the woman she was always meant to be.

"Come on, pour me a drink," Cassandra repeats, tipping her chin up to me as she lightly tangles her lips with mine. "I can always taste it on your tongue, but I want to try an actual drink and see if I like it."

She thrusts her tongue into my mouth, and I groan my appreciation, drinking in the wine on her lips. She always tastes so fucking good. I'm going to devour every inch of her body tonight.

An idea pops into my mind as I break our kiss with a dirty smile. "Let me get you that drink, sweet cheeks." She watches me curiously as I don't pour her a glass like she expected. Instead, I take a large sip of the amber liquid and tilt my chin to her.

"Another kink released to the wild," she squeals, and I have to fight back the urge to laugh so I don't spray this all over her face. *I'll save that dirty image for later.*

She turns around so her back is pressed to my groin, and I gently grip her neck and tilt her head back against my chest, clutching below her jaw firmly with my hand. She parts her lush red lips as I purse mine and drizzle the whiskey that's now warm from my mouth into hers. The sound of it trickling against her tongue causes my cock to press harshly into her lower back.

When I finish, she closes her lips and turns around to face me, delicately dabbing at the droplets on her chin. Her face suddenly contorts as she aggressively shakes her head. She beats her fist on her chest as she forces herself to swallow. "Not a fan," she blurts out, blowing whiskey breath all over my face. "It's going to be a hard pass on whiskey from now on." She coughs and wrinkles her nose. "I think I would have preferred your spit."

My body shakes with genuine laughter at how she just took

the sexiest moment I've ever experienced with a woman in my life…and made it hilarious…yet somehow even sexier.

God, I'm into her.

My glass clunks against the marble countertop as I set it down. Without pause, I reach out and grip the back of her neck, yanking her to my lips. I suck on her tongue and kiss her passionately for a moment before murmuring, "Just as I suspected, you taste incredible with whiskey on your tongue."

"Well, don't get used to it, Zaddy," she says, her eyes hooded with arousal as her hands twine around my neck, and she presses her supple breasts into my chest. "I'm more of a White Claw Queen these days. That watermelon flavor hits different."

Growling under my breath, I slide off the counter, my hard cock dragging against her body as I grumble, "I need to fuck you now, Cozy."

"Oooh, you called me Cozy. Someone's feeling very confident with himself," she sing-songs and giggles as I pull her behind me to the staircase in the foyer, feeling like I'm going to lose my mind any second.

"It was my White Claw comment, right? It makes me super relatable—" I silence her by wrapping my hand around her throat and pinning her up against the wall next to the foyer table right at the bottom of the grand staircase.

Her lips part as she releases a throaty moan, and her eyes fill with fiery passion in the dark foyer with only the light shining in from outside.

"This turns you on, doesn't it?" I ask, my fingers twitching around her neck, holding her firmly but never squeezing. "Does this make you wet for me?" Her eyes close, and I squeeze her tender flesh a tiny bit more. "Answer me, sweet cheeks."

"Yes," she whimpers, pulling my hips into her as she arches toward me.

"Good girl," I rasp, my heart pounding at the sensation of her pulse beneath my palm as I stare down at her chest heaving with excited breaths. "You like when I control you?"

"God, yes," she cries, wrapping a leg up around my hip to grind her clit against my cock.

God, she really is so fucking good. A grunt vibrates in my chest as I thrust against her. "Do you feel how hard you make me?" I whisper against the shell of her ear and trail my lips down her neck, sucking lightly for a second, just barely resisting the urge to bite until she screams. "You smell like the fucking beach, and it drives me *wild*."

"Max." She pants out my name, thrusting her pelvis into me. It's her next word that sends me into a frenzy. *"Please."*

I release my grasp on her throat, and our hands collide as we wrestle with her jeans. She shakes out of them and tosses her thong as our lips collide in an erratic, desperate kiss. Our tongues swirl against each other as my cock pours out of my boxer briefs. I don't even fuck with our shirts before lifting her onto the table beside us and spreading her legs wide.

Yanking her hips to the edge, I impale myself deep inside her, plunging to the hilt with all the finesse of a fucking animal.

Fuck, going bare inside her is another goddamn level. She's soaked for me, her body accepting me like I belong right fucking here all day, every day. I have a carnal reaction to knowing I'm the only man who's had her like this. I like that fucking feeling. I like it too much as I pull out of her slowly and slam back in.

Her cries echo off the vaulted ceiling as I press my head to her chest and watch our bodies connect. Her arousal drenches my shaft, showing me just how turned on she was by my hand on her throat. She grips my arms as I squeeze her soft thighs and look up, our eyes connecting as I pound her hard against the table.

Eye contact used to be my thing. I needed it to trust that the woman wanted me and wasn't forcing a feeling between us. But I don't worry about that with Cassandra anymore. She fucking bled for me at dinner tonight, opening up about something from her past that was raw and painful. There's a vulnerability in her gaze that I've never experienced with a woman I've been with before. Not even Jessica. It gives me everything I need to trust that she's in this with me. Tonight was the final missing puzzle piece, and now all the things I've been falling for in Cassandra make even more sense.

I see her fully for all that she is and all that I know she will be.

Her pussy clenches around my shaft as she screams through the climax that ravages her body in record time. It's all the reassurance I need before I groan loudly and pulsate inside her—twitching violently as her sweet channel sucks every last drop from my cock.

Our heavy breaths are the only sound reverberating off the walls until Cassandra's sexy voice croaks, "Yes, Zaddy," and reminds me that there is never a dull moment with this woman.

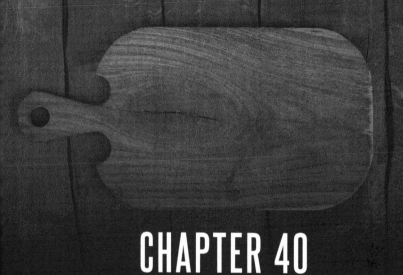

CHAPTER 40

Cozy

"**A**nd then I did a walk of shame back onto his private jet this morning." I cover my face with my hands and lean against the counter at Dakota's T-shirt shop, unable to look my bestie in the eyes after I just divulged *in great detail* everything that happened to me in the past twenty-four hours. I had to stop myself from texting her today while I was taking care of Everly because this is not the kind of story you text a bestie.

I murmur into my palm, "I'm pretty sure the flight attendant was laughing at me."

"This sounds like straight-up fiction." Dakota slaps the counter, demanding my eye contact. "Except for riding home on a private jet in the same clothes. That's not hot."

"Max didn't tell me to pack a bag!" I exclaim. "And I actually tried on one of his dress shirts he keeps in his Aspen house, thinking I could wear it home and be all 'dress shirt chic' like the hot women you see in the movies, but it wouldn't button over my gigantic ass."

Dakota peals with laughter. "That's so embarrassing."

I frown and smile at the same time because embarrassment didn't even factor into the moment. In fact, there was no self-consciousness at all this morning when we woke up in each other's arms with the Aspen sun pouring in through his giant bedroom windows that got quite a show once we finally made it up the stairs.

"Actually, it wasn't embarrassing," I interject, a smug smile spreading across my face as I realize that somewhere between the private jet and Max spitting whiskey into my mouth, I finally accepted the fact that he likes my body just the way it is. "I'm pretty sure Max was turned on by the fact that the shirt didn't fit. I thought he was a breast man, but he might be an ass man too."

"Or he's a Cozy man," Dakota replies with a stunned look that has been on her face since I arrived here this evening. "Not to discredit your impressive ass, it's a sight to behold, but Cozy...you do realize you're living in a Mercedes Lee Loveletter novel, and you need to marry this man like right now."

"Okay, calm down now." I laugh, trying to bring this gabfest back into focus. "No one is talking marriage. We haven't even given whatever we are a label yet. As far as I know, we're still just in the dating stage."

"Does Everly know he took you to Aspen?" Dakota asks, waving to a customer who walks in the door and begins shopping.

"No," I reply quickly. "We both agreed that we should definitely keep this from Everly until I'm done being her nanny."

"But you're still going with him to that charity thing next weekend?" she presses.

"Yes, Everly is staying at her grandparents', so she won't be around when we leave." A nervous flutter takes flight in my belly. "The Tatianna gown I picked out is incredible, Dakota. And Tatianna was so sweet. I can't believe I've never met your friend before. She was amazing."

"Well, you were kind of MIA after you moved to Denver," she responds knowingly, and then her face grows serious at the mention of my past life. "I'm really happy you finally told him about your stroke, Cozy. It feels like an important step for you to put that awful experience behind you."

"It does," I agree, marveling over the fact that a couple of months ago, anytime my past job was brought up, I'd feel my body tighten with anxiety. But just now as I retold my whole night with Max to my best friend, I feel surprisingly at peace. "I think I'm ready to finally call Kate back and get going on this charcuterie project."

"Dayummm," Dakota peals dramatically. "Zaddy's dick must have some magical healing powers!"

"I'll take a little credit, thank you very much." I laugh and wrinkle my nose. "But you're right…his dick is magical."

Dakota giggles, and I sigh inwardly as I realize for the first time that I'm not necessarily like my old, younger self, and I'm clearly nothing like my Denver self…but perhaps a new hybrid version that's stronger and more capable of achieving goals and setting boundaries. The perfect room temperature Cozy—as long as Cinderella's coach doesn't turn back into a pumpkin anytime soon.

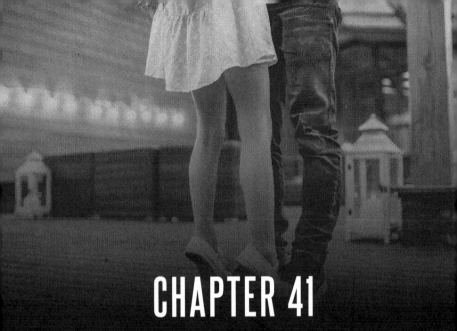

CHAPTER 41

MAX

"Y ou sure you're okay with fifty people, Max? Maybe seventy-five?" Norah asks, standing in the middle of my backyard on Saturday afternoon. The July sun is scorching so I lift my hand to block the light.

"Whatever you want, Norah," I reply, and she turns a bright smile to her mom as they point down by the creek.

Dean elbows me and nods. "Good answer. Just do a lot of nodding and smiling, and we'll both hopefully get out of here alive."

"We're going to go do some measurements down by the beach," Norah's mom shouts, and the two of them head down toward the sandy area by the creek.

My gaze slides over to the tiny house near it. I wonder how long this wedding planning will take today because Everly is at a sleepover at Claire's, which means I have unlimited access to the hot nanny. She's currently in my garage doing some woodworking, which means…*she's horny.*

And so am I.

"Hey, do you have any whiskey in that house? This wedding

planning with my mother-in-law is stressful as fuck." Dean adjusts his glasses and eyes me with the look of a desperate man.

"It's five o'clock somewhere," I respond with a laugh and slap him on the back as we make our way inside.

We situate ourselves across from each other at the kitchen island, and I can smell the scent of charred wood drifting in from the garage.

Dean sniffs loudly as I hand him a finger of whiskey.

"Cassandra is probably burning one of her charcuterie boards." I answer his silent question and sip my own drink, savoring the spicy burn on my tongue. It's the best kind of burn. A burn that tasted even better on Cozy's tongue a few days ago.

Dean gets a wicked glint in his eye. "What's the status update there? You've been a little radio silent since poker night."

I inhale through my nose. Might as well rip the Band-Aid off because I've been kind of dying to talk to someone about it and my brothers are useless when it comes to advice on women.

"We're kind of…dating."

Dean chokes on his whiskey. "You're actually dating the nanny?" he exclaims, coughing.

"Use her fucking name, asshole." My tone is lethal and totally hypocritical because I love calling her the nanny in my dirty thoughts. But from Dean, that label sounds cheap. And Cassandra is obviously so much more than the nanny now. Hell, she's slept in my bed every night since we returned from Aspen. It's been tricky too because even though we're not just banging it out anymore, we've still decided not to say anything to Everly, so it's still a lot of sneaking around.

Our current plan is a lot like our old plan, except now we're in my bed instead of hers. Cassandra comes over after Everly goes to sleep, and I worship every inch of her body. Then she slips out my patio door around five thirty every morning, looking well-fucked to go get ready for the day at her place.

It's been a pretty good plan. Satisfying for all parties involved… except for one little incident yesterday.

I thought for sure we were busted when I woke up in the middle of the night to find Everly staring at me while I slept. I shot out of bed and woke Cassandra up in the process who hid under the covers even though we were already caught. Everly mumbled something about Millie eating her blanket and it took me a second to realize she was sleep walking and talking.

So I gently guided my little princess back upstairs to her bed where I was happy to discover there was no goat eating anything. I tucked her in, kissed her head, and came back downstairs to stress about what we were going to tell Everly the next day. I also turned up the notification volume on my phone because my camera alerts should have told me she was coming. I'm getting sloppy.

I stared nervously at Everly while she ate her oatmeal, waiting to see if she had any comments about last night.

She remembered nothing, reminding me once again that kids are a strange breed.

But regardless of that little hiccup, sneaking around is for the best. For one, she's still my daughter's nanny for the next several weeks so it might feel strange for Everly to have us dating. I don't want to spoil her summer with Cassandra by blurring the boundaries between them.

Not to mention, I've never introduced Everly to a girlfriend before and I have no fucking idea how that is going to go.

Also, I still can't get a read on where Cassandra wants all this to go. She's so chill about everything in life and as much as I love that about her, I also hate it because it leaves me feeling uncertain. I like order. I like a plan. I'd like to flash into the future and see where this whole thing ends up because the suspense of the unknown is painful. And is all this even what I want? To put myself out there with someone again? Fuck…it's all scary as hell.

Dean shoots me an apologetic face. "I'm sorry about the nanny word. I didn't mean anything by it. You just shocked me. I didn't expect you to be dating her."

"You're the one who told me to go after her," I retort, my brows furrowed. "Hell, you all but shoved me out of my house on poker night to go chase her down."

"I know, but I didn't expect it to turn into a dating thing." Dean blinks away his shock. "You're usually a hit and run type."

"That's how it started." I pinch the bridge of my nose and sigh as memories of the past few weeks circulate in my mind. So much has happened. "But then it kept going and next thing I know, we're on my plane to Aspen so I can buy her a dress for my charity gala next weekend."

"Holy shit," Dean laughs, and I feel his eyes on me as he says, "Are you in love with her?"

"Why would you say that?" I pierce him with a severe look and instantly realize that I'm not denying his question, only asking him why he's asking it—which is probably very telling.

His eyes are wide and probing as he answers, "Because you don't date. Ever. And for you to take a chance on the person who's your kid's nanny means you must think she's worth taking a risk for." He pauses for a moment and then adds, "This is the first girl you've talked about seriously since I've known you. I have to assume she's important."

"She is," I reply honestly and run my finger around the rim of my glass. "She's like a magnet I can't stay away from. As different as we are, I find myself craving her freestyle nature like a drug to soothe my own stress. The problem is, the timing is awful. When I close this deal with All-Out Properties, my entire life is going to change. I'll kill myself to find quality time with Everly. Plus, Cassandra has a major past trauma with her old corporate job which means none of this meshes well together. Am I better off ending it now to save us both the pain of ending it later when I get too busy?"

Flashbacks of everything she shared with me over dinner earlier this week hit me at full force again. So much of what she said sounded eerily familiar. When I launched my company, the people who I employed worked long hours right alongside me. We were burning the candle at both ends because there was an adrenaline rush that came every time we surpassed our goals and hit the next level.

Did I pay enough attention to their health and welfare? I'm not so sure. I'm pretty sure I do a good job now. But I'm essentially starting that painful growth process all over again with this merger, and what happened to Cassandra has lit a new fear inside me for my staff members.

Two months ago, I was charged and ready for the frenzy of incorporating their business into mine. Now…I'm having second thoughts.

Dean hits me with a disbelieving look. "I thought you were a guy who likes a challenge."

I scowl at my friend. "I think my first relationship in close to a decade constitutes as a bit more than a challenge, don't you? This is a fucking mountain to climb."

Dean shrugs dismissively like we're talking about the weather, not my entire life. "Max, you're a single dad, a well-respected boss, friend, brother, son. Hell, you even do charity work beyond what the rest of us do. Why do you think this is one thing you could fail at?"

"Because I might not be enough for her." Those words feel heavy in my mouth as the reality of my deepest fears come to light again. The insecurity I have in the idea that even if I go all in with her, she still might want someone else. It's happened before. I inhale deeply and add, "She's been through a lot, and she might want someone with less burdens."

He sets his glass down and shakes his head. "A good partner in life can help lift those burdens."

His words cause a frisson of anxiety to shoot through my chest. Is this really what I'm ready for? A partner? Someone to share my life with? Just the thought of committing to someone again like I did with Jess feels like a foreign concept. I was so young when I last did it. I've lived a thousand lives since then. And who's to say Cassandra wants this life with me? Who's to say I'm even in love with her yet? I'm not even sure.

My voice is grave when I admit the fears that still live deep inside me. "What if I'm a shitty partner? I failed once, you know."

"You didn't fail." Dean eyes me thoughtfully. "You succeeded in allowing Jessica to be comfortable enough to be honest with you about her true self. That's not a failure, Max. Her happiness now is a success story. And you deserve to find your own happiness. You've fucking earned it, my friend."

Our attention is ripped away from each other when the sound of the door that leads into the garage opens. Cassandra's eyes are wide, and she spots Dean and me.

"Sorry, I thought you guys were outside," she says, looking guilty. "I was just coming in to refill my water."

"No need to be sorry," Dean responds with a friendly smile. "I was just heading out to go save my fiancée from her mother. Weddings, amiright?"

"I wouldn't know," Cassandra laughs politely and walks into the kitchen as Dean heads out the back door, looking really fucking obvious. She stands at the refrigerator and refills her water. "Didn't mean to chase him out."

"Were your ears burning?" I ask, my eyes drifting down her sexy body that's covered in sweat and sawdust.

"No…why? Were you talking about me?" she inquires, turning to face me with concern in her eyes. "I thought we were keeping this a secret."

I shrug. "From Everly, yes. I didn't think that it mattered if I told Dean. Have you not talked to Dakota about any of this?"

"Yeah, I guess I have." She bites her lip and glances down at her water bottle. "So what were you talking about exactly?"

"Life," I reply with a laugh. "The future."

"The future?" Cassandra looks nervous.

"Yeah." My eyes narrow on her. "Like, what do you want out of life?"

Her cheeks turn pink as she leans against the island counter. "What do you mean?"

"Career, marriage, babies?" I lift my shoulders up and down like I'm talking about the weather now.

Her eyes widen. "Jesus, we're skipping some steps here, aren't we?"

I shrug again, feeling suddenly very motivated to push her on this, like this conversation is going to be the determining factor in my feelings and whether or not I press on or pull back.

"I'm not saying you have to be thinking about any of this with me," I add, trying to soothe her anxiety. "But I'm just curious what you want out of life."

"Did you forget I subscribe to the willy-nilly lifestyle?" She laughs nervously and takes a long drink of her water.

"But surely you know if you want kids," I press, not willing to let her joke her way out of this.

Do I want kids? My eyes instantly lower to her belly and the idea of it swollen with a baby of our own makes my cock thicken in my jeans. *Jesus, is this a breeding kink? Is that a thing?*

She licks her lips thoughtfully and lifts her brows. "I'd probably like a kid if I could be guaranteed he or she was as cool as Everly."

I smile and nod. "I can't find a fault in that."

"Are you trying to find a fault?" she asks, her brows pinched together.

"I'm trying to find similar end goals," I answer firmly. "I don't like sneaking around, and I want to make sure we're on the same page here."

"Meaning?"

"Meaning that you have real feelings for me and I'm not just a summer fling for you during your Great Defrost."

"You're not a summer fling," she snaps defensively as she wipes at a bead of sweat that's fallen down her temple. "You're like…the most unexpected, shocking, sexiest, best surprise of my life."

Her words send a rush of heat through my body as my lips pull back into a smile. "Do you mean that?" I inquire, stalking toward her to close the space between us. No kid around means I don't have to give my curvy girl any space.

"Yes, I mean it," she replies with a laugh as I cage her in, my hands pressed on the countertop on either side of her. "You are an even better surprise than Kate asking me to make cocktuterie boards."

My brows lift. "Cock what?"

She laughs again and sets her water bottle down on the counter and wraps her hands around my neck. "These crazy charcuterie boards Kate wants me to make. Max, I don't think you realize that I'm not sure I'd be ready to dive into this adventure with her if it wasn't for you."

"Me?" I ask, desperate for her to elaborate. "What did I do?"

She inhales deeply and smiles. "You've inspired me to start dreaming again." Her voice catches, so she looks away as she shakes her head in wonder. Narrowing her eyes, she gazes back up at me. "These feelings I have for you are real and intense, and they make me imagine a completely different life for myself that I wouldn't allow myself to imagine after my stroke."

"A good life?" I pry, needy and not giving a fuck about that fact.

I want to be a thousand percent sure that this woman is worth risking my heart for again. Because I can feel it hanging tenuously by a thread, just waiting to be beat to a pulp again.

"I'm imagining a great life." She runs her finger over top of my brows, a bizarre sign of affection that is distinctly Cozy. "But let's put the future talk on ice until we, you know, have another date or something?"

I growl and lower my lips to hers. "I'll allow it. For now."

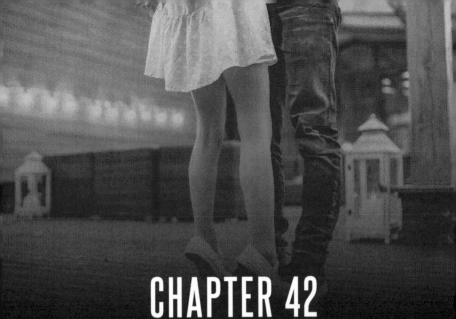

CHAPTER 42

Max

"Evie-Bear, you're here!" my mom Johanna peals from her front door as I stand in my tux holding a pink overnight bag. Everly wraps her arms around my mom's slender frame.

"Doesn't Dad look like a movie star, Grandma?" Everly looks back at me with her hands still wrapped around my mom, and I run my hand over my tuxedo, adjusting the bow tie that I still need to do up.

"He sure does," Mom responds dramatically. "He looks like James Bond."

"Who's that?" Everly's nose scrunches up, but she doesn't wait for my mom to answer before looking inside. "Where's Hershey?"

"He's in the backyard," Mom answers, referring to their small shitzu. "Why don't you go find him while I talk to your daddy."

"Bye, Daddy, love you!" Everly exclaims, barely even waving to me as she takes off in search of the family dog.

"Damn, that stings." I press my fist to my chest in mock pain.

Mom waves her hand. "A kid crying and clinging to your leg when you try to leave is what stings. That right there is called a content kid."

I smile proudly, and my focus shifts over as my dad joins my mom in the doorway. He looks me up and down. "Snazzy tux. What's the occasion this time?"

"The annual Rainbow Project Gala."

Mom frowns. "You're going to that even with Jessica out of the country?"

I sigh and shake my head. My parents took the news about Jessica pretty well. They're not closed-minded people. But they seem to struggle a bit with our modern co-parenting and how we still intermingle in each other's lives.

"I'm on the board of the charity with or without Jessica, Mom."

She smiles and nods her head. "Are you taking a date?"

"Yeah, just a friend," I reply casually.

My mom gets a sad look in her eyes. This is a constant battle with her and my brothers. She wants us all married and settled down. I don't get the pressure quite as hard because I at least gave her a grandchild, but my brothers aren't pulling their weight by filling up my mother's home with screaming babies like she dreams.

I would *love* to sit back and watch the three of them fall in love and start families. They collectively seem determined to be single, tattooed, bearded mountain men who are the cause of a flannel shortage in the United States and whose preferred form of communication comes in the form of grunts. They have no idea how quickly a woman can flip their world upside down.

I sure as hell didn't.

"Everything going okay with that merger you have coming up?" Dad asks, his brow furrowed as he braces himself on the doorframe.

"So far, yes. Won't be long now before we sign on the dotted line."

"You're going to have to move office buildings, right?" He's giving me that judgmental dad voice. The voice that says, "I don't care how much money you make every year, I'm still your father and I know better."

"Eventually, yes. The Denver staff will stay there until Jenson and I find a location that will fit everyone. I have a couple of properties we're going to look at together."

"Your staff size will double?"

I nod.

"Better you than me, kid," he scoffs. "I have a hard enough time getting your brothers to show up for work."

I grimace at that. "It's never easy working with family."

"You can say that again."

"Enough shop talk." My mom waves her hands. "Max needs to go, and I need to go spoil my only grandchild!"

"No soda before bed, Mom," I assert. "She sleeps like crap when she has soda at night, and then I'm paying for it the next day."

She rolls her eyes and waves goodbye as I turn to leave.

"Hey, Max?" Dad calls out.

"Yeah?" I answer, turning back toward him.

"You sure you want all that?"

"All what?"

He sighs heavily. "The new company, the added responsibility. All the changes."

My brow furrows. "Of course, Dad. Why are you asking?"

He blinks seriously at me. "Because you look happy right now, and I'd hate for the stress of this expansion to take that away from you."

I grip the back of my neck and shrug. "Well, I'm probably happy because I've had Everly home with me all summer. It's been nice seeing her more often. All that will change once Jess gets back, though."

"I know." Dad shoots me a wobbly smile. "I just want you to really think about this before you commit your life to it. Everly is growing up so fast, and I can tell you from experience if I could go back and flip less houses to be around more for you boys growing up...I would. I don't live with many regrets...but I do live with that."

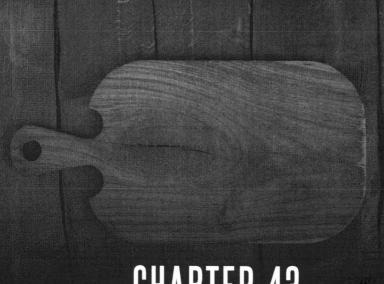

CHAPTER 43

Cozy

The Butterfly Dress is a two-piece gown with a colorful blast of swirling pastels and a shaggy tulle fabric overlay. The top is a corseted sweetheart neckline with dramatic off-the-shoulder straps that drape down to my elbows. The full A-line skirt makes a statement of rainbow-like colors. It's giving "Grecian Goddess at Pride Week" vibes all the way…at least, that's what Tatianna said. But she's right.

This dress makes a statement. Max told Tatianna beforehand that the attire at the Rainbow Project Gala goes anywhere from sleek glamor to *RuPaul's Drag Race*. This dress is like the perfect combination of both.

And when I open my tiny house door to Max Fletcher standing before me in a muted dusty-blue tuxedo with a black bow tie hanging around his white pressed shirt, I forget all about his reaction to my dress…because he doesn't just have a tie hanging around his neck…

It's a bow tie.

Swoon mode activated.

"Cassandra, you look—"

Max doesn't get to finish his words as I grab the tails of his tie and pull him down to my lips. Our tongues instantly find each other like two old friends who haven't been together in years, when in fact, this man kissed me in the garage this morning while Everly was inside. He walked into my workshop, pressed me up against the closed door, gripped my jaw and took what he wanted from me.

And I was happy to give it to him.

Max isn't a sexual dominant by any means, more so, a born leader. The past couple of weeks together have revealed a confidence in him that wasn't there when we first became intimate. When we were first banging it out with each other, it was wild and exploratory...sort of a fun guess and check as we discovered each other's desires. And "kinks," which I love that he uses that term generously now.

Now, it's like he always knows what I need—even if it's just a stolen kiss that lasts ten seconds. It's everything.

And the cuddling...I've never felt more cherished than when I'm sleeping with Max. Perhaps it was because the only sleepovers I really had with men were when I was working at my corporate job, so I was too exhausted to really acknowledge the feel of a strong man's arms around me, or the sensation of his heavy breaths in my hair, and the sounds he makes when he stretches and yawns. God...if I would have never experienced those moments with Max, I think I would live a life with an uncomfortable sensation of missing something I never had.

I break our kiss and Max says, "Beautiful." He pulls in a large breath of air and adds, "Cassandra, you look beautiful."

Simple.

Classic.

Just like Max.

I glance down at my hands still gripping his tie. "You know what these loose ties do to me."

A sexy smirk lifts the corner of his mouth. "Exactly."

The drive to Denver is charged with sexual tension that makes it feel stuffy in Max's SUV when in fact, the A/C is on full blast. Last weekend, Max hit me out of nowhere with talk about our future. At the time, I felt cagey and had to force myself to stand there and re-assure him. It wasn't easy.

The truth is, I'm still learning who Max is. Yes, he has surprised me by not being as consumed by his work as I expected of a CEO at his level to be, but I don't know what that means for him long term. I know he has some big merger coming up that I struggle to hear him talk about because it feels triggering to me. But will he be able to manage all that and still be the man beside me right now? I sure hope so. Because when I saw him in his tux tonight, it was impossible for me not to picture him as a groom. And the woman walking down the aisle toward him in that fantasy was one-hundred-percent me.

I know it's crazy early to be picturing our future already, but I have been flexing my imagination all summer long with Everly and this was an involuntary daydream I fully enjoyed. Zaddy Max is mar-riage material for sure. I just hope he continues to prove that to me.

As we pull up to the valet and the grand hotel where the event is being hosted, Max hands his keys off to the attendant and laces his fingers through mine to lead me inside.

"Will any of your friends be here tonight?" I ask, looking up at Max as he leads me through the grand foyer of the hotel toward the event room.

"No, but my brothers come every year," Max replies, head nod-ding to someone we pass.

"Your brothers?" I repeat with a smile. "Big, burly mountain men at this kind of event? I bet they are wildly popular."

Max narrows his sexy eyes and pulls me in close, his hand wrap-ping around my waist. "You better not be calling my brothers attrac-tive or I'm going to find a coat closet to remind you who is number one in the Fletcher family."

I laugh and shake my head. "Oh, trust me, I already know... *Zaddy.*" Max's deep laugh gives me goose bumps just as we round the corner and enter the event room.

My lips part at the stunning display in front of me. People dressed to the nines float around an elegant ballroom that's teeming with color. Large round banquet tables are adorned with bright, feathery centerpieces and giant crystal chandeliers hang low and reflect rainbow lights swirling throughout the room. It's like an elegant nightclub and mardi gras had a baby in here. There's a singer dressed in drag up on the stage, filling the room with the sweet sounds of Alicia Keys.

"Drink?" Max offers, placing his hand on the small of my back as he ushers me over to the long bar. We both select one of the pink signature drinks with gummy bears floating inside and clink our glasses before turning around to enjoy the view.

"Max, this is...so impressive," I say, eyeing a long table of items that look like they're set up for a silent auction. On the opposite side of the room, there's a runway where models are showcasing various outfits that I expect must be created by LGBTQ+ designers. "How involved are you in planning all of this?"

Max clicks his tongue. "I'm more the money than the creative vision, but we all have our roles to play. Jessica and I joined the board when Everly was five so I've learned over the years that I'm most helpful on the financial side of the charity. Jessica is usually a big part of the event planning."

"You do all this with Jess?" I ask curiously.

Max nods. "Yeah, she joined first and then hit me up for a donation, and after that I was pulled into the fold."

"That's amazing," I sputter, realizing that with Jessica gone all summer I haven't really had much of a chance to see Max and Jessica interact. "You two must get along well."

Max nods again. "We're not perfect by any means, but I told you in Aspen that it's important for me to support Jess and her wife and be a part of this community in a real way...not just...I know someone gay way. You know?"

"Yeah, I know," I reply, and take a fortifying sip of my fruity drink wondering once again how Max Fletcher is even human.

My eyes widen when I spot Max's brother waving at us from a table up by the stage. "Shoot, your brother is coming over," I murmur into Max's shoulder and feel my body start to twitch. "We should have talked about this. What do I say?"

"About what?" Max's sexy brows furrow down at me.

"About why I'm here," I respond quickly, knowing there's no way in hell Max told his brothers about us. They see Everly every week, they can't be trusted with this highly secure information. "Should we tell him your Aspen girl got sick and I'm filling in?" *Excellent plan, Cozy.*

"Oh…um…" Max gets a funny look on his face as his brother appears beside him and gives his shoulder a playful shove.

"How are you late to your own fucking party?" Calder says, looking at me and shaking his head knowingly as he stretches past me to grab a signature drink off the bar.

My cheeks feel hot as I stealthily pull away from Max who's just draped his arm on the bar behind me. I take in Calder's tattooed wrists peeking out of his sleek, black tux. It's quite a sight with that pink martini drink in his hand.

I open my mouth to give him my stellar excuse for being here when Max's warm hand touches my back. "Calder, you remember my girl, Cassandra, right?"

My girl?

Did Max just refer to me as his girl?

Calder smiles and winks at me. "Oh yes, I remember you. You had my brother's panties all in a wad on poker night."

"What?" I croak, feeling my stomach literally fall out of my ass. I glance down to check. "I didn't touch his panties."

"No panty touching that night?" Calder frowns and looks at Max, who appears completely unphased by this interaction. "Dammit, I owe Luke five bucks."

"He doesn't even…I mean…I wouldn't…" I'm stuttering like a moron, and I need to close my mouth.

"Relax, Cozy," Max laughs and touches the top of my head as he kisses me on the temple. "I texted my brothers last week and told them you and I are together."

He props his elbow on the bar and rakes his eyes over my body like he's internally enjoying this entire moment. What the hell?

I slap my hand over my artful makeup that took me an entire hour to apply. "You could have mentioned that to me before I started stuttering like an idiot."

He licks his lips and waggles his brows. "I never miss an opportunity to watch you squirm, sweet cheeks."

My face heats at that sexy look in his eye when Calder deadpans, "Okay, I'm not drunk enough for this." He downs the last of his pink drink and pushes between us to grab another one.

Wyatt and Luke join us at the bar a second later, and I'm greeted by Luke with, "I called it first, just so you know."

"Called what?" Max asks, narrowing his eyes on his youngest brother.

"You and her...you were so obvious that night I picked up Everly."

My brows furrow. "Nothing had happened at that point yet."

Luke shrugs. "Max was like a lost puppy."

Wyatt grunts his agreement, continuing that brooding, man of few words vibe he puts out as he sips a pink drink through his thick beard. Another stunning sight. Honestly, Rainbow Project should put these brothers on their event fliers. They'd sell tickets like crazy.

"Did you guys bring dates tonight?" I inquire, glancing around for three women who look like they've been abandoned.

"Hell no," Calder answers with a laugh. "We come to this thing every year, dump a bunch of money on the auction stuff, and hit up downtown in our tuxes. Three dudes in tuxes is like a fucking bat signal to the single ladies in Denver. It's a win-win because we don't have to buy a ticket for some random chick to the event, and we still get laid because of the tuxes." Calder snaps his fingers proudly and I laugh.

"Ignore him," Max huffs, rolling his eyes. "And I regret to inform you they are seated at our table because I can't trust them alone with anyone else."

"It's for a good cause," I offer helpfully.

Wyatt lifts his glass to mine and clinks it in a silent cheers of agreement.

"Speaking of which, we should probably go find our table," Max says, looking over the top of my head. "My business partner should be here with his wife by now, and I really should give him some face time."

An odd shiver shoots up my back at his mention of work stuff, but I do my best to shake it off. This is Max's world, and if I want any chance of what we have turning into more, I need to get used to mixing business with pleasure.

Max

The live auction begins, and I watch my brothers huddle around the brochure that lists everything up for auction tonight. The sight of them at this event every year makes me prouder than they'll ever know. None of them have a ton of money, though they aren't broke by any means. I've helped them invest in various homes they've flipped throughout the years so they can maintain some passive income and don't have to rely as heavily on booking new projects all the time. But when they come here and drop a few grand each on weekend getaways to Colorado Springs, or a wine club membership, it's not because they have money to burn.

They do it for Everly.

As different as my life is from the three of them, they have never, not once, made me feel like an outsider. I love those weird assholes.

The text thread between the four of us when I told them I was bringing Cassandra tonight and would appreciate them not being pains in my ass about it was amusing to say the least.

Wyatt communicated mostly with emojis, which was weirdly more expressive than his actual spoken language. Luke sent a lot of "I called it" GIFs, and Calder accused me of watching too much nanny porn.

He really is the biggest asshole of them all.

But fuck it, after my talk with Dean, I realized that if I didn't at least try to go all in with Cassandra, I would always wonder what-if. And I would rather try and fail with her than never try at all.

I check my watch, wondering where Jenson Hunsberger and his wife must be. The event is nearly over, and I heard from him earlier this week that he was looking forward to coming. I hope nothing bad happened to them.

Cassandra's hand finds mine under the table, and I lace my fingers through hers, smiling softly at the oddly natural feeling it is to have her here with me tonight. I haven't had a real girlfriend since Jess, and what I feel for her is nothing like what I felt for Jess. And I don't think that has anything to do with Jess's sexuality. I'm starting to realize she just wasn't my person. I was forcing her to be because I cared about her and thought we made sense. We were both driven and focused, had big goals in life.

I don't have those commonalities with Cassandra, but I find that I like the feeling of being challenged by her. And the chemistry that sizzles between our palms right now is fucking addicting.

She is beautiful tonight. Her short dark hair is curled and pulled back in a colorful headband that goes perfectly with her dress. A dress that was more than worth the quick trip to Aspen. Honestly, how I ever thought I could simply bang it out with Cassandra and be satisfied is laughable at this point. I'll never get sick of her.

Cassandra leans close to me, her pink lips looking extra kissable as she whispers, "This might sound weird, considering you're my boss and I'm your employee, but I'm really proud of you, Max."

My brows twitch with that odd remark. "Proud?"

"Yeah…you've got it going on."

"Do I?" I practically growl as I drape my arm around her chair to cage her into her seat. "In what ways exactly?"

Her lips twitch with a smirk. "Oh, you want a list?"

"Yes, I'm afraid I need one…not all of us subscribe to the willy-nilly way of life."

She narrows her sexy eyes at my mouth. "I'll have my assistant fax you over a list in the morning."

"No one faxes anymore, Cozy." My fingers tease the back of her neck, causing her to bite her lip and shiver.

I lean in to take her teeth's place when suddenly a hand lands firmly on my shoulder.

"My man, Max!" Jenson's voice booms from behind me, and I quickly pull back to turn around.

"Jenson, you finally made it," I state, standing up to reach my hand out to his. Jenson is a solid five inches shorter than me, so I always have a nice view of his receding black hairline. "I was starting to worry."

"No need to worry." He laughs and leans in close, drenching me with the scent of vodka. "Just had a little pre-party before the real party. You know how that goes."

"Where is your wi—" My voice trails off when I see a tall, young blonde standing behind him that is most definitely not his wife.

"This is Paisley," he says, pulling on the girl's elbow so she moves in to stand beside him. "She's been my right hand for years. Libby wasn't feeling well tonight so she stayed home. I thought it'd be good for you to meet one of your future team members."

He wraps his hand around her waist, his fingers drifting low on her hip as he secures her beside him. Jenson isn't a bad-looking guy, but something looks off between this girl and him. Not to mention, his hands seem a bit too intimate for a platonic boss, employee situation. Especially a boss who's married.

Then again, am I one to really judge?

Paisley forces a smile and shakes my hand, her fingers limp in mine. "Nice to meet you, Paisley. Let me introduce you to my girlfriend." I step back to reveal Cassandra, and my face falls when I see her staring up at us with the most stricken look I've ever seen on her face.

"Cassie!" Jenson bellows, bumping me in the shoulder as he moves past me to lower himself into my vacated seat. "Is that really you?"

My chest tightens as I watch Cassandra's arms cross over her waist. Her brow is furrowed, and she looks like she could be sick as she replies woodenly, "Hello, Mr. Hunsberger."

He barks out a dry laugh and drapes his arm over the back of her chair just where mine was a second ago. "You don't work for me anymore, girlie...call me Jenson."

"Work for you?" I repeat, feeling all the air escape my lungs. "When did she work for you?"

Jenson's face screws up as he thinks. "How long ago since you left? A year?"

"Seven and a half months," she corrects, staring at the table like a statue, her cheeks hollow as she seems to struggle to maintain her composure.

"How have you been, Cassie?" Paisley asks, stepping up closer, her eyes wide and sad on her former coworker. "You look so good."

Cassandra blinks up at the blonde, looking a bit shocked by her kind words before biting out, "I'm fine."

"Cassie was one of our best asset managers, weren't you, Cas?" Jenson brushes her shoulder, and I flinch when I notice she contorts her body away from his touch.

"Your former employer was All-Out Properties? This was your last boss?" I ask, my head throbbing with realization.

Cassandra's eyes are red rimmed as she struggles to look at me.

"Why didn't you tell me?" I rasp, my hands flexing at my sides. I know I've mentioned the name of the company I'm merging with to her multiple times. How could she keep this from me?

"Is there a problem here?" Jenson inquires, his beady eyes narrowing on Cassandra in a way that I do *not* fucking like.

"Just a little misunderstanding," I reply through clenched teeth as I glance around the table and see my brothers watching this exchange with charged interest. "I knew Cassandra worked in asset management, but I didn't realize she worked for *you*."

"You work at Fletcher Industries now, Cassie?" Jenson asks, elbowing her as he picks up a mint off the table and begins to unwrap it.

Seriously, if he touches her one more fucking time.

She jerkily shakes her head.

"What are you doing with yourself then?" he presses, clearly not picking up on her tense body language.

She inhales a deep breath and sits up a little straighter as her eyes find her former boss's with renewed strength. "I'm a nanny for Max's daughter."

"The nanny and the girlfriend?" Jenson barks out a laugh and tosses the mint into his mouth. "That's an interesting career shift."

"That's enough of that," I grind out, my hands balling into fists at my sides as I struggle to stay calm. The auction is still going on, and our table is smack dab in the middle of all the action. We don't need to draw more attention to ourselves than Jenson's late arrival already did.

Jenson holds his palms up to me. "I mean no harm. Just wanting to make sure you know that you're sitting on a valuable asset here. You should put her to work at your company, Max."

"Would you excuse me," Cassandra says, and her chair falls backward as she rises up too quickly. I rush over to pick it up and hear her voice tremble, "I'm just going to use the ladies' room."

"Paisley, why don't you go score your old boss some drinks. Is there no table service, Max?"

The muscle in my jaw jumps as I watch Cassandra's dress float behind her as she scurries off. My mind is reeling with this new information. Is this something Cassandra was hiding from me? What was her plan here? To let me finalize this deal with the asshole who nearly killed her? For what purpose? Maybe she wasn't planning to stick around long enough for the deal to finish.

Maybe she isn't as invested in this relationship as I am, and I'm getting played a fool for the second time in my life.

I have about twenty-seven more questions that I won't find answers for here at this table.

I don't even bother excusing myself as I storm out of the event room. When I step out into the hallway, I see Cassandra's frame retreat around another corner, so I jog over to catch up and watch her exit a door at the end of the hall.

"Cassandra, what the hell is going on?" I growl as I find her pacing outside in the hotel courtyard. It's dark out, and a couple of glowing fountains trickle loudly by the doors, mimicking the ringing in my ears. A couple cuddling by the large gas firepit stare at me and glance nervously at Cassandra before scurrying out of the garden area and back inside. I walk over to where Cassandra is pacing in front of a row of manicured bushes. "Is that your old fucking boss? The boss that nearly killed you?"

"Yes," she answers, her head bowed as she fiddles with the tulle on her dress. "And one of my coworker friends who I never heard from again."

"Why the hell didn't you tell me about this connection?" I exclaim, frustrated beyond belief that she kept this from me.

Her watery eyes find mine, flickering brightly in the firelight. "I didn't realize that All-Out was the company you were partnering with!"

"Seriously?" I snap and jam a hand through my hair. "I've mentioned All-Out Properties multiple times."

"Not to me!"

"Yes, I have."

"Max...you haven't, I swear," she repeats, her face full of panic. "I didn't even know what type of business you were acquiring. I thought you were in franchise development."

"I am. This would be another branch of my business. I'm sure I've mentioned it to you before."

"Well, why didn't you put two and two together when I told you about my old job?" she hisses, her nostrils flaring angrily.

I shake my head and shrug. "Because there are loads of commercial developers in Denver. I just assumed it had to be one of the other ones because I've mentioned All-Out before."

"Well, if you did, I probably blocked it out. I tend to block out everything you do for your company. It's a survival tactic."

"Survival tactic?" My head jerks back at that odd choice of words. "What do you need to survive from? I'm not like your former company. You don't need to protect yourself from me."

"Of course I do," she peals loudly, her eyes wide and wild as she steps closer to me, her scent invading my nose and confusing my thoughts even more. "You might not be as vile as Jenson, but you two have similar end goals. You both have that entrepreneurial drive to expand and grow and get bigger and more powerful. That represents everything I hate, Max. Everything that screws over employees and put me in a hospital. I knew that side existed in you, but I've been shielding myself from that part of you so it wouldn't change how I feel about you."

A pressure builds in my chest at the insane words she's spewing. She's saying that my career—my life—is something she can't stand to even hear about. I know what happened to her was horrific, but this is a giant boundary that I had no idea she placed between us.

"Cassandra, my company is important to me. And I'm fucking proud of it and my employees," I state, my voice firm. "If you're saying you don't respect what I do, then we have a serious problem here."

"Maybe we do," she huffs defensively. "Because if Fletcher Industries is becoming partners with All-Out Properties who put profit over people, then it won't be long before you're just as toxic as he is."

Her tone is scathing and unapologetic. It causes my lips to curl up in disgust. How could she think so little of me? After everything I've shared with her. It's like she doesn't even fucking know me.

I exhale heavily. "You're prosecuting me before I even commit a crime."

"Am I?" She laughs, and her face twists in pain as she wraps her arms around herself. "You flew me to Aspen on a company jet for a date. You paid a designer who knows how much money for this dress. None of that was for business, Max. That was you living the high life. That's shit Jenson would do. That's corporate greed."

"That you fucking enjoyed," I roar, thrusting my hands through my hair and taking a step away from her. "I'm not going to feel bad for enjoying what I've worked hard to earn. Being this successful is what makes it possible for us to raise over a million dollars in scholarship for marginalized kids tonight."

Her eyes fill with tears as she replies quickly, "But being at your level of success puts you in boardrooms next to greedy assholes like Jenson Hunsberger. What do you think will happen to you if you associate with someone like him on a regular basis?"

I look away in disgust. "There are greedy assholes in all socio-economic brackets, Cassandra. You're a smart girl, you should know that much."

She inhales sharply. "And you sound just like him, *Mr. Fletcher.*"

I jerk back, feeling like she just slapped me. I move toward her to touch her, to apologize for my words, but she holds her hands up to stop me.

Tears fall down her face when she adds, "This is the last time I let any man in power have control over my mental health."

Cozy

My chest heaves with anxiety as I make a beeline back into the event center to get my cell phone so I can call a Lyft and get as far away from this night as I can. What started out as a night full of hope and dreams of the future and charity has quickly turned into my worst nightmare.

I swipe quickly at my cheeks, trying hard to fight the pain that's enveloping me over the words I just exchanged with Max. We were doing so good. We had compartmentalized our lives so perfectly. I spent my days with Everly, and he spent his at the office. When we came together at night, neither of us discussed our work. We discussed literally everything but work. It was perfect. That balance in Max made me think this could be real between us. We could actually be happy together and not consumed by our vast differences. How could I be so blind?

Him partnering with Jenson of all people? The man whose name I can't even say without shuddering. That is not something I can overlook.

I steel myself as I approach my former boss who's still sitting at the table. Paisley lifts her hand to me with a small smile, but I ignore her, jutting my chin high and moving past her and Jenson with determination to grab my phone and handbag off the table. My eyes connect briefly with Wyatt's that are full of so much concern, it makes my chin tremble.

Grabbing my bag and phone, I turn to leave before the waterworks start when a clammy hand wraps tightly around my elbow, sending chills down my spine. "What are you saying about me out there to Max?" Jenson's voice is like nails on a chalkboard, bringing me back to the nights when his voice haunted my dreams.

"Nothing," I snap, pulling my head back for some space away

from Jenson's putrid breath. I try to jerk my arm out of his hold, but his grip only tightens more.

"Bullshit," he growls with a smile that doesn't reach his eyes. "Don't forget I was your boss for six years, Cassie. I can still tell when you're lying."

My knees feel weak, reminding me of how I always felt when I was around Jenson in the past. Insecure, rushed, scared of screwing up. I hated that girl. I'm not that girl anymore.

"I'm not discussing anything with you." I attempt to free myself again only to have him yank me backward, causing my shoulder to fall into his chest. Out of the corner of my eye, I see all three of Max's brothers stand in unison.

Jenson's breath is hot in my ear when he rasps, "If you fuck this deal up for me because of one of your little panic attacks, I'll make sure you never work in the industry ever again."

His comment shocks me in the most unexpected way. Instead of breaking my will down further and causing my anxiety to flare up like it would have in the past, I actually throw my head back and laugh.

Jenson's nostrils flare with irritation, and I notice Max's brothers all staring at me in confusion.

"Cozy, you good?" Wyatt eyes me seriously, gifting me his very coveted words as his chin drops like a tiger waiting for the signal to attack.

"I'm great, Wyatt," I answer as a euphoric sense of power settles over me. The strength and confidence I've regained since leaving the corporate world washes over me, and I take a cleansing breath at that wonderful realization.

I glance down at my ex-boss's clammy hand still gripping me like he thinks he has an ounce of power over me. My eyes lift to his as I harden my glare. I push his chest hard enough that he has to take a step back and release my arm. "Jenson, I couldn't give a flying fuck what you tell anyone in the industry about me. I've got a bright future making beautiful wooden cocks that I'm sure look nothing like yours."

The corner of his mouth tips up into a sleazy smile eliciting the exact opposite reaction I was hoping for. Typical narcissist. His eyes fall to my chest as he leans in close, his hand cupping my hip when he says, "If I knew you sucked CEO cock, I might have offered mine up. I don't mind being a chubby chaser every once in a while."

Heat rushes through my body, setting my face on fire. I don't think, I just react. I barely hear Paisley gasp as I rear my hand back, ready to slap him with everything I have.

My hand swipes the air in front of him as strong arms band around my waist, hauling me back against a rock-hard body.

"Touch her ever again, and it will be the last thing you fucking do," Max growls, his neck veins bulging angrily as he shoves Jenson in the chest, causing him to fall back into his chair. His hand reaches back to hold me behind him as his body vibrates with rage.

My heart thunders in my chest watching Max react so violently for me. It's part shocking, part inspiring, but mostly, it's terrifying. This is Max's future business partner, and he just…went off on him.

Jenson gapes up at us, his eyes a mixture of horror, anger, and humiliation. His nostrils flare as he sputters, "We were just talking, Max."

"She is mine," he seethes, the veins in his neck bulging angrily. "And you don't speak to her, touch her, or even look at her ever again." Max turns and slides his fingers into my hand, his eyes pools of darkness that I've never seen before as he states firmly, "I'm driving you home now."

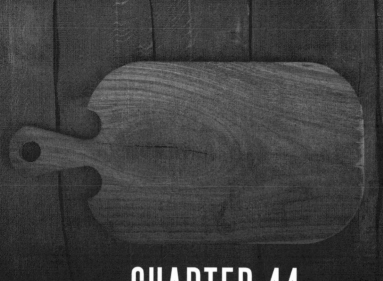

CHAPTER 44

Cozy

T he car ride is painfully silent all the way from Denver to Boulder. Max's knuckles are white on the steering wheel as his body vibrates with anger. Meanwhile, I'm over here, trying to figure out how the hell I can crawl out of this vehicle and go back in time.

Back in time to before I agreed to the date with Max, before I agreed to bang it out with him, before I wanted him to kiss me. Hell, I'd like to go back in time and never walk into that boardroom and interview for that job. All of this was a mistake. What started off as a favor to my sister and a way for me to dip my toe back into the real world has quickly turned into a nightmare of epic real-world proportions.

Max almost got in a fight with Jenson tonight…over me. This is the man whose company he is merging with, and he just literally threatened him…because of me.

I don't know how I feel about that…other than terrified. And guilty and a million other emotions that I'm currently drowning in, and my doggy paddle isn't enough to save myself this time.

What have we been doing these past few weeks? How did we

get this deep in whatever this is and not connect these very significant dots?

Oh…I know…because I hid my past from him like it was some dark, dirty secret I should be ashamed of. Like somehow suffering with anxiety and admitting that a job was too much for me and no one there gave a shit about my well-being was some admission of failure I couldn't share.

I had nothing to be ashamed of. And when I looked at Jenson and Paisley in the eyes tonight for the first time since my Great Defrost, I saw just how little power they have over me now. And that is a liberating realization.

CEO Max Fletcher, on the other hand? The power he possesses is another story altogether. These emotions I'm drowning in are not the result of Jenson reappearing back into my life out of nowhere. They are because of the man beside me giving me the silent treatment.

Max pulls into his garage and shuts the car off. As we get out, I pause by the passenger side door and watch him head inside. I hesitate for a moment before turning to walk outside and back to my tiny house where I feel safe. Alone time would be good for both of us right now.

"Where are you going?" Max barks, and I look back to see him holding the door to his house open.

I swallow the knot in my throat. "I'm going back to the tiny house."

"Alone?" he asks, his eyes swimming with so many emotions that I know I'm the cause of.

I nod woodenly, wishing more than anything he could come with me, and we could go back to the nights where it was just us in the tiny house after Everly went to bed and things weren't so complicated. When we "did less," it was easier. Willy-nilly was working for us. Why did we try to turn this into something more?

He grips the back of his neck and shakes his head. "So what does that mean?"

I shrug, hating the fact that he's making me say this all now, but knowing I can't lie to him either. I'm not okay right now. "I don't see how we can make this work, Max."

"Make what work? Us?" he inquires, his eyes severe even from a distance.

My slow nod causes him to slam the door shut and storm over to where I'm standing on the driveway. His tie is loose around his collar, his blond hair disheveled from the countless times he's thrust his hands through it, and the house lights showcase the tight stress lines in his forehead.

He looks beautiful.

"Look at me, Cassandra," he snaps, his body looming over me in all his vibrating alpha presence. "Are you ending this because you think I'm like Jenson Hunsberger?"

"No, I know you're different than him, Max." I inhale a deep breath, my voice weak when I add, "But that doesn't change the fact that your company is growing. And your life is about to get a lot more complicated. I know what corporate growing pains are like, especially when you're growing with All-Out Properties. They are ruthless and only care about money. Profit over people is their motto."

"So I'll fix the problems," he responds hotly, throwing his hand out wide. "I'll hire a company culture expert to help with the merger. I'll add more HR. Believe me, I run my company vastly different than the man you described to me in Aspen. And just because you had one bad experience with one corporation doesn't mean all corporations are run like that. What happened to you was horrific, Cozy. I could kill Jenson for how he handled what happened to you. But when I tell you that my assistant's husband had his hip replaced last year and I went to the hospital with fucking Chipotle because I remember Marcia telling me that's his favorite, I'm not lying. Not all CEOs are the fucking same."

"Your waiting room kombucha is for clients, not staff," I blurt and then cringe because that is so not what I should have replied with, but I have to add for clarification, "That's something shitty that I could see Jenson doing."

Max barks a disgusted laugh. "That kombucha is the product of one of our clients, and no one likes it. We put it in the waiting room in hopes that visitors will drink it so we can get rid of the shit. There are beverages in the employee break room that anyone is welcome to, even that shitty kombucha."

My brows crinkle. That kombucha is such a silly thing that I have fixated on since my interview. I used that moment any time I wanted to swoon hard over something Max did for me—like make me coffee every morning or the fact that he even attempted to do bubble braids in Everly's hair. Tears sting my eyes at those painful memories. The stupid kombucha memory was there to remind me that he could still be a douchey corporate asshole, just like Jenson.

How does he have an answer for everything?

"Fine, you're nice to your staff," I reply flippantly, flinging my hands out wide in surrender. "But that doesn't change the fact that you and I want different things. I want to do less. You want to do more. I want to go slow. You want to go fast. We've been living in a fantasy this summer. An alternate reality. Everly will go back to her mom's soon and you'll be consumed with your merger. This coach is turning back into a pumpkin. I'm not going to be what you want when your life goes back to normal."

"Don't tell me what I want," Max bites, his jaw muscle ticking angrily. "It's taken me *years* to even want to try something with someone again, Cozy. That fucking means something."

"But it doesn't change the fact that we want different things," I cry, knowing I have to be firm on this because Max is a man who gets what he wants. I let him steamroll me once into going on that date in Aspen, and then I got lost in him. Lost in us, in our connection, in our passion. In the incredible, mind-altering sex and the way he looks at me in the mornings when I leave his bedroom. I got lost in the fantasy that I could be a part of him and Everly…have an instant family.

But the truth is, Max will always be a CEO, and that kind of lifestyle will always put me on edge. I don't want to be near that life again. I have to be strong to protect my mental health. There is no reality where Max Fletcher and Cassandra Barlow work.

Max tilts his head and eyes me harshly. "Do you even trust yourself to know what you want, Cassandra?"

"What the hell does that mean?" I snap petulantly, feeling tiny pricks of discomfort all over my body.

He steps closer to me, his nostrils flaring like an animal getting ready to attack. "I think you're making excuses not because we want different things but because you're scared." His voice cracks, and he sniffs loudly, his face twisting with pain that I feel in my gut. "You're scared because my life slightly resembles the thing that almost killed you, so you think you're going down a path that will leave you broken again. But at some point, you have to admit to yourself that your wil- ly-nilly lifestyle isn't protecting you from anything. The real world will still be out there when you finally admit the truth you refuse to see."

"What truth?" I whisper, my throat tight with pain at the way his eyes are locked on mine so intently. I inch closer to him, desperate for the next words that will come out of his mouth. His gaze dips to my lips and then rakes over my face, taking in every tiny millimeter of my features like he's committing them to memory.

His voice is guttural when he answers, "That the only reason you do less is because you're afraid to want more."

His words pop our bubble of tension where we were suspended from time and space. They poke a deep bruise inside me that I didn't even know existed as I'm thrust back to reality. I pull back and my vision blurs as my eyes well with tears.

His words assault every part of me that I've been proud of the past seven and a half months. He thinks I'm afraid to want more? Then he doesn't understand me at all. I don't live this way because of fear. I live this way to survive. He doesn't get it because he's still in that world that I left behind. Which is why I can't be with him. I don't want a front row ticket to that life.

I suck my cheeks in and shake my head, ignoring the tears falling down my face. "Even if everything you said is true, Max, it doesn't change the fact that Jenson will be your partner soon, and I can't be anywhere near him ever again."

"Well, give me a damn minute to figure that part out, okay?" he bites, his eyes glowering at me as he steps back and begins pacing in front of me. "I just found out tonight that I'm going into business with the man who almost killed the woman I love, so I need some time to figure out what the fuck I can do to fix that."

"Love?" I gasp, my entire body erupting in goose bumps at the word that just tumbled out of his mouth. He couldn't have meant that. It was a slip of the tongue for sure. My head jerks as I stutter, "You don't mean that."

He stops pacing and pushes a hand through his hair as graveness casts over his features. "Shit, Cozy...it has to be obvious. I practically assaulted the asshole for you tonight."

Panic sets in over my whole body at how quickly this all escalated. How did I go from taking a summer job as a nanny for a rich guy to standing in his driveway, hearing him confess his love to me?

I'm not ready for this. I'm not healed enough. I just finally decided to make cock boards two seconds ago. Now Max wants to drop the l-bomb on me?

Love?

This can't be love. Love means losing yourself to someone. Love means putting them first over everything. Love means diving in headfirst. I'm still learning how to swim after drowning in Jenson's company. I can't let love factor into my life right now. And I know that if I let Max Fletcher love me, like fully love me, I will drown all over again.

I'm just the nanny. That's all this was supposed to be.

My chin trembles as I struggle to find my voice. "Well, whatever you decide to do on your merger with Jenson, please don't make any rash decisions on account of me," I croak, my face twisting up in pain. "I shouldn't factor into your choice at all."

The cold look on Max's face as he stares at me for a long, pregnant pause hurts every bone in my body. I curl in on myself, fighting off the discomfort his disappointed eyes are causing me.

He nods once, and his voice is cool and detached when he says, "Then it's good we hid this from Everly. It'd be a shame to break her heart."

And with that, Max strides back into the garage, closing the door behind him and closing off whatever piece of his heart that he might have been offering, but I'm not defrosted enough to accept.

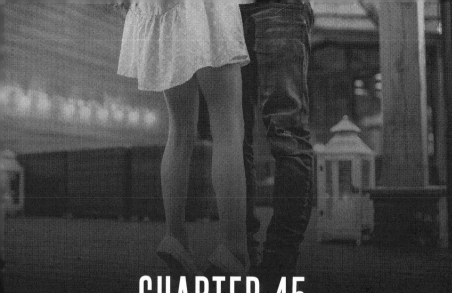

CHAPTER 45

Max

"Dad, why are we going to Aspen this weekend?" Everly asks, sitting criss-cross in the seat across from me on the company jet.

"You love Aspen." I frown and set my phone down to give her my undivided attention.

"I do, but we haven't gone anywhere all summer, so I wondered why we're going now?" Her blue eyes watch me curiously like she can see directly into my soul.

"That's exactly why we're going. I haven't taken my kid anywhere all summer, and I feel horrible about that." I force a smile that I don't feel as I reach over and tug playfully on Everly's braid.

She looks out the window thoughtfully as we begin to taxi out. "You don't have to feel bad, Dad. I like doing nothing, and I'm really good at it."

Her words sound horribly familiar, and my chest does that knocking sensation that happens every time I think of her.

The nanny.

It's like a fucking defibrillator pressed to my chest when she darkens my thoughts this past week.

I turn my head to look out the window as well and hope I'm as good at hiding my pain as I think I am.

The past seven days have consisted of work and Everly. Work and Everly. Rinse and repeat with a splash of an Everly night out with Uncle Calder…giving me more time at the office.

Then back to Everly and work.

It's all I can handle.

I don't look at Cassandra. I don't talk to Cassandra. I rush out the second she enters the house. I give the obligatory thumbs-up to the text messages she sends me about how Everly's days are going, and that's it.

I don't even reread the texts before bed at night like I used to because it's too painful. Reading her words, even in her stilted texts, is like I can hear her voice, see her smile, feel her body next to mine in my bed…which still fucking smells like her. My entire bedroom smells like coconut still. I don't know how it hasn't faded, especially when Bettina has been by to clean the house.

Or perhaps the smell has faded, and my mind is just torturing me with the memory of that scent. None of it makes sense. And every bit of it hurts.

Which is why we're getting the fuck out of Boulder for the weekend. I even booked a hotel room with a waterpark for Everly because I was too afraid that my Aspen house would haunt me with memories of Cassandra as well.

Only a few more weeks to go…then Jess will be home, Cassandra will be gone, and life can get back to normal. I just have to keep putting on a happy face for Everly. I can't let her see what's going on inside my head. Because if she did, she would know how incredibly angry I am all the time.

I'm angry I didn't see that Jenson Hunsberger was a fucking awful human. I'm angry I never mentioned the name of that company before the charity gala. I'm angry I let Cassandra sleep in my bed. I'm angry I asked her out on a date. I'm angry I let myself fall for her. I'm angry I didn't see the walls she built up. I'm angry I let her infiltrate every part of my life…even down to my own fucking heart.

I'm angriest about that. I let myself love again, and once again, it wasn't enough.

I thought our differences were what made us work. I thought they were what I'd been missing my whole life. I was fucking dead wrong, and I hate being wrong.

Which is why I'm harnessing all this anger for my Monday morning meeting with the board of All-Out Properties. I have some revisions to this merger that they better fucking accept. Cozy or no Cozy, this is a problem that needs dealing with.

For now, it's back to all eyes on Everly as it always should have been.

CHAPTER 46

Cozy

"I've never seen so much hard cock in my life!" Kate, aka Mercedes Lee Loveletter, exclaims as she appears in the doorway of my workshop. She's holding an infant car seat against her hip as she walks over to inspect my work. "Holy shit, you've been busy, Cozy!"

I take a moment to peer at Tucker, her little ginger baby boy. He's fast asleep, and his mushy cheeks are so cute that I have to resist the urge to squeeze them. I prop my hands on my hips and turn my focus back on my work. "Well…I wanted to make a few samples so we could figure out what you think will work best for your book boxes." I fondle the "cocktuterie" boards carefully. "A phallic-shaped charcuterie board is certainly a first for me, but I think I have a few good options here. You'd be surprised how many different shapes a dick can be."

"Um…no, I wouldn't." Kate barks out a laugh. "Hi…Queen smut writer here. I have a cocktastic imagination, and I could think of an infinite number of dick shapes…some of which have been dropped into my DMs on Instagram."

I laugh and bow my head. "Pardon me, Queen of the Cocks. I hope these five are satisfactory enough for you to decide from."

A mighty howl from Tucker turns our focus off each other to the sad little baby who's woken up in the middle of our cock talk and is not happy about it. Kate unbuckles him from his seat and drapes him over her shoulder. "The smallest cocks are always the loudest."

I laugh at the very bizarre joke. It feels good to laugh. This week has lacked any kind of laughter. In fact, it's been pretty much straight misery. Made even more miserable by the fact that Max and Everly left for a weekend trip yesterday. Not that I would have spent any time with them anyway since it's the weekend, but something was horrifyingly painful about watching them pack up their car and leave me behind yesterday. I felt like an outsider looking in for the first time in weeks.

I hated it.

"Can you hold him while I do a little circle jerk of your master-pieces?" Kate asks, moving toward me.

"Love to," I reply as she slips him into my arms with all the grace of a well-seasoned mother. He tucks his face into my chest, his cheek pressing against my collarbone as I hold him against me, breathing in that new baby smell.

My throat constricts at the feel of him in my arms. Just two weeks ago, I was talking about babies with Max. I was fantasizing about having his baby. I'm horrified to admit that I went so far as to wonder what our baby would look like, how Everly would be with it. Would she be a protective big sister or a bothered teen that's annoyed by all the baby crap that would consume Max's house. I got completely carried away and now everything is a mess.

"Surprise, surprise, he's a breast man," Kate deadpans when Tucker begins nodding off in my arms almost immediately.

I turn around and sway him in my arms to hide my stinging eyes from Kate as she looks over all the boards, oohing and aahing at the fine details. I've been basically in this workshop every night this week…barely even stopping to eat, so I'm pretty proud of the work I've done.

One night Everly came into the shop with some food for me and I had to do a quick coverup of my cock boards that were more balls than cock at that time, so I don't think she realized what she was even looking at, thank goodness. When she handed me the plate of food, I had to resist the urge to ask her if it was from her or Max.

I wanted it to be from Max.

And then I spent the next hour aggressively sanding wooden shafts to punish myself for wanting the food to be from Max.

This is stupid.

I should want nothing from Max. I pushed him away. I ended what we had to save myself so I should be happy with that decision.

Why did he have to say he loved me?

"This one is my favorite," Kate says, holding up one of the maples that I liked the most too. "The deep curve of this says...yeah, I might have dick cheese...but I can still hit your brie-spot."

"Nice pun," I laugh and shake my head, cupping the back of Tucker's head to prevent him from jiggling too much. "You have to put that on a bookmark or something."

"For sure," Kate agrees, clapping her hands together excitedly. "I'm meeting with the lawyer tomorrow morning and a real estate agent in the afternoon to look at some properties downtown. This shit is finally getting underway, and I couldn't be more thrilled! I'm really hoping to find a space near Dakota's T-shirt shop. That part of town is cute and artsy and everything I always pictured for an indie bookstore. I just have to finish my book today first because I'm so close to typing "The End" and I can think of no better way to celebrate than going bookstore shopping." She exhales heavily after that long rant of a to-do list she just blasted through.

"My God, you're taking care of an infant, finishing a book, and opening up your own bookstore...how do you do it all?" I ask, staring at her like she must have five clones in the car.

"I do it stylishly, of course," she answers, gesturing to her Pizza slice T-shirt. It's a Dakota T-shop original.

She laughs and turns to look at the boards again. I can't help but pry further. "No, seriously. How are you getting all this done? Are you a ball of stress at home?"

"Are you kidding me?" Kate replies with another laugh. "Not at all! I mean, sometimes I have my little freak outs, but I'm living my dream right now. I'm doing something I absolutely love, and open-ing up this charity bookstore will be like…the thrill of a lifetime."

I nod slowly. "So you think if you're doing something you're pas-sionate about, it's less stressful?"

"Definitely. And it might still be stressful but it's fulfilling at the same time. I mean…how do you feel making charcuterie boards?"

"Horny usually," I respond with an honest answer because if any-one can take it, it's this woman. "And that was before I knew cocktu-terie boards were a thing."

"I love it!" She holds her hand up in a high five that I gratefully accept because I didn't totally perv her out with my honesty.

"But I feel fulfilled too," I add, digging in a little deeper. "Making these boards is like this strangely satisfying experience for me. After my stroke, they really brought me back to life."

"I'm sorry, did you say stroke?" Kate's eyes turn to saucers.

I nod and cringe. "Sorry, I didn't mean to just drop that on you."

"No…please," she says, crossing her arms and staring seriously back at me. "If we're going to be working together with all these hard cocks, I think it's important for me to know you, Cozy. This sounds like a big deal."

I exhale heavily, squeezing little Tucker to my chest for com-fort. "It was but I'm okay now, thankfully. I used to work in a really high-stress job in corporate and it all became too much for me. I had a stress-induced stroke in the middle of a meeting almost eight months ago."

Kate's eyes widen. "Damn, that's scary as fuck."

"I know," I reply with a self-deprecating laugh. "I'm doing great now, but what you said about doing something you're passionate about really resonated with me. Making these boards helped me with my physical therapy. I gained back all I lost making these things and ever since then, when I work on them, it's like an out-of-body expe-rience. Like an adrenaline rush of gratitude every time I get to put this stupid leather apron on."

"Sexy leather apron," Kate corrects with a warm smile. "And good for you. It sounds like you made the right career change. Creative types like us are way more fun than the suited stiffs."

She laughs but all I can do is picture Max in his suits. God, he wears them so well. And in the mornings when his hair is still damp from his shower, and he's just applied his cologne...there is nothing hotter in the universe. I miss it more than I'd miss charcuterie boards.

"Well, I'm a clean bill of health now," I respond, refocusing my thoughts. "And please don't worry about my quality of work. I promise you that I am healthy as a horse and doing better than ever."

"Cozy...you don't have to answer to me," Kate says, pressing her hand on my shoulder. "I'm not your boss. I'm your client. You're your own cock-making boss bitch and you call the cum shots on your career. Got it?"

I giggle and nod. "Got it."

"And the best part about being your own boss is finding ways to take care of yourself. Like for me, Miles and Tuck are my stress relievers. When I'm feeling the pressure of my passion...because don't get it twisted, passion is not devoid of pressure...all I have to do is reconnect with them and it's like the best natural medicine in the world."

My eyes instantly begin to sting with her words that spear through a wall that I had built firmly up around myself as images of Max and Everly fill my mind. The three of us zip-lining, baking cookies on sleepover night, swimming, dancing, laughing, cuddling, kissing—all of it has been my own natural medicine all summer... and I didn't even realize it.

"Whoa, whoa, what's happening?" Kate asks, pointing at my face that's now full-on ugly crying. "What did I say? I have a big fucking mouth and no filter, and sometimes I hurt people's feelings without even knowing it."

"It's nothing," I reply and sniff loudly, turning away from Kate. "I'm just a big, dumb idiot."

"Hey, I'm President of the big, dumb, idiot club and I haven't seen you at our meetings," Kate says, walking over and rubbing my back as she wipes a tear off my face. "What's going on?"

I lick my lips and shake my head. "I just...really screwed things up with a guy I've been seeing."

"Max?"

My face contorts at her guessing him. "Um...how would you—"

"Okay, full disclosure, I know you guys are a thing," Kate blurts, a guilty look on her face. "Max told Dean. Dean told me. I told Lynsey. Lynsey told Josh. Miles and Norah are in on this telephone game… so yeah…we all knew you guys were banging."

"Jeez," I groan in mortification.

"But it's not just sex anymore, right? You guys were like…dating and stuff?"

I exhale heavily. "Yes…were being the operative word. I ended it last weekend."

"Why? What happened?"

I shrug dismissively. "I found out his company was merging with my former horrible company, and I freaked out. It triggered me in the most horrific way. Then he told me he was in love with me, and it was the straw that broke the camel's back! I mean, when Max and I were just lusting after each other and dating in secret, it was fun and exciting. There wasn't any pressure yet. Then he dropped the love bomb and suddenly, I felt weak and unsafe, just like I felt as an employee under that asshole, Jenson Hunsberger. It's like I could see myself on the floor of my former office all over again. Letting Max love me means my mental health is at the mercy of another man in power. That is way too scary of a thought for me. Romantically or in business, I'm terrified of being hurt again."

"Of course you are, you had a fucking stroke," Kate confirms bluntly, her tone fiercely supportive. "A stroke is going to fuck with any one of us for a while."

"Which is why I had to end it. He deserves to find someone who's stronger than me. Someone who can handle his corporate lifestyle and the inevitable assholes that come with that territory…like my former boss. He deserves to find someone strong enough to love him back without fear of everything falling apart." My chest aches at the idea of him opening his heart to someone else. He has so much to offer a woman and I just happened to be the willy-nilly hot mess that stumbled into his boardroom.

"You think there's a woman stronger than the one who made me five cocktuterie boards in a week?" Kate deadpans. "No such woman exists. She would be a fearsome thing to behold, though."

I groan in frustration. "These boards are different. I feel safe here. I do not feel safe with Max. I feel like I could be swallowed whole by him and lose sight of all that I've fought to gain back in my life."

"I think you're forgetting one very important fact, Cozy." Kate lifts her eyebrows meaningfully as her face grows serious. "Being vulnerable only makes you weak if you're around predators. Being vulnerable with someone good and decent like Max can make you fiercely strong. Miles and Tucker make me feel like I could move mountains. They motivate me to crush my goals and go after my dreams. I want to make them proud, whether it's opening a charity bookstore or just throwing in a frozen pizza. I live for them."

I inhale sharply as the words I said in Max's kitchen hit me out of nowhere. *"You've inspired me to start dreaming again."*

I glance over at the worktable full of cocks—a strange sign of love and strength, but not entirely off brand for this stage in my crazy life.

And I have to admit, the idea of living for someone other than myself for once feels…comforting. I was so isolated and alone in Denver. Maybe Kate's right and a good partner can help with your stress, not add to it. Maybe I'm a fucking idiot who has learned nothing from my near-death experience and has destined myself to a life of solace because I was too afraid to see what was really in my heart.

My voice is soft when I ask, "What if I'm not strong enough to risk myself, Kate?"

"You're a survivor, Cozy. And survivors are some of the strongest people I know."

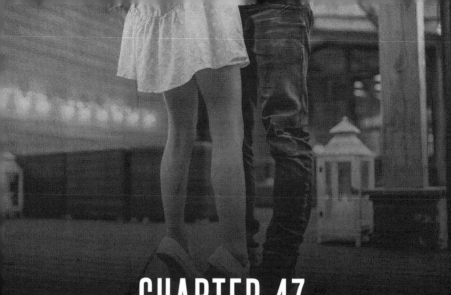

CHAPTER 47

Max

"We wrapped early!" Jessica exclaims into the phone Monday morning as I drive to Denver for my meeting with the board. "Momma is coming home!"

"Shit, really?" I ask with my brows furrowed. "Like when?"

"Like Saturday!" Jessica laughs. "But don't tell Everly. I want to surprise her. I am so excited, Max. You have no idea."

"I can hear it," I reply dryly, my chest aching at the thought of my extra time with Everly coming to a close so soon. I've seen such growth in her this summer. I don't know if it was because she was around more or because she explored different parts of her personality, but she really is turning into a young woman now. And now I'll have to go back to being a weekend dad, which sucks, but she's missed her mom, so I know this is for the best. Just a tough pill to swallow.

That thought makes me wonder... "What are we going to do about...the nanny? We hired her through the end of the summer."

Jessica hems and haws for a bit. "I think we can just pay her for the rest of the summer and dismiss her early. I'm going to want to

306   AMY DAWS

spend as much time with Everly as I can before she goes back to school."

I nod and chew the inside of my cheek as I consider that. "Yeah… okay. I'm sure she'll need time to find a place to live. This is three weeks earlier than expected. I don't know what her plans are so I don't want to stress her out."

"Can't she just stay in the tiny house as long as she needs? I mean…are you in a hurry to get her out of there?"

"No, why would you say that?" I snap, my hands tightening on the wheel defensively.

"Easy, Max, I was just asking a question."

I sigh heavily. I'm so fucking obvious, it's painful. "This is great news, Jess. Everly will be thrilled to see you."

"Max."

"What?"

"What is going on?" Jess's tone is probing, and I can already see her eyes pinning me to my seat. "You sound stressed out more than usual."

"I'm on my way to a big meeting regarding the merger. There have been some developments."

Jess tsks. "That doesn't sound good."

"It's not," I drone, hoping this meeting goes my way because otherwise, I'm not sure what my options are.

"So…nothing more about Cozy that you want to talk about?" Jess asks, her tone cautious.

My eyes narrow. "Other than her living situation, no. Why would you ask that?"

There's a pause on the other end of the line.

"Jess…you're hesitating. I don't like when you hesitate."

"Everly made me promise not to tell you."

"Jessica, you know I hate when you keep shit from me about Everly. Whatever it is, just tell me."

She moans a noise of annoyance before blurting out, "She told me she thinks you're in love with Cozy."

I nearly drive off the fucking road. "You're kidding."

"I'm not, Max. I wouldn't joke with you about this."

"When did she say that?" I ask, chills running up my spine at this surprising remark.

"A few weeks ago. Then last week she said you were sad."

Dammit, that kid is too intuitive for her own good. She must be a fucking emotional empath or something. "I'm not sad, Jess."

"You sound sad."

"The connection is bad in Bulgaria."

"Max...what's going on with you two?"

"Nothing, Jess. It's over," I state, trying to get her off this line of questioning. "I don't know how Everly knows anything because we were always very careful and very appropriate, I promise."

"Max, you don't have to sell me on this. I know you. I trust you. In fact, I was kind of excited that you were a little inappropriate for once. And I already like Cozy...not that my opinion on your love life really matters. But for the record, I think she'd be great for you."

I sigh heavily. "There's no love life, Jess."

"Why not?"

"Because we're not right for each other."

"Says who?"

"Says me," I answer harshly.

"Well, I think that sucks," Jess tuts. "I was hopeful you were finally taking a chance on someone for once. It's been heartbreaking watching you live your life alone all these years and knowing I was the one that made you like that."

"You have nothing to feel guilty for, Jess." I reach down and untie my tie, feeling suddenly like I'm sitting in the hot seat. "You can't control your sexuality any more than I can control mine."

Her voice is strained when she replies, "I know, but I know you struggled with thinking everything in our past wasn't real...and you're just so wrong about that. I loved you, Max. I loved you in all the ways I knew how to love you at the time. You are my family. Leaving you was the hardest thing I ever had to do. I considered staying with you forever despite my sexuality because I loved our family, and I loved you! But ultimately, I knew that wasn't fair to you."

"I know all this, Jess. We did the therapy. I'm good."

"I don't think you are. I don't think you've ever really let it sink in. You've read the books and done the therapy. You're an ally and a great co-parent, but you haven't forgiven our past. Our life together was not a cloudy storm. It was sunshine and rainbows. They were the best years of my life. You made me a mom, Max. We made Everly together. She is you. She is me. She is ours. Nothing about her creation should feel darkened to you."

"She doesn't feel darkened, Jess," I croak, my voice thick in my throat at just the mention of thinking of Everly that way. She is my saving grace in this crazy place called life. The one person I can count on who will always love me back.

"Then stop rewriting our family history. Let our good memories drive you to make new memories. Let them finally heal and open your heart up to be loved and desired in a full way."

"I tried, Jess," I exclaim, feeling frustrated that everything my ex is saying are things I wanted with Cassandra. "I told her I was in love with her. It didn't fucking matter. Maybe there is something about me that prevents women from really seeing me for me. Maybe I am unlovable."

"You look in our daughter's eyes and I dare you to say that to her. I dare you, Max Fletcher," Jess snaps, her voice harsh. "Everly will turn you into a puddle on the floor if you say that bullshit to her. You are loved. You are loved by her, by me, by Kailey. Your family, your friends. And if that nanny isn't in love with you, then I'm glad I'm coming home early because she's clearly too stupid to be watching our daughter."

The laughter hurts my chest, and I can't help but shake my head at this very bizarre conversation I'm having before eight o'clock on a Monday morning. "I miss you, Jess."

"I'm always right here, Max." Her voice is tender and thick, quaking at the end. "You're kind of my best friend, you know."

"You're definitely not mine," I reply with a giant smile.

She giggles, and I steel myself before saying, "I love you, Jess."

She inhales sharply. "I love you too, Max."

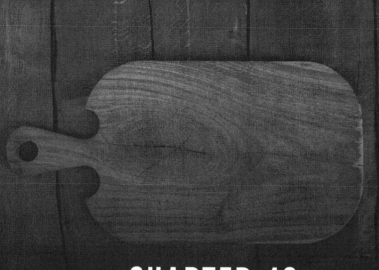

CHAPTER 48

Cozy

Tuesday morning feels like any other day. It's nearing six o'clock as I tiptoe across the deck in my loungewear with my Kindle in hand, ready for another day of nannying with a tortured heart. I've forgone the spicy romance novels I have been consuming all summer for something a bit less…well…painful.

A tragic genre by the name of…self-help.

When I slide the door open, I'm wondering how many pages it will take before I nod off while reading when Max's voice has me nearly jump out of my skin.

"Cassandra, can we talk for a moment?" My heart thunders in my chest at the view of him standing in his kitchen in a classic black suit, white shirt, slim black tie, perfectly gelled hair. He looks ridiculously handsome. I haven't seen him much since the charity gala because when I come in, he goes out. No chitchat, no morning coffee, no teasing smirks…just a view of his impressive backside.

"Okay," I reply, setting my Kindle down on the accent table to feign some semblance of confidence.

Max's dress shoes clunk along the hardwood as he makes his

way through the living room. "Let's go into the library so we don't wake Everly."

The flip flap of my sandals is mortifying as I struggle to walk in the wake of his cologne. That perfect spicy smell of naughty and delicious. I would do anything to press my nose into his neck right now and just…breathe him in.

Max perches on the edge of the pool table with the backdrop of floor-to-ceiling books behind him.

Another kink exposed.

I lean against the far bookshelf and open my mouth to say something, anything to finally dig us out of this awkwardness and maybe consider moving forward in some meaningful way…but Max beats me to the punch.

"Jessica is coming home on Saturday." Max's tone is sharp as he crosses his arms over his chest and tests the stretch of his suit coat.

"This Saturday?" My brows furrow curiously as Max nods. "But I thought…"

"Her shoot wrapped early, and she's coming home to surprise Everly. It's all very hush hush." His eyes glance at the floor, refusing to connect with mine as those stress lines between his brows deepen.

I chew my lip nervously. "So what does this mean for my job?"

His jaw muscle tics as his indigo eyes lift to me. There's pain around the edges of them that I want to reach out and touch his brows to smooth away. "I'm afraid we won't need you anymore."

Ouch.

I should have seen that coming.

He clears his throat and adds, "Jess wants to spend the rest of the summer with Everly before she starts school in a few weeks."

A painful knot forms in my throat at the realization that this means I only have a few days left with Everly. I'm not ready to be done with her. I'm not ready to be done with doing nothing. I'm not ready to leave the Fletchpad, my tiny house, this family. This is all happening too fast.

"I'll pay you through the end of the summer as originally agreed upon," Max states crisply, his face flinching slightly before he steels it behind his hardened features.

I recoil at the humiliation of that notion. Suddenly, I've gone from Cinderella to Pretty Woman, and I'm pretty sure Julia Roberts left that money on the table. I glance down at my hands, fiddling with the hem of my shirt. "You don't have to pay me."

"That's non-negotiable," Max tuts, turning to look out the window toward the backyard. "And I realize this is coming up sooner than anticipated, so you are welcome to stay in the tiny house until your next residence opens up."

Residence sounds like a swear word coming from him right now.

I fill my lungs with as much air as possible. This entire exchange is horrifying, and I sink under the weight of it. I feel like a child or worse, an employee. Not the woman who shared a bed with him for several weeks and fell in love with his daughter.

Fell in love with him.

That painful realization causes tears to spring into my eyes, so I quickly look away, pressing the back of my hand to my nose to try to stave off the emotions. My voice is garbled when I respond, "I won't need to stay."

"Really, Cassandra, it will be fine."

"No, it won't."

"Why do you say that?"

"Because you can barely look me in the eyes right now." I laugh, but it's pained as the ache in my throat threatens to tear me apart. This is Max's opportunity to cut ties with me. He's low-key firing me, and the cold, detached way he's delivering this news proves that. I've ruined any chance we had at something real. A man like Max isn't someone who forgives easily. Look how long it took for him to get over his ex. All his rules about no sleepovers and no relationships. God, I'm such a fool.

I lick my lips and add, "It's clear that you don't want me here a second longer than I have to be, so I will move out this weekend."

Max stands to his full height, his eyes twitching at my remark. "We can be professional about this."

"Professional," I croak, feeling my chin tremble at another seemingly pedestrian word that feels like a curse from his lips. "Maybe you can be professional." I lift my hands up, my eyes stinging with unshed tears. "But I'm willy-nilly, Max, so you never know what to expect from me."

His eyes tighten. "Need I remind you that this entire situation we're in the middle of is your choice?"

"Is it?" I ask, my voice barely a whisper. "It didn't feel like a choice. It felt like a forgone conclusion," I reply honestly.

Kate's words about my strength as a survivor play on repeat in my mind. I was strong enough to let Max go, but I'm clearly not strong enough to keep him.

Max shakes his head and moves toward me. "I'm not doing this."

His arm brushes mine as he walks past, and even though I'm sure I'll regret it, I reach out and grab his hand.

He freezes, facing away from me for a moment that feels like an eternity as an electric current flows between our hands, shooting up my arm like a shock. I hear his breath hitch and his jaw grow taut before he turns around to look at my hand clasping his, like it's some sort of puzzle he can't quite work out.

His eyes lift to mine, scoring over my face like a hot branding iron, showing me every emotion coursing through his veins. Pain, frustration, disappointment, confusion, desire...

Oh God, the desire.

I inhale sharply when Max's gaze drops to my lips, and before my heart beats again, his hand skates up my chest and fingers my neck in a tender caress as he backs me into the bookcase.

He pauses a moment, biting his lip as he stares at me like a cherished possession, his fingers reverently stroking the sides of my neck and jawline, immediately confirming my submission to him.

I want to submit to him. I want to be claimed by him, lost in him. I want to trust in what we can be together.

A guttural noise escapes his mouth as he seals his lips over mine. His hand maps around to the back of my neck as he angles my face upward to deepen the kiss. His body bows over mine as his tongue thrusts between my lips, harsh and demanding, taking what it wants. And I moan into it, giving him all of me. Every possible inch.

I want to give more. I want to give everything. I want to be strong enough to believe these feelings won't break me. Strong enough to let go of my past.

My hands wrap tightly around his waist, pulling him to me, the tightness in my muscles unfurling at the familiar pressure of his body flush against mine as an ache throbs between my legs.

I could kiss him forever.

Cool air blasts my damp lips as Max pulls away, a tortured look on his face as he shakes his head. "Goodbye, Cassandra."

"What?" I gasp, grabbing his suit coat and pulling him toward me, panic dotting my eyes as he pulls away from me. "You just kissed me."

"It was a goodbye kiss." He grips my hands and uncurls my desperate hold on him, piercing my heart with the horrible realization that I've ruined any chance we had. "This was never the part that was broken." He pins me with a look that silently says...*it was you.*

CHAPTER 49

Cozy

"Why do you seem sad today, Cozy?" Everly asks, stretched out on a towel in the sand by the creek.

"What makes you think I'm sad?" I push my sunglasses into my hair and peer down at her from my seat on the Adirondack chair.

"'Cuz every time you look at me, you get tears in your eyes." Everly blinks those baby-blue eyes at me, and my eyes start stinging again.

"Allergies," I scoff and turn to wipe my eyes.

I only have two more days with Everly, and she's a perceptive little thing because she's right. I have been crying every time I look at her today. I'm sad my time with her is coming to an end. And the worst part is, I can't even tell her that tomorrow is our last day together because then I would ruin her mom's surprise.

Everly turns her attention back to the friendship bracelet she's making, and I smile as she sticks her tongue out in concentration. Does this kid have any idea how much she's done for me this summer? A few months ago, I was dreading walking into that boardroom to interview for a nanny position I didn't want. I didn't want to step foot in another office, and I wasn't ready to start punching a proverbial clock again. But my sister was desperate, and I was running low on funds.

So I begrudgingly showed up.

Then I had one conversation with my little Sea Monster, and I was a goner. So much so, I would have been devastated if I didn't get the job.

This little girl has brought me back to the land of the living in a way I never even imagined. Nothing in my life has been quite as fulfilling as being a part of Everly's existence. It's been an honor.

"Did you like our summer of 'doing less,' little Sea Monster?" I croak, my voice revealing my emotions more than I expected it to.

"Uh...obviously," she replies with a flick of her wrist, and I have to bite my lip because she has been mimicking a lot of my mannerisms this summer and the narcissistic pride I feel when she acts like me is totally shameful.

"Why exactly?" I ask, wanting to make sure I suck as much Everly goodness out of her while I still can. "I mean...your parents had you in a lot of cool activities. Was there a reason you were excited to just chillax with me instead of doing all those activities with your friends?"

Everly looks up at me and wrinkles her nose. "I was in the car too much."

"What do you mean?" I inquire with a laugh at that odd response.

"Between going to Mom's and going to Dad's and then back to Mom's and then to gymnastics and then to swim team and then to school and back again. It just felt like I was staring at the back of my mom's and dad's heads all the time. And I like their faces. I especially like my dad's when he's just being normal."

"What do you mean normal?" I ask, my chest aching at the thought of not seeing Max's face anymore after I move out this weekend. So many damn emotions going on in my body today.

"I like Dad's face when he's just goofing around with me on the couch or asking me how I like my oatmeal. Or when he kisses me on the head before he leaves for work. Like just comfy stuff, you know?"

"Yeah...I think I do." My smile is tender. "Do you miss going to any of your activities?"

"Sometimes," she answers with a shrug. "I'll probably go back and do some of the stuff because I kind of get tired of reading all the time. And imagination tennis is fun and all, but no offense, Cozy... you're not as good at tennis as me, and I want to play someone who's at my level."

My belly shakes with the chortle that catches me completely off guard. "In my mind...I'm as good as the Williams sisters."

"In my mind, you need some practice." Everly giggles, and it makes me want to cry again. "So yeah, I think I want to go back to doing some stuff but just not all. I want to be medium busy."

"Medium busy," I repeat with a nod. "Sounds like a good balance."

I try not to take it personally that an eleven-year-old might have a stronger grip on her mental health boundaries than I do.

"Yours is done!" Everly squeals and jumps up onto her feet to walk over to me. That tongue is sticking out again as she ties the bracelet in a knot around my wrist. She holds her wrist next to mine and smiles at our matching set. "Friends forever."

"Friends forever," I cry and then whoosh all the air out of her lungs when I yank her to my chest for a hug.

It's too tight, it's much too tight, but she's still breathing, so she can take it. This child is one of a kind, and I will never forget how special she is.

My phone rings just as Everly begins gasping for breath. "You really like friendship bracelets!" she exclaims with a laugh. "I'm going to make Dad one now."

She goes back to her work area as I glance down at my phone to see an unknown number. This might be the guy whose house I'm trying to rent, so I better answer it.

"I'm going to take this call, Everly."

"Okay." She waves me off.

"Hello?" I stand and walk over to my deck on the tiny house so Everly doesn't overhear anything about me moving.

"Cassie?" a familiar female voice echoes through the line.

"Paisley?" My throat feels tight.

"You recognized my voice," she says with a sigh. "I'm impressed."

My brow is furrowed as a chill shoots up my spine. "How did you get my number?" I inquire because Paisley only ever had my work cell phone number, and my cell is still boxed up in storage somewhere.

She clears her throat nervously. "Um…I got it from Max Fletcher."

"Max?" I repeat, my pulse increasing instantly at the mention of his name. "When?"

"A few days ago. He was here at the office for a meeting."

"Was he?" I state knowingly, my lips pursing in disappointment. Clearly, Max is still going through with the merger, and that thought sends a shiver of sadness through my body. I know I told him not to make any business decisions for me, but deep down, I wanted him to care about me enough to kill the merger. I know that makes me a hypocrite because he told me he loved me, and I pushed him away… but I guess I'm a fool in the name of love.

If I needed a sign to know that there's no chance with Max and me, then this is it.

Paisley's voice interrupts my thoughts. "He cornered me in my cubicle and went off on me about everything that happened."

"Did something happen with the merger?" I ask, wondering if Max's actions toward Jenson put the deal in jeopardy.

"No…he went off on me about you."

Chills climb over my scalp. "What about me?"

"He mentioned your…stroke," Paisley replies, her voice tremoring on the end as she rushes out, "Cassie, I had no idea you had a fucking stroke. My God, I was sick when Max told me. Jenson told everyone at the office that it was an anxiety attack, and we were the ones who triggered you, and we should leave you the fuck alone."

My eyes fill with tears. "Are you kidding me?"

"No! He legit threatened our jobs if he found out about any of us contacting you. I felt like a monster over how protective Jenson was being of you. I had no idea he was lying."

"Paisley, this can't be real."

"It is, Cas. Jesus…if I'd known you wanted us to reach out to you, I would have been at that hospital in a heartbeat. I can't stop picturing them wheeling you out on a stretcher. It had to be completely terrifying for you."

"It was," I croak, my voice garbled with emotion as I recall how alone I felt in that ambulance when I regained consciousness. "And I was so hurt when none of you checked in on me."

"God, Cassie, I am so sorry," she cries, sniffing loudly into the phone. "The office got even crazier after you were gone because of course Jenson never replaced you. Just made all of us pick up your work…and holy shit did you have a ton of work. No wonder you had a breakdown. Cassie, you were so young, and you were doing the work of five full-time employees. It's horrifying."

I rub my lips together, feeling tears fill my eyes. "I kind of realized that a bit too late."

She sighs heavily. "I should have been a better friend to you. And coworker. I should have protected you. I should have called. I stopped by your apartment a couple of months after you left, but you didn't answer the door. I don't blame you."

"I moved back home to Boulder."

"Yeah, I gathered that. And none of us could find you on social media."

"I blocked you all because I thought you were heartless assholes," I admit honestly.

"To be fair, a lot of us are." She laughs dryly. "My heart stopped when I saw you at that charity a couple of weeks ago. Cassie, you'd never been more beautiful. Swear to God, you were the most beautiful woman in that room."

"Thank you?" I say it like a question because it's a weird thing to say in the middle of this kind of conversation.

"And I hate to admit this, but I was jealous of you for getting out. And when I saw you looking gorgeous at that table, I thought…wow, she's clearly got her life together. Then your hunk of a man dropped the bomb about your stroke, and I realized what an asshole I was."

"He's not my man," I reply dismissively.

"He was definitely coming at me like he was your man," Paisley huffs. "He was defending you like a king defends his queen, Cas. I was equal parts terrified and aroused."

My face twists up in confusion. "What did he want from you exactly?"

"He just wanted to know why none of us reached out after you got sick, gave me your phone number, and said to make it right. It took me a couple of days to build up the nerve…especially after that verbal spanking he gave me, but I was grateful for it. This phone call is long overdue."

My mind reels with all the information being thrust at me. I want to get to the bottom of Max's motivation for this, but considering this is the first coworker I've spoken to from my old job, I have to ask, "Why are you still there, Paisley?"

She sighs deeply into the phone. "Well…a bunch of us were going to stage a walkout on Jenson right when he merged with Fletcher Industries…a way to really fuck both the corporations over because we're tired of being underappreciated while these CEOs make all the money. But all that's changed now."

"Changed how?"

"Well, now that Jenson's out, we're hoping things will improve."

"Wait, what? Jenson is out?"

"Yeah…your man approached the board this week and said the only way he will go through with the deal is if the merger changes into an acquisition. All-Out Properties is donezo. Everything will be under Fletcher Industries, and Max has full hiring and firing rights. We all have to re-interview for our jobs in the next few weeks."

Blood rushes in my ears at all this new information. "Holy shit. The board agreed to all that?"

"Yeah, especially after they heard about our planned walkout. They're working on buying out Jenson's share in the company too, so he really will be gone forever. I'm nervous about re-interviewing for my job, but I'm also hoping it'll help purge the Jenson juniors in the office. Those assholes have to go."

I nod knowingly. "I didn't know about any of this…Max never said a word." Why didn't he say a word? Even a text. Something.

This must truly mean he doesn't want me anymore. Because I screwed up. Because I pushed him away, and he has bigger fish to fry than to deal with a petulant nanny who was too afraid to tell him that she loved him.

"Oh, p.s., I hope you're cool with the entire office having boss fantasies about your man because he is…*fine*."

"Tell me about it," I respond, and my throat tightens at the image of Max in front of the board, laying down the new guidelines. I bet he was a totally sexy CEO badass. And the fact that he was mine and I gave him up is a reality that will haunt me forever.

"Listen, I understand if you want nothing to do with me," Paisley continues. "But I really would love to meet for coffee sometime and catch up. And apologize in person for not being a better friend to you. We were all in the weeds together, but that doesn't mean we couldn't have reached out a hand."

I inhale a deep breath through my nose, marveling at how quickly my perspective on my old job has changed with just a simple phone call. Looking back on my time at All-Out, it often felt like I was in an abusive relationship. Abuse that I allowed to happen over and over until my body gave out.

And the worst part about my stroke was that I never really got to make up my own mind about leaving. Which means I never got closure on that past trauma.

But this phone call is doing a lot to change that.

"I would love to meet for coffee."

"Amazing. Text me your schedule next week, and we will make it happen."

"Will do," I reply softly, my heart thundering in my chest at the idea of repairing some relationships that I valued once upon a time. "I'm really glad you called, Paisley."

She pauses on the other end of the line before saying, "I'll never stop being sorry for not doing it sooner, Cas."

We hang up, and for the first time since leaving the corporate world, I don't feel anxiety and dread encompass me at the mere thought of my old job. In fact, I have hope for change. And there's a certain Zaddy that is very much the reason for that newfound hope.

Maybe it's not too late for Max and me. Maybe I need to set down my self-help book and take a page out of my Mercedes Lee Loveletter novels to try to save my own happily ever after.

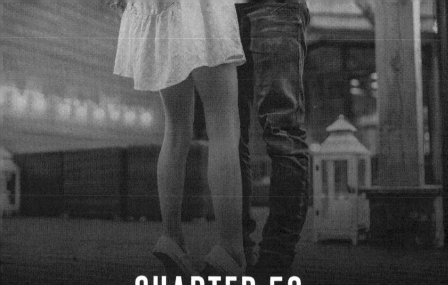

CHAPTER 50

Everly

"Okay, Uncle Wyatt…you're in charge of drinks, Luke, you're in charge of food, and Calder, you're the busboy."

"Busboy?" Calder whines. "Why do I have to be the busboy? Luke's younger than me."

I frown up at my uncle. "Uncle Calder, you talk too much, and if you're out there talking, you will ruin the romance."

"This is bullshit."

I glare at my uncle, who's acting like the kid in the room instead of me. "Behave. I'm the maître d, which means I'm in charge. Now, go set up the table by the pool and don't forget to use the placemats that I worked on last night, okay? They're very special."

My three uncles break apart as I run into the kitchen to check on Michael with the food. I requested chicken strips and french fries because it's not too messy to eat, so hopefully, it doesn't stop my daddy from kissing Cozy.

I smile to myself. Daddy and Cozy sitting in a tree, k-i-s-s-i-n-g. First comes love…then comes marriage. Then comes a baby brother that I get to love and hold and play with all by myself!

Or a sister. I'll take either, but I still don't have the hang of bubble braids, so maybe a brother would be easier.

I taste test one of Michael's homemade fries and give him a thumbs-up. I look at the clock and see that it's almost six, and Dad will be home any minute.

Music! I forgot the music! I run upstairs to grab my portable speaker and sync up one of the playlists that Cozy and I dance to a lot. It's not super romantic, but I know Daddy likes it. I've seen him watch the videos on our cameras of me and Cozy dancing, and he always smiles big at them.

This is a lot more work than when I got my friend Brooklyn a boyfriend. For Brooklyn, all I had to do was go up to the boy she liked and tell him that Brooklyn is his girlfriend for now and forever. It was easy peasy.

But Daddy and Cozy will be a lot harder, I think, because they're grown-ups. That's why I called my uncles to come help me set up their date tonight. I decided to do their romantic dinner by the pool because that's the first time I noticed how my daddy looked at Cozy. He looked at her like how I look at ice cream. But he better not lick her because that would be gross!

At first, I didn't think they should be in love with each other because Cozy can't cook, and she doesn't wear nice outfits like my daddy. So they would be a little weird together. But then I thought, I like Michael's food, and Daddy can take Cozy shopping if he wants her to dress nicer.

And I'm pretty sure they're already in love. I see how much my daddy and Cozy are always smiling at each other. And on the night of my sleepover with Claire, I saw them cuddling on the couch together. They both looked so cozy.

The last couple of weeks, they've been sad. And I think it's because summer is almost over and then they won't get to hang out anymore.

That's when I knew it was time for my plan: Parent Trap my dad and the nanny.

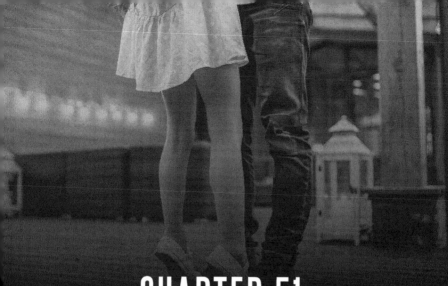

CHAPTER 51

Max

It's a little after six when I walk into the house and hear music playing in the distance. I frown when I come into the kitchen and see two plates with silver domes on top of them. Michael usually leaves the food in the oven, and I plate it myself, so I wonder what the deal is? Movement draws my eyes to the windows, where I see my three brothers huddling around a table set up by the pool.

"Good evening, Father," Everly purrs dramatically as she stands before me with her hair done up in bubble braids and one of her fanciest dresses on. "I have a surprise for you."

"Does the surprise have something to do with your uncles?" I ask, looking outside and frowning when I see Wyatt walking down toward the creek.

"No questions, just please come with me." Everly offers me her arm in a formal pose, and I laugh as I hunch over to wrap mine around hers. She leads me out to the pool deck, where Calder and Luke appear to be sniping at each other over the placement of the table.

Everly pulls a chair out for me to sit, and I do, smiling broadly at the colorful table setting in front of me. She's even picked some flowers and put them in a vase. "This is beautiful, Everly. Are you and I having a daddy-daughter date night?"

"Not exactly," Calder murmurs under his breath, and I turn to follow his eyes tracking something behind me.

My heart rate spikes when I see Wyatt escorting Cassandra up toward us. She's stunning in a black floral sundress that flows elegantly over her curves. Her cropped dark hair shines in the setting sun with a white flower clipping back the curls on one side.

Fuck.

"What's going on?" Cassandra asks, glancing nervously at me. "I thought I was having dinner with Everly. That's what the invitation said."

"You are having a dinner *experience*, courtesy of Everly," Everly chimes in, pulling the chair out across from me as Cassandra lowers into it.

"I have no idea what's going on," I state firmly, looking at my brother Wyatt whose typical silence infuriates me more than usual at this moment.

Everly stands between us, the rotating colors of the pool water as her backdrop. She crosses her hands in front of her as my three brothers line up behind her, striking a similar pose.

"Everly, your bubble braids look so good," Cassandra exclaims, her eyes full of pride. "You finally figured them out."

Everly touches them softly and gets an awkward look on her face. "I didn't do my hair. Calder did."

All eyes shoot to my brother in complete astonishment. He shrugs dismissively. "What, like it's hard?"

I laugh and shake my head, refocusing on the spectacle in front of us. "Everly, can you please tell us what this dinner experience is exactly?"

She clears her throat and smiles. "I could never parent trap my mom and dad because…well, they both like women. But Cozy, I know you like men. You told me so, and plus, I see those naked men on your book covers. And you make these funny noises when you read them, which sounds like you *really* like them!"

"I do *not* make funny noises," Cassandra sputters, her eyes wide and panicked on me as she splays her hands out on the table. "And they're not naked! They're…shirtless. But that's because some of them are athletes. Athletes get hot when they…athlete."

"Did she just use athlete as a verb?" Luke whispers under his breath.

Cassandra's gaze snaps to my brothers, her mouth opening and closing as she struggles with what to say next.

"Anyway," Everly continues, refocusing our attention as she moves to the side so Wyatt can pour the wine. Luke turns on his heel and jogs up the deck and into the house. "I want you two to take this evening of romance and think about all the reasons you should be in love with each other. Because I think you two make each other really happy, and I like seeing you both happy. Because I love you both."

Cassandra inhales sharply, and her eyes turn glassy as she looks at Everly with a soft, tender expression. "I love you too, Everly."

My chest aches at her words said so easily to my kid. Words she couldn't seem to find for me when I confessed my feelings only a couple of weeks ago. And the crushing disappointment my daughter will feel when she realizes this night was all for nothing because Cassandra doesn't care for me that way is something I'll have to deal with long after she's gone.

That realization brings that anger I've been harboring inside my body back to the forefront.

Luke sets two plates of food down in front of us and removes the dome lids with a dramatic flourish to reveal an artful display of chicken strips and fries.

"Dinner is served," Everly says, dropping down into a little curtsey before turning around and shooing my brothers away from the table.

"We don't need to stay here," I state, shaking my head in disappointment as I reach for my wineglass. "I had no idea Everly had this planned. I'll go talk to her and tell her this was inappropriate."

I take a sip and move to stand, but Cassandra splays her hand out on the table. "Can we just…indulge her for a moment?" she asks with a wobbly smile. "It's certainly a memorable send off for my last night here."

I swallow the knot in my throat at the reminder that she leaves tomorrow and sit back down. "You still plan on leaving tomorrow?" I hate that I want her to stay.

She nods, a fleeting look of sadness casting over her features. "I found a small house on the north side that should suit me. It's a rental and needs a lot of TLC, but it has a great she-shed in the backyard that I can make into my workshop. I've got a lot of charcuterie boards to get going on for Kate's bookstore launch."

"So you're doing it then? Working with Kate?" I ask curiously because I can't seem to stop caring about this woman in front of me.

She nods again and smiles. "Yeah, I'm excited about it. Kate seems like a great person to get involved with."

"She will be," I reply knowingly and realize this likely means Cassandra won't be out of my life entirely after tomorrow. I can't tell if that makes me feel better or worse. "She subscribes to your willy-nilly lifestyle a bit too, I think."

Cassandra nods slowly and then inquires, "Have you been busy with your work lately too?"

"Yes, it's been a stressful couple of weeks, but I think I have things sorted out now." I stare back at her, wondering what she knows.

"Paisley mentioned—"

"She did call then?" I sigh with relief because after the conversation we had, I wasn't sure she would follow through with my instructions. She's a spicy thing.

"Yeah, she called yesterday. I'm glad you gave her my number. It was an enlightening conversation on so many levels." Cassandra licks her lips and pauses. "Max, I had no idea you'd gone to all that work to cut Jenson out of the merger. Why didn't you say anything?"

I shrug dismissively. "You told me not to consider you with my decision. I didn't consider you. I considered myself and my staff. I can't partner with a man who treats his staff like they're disposable. And I can't employ people who foster a toxic company culture. Not now, not ever."

"I gathered that," Cassandra responds as her eyes flash back and forth between mine.

"You should have gathered that two weeks ago," I snap, the pain in my voice evident.

Her lips rub together as sadness creeps into her features. "Max."

"What?" I exhale heavily.

"I'm sorry."

I tilt my head and watch her carefully for a moment. "For what exactly?"

Her chin trembles. "For my preconceived notions when I started this job. I wanted to hate you. I wanted to judge you, and I expected to watch you choose your job over your kid all summer long. You would then confirm everything I ever witnessed at my old job."

"But?" My brow furrows as I wait for her to continue.

"But...you didn't. In fact, you turned my world upside down. I thought the only way to live a full life was to do less, want less, be less consumed by the hustle and bustle of a job. But you showed me that there are people who can do it all. You work hard, but you are so committed to Everly that it shows in everything she says and does. Honestly, I think she might be my favorite human in the whole world, and I'm going to miss her *fiercely* when I leave tomorrow." Her voice cracks as her eyes well with tears. She sniffs once and continues, "She's a testament to you, Max...and Jessica."

"Thank you for saying that," I reply, my voice thick in my throat. Despite my anger toward Cassandra, her opinion of Everly and me matters...even if she doesn't love me. "I'm not Jenson Hunsberger."

"I know," she says with a laugh, and her cheeks flush a deep ruddy color as she chews her lip nervously. "Which is why I wondered if I could submit my résumé."

"Résumé for what?" I inquire, my head jerking back at the surprising turn of this conversation.

"For a position with you." She rubs her lips together anxiously as she waits for me to reply.

"What position are you inquiring about?" I ask, wondering what Paisley must have said to her to think I wanted her to apply for a job under Fletcher Industries.

She pushes up from her seat and holds a finger up to me. "Will you wait here? I have to go get something out of the tiny house. I'll be right back."

Cozy

My heart pounds inside my chest as I speed walk all the way down to my tiny house that's all packed up and ready for me to move out tomorrow. I half wondered if the invite from Everly tonight meant she knew I was leaving. But now that I've seen this is some sort of a parent trap setup, it's as if the universe gifted me Lindsay Lohan and this incredible kid to help me have the perfect setting to make up for my life's greatest fumble.

My little Sea Monster.

With trembling hands, I grab the sheet of paper I printed off in the Fletchpad earlier today when I was alone. I do my best to walk smoothly back up to Max, who watches me the entire way over to him. And when I say watches me…I mean…he *watches me*. His eyes don't even try to hide the fact that he's checking out every square inch of my body, and I gasp for air when I realize I was holding my breath in my pursuit of him.

Breathing heavily, I sit back down in my chair and slide the paper over to him.

"Cassandra, I don't even know what positions I'll have open at the company," Max says, looking flustered for the first time since I broke his heart on his driveway. "There are still a lot of interviews we have to conduct with the new staff. And I'm not sure this is a good idea, considering our history."

"Look at the top line," I state, cutting him off. "It'll tell you what position I'm applying for."

His focus shifts down to the sheet of paper in his hands. Lips parted, he looks up at me, his eyes wide and full of so much shock and…maybe even excitement, that I dare myself to hope.

"Future wife?" His voice is thick as his eyes rake over my face.

"It's a little presumptuous, I know. But why do less when you can do more?" I shoot him a wobbly smile and shrug. "Plus, I've been reading a lot of Mercedes Lee Loveletter stories, and that woman loves a grand gesture. But if you read on, you'll see all the reasons I think I might be a good candidate for the position."

He blinks back his shock, refocusing on the sheet that I stayed up half the night creating over an old bottle of wine that I needed to polish off in my fridge. The more I drank, the more genius my idea became. And in the light of day this morning, I thought it looked crazy and I'd be a fool to show this to Max.

Then I remembered that Max likes my weird, and I am strong enough to present this to him and finally lay my cards out on the table.

I'm too impatient to sit here in silence as he reads, so I begin narrating everything I included. "I love Everly is the number-one attribute I possess. Like…love her with all my heart. Like, I've been hiding my tears from her the past few days, knowing this is my last week as her nanny. Spending my days with her has been the great-est summer of my life, and I mean that more than you'll ever know."

Max's jaw muscle tics as he continues reading and not looking at me. *Not a good sign.*

"I also think the differences you and I possess that once scared me are actually what will make us work long term. I'll be there to remind you to do less and take care of yourself when your job gets stressful, and you'll be good at inspiring me to do more and follow my dreams and maybe be a touch less willy-nilly about life?"

Max looks up at me with furrowed brows. "Is that really what you want?"

"I want you," I reply quickly, my heart pounding in my chest at the unreadable expression on his face as I repeat, "I want you."

His Adam's apple moves slowly down his neck as he looks back at the sheet to continue reading.

"I think my skills as a nanny are subpar at best, so it's probably better if I shift into a more friendship or mentor role with Everly. But I still think that will add value to my position as a future wife."

I lean over the table to peer down at the sheet to see what I listed next. "Oh yes, we both come from close families, so I think we'll understand the need to help them out from time to time or attend family functions. Said family functions will be more tolerable with each other. Don't you think?"

Max continues with that annoying unreadable expression that I'm sure drives his clients crazy in a boardroom. It's currently driving me crazy, and I talk faster because of it.

"And I know I'm not a good swimmer, but as you can see, I wrote a willingness to expand that part of my skill set with a different swim instructor since I got the impression you weren't a big fan of Ryne. Also, being a strong swimmer makes you well-suited to be my future husband because I know you can lift my dead carcass out of the water and save me the embarrassment of being dragged out. That's a big plus for you, I'm not gonna lie. Oh, and did you see that I'm also willing to do continuing education on cooking if my inability to make pancakes is a bother to you?"

His lips purse in irritation? Annoyance? Anger? God, I can't tell. I have to finish this quickly so I don't lose my nerve. Clearing my throat, I recap the last several line items. "My biggest selling point is my companion skills. All those nights you spend when Everly is with her mom and worrying about you being lonely will be filled with me. We can go on dates, watch movies, and do bubble braid tutorials. You can watch me sand wood while I watch you swim laps. We can have pool parties with your friends. I can take you to my family's farm and show you the sheep...though I think that's a better activity to do with Everly. We can jump on the company jet to Aspen, or we can drive while I give you road head. I could get involved in the Rainbow Project, unless that's just yours and Jessica's thing...that's fine too. I just want to be a part of your life, and I want you to be a part of mine."

"Cassandra," Max cuts me off, and I realize I've been rambling this entire time, and he has yet to say anything. "This isn't enough."

"What?" I gasp, my breath catching in my throat. "Oh! If you turn the sheet over, there's a list of kinks on the back. Between my affection for light choking and your obsession with marking my body, plus the number of other kinks that popped up through the course of our time together, I think this résumé shows that I am an excellent candidate for this position."

"I need more qualifications," Max states sadly, setting the paper down and sitting back in his chair like he's ending this interview.

Panic sets in, and I feel myself clawing at the table desperately. "Max, this is all I have. I want to do nothing with you. Or fight about doing more. And I promise you that I'll voice my fears from now on instead of using them as an excuse to run away. In fact, no more secrets at all! Because I don't just want eyes on you in the bedroom but in life. My eyes will be on you every day because I love you."

His eyes widen imperceptibly. "Say that last part again?"

"The eyes on you part?" I hold my breath as goose bumps erupt all over my body.

He shakes his head. "After that."

My chin trembles nervously as I realize with complete certainty that I have never loved anyone the way I love this man. Truthfully, I didn't know love was supposed to feel like this. It's why I was so alarmed by it. But now that I recognize it, I can't hold it in anymore.

"I love you, Max. I've loved you for longer than I even realized. I was just too scared to admit it because I didn't want to risk losing myself again. But if I'm lost with you, Max, I won't be afraid." I stare down at the résumé, frustrated that I thought this would work. Since he was a businessman, I thought this would be his kinky love language. For once, I didn't unlock a damn kink! Damn you, Mercedes Lee Loveletter!

"Eyes on me, sweet cheeks," Max commands, lifting my attention to him. A smirk ghosts his lips as he rasps, "I love you, too."

With that perfect reply, we both stand and eliminate the distance between us to collide in front of the pool. He crushes his lips to mine as I grip his tie like a lifeline I need to swim in this feeling. God, do I want to swim with him.

He pulls away, breathless and staring hungrily at my mouth. "You're hired."

I laugh and bite my lip. "Is that a proposal?"

His eyes widen with terror, and I laugh and pat his chest.

"Easy there, Zaddy…that was just a joke. No one's ready to walk down the aisle yet."

He growls a deep, sexy sound into my neck. "No wedding talk yet, but I think in order to conduct a thorough performance review, I'm going to need you to move in."

Now my eyes widen with terror. "But my she-shed!"

"I'll build you a better she-shed. You can turn the tiny house into your she-shed or have the whole garage. Whatever you want, Cozy. Just don't leave."

A squeaking noise has both Max and I turning back to the house where we find Everly and her three uncles pressed up against the window staring at us. As soon as we make eye contact, they all sprint off in different directions, Wyatt nearly knocking Everly over as they attempt to conceal themselves.

I laugh and turn back to Max, running my finger over his sexy brow line. "If you want me to move into the Fletchpad, you're going to have to fire me as the nanny first."

He arches a perfect brow and states happily, "You're fired." He presses his lips to mine and murmurs against them, "Pack your bags." He pulls back and gazes down at me to add, "I love you."

Is firing a kink? If so…sign me up.

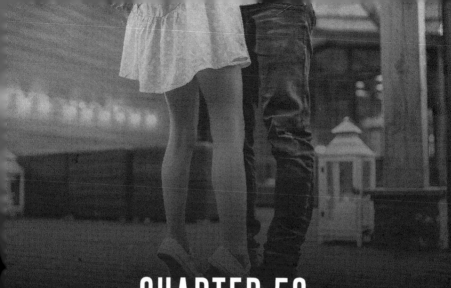

CHAPTER 52

Max

"**S**he's asleep," Cassandra whispers, glancing down at Everly's head resting on her lap as her fingers run through my daughter's blond strands, making me jealous of my own kid.

I've missed Cassandra's hands.

"Should we wake her to go to bed?"

"I can carry her," I murmur, shifting off the couch and bending over to pick her up. After my brothers left, the three of us got into our pajamas and sacked out on the couch for a movie. Cassandra made popcorn, Everly talked through most of the film, and I made a couple of dad jokes. All in all, it was a pretty boring night.

It was fucking perfect.

I stand with Everly in my arms, and she mumbles something about Uncle Calder. My shoulders shake as I turn and walk around the sofa toward the winding staircase.

Cassandra follows as I make my way up the stairs, careful not to bump Everly's head. When I reach her darkened room, Cassandra hurries around and pulls the blankets back for me to lay her in her bed.

Our hands touch as we both grab her blanket to tuck her in. I lace our fingers, staring at her in the dark for a moment, both of us absorbing the peaceful sound of Everly's heavy breaths.

We walk out of her room hand in hand, and before Cassandra can say another word, I turn and press her against the wall, my lips crashing down on hers for a desperate, needy kiss. I barely heard a word my daughter said tonight because all I could think about was that this woman loves me. The real kind of love. The kind of love I don't doubt.

We break apart, foreheads pressed together as I say, "I've been wanting to do that all night."

Cassandra breathes heavily, her hands folded behind my neck. "Pretty sure we did that by the pool in front of a captivated audience of Everly and your brothers."

"That was hours ago," I moan, dipping my head to steal another kiss. "You have no idea how much I've missed you."

She sighs deeply. "Likewise."

"It was hell being mad at you these past two weeks," I admit honestly. "Every morning you came in the house, I wanted to grab you and pull you into my room to see if I could fuck you into loving me back."

Cassandra inhales sharply at my raw confession. She grabs my jaw and forces my eyes to meet hers. "It wasn't that I didn't love you, Max. I just needed time to trust that loving you wouldn't lose me. I was getting there on my own, but honestly, that conversation with Paisley was healing for me on so many levels."

I nod knowingly. "After seeing who Jenson really was, I knew there had to be more to the story with your coworkers. I can't imagine anyone ever willingly letting you out of their life."

Her chin trembles as she scores her hands through my hair, sending shivers down my spine. "I still don't know why you love me. You're a successful, amazing single dad with cool friends and a sweet family. You could have anyone, Max. Why on earth would you see a cuddly, twenty-six-year-old nanny on the run from her past who pitched the idea of doing nothing all summer with your kid and think…that's the woman I'm going to fall in love with?"

My lips part at the bleak description she paints of herself because it's nothing like the image I see. And if it takes the rest of my life to remind her just how fucking wonderful she is, that is a responsibility I will gladly take on.

I lean back to look her in the eye. "Day one, when Everly yanked you into the pool and injured you…you still wanted to take the fall for her and act like you quit instead of me firing you for not being able to swim. Day fucking one, Cozy."

"I know but—"

"I'm not done," I state firmly, pressing my finger to her lips. She smiles meekly and lets me continue. "It was your concept of doing nothing that let my daughter blossom like a flower this summer. Both Jess and I somehow missed the fact that our daughter was burned out and begging to just be a kid for once."

"We healed together," she replies, showcasing the genuine affection she has for my kid.

"You came in at the perfect time to recharge this family," I continue, stroking her cheek reverently. "We needed you. We needed an anti-nanny. Someone to shake things up and get us out of our routine long enough to just *see* each other."

Cassandra's eyes turn glossy as she absorbs the words that I mean with all my heart.

"And you reminded me that forgiving my past to chase after a new future could be fucking worth it. I want a future with you, Cozy. You make me feel young, like I can do the family thing again and make new memories. I didn't want any of that before I met you."

"Max," Cassandra croaks, her eyes wet with unshed tears. "I want that too. I love you."

She lifts her chin to press her lips to mine, but I pull back, knowing it won't be enough. I grab her hand and drag her behind me through the house, flicking all the lights off as I go. No more whispered words outside of Everly's room. I want Cassandra naked in my bed staring into my eyes while I make love to her like I never have before.

I don't know what exactly our future holds, but if I was a betting man, I'd bet on marriage and babies in no particular order. And sooner rather than later if I have any say in it. It's about time Everly became a big sister.

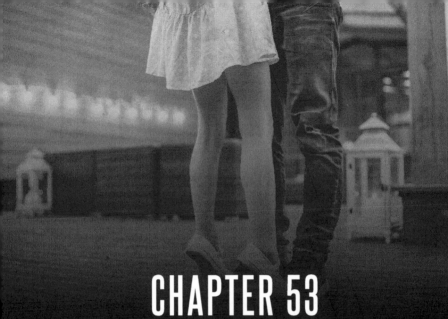

CHAPTER 53

Max

"If I was a betting woman, I would have never bet on seeing this," Jessica exclaims as she strides into the back room of Dakota's T-shirt shop with Kailey to find me, Everly, and Cassandra covered in aprons with bottles of dye in hand.

"Mommies!" Everly peals and takes off in her rubber gloves, running toward my ex and her wife, who arrived back in the country two weeks ago. They surprised Everly mid-dive into our swimming pool, and she belly-flopped, cried tears of pain, and then cried tears of happiness as they reunited. It was a hot mess.

Everly spent two weeks with them to reconnect, but we're finally back on schedule now, so I had her all weekend. Cassandra, she and I did a whole lot of nothing together the past forty-eight hours. It was perfect.

Except for tonight. Tonight, before Everly goes to Jessica and Kailey's, I was somehow coerced into tie-dying a collection of my perfectly good white T-shirts. One bad thing about having a girl-friend who has an incredibly close bond with your kid is that I am

"Stop!" Jessica and Kailey scream as they hold their hands up to Everly.

"Everly…finish the T-shirt, then hug your moms," Cassandra instructs with a laugh, and our eyes find each other over the table covered in dye. It's that silent look of understanding that two people who share a child can exchange. The one that says…*oh, my God, our kid is a crazy monster but also I love the shit out of her.*

And I realize Everly isn't Cassandra's child. But it's a look we started exchanging almost from day one of her nannying position. It's not something I could fully appreciate until I realized I wanted her to be a part of my life. And I do want her to be a part of my life. I want her to be a part of my family. I want her to *be* my family.

So I'm exchanging that knowing look with her whenever the fuck I want. It feels good to be parenting a kid with a partner. I didn't realize what I was missing all these years.

"The hoodies Everly made you guys are hanging up right behind me." Cassandra gestures with her head as she squirts a bottle of blue dye over a rolled-up sweatshirt.

Jessica and Kailey walk over to the rack and pull the rainbow tie-dyed hoodies down to admire them. Dakota printed "I Heart my Moms" on the front.

"Do you like them?" Everly asks, smiling at Cassandra because they made them sometime over the summer.

"I love them," Jess answers excitedly.

"They are perfect!" Kailey agrees.

"Dad, should I make one of those for Cozy too?" Everly inquires, her big blue eyes blinking at me curiously.

The room goes silent as Jess and I exchange a look this time.

Cassandra's reply saves us all, "The hoodie you make me should say Bestie on it, Sea Monster."

Everly nods, but her brows are pinched together. "But when you and Daddy get married, then I'll get to call you a mom, right?"

Jessica sputters out a knowing laugh, and I shoot her a lethal glare that silently tells her in no uncertain terms to shut the fuck up. She's the only person who knows I have a ring stashed in the freezer of the recently vacated tiny house, and she better pull it together and act cool right now.

Cassandra's cheeks flush red. "How about you make me one that says bae. That means girlfriend, right?"

"Dakota, can we do a Bae T-shirt for Cozy?" Everly calls out loudly, thankfully letting go of the mommy talk.

"Absolutely!" Dakota yells from her place at the front counter where she's packing up orders.

I exhale heavily when the conversation shifts to Everly's boyfriend, Hilow.

I was maybe a tad impulsive on the ring buying situation a few days ago. I don't really know what happened. I was drinking whiskey after work one night with Josh, telling him all about how in love I am with Cassandra and how I didn't go through my normal round of depression when Everly went to spend time with her moms after they got back because I had Cozy filling up all my nights.

Next thing I know, I stumble into a jewelry shop and put a twenty-thousand-dollar diamond on my credit card.

Like I said…impulsive. And maybe a little drunk.

In fairness, she did apply for the position of future wife. So it's not like this is out of left field. And at least I didn't get the fifty-thousand-dollar ring. I know Cassandra enough to know better than that. She'd kill me if I tried to give her a monstrosity of an engagement ring.

But we are settling in nicely together. I love having her in my home and in my bed. Last weekend we even went to her old storage unit and unpacked a bunch of her stuff from Denver. It went well, which was further proof for Cassandra that she is ready to move on from her old life and is done harboring the resentment she had toward her former company.

And she has her own cock-board making endeavors she's happily pursuing. Which reminds me, I need to get that coded lock on Cassandra's door. We both agreed that we don't really need to explain the ins and outs of erotic romance authors and these cocktuterie boards to my almost twelve-year-old. No judgment, just… boundaries.

Now it's just a matter of waiting for the right time to get down on one knee. I don't want to totally freak Cassandra out, but I've had some good talks with Everly about it and she has made it clear she is one-hundred-percent Team Cozy. Although in her eyes we've only been an item for a couple of weeks.

However, in my eyes, Cassandra was mine the second she moved into that tiny house. It's why I worked from home that first week. It's why I kissed her like a starved man that night of the storm. It's why I freaked out when she tried to go on a date. It's why I couldn't stay away from her after tasting her. She is mine in all the ways I've ever wanted a woman to be mine. And I want to be hers forever.

I watch her talk easily to Jessica, the two of them already acting like old friends. The day they arrived home, Jess and Kailey sat by my pool with us and heard the whole parent trap story straight from Everly's animated mouth. She is very proud of her little scheme with my brothers. She has since decided she's going to be a matchmaker when she grows up and help people find love. I think she'd be just the kind of person to pull it off.

Jessica and Cassandra knew each other already from their brief chats over FaceTime, but I could tell instantly that Jess was bonding with her. Maybe it's because she actually likes her, maybe it's just because she knew she makes me happy and that was all the approval she needed. Either way, I can see our families blending together in the future in a way that made buying that ring feel right.

I don't think I fully realized how stunted I was emotionally until Cozy came along. She pushed all my boundaries and shook me in ways that I needed to be shook. And vice versa. I don't need months to know that Cassandra is the one for me. There's never been anyone else. And there never will be.

"Cozy, I need help," Everly whines and Cassandra instantly drops what she's doing to stand behind Everly and assist her with bagging up the newly dyed shirt to soak overnight.

"This one is going to be awesome," Cassandra says into Everly's ear, who smiles happily.

She smiles a lot these days. Since Jess came home and Cassandra moved in, it's like Everly got all her favorite people right where she wanted them. And she never had to say goodbye to her nanny because she slipped easily into the role of her father's girlfriend—like she was always supposed to be there.

Last night when I was tucking Everly in, she looked up at me and touched the corner of my eyes to say, *"You're getting wrinkles here, Daddy."*

I laughed and replied, "That's because I'm getting old, kid."

"No, you're not. These are smile lines because you're finally getting happy."

It was the "finally" word that caused the tears to seep out of my eyes. But ultimately, they were indeed happy tears, so I think it's safe to say Everly was right.

Now I just have to wait a little longer before officially adding Cassandra's name to the list of incredible women who Everly can call her mom.

"Do we need more shirts in here?" Dakota asks, re-joining us now that she's done with the customers out front.

"No!" we all reply in unison. Everly is addicted to tie-dye and is in serious need of an intervention.

Cassandra looks at me and smiles knowingly. It all started with an orange tie-dyed sweatsuit.

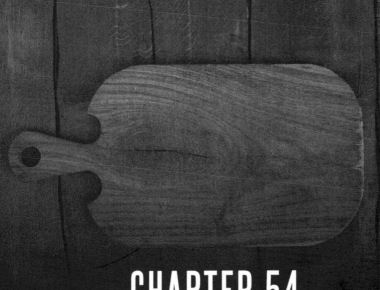

CHAPTER 54

Cozy

A Couple of Months Later

"Engaged to a millionaire and officially too bougie to wear my graphic tees," Dakota gripes as she comes striding into the bathroom of the tiny house holding two glasses of champagne.

"Make a graphic tee evening gown, and I'll be your number-one customer," I call backward, smiling fondly as the image of my two favorite graphic tees flash in my mind.

Three weeks ago, I found Max and Everly out by the pool at night. The entire area was covered in these colorful floating lights. A guitarist was playing on the deck, and they had on these orange tie-dyed shirts that said "Marry" on Max's shirt and "Us" on Everly's shirt.

I burst into tears and said yes, obviously.

It may seem fast to some, but everything about the three of us feels right. Even my sister, who I thought was going to murder me when she found out that not only did I move in with my former boss but I was also marrying him, was happy for me. And Rebecca Barlow doesn't do happy. My parents were just relieved I was working again.

They don't really get the whole millionaire thing. Not that that's the appeal of Max.

I am aware he makes a lot of money. And he's thankfully doing everything he can to hire good people to manage the extra work of his recent company growth. But that doesn't stop me from needing to have a purpose of my own in life. I've just avoided fully informing my parents that my current purpose is in the form of cocktuterie boards.

They *really* wouldn't get that.

They just need to know I'm happy and fulfilled and managing my stress as best I can. Stress is easier to shoulder with my new built-in family.

I finish curling the last of my hair that has grown freakishly fast the last few weeks and glance down at Dakota's stunning floor-length gown. "Did you come through the house? Is everyone alive up there?"

Dakota hands a champagne flute to me and sips hers gingerly. "It's chaos up there. You were smart to get ready out here."

I nod and set my glass down on the bathroom counter. "Norah and her crew needed the Fletchpad more than I did. And her mother is kind of scary."

"I gathered that." Dakota laughs and takes another sip before adding, "It was really sweet of Kate to invite me to Dean and Norah's wedding, though. This is going to be fun!"

"Kate is the best," I reply honestly. The three of us have all really hit it off with the work we're doing together for the bookstore, and I'm excited that Dakota is officially in the mix with all Max's friends.

"And Norah is a stunning bride," Dakota says with wide eyes. "I caught a glimpse of her when Max walked me through the house. She's the most beautiful pregnant bride I've ever seen. Wedding photos and maternity photos all in one go. Talk about a two for one!"

Goose bumps erupt all over my body as I bite my lip and press a hand to my stomach at the mention of Norah's belly.

"What?" Dakota asks, gaping at my hand pressed to my abdomen. She shifts her eyes to my un-touched champagne. "No fucking way."

"It's early," I confess with a cringe.

"You are not knocked up. No way!" Dakota exclaims.

I press my finger to my lips. "Keep your voice down. There are wedding guests outside!"

Dakota sets her champagne down, props her hands on her hips, and bends over. "I think I'm going to be sick."

"I've been sick enough for us both already," I respond with a smirk. When has vomiting ever made me happy?

Oh...when it means a baby is growing inside me.

"How are you pregnant, Cozy?"

I shrug sheepishly. "Usually, it's when a man lays down in bed with a woman and—"

"Shut up, you know what I mean!" she snipes, still clearly reeling at this new information. "I mean...was this planned?"

I chew my lip nervously. "Kind of? I mean...not fully. I went off birth control a few weeks ago because I read some crazy story about how it can take months to get pregnant after being on the pill for so many years. Max has made it very clear that he wants a baby, and you know...he's older than me, and this is a subject we actually both fully agree on. So I went off the pill just to give my body time to adjust and...yeah...the rest is a bit more graphic, but I can share it if you really want me to."

"Jesus," Dakota hisses. "You're my best friend, and you're marrying a millionaire and having his baby! Suddenly, my life looks really fucking boring."

"Shut up," I reply with a laugh. "You have stuff going on. Have you made any decisions about that old house you want to buy?"

"No...and I'm not going to," Dakota harumphs and then shakes her head and stands up straight. "Can we try that whole thing again?"

"What whole thing?"

"Where you tell me you're pregnant and happy and I say congratulations and hug the shit out of you because I am really happy for you?"

She rushes over and wraps me in her arms. "I really am happy for you, Cozy. God, this is so exciting. I'm going to be an aunt!"

"Hell yes, you are!"

"What did Max say?"

"I haven't told him yet," I answer, biting my lip. "I only just found out this morning, and with all the wedding setup, there hasn't been a moment to even talk to him."

As if on cue, Max knocks on the door of the tiny house and walks in. "Everyone decent in here?"

"Yes," I call out over Dakota's shoulder.

Her eyes go wide, and she turns around to scurry out of the bathroom, leaving me alone to have a tiny moment of freaking the fuck out. There's wanting a baby, and there's being pregnant with a baby. Two very different things. I could tell a couple of weeks ago something was changing in my body because my breasts hurt like a bitch when Max groped them during sex. I screamed out in pain, which he interpreted as good pain, but it was pretty much then that I thought something was up.

I reach over and grab the pregnancy test I stashed in the mirrored cabinet and tuck it down my cleavage. *Now or never, Cozy.*

"Is my girl almost ready? They're starting to seat the guests," I hear Max ask Dakota as I step out of the bathroom.

My steps falter when I take in Max in a classic black tux. His blond hair is swept off to one side, and his chin is freshly shaved, revealing that perfect chiseled jaw of his. Total groom vibes.

"Cozy, you look stunning," Max says, his eyes raking over my red strapless dress in a way that makes my thighs squeeze with need.

"I'll see you guys out there," Dakota peals and gives me a hearty thumbs-up before she slips out the door to join the guests all congregating in the white chairs placed down by the beach.

I stop beside the ladder, gripping it for balance as I buckle beneath the heated look in Max's eyes. *I know that look.*

"We have a few minutes before we need to be seated," his husky voice utters as he stalks toward me like a lion approaching its prey.

"Where's Everly?" I ask, my nipples chafing as they stiffen under my dress at just the idea of Max's hands on me.

"She's helping Josh and Lynsey with Julianna." He takes another step toward me.

I shift nervously and glance out the windows for any sign of life. "Max, people can see inside."

"Everyone's down by the creek," he replies with a wicked glint in his eye. "I'll be quick. I won't even take your dress off."

He backs me up against the kitchen counter, and his lips capture mine as my entire body alights with desire that's so intense, I hear myself moaning into his mouth. *I'm so weak.*

Seriously, is this a pregnancy thing? Because I feel like I could come any second already.

I bite my lip and grip his shoulders harshly as his hand steals under my dress and swipes inside my panties.

"Fuck, Cozy. You're soaked." His voice is guttural. "How long have you been aching for me like this?"

"Oh, God," I cry out, feeling like a live wire that will trip at any second. "Max, I need you."

"Jesus," he husks, his brow furrowed curiously at me as he unbuckles his pants. "I've never seen you like this."

"Hurry, Max," I beg, my tone breathless.

He grips my thighs and hoists me up on the counter before thrusting deep inside me.

"Oh, my God," I moan into his ear, gripping the back of his neck.

"Fuck me, sweet cheeks. You feel like goddamn heaven." He pulls out and thrusts back in, his eyes finding mine. "This is why I can't control myself around you. You always feel so fucking good," he says, pumping into me between each and every word.

"Max, I'm going to come," I whimper, my head falling back against the cabinet.

"Already? Jesus, I was just warming up." He bites his lip and rocks into me again. "Eyes on me when you do. Let me see you fall apart for my cock, sweet cheeks."

My eyes flutter open and struggle to look at him. His brows knit together as his gaze drops down to my chest, and he freezes mid thrust.

"Max, don't stop," I exclaim, grabbing his ass and pulling him back inside me. "I'm so close."

"Cassandra." He states my name plainly, his mind clearly not on sex anymore as his eyes burn a hole in my chest.

"What?" I gasp and look down to see what he's seeing.

The pregnancy test has worked its way out of my cleavage, and the little pregnant text is staring him right in the eye.

His indigo gaze lifts to mine. "Are you?"

"Prego?" I answer with a smile. "Yep."

"Holy shit, really?" he asks, his eyes instantly filling with tears. I reach up and caress his smooth face. Max's eyes often get red when he's emotional, but I never see actual tears.

I wipe a damp trail off his cheek and nod. "Looks like we're going to have a baby."

He expels a garbled noise as his lips find mine, his hands touching my belly in the most reverent way I've ever experienced. "Oh, my God, Cozy. I'm so happy. Are you happy? This happened faster than we'd planned on." He stares at me with wide, anxious eyes.

"I'm ecstatic, Max," I respond with a laugh, smoothing away the worry lines on his face. "Everly's going to be a big sister."

He sniffs loudly and kisses me again, his eyes falling to my stomach as he trembles in my arms. "I wish it was us getting married today."

I laugh again and shake my head. "In due time, Zaddy. This is Dean and Norah's day today."

He nods and kisses me chastely. "I can't wait to call you my wife."

His words feel like heaven as I lean forward and kiss him sweetly. "For now, let's just be secretly happy we're making you a daddy again."

He growls hungrily, his nostrils flaring at whatever I said that reminded him his dick is still very much inside me. I squeeze my legs around him, nodding for him to continue his earlier efforts because yes, we're having a baby, and yes, we need to come up with an epic way to tell Everly, and yes, we need to plan our wedding so we can all live happily ever after...but his cock is still inside me, and I have an orgasm to chase...so...why do less when we can do more?

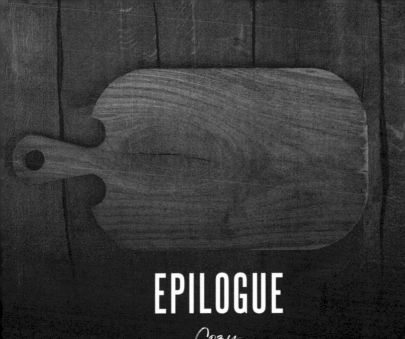

EPILOGUE

Cozy

One Year Later

"Tucker! Do *not* jump in that pool!" Kate screams from the door of the house as her wild, redheaded eighteen-month-old dead sprints for the water. Miles drops the cooler on the deck and takes off after him, but his sandal gets caught on something, and he ends up doing a face-plant in front of Dean. They all watch in horror when one second later, their little guy flings himself into the pool.

Without pause, I drop my book and leap up out of my lounge chair by the pool. I dive into the water and open my eyes to spot him as he sinks deeper underwater. What I see next has me nearly inhaling water myself as I fight back a laugh.

The little shit is smiling underwater.

Tucker's eyes are wide open, arms outstretched…*and he's smiling* like this is the best moment of his life.

I swim over to him and yank him out of the water, holding him to my chest as he coughs lightly. Thankfully, he was only under a couple of seconds, but talk about giving us all a fright!

He blinks his soaked ginger lashes back at me. "Tucker," I scold using my very impressive mommy voice but unable not to smile back at his smile. "You have to listen to your mommy. You need your life jacket before you can swim, or you can't come over to Uncle Max and Aunt Cozy's pool anymore!"

His lower lip pops out as he looks around, completely unaware that he could have drowned if he didn't have a million adults watching him.

"Cozy...you're a lifesaver," Kate gasps as she takes Tucker from my hands. Miles joins her, looking terrified. The two of them cuddle Tucker, so I turn and swim away to give them some space.

"Nice save, sweet cheeks," Max says, dropping down onto the side of the pool to stick his feet in the water.

I pause in the water to drink in his tan, chiseled chest on full display in a pair of tiny floral swim trunks. *Good God, he really is a Ken doll.*

I crawl stroke over to him, grabbing the edge of the pool between his legs. "All those maternity swimming lessons were training me for this moment right here." I pull myself out of the pool to kiss my husband on the lips.

My husband.

We've been married since Christmas, and I can't help but wonder if I'll ever get used to calling him that. I hope not because every time I say it, it makes me feel alive in ways I never imagined.

It was Max's idea we get married over Christmas. He thought I needed a new memory to mask my stroke memory. So we booked a big private jet and flew both of our families to a beach in Mexico over the holidays and got married on Christmas Eve on the beach.

It was perfect.

Max bands his hands around my waist, holding me up out of the water to deepen our kiss.

"My ass is hanging out for all to see, you know," I murmur against his lips as I feel the air on my backside. Post baby belly and a few extra pounds have made me slightly more aware of my body the past couple of months.

"Let them look," Max replies hungrily. "I've marked you, so they know you're mine."

I yank out of his arms and drop back into the water to splash him. "I'm still pissed at you about that."

"What?" Max shrieks, wiping the water off his face with that boyish smirk that fools no one. "I put them in discreet places."

I glare up at him but can't stop smiling. "Discreet for regular clothes maybe. Not swimwear."

Max shrugs happily, clearly not at all displeased by this fact when a wailing noise erupts from behind him. We both turn to look at the video screen baby monitor sitting by my lounge chair.

"Sounds like Ethan's awake," Max says, stating the obvious.

"Which probably means he's starving," I respond, feeling my breasts already letting down with milk.

"I'm hungry too," Max confesses in a deep voice, glancing down at my even bigger than usual chest. "I haven't eaten you in…"

"Like two hours," I exclaim and give his bare chest a hearty smack as I hoist myself out of the water. "Honestly, Max. I was cleared to have sex like two weeks ago, and you have been all over me. If you're not careful, I'm going to get pregnant again."

His eyes darken with desire as he leans in close. "Don't go promising me with a good time, Cozy." He bites his lip seductively. "I loved you pregnant."

Yet another kink unlocked for Max Fletcher. Honestly, if anyone got ahold of our kink list, it would be extremely embarrassing.

Max couldn't keep his hands off me when I was pregnant. Touched my belly every time we were near each other. Sat on the sofa with his hand on me, just in case the baby moved. And the sex was a whole new level as well. Lots of mirror play, lots of me on top. Lots of eyes on my belly, not eyes on my eyes. He really is such a perv.

I liked it at the time because I didn't notice any stretch marks during the pregnancy. However, after I had Ethan and my belly started to shrink, that's when they popped up. My confidence took a hit when I realized I looked different in my cropped sweatshirts that I loved to wear. So I quit wearing them.

Until Max noticed.

When I admitted to him that I felt embarrassed of my body now, he held me in front of the mirror and traced each line with his finger before reverently whispering, *"Each one of these lines is a sign of your incredible strength, Cassandra. They kept you healthy and strong so you could become a mother and give us all the gift of Ethan. These lines are our family. Please, be as proud of them as we are of you."*

I cried and let him hold me that night and remind me that he loved my body in any shape and size. The reality of being a woman sometimes is that all the confidence in the world still can't hold a candle to the reassuring words of your husband. I'm so lucky to have him in my life.

Max and I both frown at each other when we realize the crying has stopped. He helps me out of the pool, and we both walk over to the lounge chairs, dropping down across from each other as I reach for the camera monitor. We both inwardly gasp when we see why little Ethan's quiet again.

Everly has apparently crawled into his crib and has curled around his little two-month-old body. She's shushing him and stroking his eyebrows, clearly lulling him back to sleep. She leans in and kisses his head before she begins to sing softly to him.

The tears are instant in my eyes as I watch her love on her little brother like she always does. Honestly, her obsession with him is even worse than Max's obsession with my pregnant belly. We literally have to tell her to share the baby with others when we have guests come by to see him.

"I'll go check on them," Max offers, his voice thick with emotion as he kisses me on the forehead before heading toward the house.

Kate, Norah, and Lynsey join me on the loungers next as their husbands all make their way into the pool with their littles—Josh with three-year-old Julianna, Miles with wild man Tucker, and Dean is holding his six-month-old son, Hogan, while a very pregnant Maggie waddles over to us. She holds her taut belly on full display in a two-piece as Sam helps her down into her chair.

"So much for waiting," Kate murmurs under her breath,

making a jab at Maggie and Sam who swore they were going to wait a while to have kids and are now being blessed with a two-for-one special.

"Double the trouble," Lynsey declares, shaking her head. "I'm still trying to work up the nerve to have another baby but you guys having two makes me want to wait even longer."

"If you wait long enough, you'll have a built-in nanny like this one," Kate says, gesturing to me. She leans over to look at the baby monitor I'm still watching as Max helps Everly out of the crib and hands little Ethan off to her. "I'm so jealous of that."

"You should be. Everly has been amazing," I reply honestly.

Warmth spreads through my chest at that reality because Everly and I had a very tender conversation about a month before Ethan was born when she confessed she was worried I would love Ethan more than her. I was so touched because the fact that she even wants my love is still such a gift to me. My little Sea Monster really has no idea how much she fulfills me.

I reminded her that she made me a mother first…and one never forgets their first. It was also at that moment that we decided together that she could start calling me Mama Cozy. I think that was all the reassurance she needed that I am just as much a part of her life as I am Ethan's. I can't wait to see what she does in her life.

"Cozy, what did you do to your leg?" Kate barks out of no-where, pulling everyone's focus to me.

My face flushes with mortification as I try to hide the red mark on my inner thigh. "Oh…I um…bruised it."

"That doesn't look like a bruise," Kate deadpans, pulling up her sunglasses to get a closer look. "Is that a hickey?"

"No!" I exclaim, feeling my blood pressure spike as I try to invent a story that would leave a mark about the size of a mouth on my inner leg.

Suddenly, my thoughts are distracted when I catch a glimpse of Max stepping out onto the deck, holding little Ethan against his bare chest. His hair is disheveled, and his sunglasses are down over his eyes, as his arm muscles pop in the most delicious way as he rocks our swaddled baby back and forth. His thigh muscles bulge beneath the tight fabric of his swim trunks as he strides toward me, and at that moment, I realize all the ladies beside me are gaping at my husband.

I snap my fingers to divert their attention back to me. "Eyes on my thigh hickey, ladies." I smile smugly and lift my sunglasses up. "'Cuz that Zaddy is all mine."

The End

Read the BONUS EPILOGUE for Last on the List HERE
https://dl.bookfunnel.com/uol2kdz77v

More from the *now complete* Wait With Me Series:
Wait With Me—Kate & Miles
Next In Line—Sam & Maggie
One Moment Please—Lynsey & Dr. Dick
Take A Number—Dean & Norah
Last on the List—Max & Cozy

MORE BOOKS BY
AMY DAWS

The London Lovers Series:
Becoming Us: Finley's Story Part 1
A Broken Us: Finley's Story Part 2
London Bound: Leslie's Story
Not the One: Reyna's Story

A London Lovers/Harris Brothers Crossover Novel:
Strength: Vi Harris & Hayden's Story

The Harris Brothers Series:
Challenge: Camden's Story
Endurance: Tanner's Story
Keeper: Booker's Story
Surrender & Dominate: Gareth's Duet

Payback: A Harris Brother Spin-off Standalone
Blindsided: A Harris Brother Spin-off Standalone
Replay: A Harris Brother Spin-off Standalone
Sweeper: A Secret Harris Brother Standalone

The Wait With Me Series:
Wait With Me: A Tire Shop Rom-Com
Next in Line: A Bait Shop Rom-Com
One Moment Please: A Hospital Cafeteria Rom-Com
Take A Number: A Bakery Rom-Com
Last on the List: A Boss/Nanny Rom-Com

Pointe of Breaking: A College Dance Standalone by Amy Daws &
Sarah J. Pepper

Chasing Hope: A Mother's *True* Story of Loss, Heartbreak,
and the Miracle of Hope

For all retailer purchase links, visit:www.amydawsauthor.com

ACKNOWLEDGEMENTS

Oh to the vey! What a journey this book was. Frankly, all of my books are a labor of love (and a ton of pain), which is why it is so important to thank all the people who listened to my endless ramblings and gave me feedback that helped me continue writing!

First of all, Kristie from @red_between.the_wines on TikTok! I had so much fun brainstorming Max with you. Thank you for your amazing support and for all you do in the book world. You're a fantastic ray of light in this industry.

To the always spicy Jane Ashley Converse, your beta notes are so valuable and I'm so thankful to have you in my corner. To my sister-in-law, Megan who is killer at those boozy brainstorms. Can't wait to do it again soon! To my Cali girl Jennifer, who is my favorite cheerleader ever! I love your morning voicemails. My fabulous Beth, you squeeze me in every time and I'm so grateful for that. And Franci...my timeline Queen. You are my last eyeballs before editing and I love all that you catch!

I had an incredible handful of sensitivity readers on this book that I want to give special thanks to. It was important for me to honor Max's exes story in a way that honors the LGBTQ+ community. So, I thank you special readers in the community that read this book and helped me strengthen that important part of the story.

Thanks to Jenny Sims, Julia Griffis, and Lydia Rella for making this book sparkle with their sharp eyeballs, plus, Champagne formatting for making everything extra pretty. And big thanks to my PA Julia for the endless tasks you do for every release!

Also, shout out to a business in Candada called Cocktuterie! Their tik tok famous phallic-shaped boards inspired this fun idea for Kate and Cozy's business adventure together. Cock boards and smut writers are like PB&J! Check out their products at cockuterieboards. com and use Amy20 for 20% off!

And to my little family. I go from not writing a word for months to writing around the clock, which means my husband and daughter have to pick up a lot of slack around the house. And the fact that they do that without too much complaining is so appreciated.

And last but never ever least, my six angel babies. Every book signing I attend with Chasing Hope on the table reminds me that I wouldn't be writing if I didn't have the journey to loving and losing all of you. While I would much rather have been your mom here on this earth, I'm so grateful that losing all of you continues to inspire me in this career everyday.

MORE ABOUT THE AUTHOR

Number 1 Amazon Bestselling author Amy Daws writes spicy love stories that take place in America, as well as across the pond. She's most known for her footy-playing Harris Brothers and writing in a tire shop waiting room. When Amy is not writing, she's likely making charcuterie boards from her home in South Dakota where she lives with her daughter and husband.

Follow Amy on all social media channels, including Tik Tok under @amydawsauthor

For more of Amy's work, visit: www.amydawsauthor.com or check out the links below.

www.facebook.com/amydawsauthor
www.twitter.com/amydawsauthor
www.instagram.com/amydawsauthor

Made in the USA
Middletown, DE
27 August 2022

72234663R00215